THE KIF STRIKE BACK

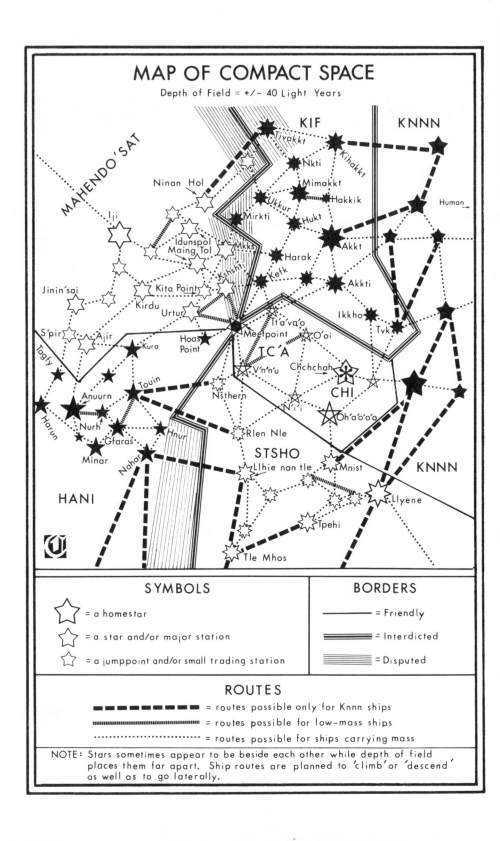

THE KIF STRIKE BACK

C. J. CHERRYH

Map by David Cherry
Frontispiece by David Cherry

PHANTASIA PRESS

Huntington Woods, Michigan
1985

THE KIF STRIKE BACK

Published by
Phantasia Press
13101 Lincoln
Huntington Woods, Michigan 48070

Copyright © 1985 by C.J. Cherryh
Map copyright © 1985 by David Cherry
Frontispiece © 1985 by David Cherry

OCT 1 5 '88

FIRST EDITION

This edition published by arrangement with DAW Books, Inc., New York, New York.

Manufactured in the United States of America

ISBN 0-932096-35-2

In Our Last Episode. . . .*

A kifish prince named Akkukkak acquired a prize and an unprecedented opportunity: an alien ship and crew fell into his hands—promising him new hunting-grounds for the kif and a new species to prey on. All he had to do was to find out where the ship came from and how powerful the aliens might be.

But the last surviving alien escaped him onto the docks at Meetpoint, and ran onto the hani ship *The Pride of Chanur*.

That was how Pyanfar Chanur met Tully the human; and how the ancient Chanur clan ended up in a fight hani would ordinarily have avoided.

It ended in a full-scale shootout at Gaohn Station in the hani home system, when Akkukkak occupied Gaohn. Chanur clan and a couple of mahendo'sat hunter-captains named Goldtooth and Jik joined forces to defeat the kif.

Akkukkak perished in that battle—or at least made an unwilling exit in the company of a species called the knnn, methane-breathers of bizarre mentality.

Tully went back to human space. Pyanfar Chanur hoped then that there would be trade forthcoming. She anticipated a whole new era of hani prosperity with Chanur clan getting rich.

But she was quickly betrayed, first by the stsho who owned Meetpoint and who barred her from that critical trading station—and thereby from access to humanity; then by her mahendo'sat partners, who went off and dealt with the humans on their own; and finally by her own kind, because a good many hani clans saw Chanur clan as a threat to their own power and were all too glad to see it impoverished.

In hani eyes, Pyanfar Chanur had done a heinous thing in bringing aliens to Gaohn: hani had been brought into space by the mahendo'sat and always resented the debt. Mahendo'sat had taken their direct influence off the hani homeworld of Anuurn,

---

*As told in: *The Pride of Chanur* and *Chanur's Venture*.

5

but hani never quite trusted them; they liked kif far less, distrusted the stsho, and wished not even to contemplate the knnn—let alone the prospect of non-Compact aliens like humans, all of which Pyanfar Chanur had brought into the very heart of hani civilization.

More, she had grown *foreign*. When a hani lord is defeated in challenge, he dies; but Pyanfar intervened when her son supplanted her husband: she took her husband offworld where no hani male had ever been permitted, and declared him part of *The Pride*'s crew. Moreover, Kohan, lord of Chanur, acquiesced to her action, a circumstance which occasioned ribald jokes at Chanur's expense and further damaged Chanur's credit among hani.

So for two years *The Pride of Chanur* and other Chanur ships made small runs and barely kept operating, sinking deeper and deeper into financial ruin.

Constantly Pyanfar renewed her applications for Meetpoint access; but she lacked money for the bribes necessary to deal with the stsho, she had no help from the mahendo'sat, not a whiff of human trade, and there seemed no hope for Chanur's fortunes.

But unexpectedly and for no reason she could fathom, the stsho sent word her application was approved: *The Pride* turned toward Meetpoint with the last large cargo Chanur could scrape together.

Once docked, Pyanfar headed immediately for the offices of Stle stles stlen, stationmaster of Meetpoint, to sign the necessary documents and reinstate her trading license.

She was accosted on dockside by Goldtooth, who dragged her aboard his ship, *Mahijiru*, and brought her face to face with Tully—back in Compact space and at a station which would erupt in xenophobic riot if it knew a human was present.

Now Pyanfar Chanur was a hani of considerable nerve, but this was more than she could bear—until Goldtooth began naming advantages to the deal, like human trade, and money, and alliance—and until a small quiet alarm started going off in her skull telling her just *who* had gotten those papers cleared, and how fast it all might collapse if she refused Goldtooth's deal.

She took it; and Tully; *and* a packet of papers; and went back to break the news to her crew.

But kif on the station arranged a riot to cover their attempt to snatch Tully from her custody. Goldtooth fled the docks; she and her crew ended up billed for damages—which she charged to the mahendo'sat government, using the papers Goldtooth had left her. Stle stles stlen was mollified—for the moment, so well-disposed, in fact, that this avowed friend of the mahendo'sat gave her one direct warning: *don't trust Goldtooth.*

The kif also approached Pyanfar with two direct offers: one, to *buy* Tully from her and, two, to ally themselves with her against a certain kif who had a bounty on her head.

It was certainly tempting. Money enough to solve their problems. A way out of their dilemma. A possible peace with the kif.

But she turned it down, dumped her precious cargo, and pulled out of Meetpoint as rapidly as she could with Tully aboard—because her credit with Stle stles stlen hung upon a credit authorization from the mahendo'sat—and *that* was only valid if she played her role as Goldtooth's courier. Kif offers or not, she had never dealt with kif and never wished to; Goldtooth, moreover, had her trapped—and Goldtooth had run, heading deep into stsho space with kifish hunters on his tail, *some* of whom were interested in her.

Then she learned that getting Tully and his message to the mahen regional capital was only part of it—

A knnn tracked them out of Meetpoint. *That* was no good news. Rumors of what she was carrying had evidently spread to methane-side. Knnn, so alien no one could talk to them, so technologically advanced no one could fight them—existed inside the Compact and outside the law. They might take exception to any move at any moment and kill a ship; and no one would do a thing about it—because no one could talk to them. It was a monumental achievement that the serpentine tc'a had once upon a time gotten the knnn to understand the concept of trade: so nowadays knnn simply contacted a station, rushed onto its methane-dock and deposited whatever they liked, grabbed whatever they wanted and left. This was an improvement over

7

their former behavior, in which they simply looted and left. Or took a ship apart.

And Tully, when questioned, avowed that humans were late getting back to Compact space because their ships had been stopped. *Someone* was conducting piracy against human ships in human space, and kif was the automatic assumption. The message and the mission seemed to have to do with a mahen determination to push through a regular, patrollable route that would bring humans to Compact space—and incidentally right *past* their old enemies the kif. All this made sense, and Pyanfar was averse to nothing that bothered the kif.

But Tully handed her his own suspicions—that it was not kif which had raided them: it was knnn, and humans had fired on knnn ships.

Pyanfar was horrified.

If Tully was right, they had a potential knnn target aboard their ship. They were carrying a message which involved knnn affairs, either one of which was about as welcome as a ticking bomb. If the knnn moved on them they were flatly done for. Moreover, the kif who was hunting them had seized the route that led most directly to the mahen capital and they had to reroute to the border station of Kshshti—far from a safe place to have a prize like Tully, a place close to kif territory and frequented by the methane breathers.

As if they needed more trouble, they had picked up another pursuer. A hani government ship captained by one Rhif Ehrran was out hunting a hani renegade named Tahar. This Tahar had sided with the kif at the battle of Gaohn, and was a well-known outlaw, said to be operating as a pirate in the vicinity of Kefk and Meetpoint. But *The Pride of Chanur* turned up under Rhif Ehrran's nose, trafficking with mahendo'sat and kif—and this policewoman of the *han* diverted herself from one quarry to another potential traitor. Rhif Ehrran's political patrons would be far happier to see the demise of Chanur than that of a mere pirate already powerless in hani affairs. So priorities were revised. Rhif Ehrran learned, probably from Stle stles stlen, that Chanur had Tully aboard—and that Chanur was in the employ of a foreign government; and Rhif Ehrran saw a chance to ruin Chanur once for all.

Ehrran commandeered assistance: Banny Ayhar of *Ayhar's Prosperity* was compelled to dump her cargo and come along as Ehrran's ally—as they headed off in the only direction now open to travel.

Pyanfar barely reached Kshshti alive: *The Pride*, long running without needed repairs, broke down under the stress of the jump and limped into Kshshti to discover a welcoming committee in port: Rhif Ehrran, Banny Ayhar—and the same kif who had tried to buy Tully back at Meetpoint.

Now, this kif's name was Sikkukkut an'nikktukktin, once a vassal of Pyanfar's old enemy Akkukkak. Akkukkak in fact had had *two* lieutenants: Akkhtimakt and Sikkukkut; and the two of them were presently contending for primacy among kif. Akkhtimakt was the one they had evaded on their way to Kshshti; Akkhtimakt had imposed the blockade not only to stop traffic, but to forestall his rival Sikkukkut—and lo! into Sikkukkut's reach came the whole mahendo'sat plan to outmaneuver the kif . . . in the person of Pyanfar Chanur and Tully.

The mahendo'sat authorities at Kshshti knew what Sikkukkut was up to, and they were anxious to get *The Pride* out of there at any cost. They broke *The Pride*'s old engine pack off the rear and began to install a new one, effectively rebuilding the ship, but as *The Pride* sat immobile in the last stages of repairs, kifish raiders kidnapped Tully and, by accident, Pyanfar's young niece Hilfy Chanur, gravely wounding Pyanfar's cousin Chur Anify.

Whoever began the fracas, Akkhtimakt's agents or Sikkukkut's, it was undisputably Sikkukkut's ship *Harukk* which sped out of Kshshti with Tully and Hilfy aboard, with *The Pride* dockbound and helpless.

Moreover, the methane-breathing tc'a delivered Pyanfar an ambiguous warning of multiple factions and connivance among kif; of danger to themselves, and of knnn involvement in the whole question.

At this depth of despair another ship pulled into Kshshti: the mahen hunter ship *Aja Jin*, commanded by none other than Keia Nomesteturjai—*Jik*, to his friends; partner to Goldtooth; agent of the mahen government and armed with enough authorizations to coerce even Rhif Ehrran.

Pyanfar still had the message packet destined for Maing Tol— but Sikkukkut's parting message indicated if she wanted to see Hilfy and Tully alive she must come instead to Mkks—even deeper into the border zone, where kif were predominant.

Jik called a conference of captains and handed the packet to Banny Ayhar with orders to get it to Maing Tol; and thrust upon Rhif Ehrran a set of authorizations that won her cooperation as well.

So one message has sped toward Maing Tol; Hilfy and Tully are held hostage on the kifish border; Goldtooth is among the missing and one more dockside has been wrecked.

They move each as they must. And *The Pride* leaves Kshshti, headed deliberately into a kifish trap.

One

The Pride came in, dropping suddenly into here and now; and Pyanfar Chanur reached for controls, half-dazed yet.

Where? she thought, with one wild panicked notion that the drive could have betrayed them and they might be nowhere at all. There were new routines to remember. There were new parameters, new systems—

No. Go on comp, fool, let the autos take her—

"Location," she said past jaws gone dry as dust.

"We're in the range," Tirun said.

The first dump came, phasing them into the interface and out again; and *The Pride of Chanur* hauled herself back to realspace with authority.

"We're alive," Khym said.

And that surprised them all.

"Chur?" Geran asked.

"Here," a voice said from in-ship com, faint and slurred. "I'm here, all right. We made it, huh?"

Second dump: *The Pride* shed more of the speed the gravity drop had lent her.

And kept going, while the red numbers reeled on the board, a passage-speed that flicked astronomical measures past like local trivialities.

"Just passed third mark," Haral said.

"Huh," said Pyanfar.

"Beacon alarm."

"No response." Pyanfar's eye was on the scan image Mkks' robot beacon sent them, positions of everything in Mkks system. Beacon protested their velocity. "Get me that line, gods rot it, can we do it?—*where's that line? Wake up!*"

The line flashed onto the monitor, red and dangerous, showing them a course that broke every navigation code in the Compact.

Alarms flashed: the siren howled. Pyanfar laid back her ears and reached frantically to controls as Haral synched moves with

11

her to get the numbers ripped loose from scan-comp and embedded in nav-. She keyed a confirmation, one press of a button. Alarms died, and *The Pride* kept going, hellbent on the line—

("We're on, we're on, we're on!" Tirun breathed—)

—sending a *C*-charged jumpship on a course straight to Mkks station, a maneuver two stars wide, betting everything they had that Mkks beacon would be accurate. They were racing the lightspeed wavefront of their own arrival, the message which that jumprange beacon back there sent to Mkks—chased that moment down the timeline as fast as any ship could dare, with enough energy bound up in their mass to make one great flare if anything Mkks beacon had not reported should turn up in their path—a nova in miniature, a briefly flaring sun.

Pyanfar let the controls go, flexed aching hands and reached in null *G* drift for the foil packet she had clamped to the chair arm. It escaped her claws and she snagged it back, bit a hole in it and drank the contents down in several convulsive gulps, shuddering at the taste and the impact on her stomach. It was necessary: the body shed hair, shed skin, depleted its minerals and moisture. Shortly blood sugar would surge and plummet, and she had to be past that point when *The Pride*'s course reached critical again.

There was no hope now of steering. They were going too fast to skew off to any influence but the star's, and that pull was plotted into their course. She wiped her mane back and rubbed an itch on her nose that had been there since Kshshti.

"Mkks nine minutes Light," Haral said.

Nine minutes til Mkks station got the news of their arrival; mahendo'sat authority would take a few minutes more realizing they had not made that critical third velocity dump. In the meanwhile *The Pride* was shortening the nine minute reply interval. In much less than eighteen minutes, they would run into the outgoing communications wavefront of a frantic station.

That was time as starships saw it: but someone had to call the kif on com; someone had physically to push buttons and get to kif authority, while in each running stride of kifish feet down a corridor an inbound jumpship traveled a planetary diameter.

"Send," she said to Khym. "*The Pride of Chanur* inbound to

12

Mkks: requesting shiplist and dock assignment. We want berths clear on either side of us. We have cargo hazard. Send."

That would confuse them: a ship behaving like vane malfunction and talking like cargo emergency. Eight point nine minutes to get that message to station. Fifteen point something by the time station could so much as reply if they were instantaneous. *Someone* had to turn a chair, ask a supervisor, report the message. She heard Khym send it out—gods, a male voice from a hani ship: that alone would confound station central. They would not have heard its like before—would be checking their doppler-receivers for potential malfunction, doubting the truth while it hurtled down on them, even techs accustomed to *C*-fractional thinking—

"Send again: Message to *Harukk*, Sikkukkut commanding. We have an appointment. We've come to keep it. We'll see you on the docks."

(Someone deciding to relay that to the kif; kifish feet racing to locate the commander: another moment to decide to undock or sit tight—An instant's consideration and a planetary diameter flicked by.)

Ten minutes to launch a ship like *Harukk* if they ripped her loose from dock without preamble: forty more to get her sufficient range from mass to pulse the fields up. *Harukk* had a star to fight for its velocity, and that star was *helping* them come in.

Another half-minute down.

At this dizzying rate, inside this time-packet, there was a curious sense of slow-motion, of insulation from kif and threats.

And a sense of helplessness. There *were* things the kif could do. And there *was* time for those things—like pressing a trigger, or cutting a defenseless throat—

The dizziness hit; the concentrate had reached her bloodstream.

"You sick, Khym?"

"No." A small and strangled voice. It was not the first time.

"Chur?"

"Still with you, captain."

"Tirun: got a realtime check?"

"483 hours in transit, by the beacon."

13

"That's 20 minutes to final dump," Haral said.

On schedule, on mark. They had worked it all out at Kshshti, before they undertook this lunacy; worked it out the hard way, in the hours before undock, and in the long hard push that sent *The Pride* out to a jump by-the-gods deep in the gravity well and brought her in gods-rotted deep in this one, in a maneuver a hunter-crew would stick at and no merchanter ever ought to try.

They were hani, all: red-gold maned and bearded, red-gold hides. All of them but one had gold rings aplenty up the sweep of their tuft-tipped ears, gold that meant experience, voyages and ventures from home at Anuurn to Idunspol, Meetpoint, Maing Tol and Kura; Jininsai and Urtur; strange ports, foreign trade, dice-throws and wide bets. But no voyage like this one. Mkks was no hani port. Not a place where any honest freighter would care to go. And no honest merchanter had that outsized engine pack they carried; or that ratio of vane to mass.

Pyanfar said nothing. She uncapped the safety switch on what few armaments *The Pride* had, and broke another law.

"Eighteen to final dump," Haral said.

"Call coming—Tirun—Tirun—*which one?*" Khym's voice betrayed strain and panic, inexperienced as he was at that board. Disoriented as well as jump-sick, it was well possible. But the switch got made and the station's voice came through, dopplered out into sanity.

Mahen voice. *"Confirm dump, confirm dump—"*

"Repeat previous message. Tell them we want that shiplist. Fast."

There were codes they might have used to get cooperation from the mahendo'sat. There was no way to use them. The kif had ears too.

So they went at it the hard way, and Mkks station began to panic, dopplered message overlaying message, continuing a few seconds yet in the initial assumption: that they had a ship incoming dead at them in helpless malfunction.

By now their own message would be flashing to the kif, who would not be so naive.

The kif might—*might*—at this stage get a ship out to run; but she had not read Sikkukkut an'nikktukktin as that breed of kif.

14

Not with prisoners in his hands.

It was a hall somewhere within the upper reaches of the ship docked gods-knew where. Hilfy Chanur knew the ship-name now. It was *Harukk*.

And she knew the kif seated before her, among other kif. His name was Sikkukkut. He sat as a dark-robed lump on an insect-chair, among its black, bent legs. Sodium-glow relieved the murk close in, casting harsh shadow and orange-pink light. Incense curled from black globes set about the room and mingled with ammonia-stench. She could not so much as rub her offended nose. Her hands were linked with cords behind her back, Tully's likewise, for all the good that he could have done if his hands were free. Tully's face was pale, his golden mane and beard all tangled and sweat-matted, his fragile human skin claw-streaked and bleeding in the lurid glow. He had done his best. She had. Neither was good enough.

"Where did you hope to go?" Sikkukkut asked. "To do what?"

"I hoped," Hilfy Chanur said, because it never paid to back up with a kif, "to fracture a skull or two."

"No fracture," Sikkukkut said. "Concussed."—whether that that was a kif's humor or a kifish total lack of it. *Harukk*'s captain unfolded himself from his insect-chair in a rustling of black robes. There was no color save the sodium-light, none, throughout all the ship. Objects, walls, clothes were all grays and blacks—*They're color blind,* Hilfy thought, *really, totally blind to it.* She thought of blue Anuurn skies and green fields and hani themselves a riot of golds and reds and every color they decked themselves in, and held that recollection like a talisman against the dark and the hellish glare.

Sikkukkut moved closer. There was a sound like the wind in old leaves as other kif moved beyond the lights and the curling wisps of smoke. She braced herself; but it was Tully the kif aimed at.

"This speaks hani," Sikkukkut said. "It tries to pretend not—"

Hilfy stepped into his path.

"And where our understanding fails," the kif said in flawless

15

hani accents, "I know you have expertise with the human. We can secure that. Can't we?" He brushed past her and jerked Tully suddenly toward him by one arm and the other. The kif's claws made small indentations in his flesh and Tully stood there, face to face with those jaws a hand's breadth from his eyes. Hilfy could smell the sweat and fear.

"Soft," Sikkukkut said, tightening his grip. "Such fine, fine skin. That might have value on its own."

Closer still.

"Let him go!"

The dark snout wrinkled and the tip twitched. Kif sustenance was mostly fluid, so outsiders said: they were total carnivores, and disdained not at all to use those razored outer jaws. Two rows of teeth, two sets of jaws. One to bite and one fast-moving set far up inside that long snout to reduce the outer-jaw bites to paste and fluids the tiny throat could handle. The tongue darted in the v-form gap of the teeth. Tully jerked and winced in silence. The long face lifted, to use its eyes at level, its jaws—

"Stop it! *Gods rot it—stop!*"

"But it will have to stop struggling," Sikkukkut said, "I can't release my claws.—*Tell* him so. . . ."

Hilfy took in her breath. But Tully had stopped resisting, stopped—all at once, betraying himself.

"Ah. It does understand."

"Let him go."

The kif sniffed, jerked Tully against his chest and flung him free all in two quick motions.

Tully stumbled back. Hilfy thrust her shoulder between him and Sikkukkut's step forward and stood her ground with her knees wobbling under her from stark fear. Her ears were back; her nose rumpled into a grin that was not at all the grin of Tully's helpless primate kind.

A dry sniffing. Kifish laughter. Sikkukkut gazed at her from within the hood, the dim light glinting off his eyes. "Implicit in the hani tongue are concepts like friendship. Fondness. These are different than *sfik*. But equally useful. Particularly I do not discount them when you have such success talking to this creature. How have you bound him?"

16

"Try kind words."

"Do you think so? I have been kind. Perhaps then my accent confuses him. Tell him I want to know everything he knows, why he came, to whom he came, what he hopes to do—*Tell him this*. Tell him that I am anxious and impatient and many other things."

She weighed it what seemed forever. She wondered that the kif's patience could last so long.

It broke. The kif reached and she blocked that reach a second time with her shoulder. "—He's asking questions, Tully," she said all in one breath. "He wants to talk."

Tully said nothing.

"Guess he doesn't understand," she said. "He gets words muddled up—"

"I was *skku* to the *hakkikt* Akkukkak in his day." Sikkukkut's voice was soft, cultured; but in its softness she heard distinctly the clicks within the throat, the clashing of inner jaws as he lifted his chin. "We do know each other, he and I. We have met—before this. At Meetpoint. Does he remember?"

"—Friend of Akkukkak's," Hilfy said. *Distract him; gods, distract him, get him off the hunt.* "—If kif had friends."

"This human has *sfik*," Sikkukkut said, unmoving. "Akkukkak failed to know this. How could so soft a creature have so much *sfik* as this, to elude kif on Meetpoint docks? Had I been there, of course, he would have fared less well. And now I am here, and he is here, and I am asking him these things."

"—He's still asking questions," she said to Tully.

"I shall be asking them," Sikkukkut said. "I do ask them." The silence lingered. Light kifish fingers touched her shoulder, stroked the fur—

—withdrew. She sucked in a kif-tainted breath, trembling. Her ears were flat. She went deaf, near blind, hunter-vision narrowed to one long black tunnel focussed on the kif. But Sikkukkut drew away. He settled down again onto his many-legged chair and tucked his legs up until he indeed resembled some ungainly insect.

Tully's shoulder touched hers and leaned there. She felt his weight, the chill of his flesh: *gods, no, stay upright, don't give way, don't faint, they'll go for you—*

The kif lifted his hands to the hood he wore and dropped it back to his hunched shoulders, the first sight she had ever had of any kif unhooded, and it was no pleasant thing, the long dark skull, the dull black wisp of mane that lay forward-grained along the centerline: he was virtually earless, stsho-like in that respect. She had seen models. Holos. None were this peculiarly graceful, ugly thing.

The eyes rested on her, apt for such a face, dark and glittering. "You will understand these things: this creature has more than *sfik*-value; it has *sfik* itself. Let me speak in hani terms: Akkukkak perished of embarrassment. Therefore I love this creature, because it has killed my superior and now I have no superior."

"Gibberish."

"I think it quite clear. It has value. If it yields me its value and tells me what I ask I shall be further grateful."

"Sure."

"Perhaps I shall keep it in my affection and let it see the death of my friend Akkhtimakt. Perhaps I shall let it eat of my rivals."

It still spoke hani. The words meant other, kifish things. Her nape bristled. She wanted out, out of here.

"Translate this."

"—He's crazy as all kif."

The thin body shook and hissed atop its insect-perch. "Bigot. I shall make my own translations. *Kkkt!*"

"*Fool!*" mahen authority screamed into com; and other, less complimentary things.

"Stand by third dump," Pyanfar said.

"*You fool, daughter ten thousand fools, what do? what do? You get report sent* han *this outrage; we report you endanger—*"

The Pride dumped speed, a breakup of telemetry—

—phased in again, into a new flood of station chatter.

"Khym. List." Tirun's voice, prompting him in his muzziness. "Shift it. *Move.*"

The incoming shiplist turned up on number two screen, Haral's transfer of data smooth and routine while station's voice suddenly grew quieter. . .

"That's two minutes Light," Geran said. They were virtually realtime with Mkks station, moving at a crawl now, within the capacity of their realspace braking thrust.

Harukk, the shiplist said. There were other kifish names. A lot of them. A few mahendo'sat. A stsho. (A stsho, at Mkks!) A flock of tc'a and chi in Mkks' small methane-sector.

"Thank the gods," Pyanfar muttered, and began to take the telemetry again, shifting her mind back to business. "Approach," she said; and when Geran delayed: "*Course clearance,* gods rot it, look to it!" She began *The Pride*'s high-*V* braking roll. "Hang on. We're going with it. Now."

"What business?" Sikkukkut asked; and Hilfy pressed close to Tully's side, hearing the shifting of bodies about them beyond the smoke and the lights. "What did it arrange with the mahe? Kkkt. Ask it. Get an answer, young Chanur."

"—He's asking about deals," Hilfy said, and shifted again, for a kif moved up on that side of Tully. She looked at Sikkukkut. "*He doesn't understand.* He can't understand, gods rot it. He uses a translator on our ship. He can't speak, he can't shape our words even if he knew what I was saying to him."

Sikkukkut gathered up a silver cup from the table, a ball-like thing studded with thumbsized, flat-ended projections. He extended a dark tongue, dipped his snout into it and drank—gods knew what. He lifted his face. A thin tongue flicked about his muzzle. He still held the cup, his fingers caressing the flat-studded surface. "Choose better words. They will harm him, young Chanur, my *skkukun*; they will. Persuade him. Break this silence of his. If there are mechanical translators needed, we will supply them. Only make him speak."

"I'm trying." She shifted again, bringing herself between Tully

19

and the circling kif. "Back off!—Tully, Tully, tell him something. Anything. I think you'd better."

—*Lie*, she wished him; *play the game, I'll help you*—She felt the chill of his body against her side. She tried to look up at him, but he looked only to the kif, perhaps without the wit left to lie at all.

"Perhaps," said Sikkukkut—A door opened, admitting sullen light: another kif came in, silhouette like all the rest.—"We should consider another private interview with him. *Kkkk-t?*"

The kif hastened past the others. Sikkukkut turned his head.

"Ksstit," it hissed. "Kkotkot ktun."

Message. Hilfy drew a breath and felt Tully shiver against her. The interloper bent its hooded head near its captain's and whispered shortly. Sikkukkut rested with his hands upon his knees. His shoulders moved with a long, long breath and his jaw lifted.

"Kkkt! Kktkhi ukkik skutti fikkti knkkuri. Ktikkikt!"

All about them the room rustled with kif. *Take them from here.* Hilfy knew that much kifish. But not the inflections. Not why, or what had happened, or what happened next.

Kif closed about them: Tully let out an unaccustomed sound as they tore him from her side.

"Claws *in*," she yelled at the kif, "you stupid clot!"—She raked a kifish shin with a bare-clawed foot. A returned blow jolted her teeth and claws bit into her shoulders. There was nothing, with her hands tied, that she could do. They were enough to carry her. They seized her about both knees and did that at the end, despite her twisting and turning.

"Bastard!" she yelled past kifish bodies. She saw Sikkukkut still sitting there like some graven image in the dark, flanked by other kif.

"They are here," Sikkukkut said.

The door came between and closed.

Mkks station was a wall in front of them as *The Pride* homed in: the berth Mkks had assigned her glowed with the comeaheads on the number two screen while the closing numbers ticked off.

—*"Please you wait,"* mahen authority had protested via com during the last part of their approach, a much, much more conciliatory tone. *"Got already advise* Harukk, *same want conference, repeat, want conference. Request reply"*—

And closer still, in their silence: *"We make request you delay dock,* Pride of Chanur, *you got problem, please, we negotiate—"*

Because there was no way a station like Mkks had to stop any ship from coming in. And worse, there were fifteen vulnerable kifish ships dead-vee at dock, attached to Mkks' very vulnerable side. Mkks would have sounded alarms by now and thrown the section-seals on its docks, fearing projectiles launched, fearing kif; and riot.

—*"Please,"* the protest went on from Mkks authority: *"you stop this make negotiate the kif. We forbid you carry quarrel here."*

But they had the berth they demanded, a clear spot with nothing directly next them on either side. There were kif at hand. *Harukk* was in the sixth berth down, within the section. Two mahen traders were docked far over on the other side of Mkks' torus. Kif ships lined the adjacent section's docks. There were more mahen ships beyond. The solitary stsho. And tc'a and chi on methane-side.

—*"We meet you at dockside. We bring security. Make negotiate this matter. We appeal—"*

Clank-thump. The grapples took, from their side and from station's; the hookup routines started. They had a docking crew waiting. And security. So Mkks Central said.

"They've stopped talking," Khym said anxiously, meaning he had done nothing to cut them off by accident, in his inexperience. "They just went quiet."

But half a heartbeat later, another call came through.

"This is kif port authority," said a clicking voice. *"You are clear. Welcome to Mkks,* Pride of Chanur. *You may even bring your arms. The* hakkikt *extends safeconduct. You will have guides. Welcome, again, to Mkks."*

"Gods *rot* those bastards!" Geran cried.

"They've got their own personnel inside Central for sure," Tirun said. "That was a valid code."

"Move. We've got no choice." Pyanfar powered her chair about and hurled herself out of it, slapped the back of Haral's seat. "Get that linkup made."

"Rifles or APs?" Tirun was already on her feet; Haral's sister, tall, full-maned and bearded, with gold rings winking from her ear. There was Geran, slight and fairer: slight indeed against the size of Khym *nef* Mahn who climbed out of his seat and towered there, wider and taller and dead grim.

"APs," Pyanfar said with a tautness about the mouth, a drawing-down of her mustaches. "But I'll take a rifle; want you with one, too. Might want a distance weapon on those docks— might want a lot of distance, huh? And I don't think we have to worry about the law here."

There were quiet laughs, a soft explosion of ugly humor. Tirun opened the locker and passed out side-arms to her and Geran, mahen weapons that fired an explosive shell, not the motley patchup of pocket guns they had had back at Kshshti: APs with the necessary extra cartridge-case on the holster belt. And the two rifles, hers and Tirun's, longer-range and capable of a precise target, unlike the APs.

Pyanfar took the rifle and checked the safety and cycled the power-test while com crackled with further instructions. "*We will meet you outside,*" the kifish voice said. Thumps and clanks went on, the securing of lines and hoses.

The kif intended ambush. They took that for granted. Ambush might come later, after they had gotten far from the ship, or it might be a kifish rush the moment the airlock opened, and gods help any mahen dock-worker caught between.

"They're moving the access link in." Haral spun her chair about. "We're in." She rose and belted on the AP Tirun handed her.

"One of us," a voice said from the door, "has got to stay here and hold the farm."

"Gods rot—" Pyanfar did not need to turn. She saw Chur clearly from where she stood. Geran's sister leaned in the doorway of the bridge, blue breeches drawstringed perilously low, beneath the bandages swathing her midsection. "Chur—"

"Doing fine, thanks." The tightness about Chur's nose and

22

mouth denied it. "*Na* Khym's worth more outside, isn't he? And *I* can bust her loose from dock if need be." Chur limped across the bridge into her sister's reach and waved off Geran's help. She reached her own accustomed seat at scan and leaned on the back of it, kept going as far as Haral's co-pilot's post and sat down. "You tell me when you want her opened, captain. I'll figure shut for myself. No mahe's getting in, huh? Gods rotted sure no kif either."

Pyanfar gnawed her mustaches and threw one look at Geran, whose head lifted in terminal stubbornness. No reasoning with either sister. It ran in the blood. No reasoning with that sudden fire in Khym's eyes, when he saw a chance more to his liking than sitting guard up here. "Fine," she said. "Get Chur a rifle. In case. And get him one. Move it.—Khym, you keep your wits about you out there. You don't *breathe* without my order. Hear? We've got one problem on those docks. *One.* Hear me?"

"Aye."

They were husband and wife at other times. Not here. Not out there. As males went, he was a rock of stability and self-control.

And Chur was right: he was helpless with the boards.

Clank-thump-clang. The accessway was firm. They had connection to Mkks station.

Geran laid a rifle into Chur's grasp. Chur lifted it deliberately, though she had done well to lift a hand the other side of jump's time-stretch. Click-click. Safety off and on again. She looked up, ears pricked, mouth pursed in a wry smile that showed hollowness below her cheekbones, substance wasted in jumpspace healing. Her gold-red fur was lusterless and dulled. Light showed through her ear-edge where rings belonged. Chur had not dressed for amenities, not even important ones like that. "Get them out, huh?" Chur said, meaning Hilfy, meaning Tully, and gave a look at Geran before all of them. "Want you all back, too." she said.

"Come on," said Pyanfar. She turned on the pocket com she had hooked to her belt and gestured at the door. She wore no finery this trip, none of the bright color she favored, just blue spacer breeches, same as the rest, excepting Khym, who wore plain brown.

23

She headed out the door without a backward look, with Khym thumping along beside her and Haral and Tirun and Geran at her back.

"Com's live," Chur's voice pursued them down the corridor toward the lift, all-ship address that echoed everywhere. Behind them the bridge door hissed shut, sealing Chur in.

"Hurry it." Pyanfar hit the lift button and held the door open, diving inside last as the door shut and the lift whisked downward with a *G* drop of its own. They were rank at close quarters, unwashed since jump. Wisps of shed fur clung to bodies and clothes; copper taste filled her mouth. None of the crew was better off, none of them fit for diplomacy dockside. The gun dragged at her hip. The heavy rifle in the crook of her arm offered no comfort at all. Gods, gods, kif outside; or mahendo'sat—honest mahen station guards trying to prevent trouble and protect their own folk. The last thing any of them wanted was to shoot their way past allies who were duty-bound to stop them.

The lift braked and let them out again on lowerdecks. They sorted themselves out into an order of instinctive precedence as they headed down the hall: herself and Haral; Khym with partnerless Geran; Tirun at the rear, Haral's sister-shadow, a little lame in a long run, but veteran of too many ports to let anything reach their backs.

And Khym—calamity waiting a chance, she thought; lousy shot, male-like; male-like, a worry in a crisis; and twice as strong as any of them if it came to a set-to hand to hand.

"Got a call from a mahen officer named Jiniri," Chur's disembodied voice boomed out from com. *"We got ourselves some mahen station guards out there and a lot of citizens. I told them keep clear; they're not—not listening—"*

"You all right up there?"

"Fine, captain." The voice was hoarse and thin. *"Fine."* Stronger that time. *"Watch yourselves, huh?"*

They reached the bend toward the airlock. "We're there," Pyanfar said to the pickups in the corridor. "Where's the kif? See any?"

"Can't tell for sure. Haven't heard a sound in the access and I've got the gain up full. The com—they say they're out there. Mahe—mahendo'sat—out there—Me, I'd just as soon they were."

"Gods-rotted trouble. Tell them get out of it. Fast."

"Won't listen—They invoke the Compact. Say—say—Gods rot, you can guess."

Pyanfar snicked the safety off her rifle; there were two echoes and a couple of different sounds as Haral and Geran took the APs from their clip-holsters, took the safeties off and sent cartridges to the chambers. "We're set. Open us up sequential."

The hatch hissed open. They herded in and stopped, facing the outer door. "Seal us out and let's go," Pyanfar said.

The way behind them closed; the facing hatch shot open on an empty accessway, a yellow-lighted passage, icy cold.

Pyanfar dashed to the last point of cover where the accessway bent; Tirun took the other side with her rifle and the two of them came round the bend together, with three more guns aimed past their backs.

No kif. Empty passage. Pyanfar jogged soft-footed as far as the debouchment, where the yellow access tube gave over to descending rampway, a slope of interlocked gratings leading down to the pressure gates, and down again, a long exposed walk to the dock. People down there. Crowd-noise. A knot of about forty civilian mahendo'sat waited at the bottom of that long ramp, with a handful of mahen guards, dark, tall, primate: black-furred and one conspicuous tasunno, brown. And, gods, an anomaly in the midst of the crowd, a white-skinned stsho in drifting rainbow gossamer. The crowd surged forward with a gibbering outcry at the sight of them.

"Smell it?" Haral muttered, at her side.

Ammonia: kif scent. The dilapidated dockside was in twilight, and a hundred doorways showed on the anti-dockward side, any one of which might hold a sniper; if the wind had not been up her back before, that smell would have sent it.

She headed down in haste, a quick thunder of steps on the old-fashioned steel rampway, Haral at her side. The mahendo'sat below shouted and pushed and shoved among themselves, attempting the ramp while the guards struggled to hold the line.

One passed, came striding forward right onto the foot of the ramp as they came down to it. "You crazy, *crazy!*" The official-looking mahe waved her hands as they came face to face; her howl rose louder than the rest, even the stsho's agitated warble. "You go back 'board, we negotiate this trouble, not bring guns this dock! You keep back our line, let our guard do, hani captain! Hear? Go back you ship! We arrange talk; come, go between talk, you, kif *hakkikt!* No go down, hear! We got accommodations—we fix—"

They had it down smooth, she and Haral: she could deal with the mahe knowing her second in command was watching the crowd; and Geran and Tirun would be watching left and right, with the known space of the ramp at their backs. Gods knew where Khym's attention was. She ignored the waving hands, the attempt to catch her arm, and brushed the officer aside. "Come on," she said to her crew, and left the ramp, parallel to the line of guards who had their hands full with agitated dignitaries.

"You no go!" the mahe cried, trying to get in front of her again. The black face contorted in anguish. "No go!"

Pyanfar shoved with the rifle, sideways-held, which drew a collective gasp from the crowd. "Private business," she said. "Get your people out of the way, I'm telling you—Go! Get! Get cover!"

"*Not bring guns! Go, go you ship, not do, not do!*"

And from the stsho, who eluded the guards to rush up and wave white arms in her face: "You break Compact law. Complaint, we make complaint this barbarous behavior—We witness—"

"Move it!"

A second shove. The stsho recoiled in a wild motion of *gtst* spindly limbs, retreating in a flood of *gtst* gossamer robes and a warble of stsho language, headed full-tilt away from the scene. "Ni shoss, ni shoss, knthi mnosith hos!—"

"Maheinsi tosha nai mas!" the mahe cried; and mahendo'sat guards turned from crowd-control to facing hani rifles with their riot-sticks, as the mob discovered they were not at all interested in getting closer. There was a low sound of dismay and the docks grew astoundingly quiet.

"Move them," Pyanfar said, gesturing with rifle barrel still averted from the mahen official. "*Hasano-ma*. Authorization from your Personage. Hear?"

The mahe had drawn back to range herself with her guard. She stood with diminutive ears laid back. But they came up at *Personage*. Fear grew starker on her face.

"You've got your tail in a vise, Voice. I advise you, now, get back to Central and stay there. Fast."

"Captain!" Haral hissed. "Your left."

A shadow advanced at her flank, from the obscurity of gantries and machinery—kif, in numbers. The mahen Voice wheeled about and held up her hand in the face of the advance. "You stop! Stop! You break law!"—as the crowd shrieked and scuttled from between, and kept going, all but the Voice and her handful of nervous guards.

The kif drifted to a stop like a shadow-flow. One kept walking ahead, a black-robed figure. The rest stayed still, rifles in their hands. The whole dock seemed hushed, but for the distant whir of fans and clank of pumps and the fading sounds of fleeing civilians.

Law. The Voice's protest echoed faint and powerless. Mkks was in this moment very, very far from mahen law. And the mahendo'sat who claimed this disputed star station depended on pretences that had teeth only when mahen hunter-ships were in port.

Not in this hour, that was sure.

Pyanfar's ears flattened. She let them stay that way. "Well?" she said to the hooded kif who had stopped a little distance removed, rifle crosswise in its hands. "We were invited here. Name of one Sikkukkut. You represent him?"

The kif walked closer. Guns leveled: Khym's; hers. Haral's and Geran's were trained on the main mass of kif; and Tirun—Tirun, rear-guard, was not in her view; but she was back there and alert, that was sure.

The kif regarded them with dark, red-rimmed eyes. Its gray

27

wrinkled skin acquired further wrinkles up and down the snout and lost them. "I have message, hani."

It held out a thin hand. It held a small gold ring between its thumb and retractable fore-claw.

Tully's. Pyanfar held out her hand and the kif dropped the ring into her open palm, no more willing than she to be touched.

"Is the human alive?"

"At present."

Hilfy too? Pyanfar ached to ask and knew better than to give a kif a hint where the soft spots were. She kept disdain in the set of her mouth. "Tell Sikkukkut I'll talk about it."

There was a long pause. The kif gave no ground. "You come to trade. The *hakkikt* will see you. We choose a neutral ground. Bring your weapons. We have ours."

It was better than might have been. It was far too good an offer and she distrusted it. "We can deal here," she said. "Now."

"This wants time discussing. You ask condition. Alive, but uncomfortable. How long delay do you wish?"

She slung the rifle marginally upward, out of direct line, and wrinkled up her nose. "All right," she said, ever so quietly, as if no hani had ever broken a kif's neck or no blood ever been shed at Gaohn. "All right. We'll add it up later, kif."

It flourished a wide black sleeve: *follow.* It headed for its own ranks.

Pyanfar started walking and heard a soft-footed whisper of pads on decking behind her as her crew followed, with the rattle of gunstrap rings.

"Captain." A patter of non-retracting claws. The Voice caught her arm again. "No go—"

"Keep the kif away from my ship. You want this station in one piece?"

The Voice fell behind. "You crazy," the outcry pursued her, echoing off the dockside walls, the gray emptiness. "You crazy go that place!"

28

Two

Kif fell in and walked as an escort about them, their black robes like a moving wall in the dockside twilight. A dry-paper and ammonia smell rose about them, mingled with the scent of pungent and oil. Weapons rattled as they went, rifles and side-arms as illegal as their own.

They had docked in the same section as *Harukk*, without a section door to pass. The twilit deck stretched out in the upward-tending horizon of all station docks, up to a towering section seal that blinked red lights: *hazard, hazard, hazard*—precaution against riot and catastrophe. Mkks braced itself.

On the rows opposite the docks, in that space usual for services and bars such as spacers used, doorways filled with kif who lounged there with hateful eyes and whispers. Windows glowered with neon, with sodium- and argon-light; the girders overhead were palled with smoke no ventilation coped with, a haze about the glaring suns of the dock's floodlamps.

"Gods-rotted mahen hell," Haral muttered, striding along at Pyanfar's side. "The place is *all* kif."

The kif chittered and clicked among themselves in some obscure accent. Not main-kifish. Pyanfar knew words enough of that, and lost this entire.

They passed other doors from which came different, grass-eater smells; and strange moans and wailings: animals, kept and pent here. Hunter-kind that hani were, it turned Pyanfar's stomach. Kif fed on live food. While it lived.

Even on their own kind, in defeat. So rumor had it.

The kif in the lead tended toward the inner wall and a side corridor; they followed into that narrower passage, among armed kif who loitered in small clusters along the wall and stood away from it as they passed.

"*Kk-kk-kk*," one said, insulting them. Khym broke step: "*No*," Pyanfar hissed; and Geran grabbed his arm. They went further, with kif closing in at their backs and in front of them. The safe-

29

ties were already off the guns and had been off, since the air-lock. But there was nothing to win here. Not even for the kif.

Doors opened for them, on a room sodium-lit and reeking of kif-stink. The distinctive chatter and clicking of kif came out to them; and a high wail that was not kif died in a sudden squeak.

"Here," their hooded guide said, beside that open door, extending a wide-sleeved arm. "The *hakkikt* will welcome you."

"Huh," Pyanfar said, and stepped inside, into the murk, slid sideways of the door and sideways still as Haral and the rest followed, in amongst a crowd of kif, in amongst deeper shadows and that old-paper scent and scent of ammonia and incense so strong they blinded the nose to other cues.

There were chairs, tables: seated kif, standing kif.

And standing at the far end of the long room, amid the hellish glare and drift of incense, two paler figures, one pale-skinned, one red-brown.

Abruptly Pyanfar's rifle tumbled from carry to her hands and rifles and guns moved with one rattle that sounded round the room in rapid sequence, a hundred-fold. Five of them were hers. The ready-lights on rifle stocks glowed like a scatter of bloody stars.

Nothing moved after that. Their backs were at the wall; and Hilfy and Tully were thrust back amid a ring of kif with rifles all about them.

"*Sikkukkut!*" Pyanfar yelled. "You here, *hakkikt?*"

One kif had remained seated in a many-legged chair. That one unfolded upward and stepped from among its legs, one hand lifted. "You amaze me, Chanur. Now what will you do? Ask me to let them go?"

"Oh, no. I'm going to stand here. We're all going to stand here like this, and no one moves, until *my* friends get here."

"Your friends."

"Couple of hunter-ships. Just to keep the odds even while we trade."

The kif lowered his hand very slowly. He was utter shadow as he moved before the orange glaring lamp. The hands spread themselves, light streaming past the sleeves. A dry sniffing reached her ears. Kifish laughter. "So *that* was your request for

30

an open berth. Good, hani. Very good." He gestured toward his prisoners. "Do you want to take them now?"

Pyanfar did not look, refusing the distraction. She kept the gun aimed at the *hakkikt*'s chest. "We can have a real good bloodbath, *hakkikt*. Let me put it in kifish terms: we've got a *sfik* item here. It's *my* ego in question. So we'll just stand here. Hours maybe. We're patient. You want to send a message? Head my friends off from docks? Fine. Or come at us. It's all over in here, then."

The kif gave a flourish of his hands and sat down in his insect-legged chair, a black lump amid the black pillars of his folk, beside the solitary wisp of white and color that was the prize. In the tail of her eye she saw a shifting there among the prisoners, and heard a sharp, hurt gasp.

"I'd stop that back there," Pyanfar said, "*hakkikt*. One of my people over there yells, might distract me, huh?"

Sikkukkut lifted a hand. "Hunter Pyanfar, you should have been a kif. I tell you, I will deal with you."

They could die, they could all die, of this kif's embarrassment. Of failing him. Or of trusting him. But it was an offer. She drew a long, even breath.

"Fine. Let's wait on my friends."

"There truly are such?"

"Truly, there are."

"You have a fast ship, hunter Pyanfar."

A kif—gave points away and halfway admitted to surprise. It was, gods help them, conciliatory. Or mockery. Or some obscurely kifish thing.

"What do you want?" she asked. It had to be the right question. Or there might none of them leave the room alive. "You wanted me here. Why? What trade?"

There was long silence. "Skokitk," the kif said. *Cease.* "*Skokitk!*"

The pale figure hit the floor, a thudding tumble to its knees. The red-brown moved and crouched low beside it. Pyanfar never turned her head.

"Hilfy," Haral said. "Very carefully. Get up and get him over here."

31

C. J. Cherryh

"*No*," said Sikkukkut. "This would not be wise."

"Then we'll wait," said Pyanfar. "He all right, Hilfy?"

"So far," Hilfy said, a hard, thin voice. She heard the spasms of breathing, saw the paler figure rise again, assisted to his feet. "So far."

"Let us," said Sikkukkut, leaning an elbow on the high arch of a chair leg, and resting his long jaw on his hand, "—let us settle this matter. Let us dismiss this inconsequence and talk like allies."

"Allies in a mahen hell."

"Mkks is neutral ground. Let us welcome your friends when they come."

"We'll wait."

"They really are coming."

"Absolutely. And your ships still have their noses set to station. Still sitting targets."

"If you had meant to die you would have killed your kin first."

"Maybe."

"So these allies will not fire on our ships, no more than you did. You intend to get out of here. So do I. Therefore your prizes are intact. And mine is."

Kif-thought. It made mazes. "*What* prize, kif?"

"You," said Sikkukkut. He leaned toward the upright and rose from his chair ever so slowly, a smoky drift against the glaring lights. "You are here. And your allies are. I am no merchant. Trade—does not interest me. I make other transactions. Young Chanur—*you* may cross the room. Do so slowly."

"Tully—" Pyanfar heard Hilfy say. "Come on."

"No," said Sikkukkut. "He is ours. You may go, young Chanur."

Silence then.

"Hilfy," said Pyanfar. Her eyes never strayed from Sikkukkut; the gun barrel never moved. "Get over here. Now."

"He—"

"*Now.*"

There was slow and careful movement. The kif stirred and eclipsed Tully's white shape. Pyanfar never let her eyes stray,

32

trusting Haral and the others to watch the other kif. She had her own target all picked out. She heard the quiet movement reach her side, heard Hilfy's harsh breathing.

"Give me a gun." Hilfy's voice, hoarse and strained, with mayhem in it.

"Stand fast," Pyanfar muttered. "Just stand still, imp—Don't get in front of anyone."

"Get Tully out of here."

"In time," said Sikkukkut. "Perhaps."

"What perhaps?" asked Pyanfar.

"How soon," asked Sikkukkut, "these *friends* of yours?"

"Inbound now," Pyanfar said. Sikkukkut made a flourish of his sleeve, a sweep of his robe, an acceleration of small moves. "Stand still, *hakkikt.'*

"Ah."

"I advise you. Stay put." The shot she fired would take out Sikkukkut. The returning barrage would do for her, her crew, and the wall behind them. "Not a convenient time to leave dock, even if you could get to your ships. *Hilfy, get. Get out.*"

"With your allies," Sikkukkut said, "I will also deal. There is no need for haste." He paced aside, the only moving figure in the room. "After all." He moved again. Closer. Spread his arms in a dark flourish. "*Fire,* hunter Pyanfar. Or admit I have judged what you will do."

"Don't push me, kif."

"*Civilization.* Is that not your word for it? *Friendship?* The mahendo'sat who will die of your rashness are your allies. Your own life is still more precious. *I* shall be your ally, hunter Pyanfar, as I was at Kshshti. Is it not true? Others aimed at this young hani and this human. *I* took them. Therefore they were safe. Is this not a *friendly* act?"

"You want us out of here before the rest of us reach station. Is that it?"

"I will deal with *you,* hunter Pyanfar. Nankhit! Skki sukkutkut shik'hani skkunnokkt. Hsshtk!"

Rifles lowered, one by reluctant one, among the kif. A tremor came to her muscles, a long, long shiver; her heart thudded against her ribs. But the rifle stayed steady.

33

"You may go," said Sikkukkut.

"Haral. Get them out. Get everybody out."

"Captain—"

"Move it!" She heard a low rumbling. "*Khym*. Out."

"Come on," she heard from Haral. She drew in her breath, heard the sibilance of cloth and quiet hani feet, the slight rattle of arms.

She was alone then. Herself. A roomful of kif. Tully and Sikkukkut.

"You plan to die like this?" the *hakkikt* asked.

Her nose rumpled into a hani grin. "Scare you, kif?"

Sikkukkut walked again, laid a hand on Tully's shoulder, where he stood in the others' grip. Gently. "One last prize. I shall keep this one for a while, and give you another, perhaps, for your *sfik*.—Your crew is still outside. Do they pick and choose your orders?"

"They understand me."

The kif stared at her within the shadow of the hood, faceless against the glare.

And laughed his dry laughter then. The hand fell from Tully's shoulder. "Hunter-ships."

"They'll come."

"Skhi nokkthi." Sikkukkut retreated again to his chair, the while a rustling of cloth told her of movement at her side. The kif reached to the table beside the many-legged chair, where a meshwork bowl stood. Something in it raced and scrabbled madly; squealed as the *hakkikt*'s hand closed. The squeal ceased abruptly. He popped it in his mouth, the jaws worked rapidly a moment. Then he took an ornate cup and spat into it.

She laid her ears back.

"Would you join me at table?" asked Sikkukkut. "No, I thought not." A bony-knuckled hand gestured Tully's way. "You know he has not spoken since the day we took him. Not a word. He utters sounds, sometimes. I cherish such *sfik*. His words are precious. Perhaps he will give them up."

Take him from me, the kif meant, *do something about it, if you can.*

"The mahe gave you this passenger at Meetpoint," Sikkukkut

went on. "Was that all? Was that all *Mahijiru* brought you? Goldtooth. Is that not what you call that mahe? Ismehanan-min is his name. We are old acquaintances. I spoke to him about alliance. He was doubtful." Again Sikkukkut raised the cup and thrust his snout inside. He lifted his face after. "I think this bigotry."

"Think what you like. Let's talk about Tully, shall we?"

"I was *skku* to Akkukkak. Vassal, you would say. And potential heir—to use hani terms, which mislead. You did me a service."

"Killing Akkukkak, you mean."

"Even so. Often our interests have been mutual. This human, for one. And have you noticed the stsho here? Uncommon. *Stsho* send emissaries about. Even here to Mkks. When the grass-eaters raise such dust, expect fire. And there is fire, hani. From Llyene to Akkt to Mkks. Even Anuurn. A fool would reject my offer. You are not a fool."

"No. I'm not."

He set the cup aside. "Is *Mahijiru* one of these ships?"

"No. *Lost*, I thought you told me."

"Perhaps. Ismehanan-min is full of surprises."

"And Tully's folk? What happened to them?"

A kifish shrug.

"You had a ring, gods rot it. It came from *Ijir*. What's your part in that?"

"I have my agents. Even among Akkhtimakt's spawn. That ring *has* traveled, hasn't it? Like Tully himself. Perhaps you'll give it back to him."

"Did you take that ship?"

"I? No. That was Akkhtimakt. *He* has that prize. I have mine. Go back to your ship. I'd hate to have a misunderstanding with your allies coming in. If my ships should be damaged at dock— you understand. It would be a great mistake."

"So would harming him. You want talk. All right. Return him now. You'll get talk. You'll get something more. I'll *tell* you we won't fire."

There was long, long silence. "Ah. *Promises*. Another hani term. Some hani put *sfik*-value on a promise. Mahendo'sat are another matter. I will keep this human. To assure good behavior. But for your promise I will give you one of mine."

"I get him back. Alive. And well."

"There's no kif word for promise. When your allies are here. I promise." Wrinkles chained up and down the kif's dark snout, limned in light. "I do tell you truth. You should thank me, hani. Someone else might have gathered up your people, there on Kshshti dock. I found them in an alleyway. But it was not I who aimed at them."

"Akkhtimakt."

"His agents. If he had taken them, there would be no help for them. I've protected them. Comparatively."

"Tully." Still she did not look at him. She did not want to see that look, that blue-eyed trusting look that confounded her and knotted up her gut. "Tully. They want me to go. Few hours more. I get you back, Tully."

"Fine," he said, a faint, slurred voice. "Py-anfar. Go."

"Kkkt. It *does* talk."

She stood very still. Points, gods: Tully scored on the *hakkikt* and maybe did not know it. She held the gun constantly toward Sikkukkut, not daring look Tully's way.

"Promises," she said. "Your ships are safe. Safe as Tully is."

The silence hung there. "We will talk," Sikkukkut said then. "He and I. While we wait on your agreement. Go back to your ship. You have no choice, hani. See that nothing happens."

"Likewise." She backed for the door, reached the archway where the brighter light of the twilit hall fell on the corners of her eyes. There was light to one side of that vision, hani red and blue and brown. There was kif black to the right. She kept the gun trained on the *hakkikt* inside the room. "You want a deal, kif," she said into the murk. "An alliance. I'll ask my allies. Don't foul it up, huh?"

Silence from the room. Perhaps the majority expected her to fire and scour the room. Most kif would, losing points by it, in Tully's case. Destroying all, both gain and loss.

A very arrogant kif might not.

Or a hani with a friend in there. In his own arrogance, Sikkukkut was confident he knew hani. She stared constantly at

36

that single seated shadow beneath the lights. At the *hakkikt*'s right, among the guards, she saw Tully's pale face and never focussed on it. About the room the LED ready-lights of a hundred rifles glowed a wicked, unblinking red.

She dived aside, rolled her shoulders against the wall and bounced off it, headed at a trot for her own crew while they covered the kif down the hall.

"Tully—" Hilfy said.

"We can't get him yet."

"Give me a gun." Hilfy caught at Geran's wrist. "For the gods' sakes—"

"Gods rot it, *move*." Pyanfar tore Hilfy away one-handed and dragged her along the hall. Hilfy dug her claws in, roundhoused a swipe at her and Khym caught her by that arm.

Hilfy fought without a sound. Her feet went from under her in their haste and Khym hugged her against his side and kept her moving, down the hall, round the corner.

Further still, as they reached the open docks. Hilfy still struggled, but more weakly now, as Khym maintained his grip.

Pyanfar never let them slow. There were kif, kif everywhere, in the doorways off the dock, standing about by the gantries of the ships.

Up ahead—far distant—blue lights blinked on the wall above two shipberths: incoming ships, one on either side of *The Pride*.

"We'll get him," she promised Hilfy, herself hard-breathing as they strode toward that goal. "We'll get him out."

Hilfy's rage sank away to gasps. She thrust away from Khym's side as he let her go, staggered free, weaving in her steps ahead of them.

Rage; and grief. It was not the youngster she had lost and found. It was all too profound for light-hearted Hilfy. Pyanfar's gut hurt, seeing it, seeing the bowed shoulders, the hurt no one could hold and cure.

She had grown too old for comforting, the niece who used to swing upon her belt-ends and laugh and ask for tales, where the ship went, where she fared, what the stars were like.

Hilfy strode on ahead of them, staggering now and again.

There was bloodstain on her trousers and her fur, across her shoulders. Her mane was tangled and matted with it.

And the ships were coming in.

"Chur," Pyanfar called on pocket com, there at the foot of the ramp. "Chur—We're coming in." She cast a glance back; Tirun was still behind them, gun live, covering them against the chance of attack from the shop-lined far side of the docks, over among the shadows and the kif. The mahendo'sat and stsho had gone, hidden, abandoning them.

"*You get 'em?*" The voice coming back from the bridge was faint and full of breath.

"Hilfy's with us," said Pyanfar. Hilfy's ears had come up as they started up the ramp, pricked forward with the first liveliness she had shown. "Had a little problem getting Tully loose. We're working on it."

The ears went down.

"*Hhhuh,*" Chur said, or the com lost something. "*Hatch is open. Vigilance and Aja Jin are headed in; they haven't dumped down yet. They want our instructions.*"

"Huh." From her side. "Confirm as agreed." An unshielded pocket-com was not the way to talk *that* out. She strode up the chill ramp plates with one glance back to every three steps forward. Tirun had stationed herself in the cover the start of the ramp afforded, there by the gantry control console, rifle slowly sweeping the dock. They entered the covered accessway and Pyanfar glanced back yet again, Haral standing by her side with AP in hand. "Tirun!" she called out, and Tirun ducked about and pelted up the echoing metal plates.

Inside, then, Tirun still out of breath as they hurried through the lock into *The Pride's* safe inner corridors. Geran swore in relief. Tirun clicked the safety back on her rifle and used it for a stick as she walked: "Not good for sprints anymore," Tirun muttered as they holstered the APs and slung the rifles back to carry-straps. Hilfy went on through the corridors ahead of them, ears down; got into the lift first and held the door for them, tempers past. But no one touched her. *Welcome home, kid. Welcome back. Glad you're all right, at least.* No one ventured it.

Neither back nor right, Pyanfar thought, with profile view of that young face as the lift went up: ears back, mouth tight on silences. *Gods rot it, niece, I got everything I could.*

The lift let them out on bridge level. They trudged out in no particular order. Khym stayed with them, past his cabin and baths and all such allurements. They were filthy, cold from the docks, and stank of kif. They brought *that* smell onto *The Pride* along with them.

Chur powered the co-pilot's chair about when they came in, inexorable move of machinery cradling a bandaged hani who lay shrunken and feeble against the cushions. But her ears came up and she lifted her head.

"Good to see you, kid."

Hilfy crossed the bridge and bent down to clasp Chur's arm. "Good to see you," Hilfy said hoarsely. "I thought they'd got you. Gods, I thought you were dead."

"Huh. No." Chur laid her head back as they gathered around her. She shut her eyes and opened them refocused on Pyanfar. "Captain. I sent the confirm-message. Not a rotted bit of help from the mahendo'sat on-station. 'Cept traffic control. Central's staying real quiet. They've been real upset ever since our friends dropped into system. Scared. Not saying a thing but necessities."

"Huh." Pyanfar laid her hand on the chairback. "Best you get to bed, right now."

"Food," Chur said. "Lousy c-stuff. I want a cup of gfi."

"I'll get it," Khym said, and set the rifle down (gods, on the counter, loose) and headed off.

"Secure that!" Pyanfar snapped. He jerked to a stop and looked about, looking for what he had done. But Tirun took the gun along with Chur's.

"Got it, captain. He gave it to me."

Pyanfar nodded and collapsed onto her rump on the console edge as Khym headed off. She gave him no mercy. None. Crew covered for him; and they did it not because he was male, or hers, but because he had just earned it out there, if he had the sense to know it. That warmed some of the cold at her gut.

Some. That beaten weariness in the slump of Hilfy's shoulders, that bleak, all-business stare—that was out of reach.

"How close are our friends to final dump?" she asked Chur, and handed her rifle on to Haral. "We got anything trustable out of Central?"

"I marked the first alarm," Chur said, gestured loosely toward comp, a ticking chronometer on the number two monitor. "Figure—figure our ships'll be dumping down about now, but Jik may freehand it. Don't trust the kif to tell us, huh?"

Understatement. Complicated comp operations from a crew-woman doing well to be sitting upright. "You're going off-duty. Shift's Haral and Tirun. Rest of us clean up, then turn about. Move it. We've got company coming."

There were minute delays, a quick dart of Haral's eyes.

Questioning. *What do we do? Sit here?*—because sitting here at dock was not altogether sane. *Think there's a chance of pulling the rest of this off?*

"Send," Pyanfar said. "Us to both those ships. Tell them we're back aboard. Tell them we've talked to the kif and we've got *half* the job done. Kif wants to go on talking."

"*Tully's left there,*" Hilfy said, of a sudden turning about and leaning toward her on the counter edge. Hilfy's voice cracked and spat. "Four *days*, aunt—four days they worked on him. . . ."

"Then we made good time," Pyanfar said, cold, very cold, because Hilfy wanted heat. "I'd have figured five. We'll get him out."

"They're taking him apart." Hilfy stood up and back. "That bastard kif's got time to do it in."

"We got what we could."

Hilfy drew one long breath. "Yes," she said, and was all quiet, all the way through.

"Send that message," Pyanfar said to Tirun, and unbuckled her AP and passed it to Haral to put in the locker with the rest. She turned back to Hilfy. "Go wash up. *We're not through yet, niece.*"

"Aye," Hilfy said, and turned and walked off.

"You too," she said to Chur. "Geran, get her out of here."

"Want the gfi," Chur protested.

"Fine. It'll come back there where you are, just fine." She stood there while Geran helped her sister up from Haral's chair and supported her toward the door. "Stay to Khym's cabin, huh? I want to keep you near controls. Might need you to sit watch."

"Aye," Geran said on Chur's behalf, a departing glance.

The situation was not what they had feared, in all: hostages murdered, Mkks with major damage—That was what could have happened even before they made dock. It was little short of a miracle they had worked, getting in and getting Hilfy free.

But it was not good enough.

Haral slid into the chair that Chur had left, powered it about again and got to work in Haral's own unflappable fashion, mind going instantly from dockside to those boards with no glitch-ups likely. Pyanfar tested the weapons-locker door and heard the electric tick of the resisting latch. "That access camera and the motion-sensor better stay on. We don't control those gates down there."

"Right," Haral said, and reached and keyed mode and number without a beat missed, while the numbers ticked by on comp's other sections.

"Got a confirmation on that final dump," Tirun said, holding the complug to her ear. "Captain, just got the confirm from *Aja Jin*. Captain's compliments and he'll see you here soon as he gets in."

Pyanfar looked at the chronometer. They were down to two minutes Light on response-time between themselves and the incoming ships. "Understood," she said. Two minutes as light moved. A good deal longer for a ship that had blown off its *C*-fractional energy to move into station's slow-going frame of reference, and longer still to dock. "I'm going for that bath."

Mayhem and chaos might erupt. There might be attack. There were wobbles in her knees, deprivations coming due. There was still time for a bath, a cup to drink; in the meanwhile it was *The Pride*'s seniormost crew at controls. No flap, no emotional decisions, no foulups. Thank the gods.

She dumped it all into their laps and headed down the corridor untying belt-cords as she went.

Hilfy had gone below, to the empty crewquarters. Alone. She would not have had that. But there was nothing else to do, nothing else to offer.

So we throw the party later, kid. When it's due.

Gods help us all.

She thumbed the door open and headed straight for the bath, shed trousers into the bin, hung the com on the bathroom wall within reach of the shower cabinet and turned on the warm mist with a melting sigh.

Fur by the fistful swirled into the drain at her feet—gods, only half of it was left from jump: the kif business had scared the rest off. And the while she lathered and rinsed under the warm flood she tried to collect her jump-scattered wits, plotting and replotting how to bet the next dice-throw. The kif would have a trick or two. She knew.

And the com beeper went off as she reached to cut in the drying-cycle.

"Gods, what?" she asked, snatching the com, shedding water on the floor. Her heart thudded. Showers—*any* offduty indulgence—had begun to make her paranoid. They knew; somehow the whole universe knew the moment her guard went down.

"Got a kif outside in the accessway," Haral's voice came back. "Captain, it swears it's *yours.*"

Three

"You. Kif." Pyanfar leaned above the com console, and saw the intruder on the camera they had rigged back at Kefk, a huddled black-robed silhouette in the yellow glare of their access tube. It was cold out there, no place for standing. The kif's breath frosted against its own darkness. "Kif, this is Pyanfar Chanur. You can talk back from there. You got some news for me?"

"Skkukuk is my name. Let me in, Chanur. The *hakkikt* an'nikktukktin has sent me."

"In a mahen hell."

"I must freeze then."

"*Get your freezing carcass out of my accessway!*"

The kif stood still. Lifted its arms. The sleeves of the black robes fell back, disclosing black, hairless arms and long, retractable-clawed hands. "Chanur's safety is mine. I offer it my weapons."

"Library," she muttered to Haral; and Haral dived for the comp, looking to see what Linguistics made of that as a formula. Meanwhile she stalled; and the hair on her backbone stood up. "Kif. Skkukuk. What do you expect from me?"

"I wait to discover."

—"Captain," Haral muttered, "library's blank on that idiom."

—"Fine. Gods rot.—*Kif, you take my orders, do you?*"

"I am Chanur's."

She killed the sound. Straightened. "Gods know what that means either. We've got a Situation," she said; and as the number four screen carrying the routine output from station central and traffic control suddenly went all to kifish letters, her jaw dropped. "Gods fry them—"

Tirun snatched at controls. Nothing better happened. "That's the station nav output," Tirun said, hitting keys as fast as her fingers could move. Translation came up: *Transmission difficulty.* Lights started flashing elsewhere on the com board, urgent com-

43

munication arriving from incoming *Vigilance* and *Aja Jin*, which had just seen their navigation monitors go totally kif.

Things went chaotic for the moment: Haral swore and started switching systems. Images flickered on the monitors in rapid sequence. "Gods!" Pyanfar hissed, putting kif and airlocks out of her mind in the press of worse disasters. She rang the general alert to bring the crew up. "We got anything to give them?"

"Station's not jamming us," Haral said. "We can output our own scan to our friends out there, but it's not much, in our position. We can beacon them in to dock right enough."

Aft, the lift was working, crew on the way from lowerdecks to the bridge as fast as feet and *The Pride*'s lift mechanism could carry them. The alarm bell rang in spurts, drowning other sound at intervals.

"Message from central," Tirun said. "Kif say—say: compliments of the *hakkikt* and they won't interfere with the docking of our ships. This is relayed . . . We've got another call: stsho— that's a protest. Mahendo'sat—a group is protesting to the kif and wanting rescue. They're stuck in some shops down the way and they're afraid to go outside. They want police. Meanwhile the kif are saying mahen crew will handle docking for *Aja Jin* and *Vigilance*—The *hakkikt*'s compliments again."

There was a soft noise, a wheeze of leather upholstery: Chur made it back alone and took a post. There were running steps in the corridor behind.

"What we got?" Chur asked straightway.

"Got a kifish takeover of the whole gods-forsaken station," Pyanfar muttered. "Got a gods-be kif in our gods-be access—*Get back to bed!*"

"Give me that," Chur murmured to Tirun, all business; and business went on in mutters and com-chatter.

A thunder of steps, scrape of claws on decking; more bodies hit the cushions, one, two, three: Haral delivered a terse briefing to late-arriving crew and Pyanfar let it go, finding more and more information popping up on her screens as stations came alive. *Vigilance* and *Aja Jin* were still proceeding on their approach toward docking: "Negative. No fire," she answered the query from the inbound mahendo'sat. "Brief them on it, Tirun."

She spun her chair half about and saw *The Pride*'s bridge more crowded than it had been since Kshshti: Hilfy and Khym were both at posts.

"Kif are counting on us to calm it down," she muttered to the lot of them. "Gods rot it, they're pushing us hard as they can push. Gods-cursed kif bastard *knows* we won't fire cold."

Hilfy swiveled her head half-about. "He's got Tully," she said, once and tautly. So it was said. The line was drawn.

And gods be feathered if she wanted to be put under pressure to do what she already told herself she was crazy for doing on her own. Like sitting pat at dock instead of tearing loose and running with what she had.

"So we've got our own detainee," Pyanfar said, puzzling Hilfy: she saw the ears cant in bewilderment. She opened a channel below to the accessway com. "Skkukuk. What do we do with you?"

The kif had tucked down in a ball. It stood up and straightened. "I am freezing, hunter Pyanfar."

"Good. What if I blow your head off? Would the *hakkikt* like that? You offend him somehow?"

"I lack all status with him."

"Hope to gain it, do you?"

"I am hopeless, unless your *sfik* is greater than it seems."

She laid her ears back. "Kif, you want to live?"

"Naturally."

"Strip and get inside that lock. Leave the robes in the lock. Walk into main corridor. And wait there."

It bowed, hands tucked away again.

She leaned and keyed the outer hatch open, powered the chair around and met Hilfy's quick, flat-eared stare. "Got ourselves a *sfik* item down there. Tully it isn't. We'll see what we've just been handed. Tell *Vigilance* and *Aja Jin* we're playing this business out and staying at dock; they can do what they like about it."

"We've got scan image going out," Haral said. "Jik says affirmative, he's still coming in."

"Gods hope he isn't kidding," Geran said.

"Gods hope," Pyanfar muttered. Visions of attack assailed her.

45

One swift blast at the dock from either of her two incoming allies and it was all over. But she trusted Jik. She hoped. "Khym. Come on."

"You going down there?" Hilfy asked, turning her chair about.

"Nose to that board, youngster. *Stay put.* Come on, Khym. This one's yours."

Khym's ears came up. He had not looked so cheerful since they took him into fire on the docks in the Kshshti mess.

She had her pocket gun in one hand, a com unit at her belt with the gain turned up full as the two of them rode the lift down. Khym had his bare hands; and those were not bad odds—unless, she thought, the kif down in their airlock had a knife or worse: gods witness, they were not a warship, to have security precautions and detectors. They went on guesswork, took the gamble—

—lunatic, a small voice said. For a bedraggled, half-crazed human's sake, to risk *The Pride.*

"Don't push it," she said to Khym while the lift was on the way down. She thumbed the safety off the pistol. "Gods forbid it's called our bluff and brought us a grenade."

"What do you do then?" Khym asked.

"Throw it back, for godssakes! How should I know?" The thought ruffled her nape-hairs. And punching the button on the in-lift com: "Haral—Stand by that inside hatch release!"

The lift door whisked open. She walked out after Khym with her gun ready in her hand.

"Now, captain?" Haral asked.

"Now."

A corridor and a half away the airlock's inner hatch opened. Pyanfar grabbed Khym by the arm and jerked him over to the side of the corridor where there was vantage.

Like a black slither of freefall oil, the kif rounded the corner and stood there a good distance down the longest corridor *The Pride* had—stood there, all gangling gray-black nakedness, hands out to show that they were empty.

"All right," she said, never taking the gun off the kif's middle. "You keep those palms out, kif, and keep them in plain sight."

"The air stinks."

"It stinks out there too, kif. Just come a bit forward. Stop right there. Khym, go to the lock and get its clothes. Search them for weapons."

"There is my knife and my pistol," the kif said.

"Fine. Move it, Khym."

Khym went—not without queasiness, that passing in the corridor. Khym flattened his ears as he went by the kif. The kif half turned its head, the hunched shoulders, the forward thrust of the long jaw become something strangely serpentine and graceful. The kif continued the motion in reverse, swinging back to her. The hands lifted, showing empty palms.

"You're mine, huh?" Pyanfar said sourly. "What's Sikkukkut got in mind in this exchange? I don't trade my claim on the human. Hear?"

It made a slow move of its hands. "I hear."

"So answer, you earless bastard. What are you doing here?"

"Waiting," it said.

"On what?"

It gave a kifish shrug. "I don't know."

"You hand me puzzles, kif, I'll skin you."

Khym reappeared in the corridor behind the kif with his hands full of black cloth and leather. "Knife and gun," he called out. "Nothing else."

"Bring its robes. Give them to it."

He brought them. Dropped them at the kif's side.

"May I?" the kif asked.

She motioned with the gun. It bowed its head and moved very slowly, gathered its belongings and held them to its chest with that hunch of shoulders and lowering of head peculiar to kif. It looked sinister in one instant, beaten and pathetic in the next, in each shifting shadow on the gray-black, wrinkled skin.

The hairs rose on her back. "Khym. Open up that washroom. Skkukuk. Inside with you."

The head lifted. "It is waste," Skkukuk said. "Give me my weapons and I shall give you your rivals."

47

"*Inside.*"

"I serve a fool."

"Not a great enough fool to turn my back on you, kif. Either Sikkukkut sent you or Sikkukkut threw you out; and in either case I don't want you."

Skkukuk's head drew down between his shoulders. With that same serpentine grace he turned away and passed the open washroom door. But she thought that she had scored.

"Tully's old quarters," Pyanfar said to Khym, who lingered outside. "Toss it the rest of its garb."

"We *keeping* this thing?"

"Heave it."

Khym tossed boots and belt through the door. The pistol and knife he kept.

And shut the door and locked it. "It'll probably wreck the room," he said.

"That's the least of our troubles."

"What's it want, for the gods' own sakes?"

"You guess, you tell me." She thumbed the safety back on her pistol, discovering her knees had gone to jelly. "Gods *rot*, I got a kif on my ship, and he wants to know what for. How should I know? I got ships incoming, I got a station in kif hands, and the kif are playing tag." She turned and stalked back toward the lift, turned again. "Stand guard down here. Doublecheck that gods-rotted lock that it's closed, put that stuff away, and for the gods' own sake you open that washroom door—I don't care if the kif blows up, you open that door I'll space you first, then the kif! Hear me?"

His ears went down. His jaw dropped.

She walked back into the lift.

"And next time," she yelled back down the corridor, "when I say give a thing you don't drop it, hear?"

The door closed. He was still staring.

She leaned on the lift wall as the car slammed up. She was shaking, gods, and *food* occurred to her. Desperately.

But there was no time for that.

"Haral. What's going on?"

"*They're entering critical approach.*"

"*Both* of them?"

"*Aye, captain. Both incoming.*"

So it was not attack. *Vigilance* and *Aja Jin* were both committing themselves to dock and there was nothing left to defend their vulnerable backsides.

The car stopped; the doors opened. She stalked down the corridor toward the bridge.

"*They're on our beacon,*" Haral's voice continued from the com, tracking her on speakers down the corridor. "*Kif are outputting guidance now. It jibes with ours. So far. Captain, we got another problem. Station-folk. We got our boards jammed with queries. We got panic out there.*"

She muttered oaths and quickened her pace. Station riot. It was enough to coagulate any spacer's blood. "We've got to hold this dock," she said, arriving through corridor's end onto the bridge; and not a harried head turned when her voice acquired a body. "Hilfy. Be polite. Tell the station-folk we got a sniper problem on this particular stretch of dock and keep off it." She flung herself into her own chair and sent it whining about into position. Screens showed her what information *The Pride* could gather with station output reduced.

"Kif might agree to damp those station calls down," Haral said.

"Better they get through. Less panic that way. Ten thousand citizens pouring down here after news is the last thing we need."

"Uhnn." Haral sent another list her way. "Messages you might want to see."

She scanned it.

—*Compliments of the* hakkikt, *system scan transmission is resumed for incoming ships. It will be accurate.*

—*The Personage urgently requests information—*

—*We make protests this insane and irresponsible action. Protest will be filed stsho authority—*

—*Compliments of the* hakkikt, *docking crews are ordered into position—*

Thank the gods.

49

Jik of *Aja Jin* entered the bridge, Jik—alone: he wandered in like some bewildered spacer hunting a proper bar, his black face doleful and worried as ever. He wore a gold collar and half a dozen bracelets; a broad gold and bronze belt above a kilt of purple and bronze stripes; carried an AP gun in its black holster over all of this, weapon enough to take out half the bridge; two knives—Jik rarely underequipped himself, and the condition of the docks out there did not encourage optimism. "About time, Jik," Pyanfar said to him.

"See? Tell you that new engine hold, a? You number one sharp, Pyanfar, handle this ship good. *Ker* Hilfy, good see you 'live."

"*Na* Jik." Formal and self-contained. "Good to see you."

Not *when do we go in, how soon? Give me a gun.* Hilfy kept to drill, part of crew. But if she had smiled since her rescue, it was perfunctory, tightly measured.

Through the several waiting hours.

Everyone waited. They waited still, disposed about the bridge, even Chur, who sat propped up in bandages—"You damn tough," Jik vouchsafed, nodding Chur's way. Chur flicked her ears. "I pass *na* Khym, a, say he got stand guard down in lower corridor. Ehrran clan all same got you airlock secure." Jik leaned this rattling magnificence against the nearest counter edge, bit at a hangnail of one non-retracting claw. He looked weary as the rest of them. His eyes had wrinkles about their edges. There were deep creases by the corners of his mouth. "Also got hani guard take position on dockside. That Ehrran, she got 'nough security both us, a? Same got quick trigger. Make me worry."

"Gods rot it, Jik—you had a look at this dock?"

He shrugged. His brow rumpled as he glanced up. "Got trouble, sure. Got lot calls, station folk lot panic. *Kif.*" Back down the hall the lift worked. "You do number one fine job get in here, hani. Number one fine job get *ker* Hilfy out."

"We're not through yet. And *we've* got to get out of here again." She canted her ears toward the recent noise of the lift, turned a glance in that direction. Khym was striding down the corridor with a dark look on his face. She matched the scowl as he walked onto the bridge: he had left his post unasked. But the lift had gone down again, on call. She heard that too.

"Begging pardon," Khym said tautly. "Ehrran's headed topside. I locked up."

She took that in the coded way he meant it: he had left the washroom unremarkable to outsiders. Politics and intrigue: he was no fool in that department. Jik did not ask further, in his own indolently gracious way, and bit another hangnail. The lift worked again. Tirun and Geran got to their feet; Hilfy was already standing. Haral stayed by her board. "She fine captain," Jik murmured, of their arriving guests. "Come in right on mark; good ship, *Vigilance*. Also damn fool. I like maybe leave one ship undock, little way out—scare these kif. But this hani scare *me*, a? Same like have chi for ally: crazy. So I got make her come in dock too. Keep eye on her. She hate you, Pyanfar. Maybe want you have accident."

Pyanfar's ears went down. Ears all round the bridge flattened, excepting the minuscule ears of the gold-glittering mahe. "She's a bastard," Pyanfar said, "but *that* far, no. She'd like the kif to settle it."

And down the hall the lift let out a red-gold, black-breeched crowd of armed hani.

"Sure brought crew enough," Tirun muttered. "How many's she got on that ship, anyhow?"

"I checked library back at Kshshti," Haral muttered. "*Vigilance* runs a good hundred fifty crew. All those offices, you know."

"Funny," Geran said, "when we were short-handed they never had crew to spare."

"Funny," Pyanfar said. "I'd have enjoyed turning them down."

The Eyes of the *han* walked onto the bridge, immaculate, her silken mane and beard in bronze ringlets; her black silk breeches, Immune clan uniform, were crisp and new; the AP gun hung at her hip in well-polished black leather. Elegance. Wealth—*Trying to do what?* Pyanfar wondered. *Attract bandits and kif?* Her ears refused to prick up. Her pulse refused to stay at level. Gods rot the Immune and all her ilk. Government officials. Note-takers.

"Best if we could have avoided this," Rhif Ehrran said: *You*

51

botched it, that meant. "Our transmissions from central are *all* kif. Do we propose to negotiate under these conditions?"

And Rhif Ehrran looked at Jik, deliberately and exclusively at Jik, past Pyanfar.

"We'll manage," Pyanfar said in Jik's silence, and Rhif Ehrran turned her head with just enough slowness.

"I hope so."

There was no profit in argument. The Immune was only collecting complaints on Chanur clan dealings. Even yet. The list was already long.

"We go," Jik said. "Maybe time we talk be already long time the way this human reckon, a? Want him back. Val-u-able, a?"

"We just walk in there."

"Won't be a problem," Pyanfar said. Deliberately she settled on the arm of Tirun's vacant chair, informal as Jik, leaving the Immune and her crew standing. "We just walked in, walked out. Kif's real friendly."

The *han* deputy turned, her be-ringed ears flattening. "You want to walk in and do it again, Chanur? Maybe you can finish the job this time."

"Fine. It'll be just fine. You're delegating to Chanur, are you?"

Jik stood up, abruptly, with a rattle of his weaponry. "No joke," he said, moving into the midst. "Got number one serious problem. Not got time hani quarrel. Got one human got bad trouble. Got damn bad mess, kif got station, got plenty scared people, got long time not hear from mahen authority this station. You got way get in there, a, friend Pyanfar?"

"Sure. *Ask.* That kif'll let us in number one quick. It's getting out again I can't vouch for."

"How many kif?"

"Last time, maybe a hundred, maybe more. That I saw in that room. Up and down that dock, you're talking—oh, maybe four, five thousand. Maybe worse. You got current stats on Mkks?"

"It's crazy to go in there," Rhif Ehrran said.

"Got idea?" Jik asked.

"I had the idea," Rhif Ehrran said, "that coming into dock with all three ships was crazy in the first place, but you had other opinions."

"What you want? Shoot up dock? Got *cit-i-zen* here."

—"Captain." Haral spun her chair about. "I got a blip."

Pyanfar's eye was already moving, already taking in the scan-image that flashed to main-screen above all the seats.

Every eye was. Crew dived for posts without an order. Pyanfar did, abandoning Jik and Rhif Ehrran and her lot to their own devices.

"Get ID, gods rot it, what's the output?" She spun her chair about and felt the press of a large weight on the shoulder of her chair. Jik, getting view of the screens: she made no objection, too busy to take account of distractions.

"That's *stsho* output!" Hilfy exclaimed.

"We gods-blasted hope it is," Tirun said. "Kif could've—"

"Send to station," Pyanfar said. "Query."

A light on com-output lit: confirmation of the outgoing message. "This is *The Pride of Chanur*," Khym's deep voice rumbled, while other lights signaled activity from other crew. "What's that ship doing out there?"

Not proper com-etiquette, gods knew, but direct.

"Khym, give me the response," Pyanfar said, and as Rhif Ehrran moved up close and offered some advice: "Get clear. We're working, rot it."

—"—*of the* hakkikt, Pride of Chanur, *this information is private.*"

"Give me output!" Pyanfar said; and it arrived. "*Kif*, compliments of Pyanfar Chanur, you by the gods lay a hand on that stsho we'll yank loose and take your wall out! *What's going on over there?*"

Prolonged silence.

"Give me that contact," Rhif Ehrran said, and leaned on her chair back.

"Not on my bridge."

"Stsho's pulling out," Haral said. "That's outbound, vectored nadir. . . ."

Better news.

—"*the* hakkikt, Pride of Chanur, *the stsho undocked without clearance or docking assist. This is not an attack. This was not authorized. It was unprovoked.*"

"Got station damage, central?"

Silence a moment. *"We are authorized to report so."*

"Got a problem, don't you, kif?"

Silence.

"Don't provoke it," Rhif Ehrran said. "Chanur, give me that."

"Hhhhuh." From Jik. "Let be. Get ship code. No contact."

"That's *Nsthenishi*," Hilfy reported. "Comp says Rlen Nle's its home port."

"When rain falls up," Ehrran said. "Stsho never give ports further in than that. Eggs'll get you pearls it's Llyene. That ship is straight from the capital."

"Stsho personnel was on the dock," Pyanfar said, "when we came in. I don't know where it came from."

—*"Message from the* hakkikt," the voice from central said. *"The situation on this station is already conducive to incidents. Your allies have been permitted contact with you. Are you prepared now to meet and negotiate face to face, or do we expect more delays?"*

"No more delays. We'll come with our weapons, kif."

Silence. *"The* hakkikt *says: All sides will be armed, hunter Pyanfar."*

"We'll be there," Pyanfar said. "About a quarter hour." Rhif Ehrran leaned forward. Pyanfar brushed her aside with a forearm and stayed over the directional mike.

"Rot you—" Ehrran said.

"This is acceptable." From the kif.

Pyanfar cut it off. "That stsho still headed?" she asked rightward.

"Still," Haral said.

"Monitor that output." She swung the chair about, looked up at Jik. "So we try for Tully this time. We ready?"

"You have no authority to negotiate," Rhif Ehrran said. "Leave this to us from here on. You got as much as you can get easily. You'd serve us better staying here."

"Easily, huh?" At the boards the tracking and translating went on. Pyanfar stood up and stared at the backs of her crew. "Shut down to Hilfy and Chur's posts. Shunt command to Chur, Haral. We're going on a walk down the docks, we are." And

when Hilfy turned her chair about, mouth open. "Hilfy, niece—
you're a provocation to them, and I think you know it. You're
staying here."

"Aunt—" Hilfy got to her feet.

"*Sfik*, niece. You're a prize in this, like it or not, and bringing
you back into the *hakkikt*'s reach is asking for more kifish
tricks. Sit tight. And let Chur do the talking to central. Let's try
to get Tully *out* of there, huh? Efficiently and quietly. For his
sake."

Hilfy's jaw clamped. Her ears were back, her claws dug into
the seatback. But: "Aye," she said. Everyone but Chur was getting to her feet. Khym too. And the Ehrran crowd stood there
aftward on the bridge, blackbreeches among whom *ker* Rhif took
her stance, still scowling, while Jik leaned his rump against a
cabinet and rubbed behind one ear.

"Is she running this?" Rhif Ehrran asked indignantly.
"Captain Nomesteturjai, I undertook this business on your
government's request, understanding you personally requested—"

"My government same request you go with," Jik said. "Same
request you got patience, honorable. Chanur got thing organized,
a?"

"Come on," Pyanfar said. "Guns, Tirun. Let's get this moving."

"Aye," Tirun said, and brushed Ehrran crewwomen out of the
way of the locker door.

"Got positive ID on that stsho freighter," Chur said. "And
they're not stopping for anything."

"It go *home*," Jik said, "got plenty disturb."

"Gods rot," Ehrran said, "what more did it need? We've got a
stsho in the middle of this incident, tc'a and chi—."

"Got also mahendo'sat cit-i-zen on this station," Jik said
pointedly. His smallish ears were flat. "Maybe same got mahen
agent, a?"

"Yours?"

Jik shrugged. "Maybe. Maybe not. I got check files. But I got
other bet: when Sikkukkut come in here, some damn kif escape
tell kif authority at Harak system. Four, five day ago. Maybe

'nother go Kshshti. We got move, get thing fix right, a, Pyanfar? Soon maybe got whole damn lot kif here."

"Let's go," she said. She took the rifle Geran passed to her, while Haral buckled on an AP. Khym took his rifle from Geran's hand and checked the safety in rapid order.

"Wait a minute," Rhif Ehrran said. "Chanur. You're not taking *him* out there, are you?"

"I'm not taking him anywhere. He goes on his own."

"Chanur, that's the limit. I've got a file on you that goes—"

"I'm sure you do."

"Look here, Chanur." Ehrran's ears were back and pricked up with a twitching effort. She lifted a hand, one carefully controlled foreclaw crooked. "Practice your cockeyed social theories on your own ship; that's your business. But when you plan to bring *him* into a sensitive negotiation and hand him a rifle into the bargain—"

Rot it, speak up, she wished Khym. But he would not. His ears were down in outrage. It was all dammed up in him: and the temper it deserved if it came from him—would only confirm all the old prejudices Rhif Ehrran served. Unstable males. Hysteria. Berserker rages. He just kept his head down and threw the safety on again. And looked her way.

He was a lousy shot. But kif were afraid of anything his size. Justifiably, if he got into it hand to hand.

"I'd rather have him at my back," Pyanfar said studiedly, "than some." She slung the rifle into carry, deliberately looking elsewhere, finding it convenient to throw a glance in Hilfy's direction. "Stay topside, will you?"

Because, o gods, they had a kifish guest below; and the last thing she wanted on her mind was worry over Hilfy and Chur with a kif loose on the ship.

"Get him out," Hilfy said.

"I'll do that."

"Chanur," Rhif Ehrran said, "for the record, his presence and your insistence is going in the report."

"Fine. Maybe you'll be able to deliver it to the *han* in person. Or maybe none of us will ever have to worry about it, huh?" She waved her left hand. "Out!"

56

"You don't give the orders on this."

"We go," Jik said, bestirring himself from his cabinet-edge.

"That quarter-hour's getting short," Pyanfar said. She lagged behind, seeing Ehrran's blackbreeched lot out the door, and Jik, and her own crew. She paused for a backward look, then strode through the others to overtake Jik halfway down the hall.

"Got few my crew wait outside," Jik said as she came even with him. "They watch the ship."

"Maybe," Pyanfar said reluctantly, "Chanur and Ehrran *ought* to go in there solo and let you and yours hold the dockside. Kif know you, Jik. Know you real well. You stay here, back me and Ehrran up; that's all we need."

Jik rubbed his nose. "Long time I hunt kif. Sure thing they want me. Same want you, Pyanfar. Want bad. Maybe even want *han* deputy, a? But kif mind, that be crazy thing: we kill kif, no matter: that give us lot *sfik* with them. We not got *sfik*, they eat our heart number one sure. We got *sfik*, they *want* eat our heart—but same time think maybe they get *sfik* off us 'nother way. Like deal with us. Like they hope maybe we make more trouble on their rivals, a, than we make on them? We all go talk to Sikkukkut. We lose *sfik* else."

"You know what you're doing," Pyanfar said.

"Sure," Jik said cheerfully. "Number one sure."

It gave her no reassurance. Neither that nor that washroom door they passed in the lower corridor on their way to the lock: she glanced that direction, and the hair bristled on her nape.

Kill it, instinct said. Kill the kif hostage outright, let it vanish without a trace. Keep Sikkukkut guessing.

But where was the *sfik* in that, and what was she supposed to do with such a gift?

Be a fool and let it loose?

One stsho merchant was already loose and running, bolting dock. If one shot went off on that dock and panicked the traders, more ships might break loose from Mkks dock . . . ships lacking the stsho's obsessively pacifist tendencies. There were the methane-breathers, for one large instance.

It was a trap, of course. They had suddenly lost the rhythm of things and kept the kif's schedule, for a prize the kif still held.

57

No kif ever yielded anything without gain.

Four

An eerie quiet persisted on the docks. A few blackbreeched Ehrran clan personnel were visible in vantage points, armed with rifles; doubtless a few such were not visible at all; and there were two more Ehrran crewwomen stationed up inside the ramp, guarding *The Pride*'s airlock and accessway. Less ominous and more, a solitary, AP-wearing mahendo'sat slouched her way up to her captain in specific. Sleekly black, gold-glittering as Jik himself, she had half an ear missing and a bald streak on a burn scar down her jaw.

Jik spoke to his crewwoman rapidly in some language they both shared, of Iji's great multitude. "A," the woman said, and with her hand on the AP gun's butt, moved off again into shadows near the gantry.

"Khury," Rhif Ehrran muttered to her aide, "get back to the ship; take charge. And if we don't get back, get home directly and make a thorough report to the *han*."

It was Enaury hani the Ehrran spoke; Pyanfar caught it: so would Geran, but not likely anyone else. And Pyanfar ducked her head and rubbed her nose—better say less than one knew than more, she reckoned. With the *han* deputy it was certainly the case. There were already mounds and mountains of reports aboard that ship, to the delight of Chanur's enemies when Ehrran got back to Anuurn and that collection of complaints got to the *han* debating floor—

And a certain stsho check was on its way to a mahen bank at Maing Tol, if it had not gotten there already. When *that* hit the desk of a certain Personage—

The *han*'s deputy had not discovered that small matter yet.

Nor had Jik.

Pyanfar lifted her head and the oncoming kif welcoming committee looked almost friendly in that light.

59

They did not turn in at the same corridor as before. The half-dozen kifish guides brought them further and further down the open dock, and the paper and ammonia smell even surmounted the cold in this sector. The light was dim and murkish orange-gold, the only visual warmth in the gray and black of their surroundings. The signs were kifish, in crawling, dotted script.

Kifish ships were docked along the row at their left; kifish dens lined the right hand, deserted and quiet, which lent no reassurance at all. The hair prickled down Pyanfar's back as more and more of the horizon unfurled; it went all bristled as all the missing kif suddenly showed up past the curtaining overhead girders of the station's curve—a dark mass ahead, a gathering of thousands on the docks.

O gods, she thought. Her legs wanted to stop right there; but Jik had not even hesitated, nor had Ehrran—perhaps they waited on her, on Chanur, who they thought had been this route before.

"More of them than last time," Pyanfar said, breaking the spell of caution. "Gods-rotted lot more of them."

Jik made some sound in his throat. A noise grew ahead, like nothing she had ever heard—clicking and talking all at once, the roar of kifish speech from thousands of kifish mouths together. And they were obliged to walk through this congregation. She was conscious of Khym at her back, hair-triggered; of Haral and Tirun and Geran, steady as they came. And Rhif Ehrran and her handful; Jik striding along with legs that could match a kifish stride and instead kept pace with theirs, holding their guides to a hani pace.

She slipped the safety off her rifle as the scene came down off the upcurved floor and straightened itself out in the crazy tilting of things on station docks. It became flat, became distinct as hooded, robed kif standing about, became kif on all sides of them, close at hand, turning to stare at them as they passed with their escort. A clicking rose—"*Kk-kk-kk. Kk-kk-kk.*" Everywhere, that soft, mocking sound.

Kif territory for sure. Outnumbered, out-gunned a thousand times and three. If it got to shooting here—gods help them. Nothing else would.

And if they had to enter one of the ships at dock to do their bargaining—they were in no position to protest the matter.

The kif guiding them brushed other blackrobed, hooded kif from their path like parting a field of nightbound grass; and indicated a double-doored passage into a dark like that other dark hole, into a place thicker with kif stench and the reek of drink.

Kokitikk, the flowing sign above the door proclaimed—at least the symbols looked like that. *Entry prohibited*, mahen letters said. *Kifish service only.*

Gods, that would keep the tourists out.

"Meeting-hall," Jik said.

Kifish noise rose about them as they entered, noise from tables at either hand. There was a clatter of glasses—the smell of alcohol. And of blood.

"Gods save us," Geran muttered. "Drunk kif. That's the last."

Pyanfar walked ahead, rifle at carry, keeping close by Jik's side. Rhif Ehrran caught up with a lengthening of her stride. There were chairs all about of the sort Sikkukkut had used; there were lamps and smoking bowls of incense that offended the nose and sent smoke curling up against the orange, dirty light. Kif shadows, kif shapes—*kkkt,* they whispered. In mockery. *Kkkt.*

And their half-dozen kifish guides drifted ahead like black specters, clearing them a way. The muttering grew raucous. Jaws clicked. Glasses rattled with ice. There were red LED gleams about the fringes of the hall, rifle ready-lights.

"It's a gods-cursed *bar*," Rhif Ehrran said.

The crowd opened out, creating a little open space. In the midst were kifish chairs, a floor-hugging table.

A kif sat alone at that table, beneath a hanging light.

Its robed arm lifted and beckoned.

There was a stirring all about the room as kif rose from chairs for vantage.

"Sit down," the kif at the table said. "Keia." It was Jik's first name, his true one. "Pyanfar. My *friends*—"

"Where's Tully?" Pyanfar asked.

"Tully. Yes." Sikkukkut moved his hand, and kif about him stirred. There was a mahen shout, unmistakable; a yelp of something in pain. "But the human is no longer the only matter in contention."

The dark crowd parted near doors to the rear; and those doors opened. Dark shapes not kif were thrust forward and held fast— mahendo'sat prisoners, some in kilts, several in the robes of station officials. One had badges of religious importance. And a solitary stsho, pale, its gossamer robes smudged, its pearly skin stained with kifish light and smeared with dark patches. Its state was dreadful; it swayed and kif held it on its feet.

"A," Jik said. "So the stsho leave Mkks got reason."

"Mkks station," Sikkukkut said, "is mine. Its officials have formally ceded it to me in all its operations. Sit and talk, my friends."

It was Jik who moved first, walking forward to settle himself on one of the several black, insect-legged chairs that ringed that table. Pyanfar went to Sikkukkut's other side, and set a foot on the chair seat, crouched down seated with the rifle over her raised knee and canted easily at Sikkukkut. There was one seat left. Rhif Ehrran filled it. Haral and Tirun moved up at Pyanfar's back; Khym and Geran and the rest of the Ehrran hani close about the table, with a wall of kif behind.

"You let folk go," Jik said. He opened a pouch one-handed, took out a smoke and fished up a small lighter. It flared briefly. Jik drew on the stick and let out a gray breath of smoke. "Old friend."

"Do you propose a trade?" Sikkukkut said.

"I not merchant."

"No," the kif said. "Neither am I." He made a negligent move of his hand, and Pyanfar caught a whiff of something else, something strange and hers and scared, half a breath before another white thing was shoved into view through the wall of kif. Tully crashed down with arms on the table-edge between her and Sikkukkut. "There. Take him as a gift."

Pyanfar did not stir. Hunter-vision was centered only on the kif, the trigger under her finger, with the rifle against her knee. If Tully raised up too far, Tully would be in the line of fire. It was intended. She knew it was. She adjusted the knee and the rifle into a higher line. Sikkukkut's face, this time. "You want your hostage back?"

"Skkukuk? No. That one is for your entertainment. Let's talk about things of consequence."

Rhif Ehrran's ears had pricked. Jik let out a great cloud of smoke that drifted up and mingled with kifish incense. "We got time."

"Excellent. Hokki." Sikkukkut picked up his cup from the table and filled it with something that reeked like petroleum and looked rotten green. He drank and set the cup down, looking toward Pyanfar. "You?"

"I've got plenty of time."

"Even before Kshshti," Sikkukkut said, "even before that, at Meetpoint, I had converse with Ismehanan-min. Goldtooth, hunter Pyanfar calls him. I advised him to avoid certain points and certain contacts. You'll have noticed that the stsho vessel has deserted us now."

"Same notice," Jik said dryly.

"You'll have noticed a certain distress on the part of this stsho who remains with us—kkkt, perhaps you would care to question this one. A negotiator, *gtst* claims to be—"

"You tell," Jik said, puffing a cloud of smoke. "You got something drink, friend kif?"

"Indeed. Koskkit. Hikekkti ktotok kkok.—" A wave of his hand. A kif departed. "Were you always at Chanur's back?"

"No, not. Crazy accident I come Kshshti. Friend Pyanfar say she got trouble. So I come. Bring this fine hani." A nod Ehrran's way. "You remember, a?"

"Meetpoint," Sikkukkut said. The long-jawed face lifted. There was no readable expression. "Yes. This hani was dealing with the grass-eaters."

Rhif Ehrran coughed. "By treaty, let me remind you—"

Sikkukkut waved his hand. "I have no desire for treaties. Operations interest me. Chanur interests me."

"Hunter Sikkukkut, there's been a persistent misunderstanding of hani channels of authority."

O gods, Pyanfar thought, and felt sick at the stomach. *Hunter,* indeed. Rhif Ehrran demoted the kif in a word, in front of his subordinates.

"It seems mutual," Sikkukkut said, with equanimity and heavy irony, and pointedly turned his attention from Ehrran. "Hunter Pyanfar, I will speak with you. And my old friend Keia. When did we last trade shots? Kita, was it?"

"You at Mirkti?" Jik asked.

"Not I."

"Kita, then." Another puff at the stick. Jik flicked ash onto the floor. "We got shoot here?"

"Mahen bluntness.—That thing is a foul habit, Keia."

Jik laughed, replaced the smokestick in his mouth. "True." He glanced aside as a kif approached him with a glass. He sniffed it and drank. "Mahen. Nice stuff."

"Ssskkt. I appreciate it now and again."

"What got?"

"My business? Very serious business. Mahen interference. Stsho connivance with hani. This *humanity*—" Sikkukkut reached down and lifted Tully's chin. "How are you faring? Are you well, kkkt? Understanding this?" He let go and Tully kept his head up, white-faced and sweating and incidentally in the line of fire til he slumped and rested his arms on the table. "This humanity is a problem. Not alone has their presence disrupted trade: we do not, ourselves, depend so much on trade. . . . kkkt? But stsho do. Stsho fear anything that comes near them. So the balance of the Compact is upset. And when that balance tilts, so agreements fall; and when agreements fall, so authorities give way—so there is disarrangement. This is our perspective. And our opportunity. Akkukkak first brought this creature into Compact space. Had it been my doing, of course, I would have fared better, kkkt?"

"Akkukkak dead. Lot dis-arrangement, a?"

"We trust that he is dead. The knnn are unpredictable. Perhaps he will turn up in a bazaar in some trade—but let us assume he is out. Presently there is Akkhtimakt. Akkhtimakt styles himself *hakkikt*, holds Kita, disrupting traffic—"

"—make lousy big trouble," Jik said.

"Have you dislodged him?"

"I maybe do. Maybe not. Why you raid Kshshti dock?"

"Ah. Now, there you are mistaken. The Kshshti Personage has a traitor on the staff—"

"Not got now."

"Kkkt. You redeem my opinion of you. But this spy was Akkhtimakt's operative, not mine."

"Ummmn. You same got spy at Kshshti?"

"Not now. But then I did. When the human was crossing the docks—Akkhtimakt's agents moved to seize him. And I, fortunately, foreknew it. So I was on the hunt as well. Kkkt. Would Kshshti have fared so well in that firefight if kif had not fought kif on that dock? Mahendo'sat have me to thank; I believe thank is the expression—at any rate I stepped in and gathered up the prize before Akkhtimakt's agents could seize it. There was no negotiating there, at Kshshti, with everything astir, with every probability Akkhtimakt's agents would presently report all this—I am discreet no longer. By this intervention at Kshshti I have challenged my rival openly. Now I contend with him. And I surmised correctly that you would follow me, hunter Pyanfar, as soon as your ship could move."

"What's the deal?" Pyanfar asked.

"You might, you know, put the safety on that thing."

"Huh. Might. But I'm comfortable, *hakkikt*."

The snout wrinkled in what might be humor. "You don't trust my word."

"The deal, *hakkikt*."

"Ah. Kkkt. Yes. In simplicity: I have chosen Mkks as my temporary base. And my motives and yours coincide."

"Do they?"

"Kkkt. There are fools at large. Many fools. Stsho seek a way to prevent humankind from going through their space. Stsho connive with hani—am I right, deputy?—against mahendo'sat, who would wish to bring humans through at *our* backs, for reasons not lost to us. How quickly Keia distracted me when I mentioned stsho negotiators! But we know. To gain a foothold at Meetpoint, mahendo'sat route humans through tc'a space. Unwise. Vastly unwise. Stsho will not tolerate this any more than the other—and the very possibility of a human route approach-

65

ing *their* territory or even their neighbor and ally tc'a—agitates them beyond rationality. Akkhtimakt operates with the fist. I, with the knife. Akkhtimakt wishes humans barred. But I am, among kif, your friend. Our motives frequently coincide. Is this not a better definition of alliance than friendship?"

Jik let out a puff of smoke. "You wrong, friend. Human got own idea. Damn stupid. But they *want* come through."

"They have urging. Do they not?"

"Who know? I tell you got number one serious thing, methane-breather upset. We got trouble. Kif got trouble. Not all profit, either side. A?"

"You are willing to deal."

"Maybe." Another puff of smoke. "What you got I want?"

"Mkks."

Jik flicked ash. "A. Now we talk kif logic."

"You understand."

"Sure thing. You no trade. Maybe give gift. You give me Mkks. I then got plenty *sfik*. I make good ally, a? Maybe do something more."

"Take Kefk."

Jik's heavy brow shot up. The stick hesitated on its way to his mouth. Arrived. "So. Maybe."

Take Kefk. Only take the only kifish gateway to Meetpoint, the one kifish channel to the biggest trading point in the Compact—a major station and probably the most sensitive spot in kifish space outside Akkht itself. Pyanfar kept her ears erect with the greatest of efforts, kept a bland look on her face; and counted the kif and her ally stark mad.

"You think it possible," Sikkukkut said.

"I got allies. You got same. We go take Kefk." Jik took a final drag on the stick and drowned it in the dregs of the drink. "Personnel this station take back jobs. Then I take Kefk. You want?"

"Wait a minute," said Rhif Ehrran. "*Wait* a minute."

"I talk to her," Jik said without a look in that direction. "Got same good friend Pyanfar, one tough bastard hani. You want Kefk, fine. You get."

"Alliance," Sikkukkut said. "Myself and your Personage."

66

"You got."

"It's more than *talk* we've got to do," Rhif Ehrran said.

"The *han* deputy wants to know her advantage in this," Sikkukkut said. "But hani have allied with kif before. The deputy knows whereof I speak. Hani have formed various associations."

Pyanfar slid a glance Ehrran's way; the deputy's ears were down.

"What," Ehrran asked, "does the *hakkikt* know about hani allied with kif?"

"One word. *Tahar.* Does that interest you?"

"Where is Tahar?"

"In service to Akkhtimakt. *Moon Rising* is one of his ships and Tahar one of his *skkukun.* Not high in his estimation—but of some use to him."

"Gods rot," Pyanfar muttered, and looked at Sikkukkut herself.

"A hani famed for treason—*treason*, is that not the word?"

"It's close enough. *Where* is she?"

The kif shrugged, smooth as oiled silk. "Where is Akkhtimakt? Now does confrontation interest you?"

"She do fine," Jik said, studying the ice in the glass, in Rhif Ehrran's silence. "What say, *hakkikt*?"

"Ssko kjiokhkt nokthokkti ksho mhankhti akt." Sikkukkut waved a hand. "The station personnel are free to go."

"A." Jik twisted half about in his chair, leaned back within view of the mahendo'sat and stsho. "Shio! Ta hamhensi nanshe sphisoto shanti-shasti no."

There was babble. The stsho shrilled; and the mahendo'sat left the kif's hands and headed for the door, walking at first, then moving with increasing speed. The stsho ran, fell, scrambled up and fled through the chittering crowd even before the mahendo'sat.

Jik turned around again when the jam in the doorway had cleared. He pulled another stick from his belt and lit it. "How many ship you got?" he asked.

"Here? All kif here are mine but one. And that one is disabled; its crew—is presently rearranging its loyalties."

"Fourteen ship. We got three. No problem. Akkhtimakt maybe

67

come Kshshti; maybe come Mkks. Not good you stay here, all same. Advice come free, a?"

"So Mkks will fall again—if Akkhtimakt comes here."

"He not stay. Got no reason stay." Another expansive puff of smoke. "He quick learn we go Kefk, a? So he come. He leave Mkks, come Kefk number one quick, pay you visit."

Wrinkles chained up Sikkukkut's snout. "So by aiding me you aid Mkks."

"You right, friend."

"Hunter Pyanfar, where are your loyalties in this?"

"Myself. My crew. My friends. Jik wants us there, I don't doubt we'll talk about it."

"So. And a promise. Will you keep it?"

"Thought kif didn't have the word."

"You do."

She scowled. "I do."

"Then take your human as a gift. Join us. I will give the orders in this attack. I will personally provide you information on Kefk defenses."

"Jik?"

"You promise. Got no problem."

She shot Jik one long, burning look. But he did not look her way, studying instead the contents of his glass. She looked back over the rifle barrel balanced on her knee.

"Jik and I will talk about it."

"You go," Jik said.

"Huh," she said.

"She promise."

"Excellent." Sikkukkut unfolded upward from his chair. There was a stir among the kif. "You are all free. Take that as my gift."

He drew back. Blackrobed kif surrounded them.

"Tully." Pyanfar reached out and nudged Tully with her foot, her rifle in both hands. "Tully. Up. We get you out of here. You walk, Tully."

He gathered himself up, holding to Sikkukkut's vacated chair, and stood wobbling on his feet. No one said anything. Likely Rhif Ehrran was choking on what she wanted to say about the situation, but it was not the time or place for it. Pyanfar stood up and let her rifle hang at carry, laid her hand on Tully's bare, claw-streaked shoulder. It was icy cold. There was a deep and healing wound on his arm. Come on," she said. "With us."

He walked. Geran took his arm with her left hand, her right on the butt of her pistol. Jik was up—he had the stick still in his mouth, and drew yet another puff on the foul thing. Rhif Ehrran was on her feet and drew her own crew into retreat.

It was a long walk through the silent kifish crowd to the door, a slow one, at Tully's pace. But they made it out into the comparatively bright light of the docks, the atmosphere laden with oils and volatiles that hit like a gust of fresh air after the closeness of the meeting hall.

Khym walked along with them, Haral out in front. Tirun carried her rifle left-handed to keep Tully on his feet, with Jik and Rhif Ehrran bringing up the rear. Pyanfar cast a look back: gods, Jik was puffing on that filthy thing all the way and scattering ashes as he went. But kif kept hands off them. There were stares from the crowd outside, and there was muttering, but nothing worse.

"You get quick you ship," Jik said, as Pyanfar fell back to walk beside him. "Got lot work, hani, *lot* work."

"It's your intention to go through with this," Rhif Ehrran said.

"Number one sure. You want wait here, say hello Akkhtimakt? Got also other big trouble. That stsho go out from here. Maybe go Kshshti—maybe instead go Kefk, a, on way to Meetpoint. Maybe talk too much. Stsho lot talk. Not good thing we get compli-cation. Stsho make same, a? Go."

"There's a limit to what treaty makes me liable to. We'll discuss this, *na* Jik."

"Fine. Same time you lay course. We do same. I tell you, I bet some kif leave here, go Kshshti. They tell Akkhtimakt what happen here at Mkks, we got small time. Akkhtimakt got fast ship. Same got trouble with kif maybe go Harak. Same trouble stsho go Kefk—lot smart, stsho: maybe got rumor already Akkhtimakt come Kshshti, so run damn quick go Kefk, go Meetpoint—

maybe Tt'a'va'o, maybe Llyene—Bet Sikkukkut lot unhappy not stop that ship."

"You've stopped coinciding with *han* interests."

"A. Then maybe wish you goodbye, lot luck. Akkhtimakt eat you heart."

"You foul this up—"

"—he eat mine. Number one sure, hani. Akkhtimakt want me, long time." He put his hand amid Rhif Ehrran's back and hastened them along. "Best we move, a?"

"Kefk, for the gods' sake," Pyanfar muttered.

"Easy stuff."

"*Then why for the gods' sake hasn't Sikkukkut done it?*"

"*Sfik.*" Jik took the stick from his mouth and blew a cloud of smoke. "Need *sfik*, make convince other kif, a? Now he got *us*. We all got lot *sfik*, le-gi-ti-macy, a?"

"Lunacy," she muttered.

"You run, good friend?"

"Gods rot it, you'd find some reason why not."

Jik grinned and put the stick back in his mouth. "You owe me. When Chanur ever default on debt, a?"

"Gods rot your hide."

She strode along by him, cast occasional looks back, as Ehrran's crew did. *Gods, get us off this dock.* More and more kif appeared along the way, all chittering and chattering among themselves. *Our allies. Gods!*

And Tully limped along at his own pace, doing the best he could.

There was the safe area ahead, that portion of the dock under surveillance from their own guns. They reached it, and Pyanfar looked back. The kif had not followed them across that imaginary line . . . thank the gods.

"We're safe," an Ehrran crewwoman said. Ehrran crew stood out from cover on the docks; a few of Jik's were visible.

"We're all right," Haral said by pocket com, now that they came in range of *The Pride*'s dockside pickup. "Haral speaking. We got him. He's all right."

Some answer came back. Pyanfar did not hear. She saw Rhif Ehrran sweep a signal to her own crew as they passed the dockage of *Ehrran's Vigilance,*—not a signal to turn in there, but to come with her. Rhif Ehrran lengthened stride; and stopped Tirun and Tully and Geran at the foot of *The Pride*'s docking area, with a grip on Tully's arm. "The human's safer in our keeping," Rhif said. "We'll take him."

"No," Pyanfar said, overtaking. "Gods rot it, Ehrran, we'll discuss it somewhere else. Get out of the way. We got kif back there—let go of him. He's had enough! Gods fry you, that's *crew* you've got your hands on." She launched a blow of her own and it brought up on Jik's out-thrust arm.

"I take," Jik said. "*I* take, hear."

"By the gods you don't. *No!* He's listed crew of mine. Gods rot you, let him go—"—as Haral decked an Ehrran crewwoman and mayhem broke loose, one brawling knot with Tully in the midst. Pyanfar elbowed Jik and shoved her way in as Khym did.

"*Out!*" Khym yelled, a male hani voice that shocked echoes off the overhead; he dived amid the mess and snatched Tully to himself. He grinned at Ehrran, ears flat, with Tully crushed against his chest.

It stopped. It all stopped.

"I'm crazy," Khym said. "Remember?"

And it was in Pyanfar's own head that he truly might go berserk. She opened her mouth, shut it. Tully was not struggling. He held on, fists clenched in the fur of Khym's shoulders. And Ehrran waited for the bloody bits and pieces to start flying. Male and male. Tully hanging in Khym's grip like an unstrung toy.

"He's Chanur crew, isn't he?" Khym rumbled. "Like me." He swung Tully up into both arms, the rifle swinging loose from his elbow—good gods, the safety off on a gun fit to hole armor plate. Tully's head lolled back, his limbs suddenly gone loose. "We going inside, captain?"

"Move it," Pyanfar said. Her heart started beating again.

"Hhhunnh. Excuse me." Khym walked deliberately through Ehrran's ranks, swinging to clear Tully's legs.

"Chanur," Rhif Ehrran said.

"I know. You'll file a protest. Get your crew out of my crew's way, or they'll be picking fur out of the filters all over Mkks."

71

"Damn fool," Jik muttered. He pinched out his stick and dropped it into a pouch. "Move! You think we got no witness?" He jerked a hand toward the watching kif, far off down the dock. "What want? Entertain them?"

Rhif Ehrran made an abrupt gesture upward. Rifles clattered out of the way. Her eyes were amber rings around black. Her rumpled mane stood out in curling wisps as if charged with static. "We'll settle it later, Chanur."

"Fine." Pyanfar led her own crew through, lingered at the rail of the upward ramp and turned her head to see nothing happened behind her. The Ehrran crewwomen stood stock still. *Ker* Rhif herself stared with ears flat, promise in that look. Geran came last, not without a backward glance on her own. "Get in," Pyanfar said in Geran's slight hesitation: *Need help?*, that delay implied. Geran went; she followed, and as they came into the accessway she remembered the Ehrran guards in lowerdeck. "Gods," she muttered, and started running, sweeping the crew with her.

Khym had gotten to the airlock with Tully in his arms. The hatch stood open; and two Ehrran guards stood there with rifles uncertainly in their hands and panic in their eyes.

"That's all right," Pyanfar said equably, taking her breath. She pursed her mouth into a cheerful smile for the guards, all innocent of the fracas outside. "Hold your post. Come on, Khym. Need help with him?"

"He doesn't weigh much." Khym shifted his arm to roll Tully's head up against his chest as they went on through the lock and into the inner corridor. Tully moved, a limp wave of his hand. "Py-an-far."

"We've got you," Haral said, gently disengaging Khym's rifle from his arm, taking the weapon to herself before it blew a hole in the overhead. "No more worry, Tully, we got you."

The lift worked as they walked on into main corridor. Hilfy came out and headed for them at a run.

"He's all right," Geran said.

Hilfy slid to a worried halt in the face of Khym and an evident Situation; but Tully reached out his hand and she took his arm, Khym or no. "Hil-fy—" Tully tried to grasp her arm,

72

awkwardly, with Khym's holding him and walking again. "Hilfy—"—over and over again.

"Huh," Pyanfar said. It was good to see Hilfy's ears up, her eyes bright like that. As if something was repaired. "Gods, get him to bed. We got other problems."

She leaned back against the corridor wall when Khym had taken the whole Tully-business away. Across from her Tirun sagged, standing on one foot. The wound Tirun had gotten at Meetpoint two years ago, the wound they had never had time on that voyage properly to treat—gods, they ran scared again. She thought of Chur, patched together at Kshshti. Like *The Pride* itself.

"Kefk," Haral said, going to lean against the wall beside her sister. "That's going to be one bitch, captain."

She listened. Geran overtook them and joined the lineup, the several of them. She felt numb. Her gut hurt from long walking, and from the earnest desire to break Rhif Ehrran's neck. "Gods rotted right one bitch." She shoved off from the wall and walked along the corridor toward the lift, alone.

Gods, the worry and the trust in Haral's eyes. Oldest of her friends and truest, Tirun next by a year; Geran and Chur after that by two. Five hani, with a few gray hairs round the nose and aches when they ran; a young fool kid. A stray human and a hani male past his prime—There had been a time, when she had gotten into this, that she had had ambitions—trading deals with mahendo'sat and humans, to repair Chanur's financial damages; get the ship up to standard—well, *that* much she had done. And *The Pride* had altered outlines, wider vanes, alien systems that would put a kink in Chanur's enemies for sure—if it came to a conflict in space.

But there were other kinds of enemies—like on the debating floor of the *han*, when the Rhif Ehrran stood up to declare charges and bring Chanur down.

Khym, gods, Khym—she hugged the moment to herself, his defiance of Rhif Ehrran on the docks. But it cost. It would cost plenty when Ehrran and *Vigilance* got home. Chanur had staked much on this dealing with outsiders; risked too much. Chanur

73

had become like *The Pride* itself, half-hani, with alien outlines. Foreign wealth bought those changes.

—but go home again? See her clan-home again? Deal again as hani and not some mahen agent bought and paid for?

She pushed the lift button. Turned. The crew had stayed where they were down the corridor, not following. Maybe they sensed her mood. She beckoned and Haral saw and brought the others.

Another hani ship had gotten cut off from hani kind two years ago: *Tahar's Moon Rising*. *Moon Rising* served the kif nowadays; and time was when she would have gone for Tahar on dock or in open space and known that she was right.

The lift arrived; her crew did. Another thought occurred to her and sent the wind up her back. "We've still got that kif aboard," she said.

"We can throw it out," Tirun said. "We've got what we want."

Pyanfar thought about it, her claw hooked into the lift-switch. But small alarms went off in everything she knew about the kif. "*Sfik*," she said. She let them into the lift and got in after. "If we turn it out, we lose a *sfik*-item, don't we, whatever by the gods that means. Status. Face."

"What's that kif want we do with it?" Geran asked in disgust.

"What he did with Tully," Haral surmised in the general silence as the lift went up. "Maybe worse. What's a kif care? It's to salve our pride, that's what."

A chill spread through Pyanfar. "Gods."

"Captain?"

"He talked about a kifish ship not his." The lift stopped and the door opened. "Rearranging its loyalties. He said."

"That kif's one of *Akkhtimakt's?*" Haral guessed, right down her own track.

"Bet you."

"Good gods, what do we *do* with the son?"

Pyanfar walked out and threw a glance over her shoulder on the way to the bridge, to Chur. "If you figure out what a kif's mind's like, let me know. It says it belongs to Chanur. If we let it go we lose *sfik*. And we got a stationful of kif at our throats if we do."

"We could space it," Tirun muttered longingly.

"We could give it to Ehrran," Geran said.

Pyanfar looked back, short of the bridge door. "That's the best idea I've heard yet."

"We do it?"

She bit at her mustaches, gnawed and gnawed. "Huh," she said, storing that thought up. "Huh." And walked into the bridge.

"*Kefk?*" Chur asked, turning her chair about.

"I got him for you," Khym said, huge, dishevelled, hands hooked into the waistband of a tatty and snagged pair of brown breeches. His much scarred ears were slanted half-back, his scarred nose ducked in embarrassment. Hilfy came and fussed his mane into order, and the ears came up, there, in that room with another male, with Tully lying still on the bed and witnessing all of this.

"You were marvelous," Hilfy said.

"Huh," Khym muttered. "Huh. He smells awful. So do I." And with one shrug of his great shoulders he meandered out into the corridor.

Hilfy shivered then. And she thought of killing kif, which had become a constant, burning thought with her.

"Hilfy." Tully made an attempt to get up from where Khym had disposed him, on his own bed in his own quarters, on a coverlet soiled with blood from his poor back. She looked his way and he made a face and tried to stand. He sat down again, hard, and caught himself on one elbow.

"Gods." She snatched at the pocket com she had and punched the translator channel through. "Tully. Lie still." She came and put the com into his hands, so that he could speak and understand, with that unit to relay to the computer on the bridge.

But he let it fall and grabbed her about the shoulders and held on, just held, the way he had done when he had been hurt; or she had; or the kif threatened to separate them. "It's all right," Hilfy said. She held to him, which she had done in their dark cell when he could understand little more than that. "It's all right. We got you. No more kif."

He lifted his face finally and looked at her, alien and awful-smelling and his mane and beard, his handsomest feature—all wispy gold when it was clean; but it was all tangled. His strange eyes were reddened and spilled water down his face—kif-stink hurt her eyes too, and his rags of clothes were full of that and kifish incense. "Pyanfar," he said, "Pyanfar—friend these kif?"

"Gods, no."

Tully shivered, a shudder apt to tear his joints apart. She held him tight, talisman of her own safety. She was aware of his maleness as she had been aware of it in their prison on *Harukk*, in a vague, disturbing way; but Anuurn and home and men were very far away—excepting Khym, who was enough to remind her of such things though he was Pyanfar's, and far too old. As for Tully, whatever humans felt, it was complex and alien and gods knew whether he even thought of her as female.

But someone should defend him. Hilfy had known all her life that men were precious things; and their sanity precarious; and their tempers vast as their vanity. *Na* Khym was—well, *exceptional*; and gray-nosed and sedate in age, whatever Pyanfar believed. Young men were another kind. One made a place for them and kept all unpleasantness away; and they wore silks and hunted and made a woman proud. They fought only when their wives and sisters had failed, when disaster came. And they were brave with the bravery of last resort, no craft—no one expected slyness of males. Not when the madness took them. Not when they were young.

Her Tully was clever. And brave. There had been a time kif had laid hands on her and Tully had thrown himself at them, clawless as he was. They had batted him aside, but he had tried to defend her till they knocked him senseless.

And she could not reach him then. That hurt with more than the pain of the bruises it had cost. They had drugged her. And she had been helpless when they took him to question.

"Chur's all right," she said—remembered to say, for he had not gone up topside yet to learn it. "Tully, she got out."

He looked at her and blinked. "Chur safe."

"Everyone."

He made a sound, wiped his face and ran his blunt fingers through the tangles of his mane. "# # #," he said, something the translator mangled. He edged one foot and the other over the side. "I # crew. I crew, Hilfy, go work—Want work—understand."

He got himself on his feet. He wobbled in the process, caught his balance on her offered hand, then: "Bath," he said. And headed that direction.

She understood that.

"I'll wait for you," she said.

So they were all a little crazed. She felt like collapse herself and felt the dizziness a lump on her skull had left. But *The Pride* was close to moving. They would be pulling out and getting out of this; and she had undergone one long nightmare of jump in kifish hands—

—shut below, trapped belowdecks, with no sense of where they went or where they were or when they would die.

They were at Mkks, Chur had told her. And a host of other things—like a deal struck at Kshshti station, that had sent Banny Ayhar hellbent for Maing Tol with messages; and brought Jik and *Vigilance* with them—improbable alliance, but a useful one.

—Jik's got some piece of Ehrran's hide, Chur had said, in the long waiting for results. *He flashed some paper at her at Kshshti and she caved right fast. He's no hunter-captain, that Jik, no way that's all he is. He's got connections—got us out of port, used that fancy computer on* Aja Jin *and laid us a course that put us straight into Mkks, all three, neat as you please. We went out on our mark and by the gods we were on when we came in. Got that new engine pack back there—*

Chur had showed her that, working the cameras aft; and the sight of their tail assembly on the vid had sent a shiver up Hilfy's back.

The Pride had changed. Had become something else since they pulled into Kshshti.

Like her. And she would have wished to see the old outlines

77

back there and to have felt she had come home to something known and never changed.

Pyanfar friend these kif?

Hilfy conjured scenes—things Tully had seen and she had not when Pyanfar had stayed alone in that room of kif; and again when Pyanfar had gone in after Tully with Jik and Ehrran and all the crew but herself and Chur. *So, gods, why would he even ask?*

True, they had a kif aboard. Tully did not know that. The presence set twitches in Hilfy's lip, and a shudder in her bones. The thing was down the corridor. Just a few doors down and around the bend.

She sat on Tully's bed and hugged her arms about herself, wishing as she had not wished since she begged to go to space and got a doting father's leave—She wanted her home again, and safety, and not to see what she wanted now to do. Better hunting in the hills, that kind of killing. A clean kind. Find a mate. She was due that in her life. Have the grass under her feet again and the sun on her back where no hani she might meet would understand what kif were or the things that she had seen.

Tully staggered out again, naked. There were wounds on him that seeped blood; bruises, bruises and burns and every sort of abuse. She carried like scars. He hunted a drawer for another pair of Haral's cast-off breeches and came up with what must be the last.

"Need help?" she asked.

He shook his head, a human *no*. He sat down and tried with several attempts to get his leg in. He rested a bit, waved her off, hanging on the chair edge; and finally succeeded, one leg at least.

The door opened, unannounced. Chur stood there, all bandaged as she was. Her eyes widened; her voyages-ringed ears flicked back.

"Chur," Tully said, and got the other leg; and contrived to stand up and pull the breeches on and pull the drawstring in, with now and then a grasp at the chair back.

"Gods-rotted little we haven't seen of each other," Hilfy mut-

78

tered with a little shrug at Tully and a heat about her ears. "Him or me. It's all right, Chur."

"You all right," Tully said. He left the chair and reached out both hands for Chur. Chur winced instinctively; but he did not grab, only took her hands and clasped them in his own. "Chur, good to see you. Good to see you—"

"Same," Chur said. Her mouth pursed in a gaunt smile, and Hilfy got to her feet. "We're some sight, aren't we?"

"We *fine*," Tully said, with simplicity that ached. He grinned, tried to stop himself, got his face into a hani pleasantness. "Chur, I think you got dead."

"Got dead, no—" Chur cuffed his cheek ever so gently. "Gods, they chewed you up and spat you out, didn't they?"

Hilfy flinched, leaning on the chair. "Let him sit down, for the gods' sakes. You too. What are you doing here?"

"Got a small break. They've got data coming in up there; Tirun's on it—thought I'd take the chance to come down and see you while I had it."

"We're going out, are we?"

Chur's ears went down.

"Aren't we?"

"Got some little deal going," Chur said.

"*What* deal?"

"Jik. We got this—well, we got this pay-off we got to make. Jik's asked us to go to Kefk. He's talked Ehrran into it."

"Gods-be." Hilfy's claws dug into the upholstery and she retracted them. Fear. Stark fear. She knew it in herself, that flinchings had been set into her, bone and nerve, forever. "What's at Kefk but kif? We still following this willy-wisp of human trade?"

"Some other kind of deal," Chur said. Her ears stayed at half-mast. The white showed at the corners of her eyes. "I don't know clearly what. Captain's back and forth with Jik."

"Go Kefk?" Tully asked. He wobbled over against the wall and stood there holding himself on his feet. "Kif? Go kif?"

"*What* deal?"

"Jik's deal," Chur said. "Hilfy—we bribed you out. I don't know what's up, but it's certain we've got trouble on our tail and we're clearing out of here to lead Akkhtimakt off Mkks in the likely case he comes this way. We got two kif headed for a showdown at Kefk and Jik's taking sides. Mahen politics. And we're in it."

"Gods, no!" The room went black-tunneled. She thrust the chair skidding on its track and headed doorward, dodged Chur's hand.

"Hilfy—" Chur's voice pursued her. *"Hil-fy!"*—Tully's, that cracked and broke.

"In a mahen hell," Hilfy said to everything in reach, and headed for the lift.

Five

"*We got Ehrran agree,*" Jik's terse message had said, scantly after Jik could have gotten back to his ship and put the call through. ("Good gods," Haral muttered then. "What kind of blackmail's he using?") ("Must be good—"—from Tirun.) And straightway from Jik: "*We got hakkikt send comp feed, lot interesting stuff. We run through library. You take, we make check.*"

And arriving with that feed from Sikkukkut's *Harukk*: "*I Sikkukkut send a gift. Kefk is not Mkks. You will discover this. We leave port in twelve hours or less.*"

"*Aja Jin,*" Pyanfar protested at once, "that's a short turnaround. I *know* we're pushing, but gods rot it, we haven't got relief."

"Sorry," Jik said. "Got do. *Try*, friend. We got problem."

"What problem?"

"Like vector on that stsho."

"Went to Kefk, huh?"

"Damn right."

"Gods be." She raked a hand through her mane, leaned both elbows on the console, feeling the tension behind her eyes.

The com kept up a steady crackle of kifish chatter and mahendo'sat, the station central offices still in kifish control, but with a few mahendo'sat speaking now from dock offices. The boards rippled systems-lights with the feed from Jik's *Aja Jin*, which was filtering *Harukk* data through its own computer and checking it against records before sending it on.

"I'd like to have a look at that comp system over there," Tirun said. "One gods-rotted complicated son, I'm betting, the way it put us in here."

"Better do it twice," Haral said, "that's all I say. Khym—get that thing, will you? Help him, Geran. He's got it fouled somehow."

"It's gone. I'm sorry. I lost it out of records."

"What's one more bill?" Geran said.

Two crew down. Chur was not up to more work and Hilfy was R&R with Tully belowdecks, while the accessible universe wanted through the com system with individual complaints.

"We sue," was a frequent note.

"You gods-rotted optimist," Pyanfar yelled at one mahe more persistent than the rest. "Send your lawsuit to Maing Tol and I by the gods hope it gets through!"

Then she wished she had held her peace. Her hands shook and there was a hollow feeling at her gut that going hyper-ac after jump was guaranteed to do to a body. She ate concentrates, drank, and it did no good.

They had to sleep, no matter what; they all had to go off-shift and get some rest, and Jik's communications streamed in without letup.

"Gods-rotted mahe's got no nerves," she muttered. "He had a relief crew while he was inbound. Probably had a five-course dinner. What's he think we *are?*"

No one answered that.

And: "Gods," Geran muttered when the course plan and the Kefk information began to take shape. "That son's *mean.*"

"That's before we even get there," Haral said. "I'm betting there's more surprises in that system that kif doesn't want to show us."

"Not taking that bet," Geran said.

There was no jump-point on their way to Kefk, no point of mass where three ships up to no good could come in, go dead silent and rest and sleep a while. The route was just two stars in each other's gravitational influence; *The Pride* would ride its own jump field and Kefk's pull directly in with a vengeance. Three stars, counting Mkks and Kefk 1 and Kefk 2: Kefk was a close binary; and that made for difficult navigation at best.

"Six ships go in with Sikkukkut, Jik, and our friend Rhif," Tirun said. "We get the tailguard post."

"Alone with seven kif," Geran said. "Gods, what a party."

"Beats going first."

"How much interval we got?"

"Not by the gods enough." Haral took furious notes and Pyanfar's comp slot spat out a paper.

All she could think of was sleep, the chance to lay her aching bones on a mattress and let her mind go . . . while they sat on a kifish dockside with a kifish strike force likely inbound at their backs from either of two enemies . . . kifish authorities at Harak or Akkhtimakt's ships off by Kshshti. They *hoped* Akkhtimakt was no closer than Kshshti.

Gods only knew. If an attack caught them like this, if Akkhtimakt came to Mkks before they left or got up to speed, they were sitting targets with their nose to station and no way to get up to *V* in time—the same thing they had done to *Harukk* and all its allies.

It took no mindreading to know the practical reason why Jik wanted out of Mkks in a hurry.

But other things occurred to her: like the chance Jik knew things he was not saying, about operations in progress elsewhere; the absolute surety that Sikkukkut did.

There is fire, hani. From Llyene to Akkt to Mkks. Even Anuurn.

Even Anuurn.

And *Vigilance* agreed to join in an act of unvarnished piracy.

I surmised correctly that you would follow me, hunter Pyanfar, as soon as your ship could move.

So why us? Gods and thunders, what have we got either side wants but Tully? And Sikkukkut gave him back. Jik could have laid claim to him. And Jik backed off.

Why did Sikkukkut want *us* in this?

Kif in the washroom. Kif all about. Threatened lawsuits pouring in, because a hani merchant was easier to sue than a *han* deputy or a mahen hunter ship; and, gods knew, the kif.

"We just got a transmission from *Vigilance*," Haral said. "Official notice we got a complaint filed."

"Tell 'em eat it."

"Captain."

"No, don't tell them that. Acknowledge." She shifted her attention to another board where a systems check had just blinked clear. "Number two vane is clean." She verified Tirun's check, punched the test of number three and got back to the Kefk system data.

The schematic showed armed guard stations. Three of them at Kefk. And the robot navigation beacon in the jumprange gave no inner-lanes data to incoming ships until it got a ship ID; and if it disliked what it got, it would blank out entirely. That meant dumping speed early to avoid collision, and risking collision even at that reduced velocity. And without that incoming V they were sitting targets for anything those guard stations decided to throw at them. Gods, it was lunacy.

"It's sure something to run with clean equipment," Tirun said. "I'd gotten used to alarms."

"Huh." Pyanfar read an incoming schedule on screen two, blinked it clear, rubbed her right ear. The letters separated in a green haze and came back again. Not a complaint from the crew. A hani male sat over there bone-tired and working keys and grumbling in his throat in a kind of mindless reflex moan that occasionally became a mutter: poor Khym, too well-bred to swear like the rest of them, and doing a crewwoman's job with a woman's steady concentration, side by side with Geran. "Give me your information," his litany ran, impeccably delivered. "I'll get it to the appropriate officer."

And: "I'm sorry, that's not quite possible."

The lift worked—Pyanfar turned the chair half about to glance down the corridor, nervous reflex with a kif aboard and Ehrran crew on guard in *The Pride*'s airlock.

Hilfy was coming bridgeward in some haste. Ears back.

Eyes dark, when she had gotten past the door.

"Aunt. What's this Kefk business?"

Pyanfar swung the chair all the way about in Hilfy's direction and leaned her head back on the cushions. *Nobody* came onto *The Pride*'s bridge and used that tone to her. But Hilfy—Hilfy wanted latitude lately. Pyanfar gave it. "We're going there, yes. Got a bit of business to take care of."

"*Kif* business?"

Her own ears went down. She saw the fracture-lines in Hilfy, the unreason. And said nothing for a breath.

"Well, is it?"

"Jik's business. Look, we got a bill to pay, niece. A gods-rotted big bill."

"To *whom?*"

"Jik, for one." In spite of herself her heart raced, her ears lay back, her claws jerked half out of sheaths and gouged the upholstery. "Jik. You think I got the influence to pull a mahen hunter-ship and a *han* deputy in here to help us bail you out without some tradeoff? You're expensive, niece."

That slapped young Hilfy in the face. The whites showed at her eyes' corners. Her nostrils dilated. "What do we do, then?"

"What we do—" Pyanfar's voice cracked, utter weariness. She waved a hand. Hilfy wavered there on her feet in no better condition. It was madness. All of them were that tired. "What we do, niece, is what we're set to do, whatever we're set to do. Yes, we go into Kefk. I don't see we have much choice. Debts are being called in. We don't doublecross Jik. Even Ehrran's going on this one. Don't ask me why. To spy, that's gods-rotted sure. For us, it's what I said. Debts. We got you out. Best I could do."

"We've got a kif on this ship."

"Not my choice."

"What *is*, lately?"

She did not believe for a moment she had heard that; and then her muscles moved, one convulsion that took her from the chair. And Hilfy backed up, stood there with her ears flattened and dismay on her face, as if she did not believe she had said it either.

Khym climbed from his chair; *his* ears were back; and that was trouble on two feet.

"How much territory do I give you?" Pyanfar asked. "What are you due, huh?" Down the corridor the lift doors had opened again. Chur and—gods—Tully both were on their way to the bridge, faster than either of them ought; while all about the bridge there was a dire silence, whisper of leather as crew turned in their chairs. "You got some particular recommendation, niece?"

"No." The word got out, finally. Chur and Tully arrived on the bridge, all but carrying each other at the last.

"Maybe you better go back on break," Pyanfar said. "We've got work to do."

"Gods rot it, aunt—"

"*I got you out! Gods and thunders, Hilfy Chanur, you want to argue method with me?*"

Tully pushed off from the counter edge—feckless, fever-crazy, wandering between two mad hani. But he stopped there wobbling back and forth with panic in his eyes.

So she understood then; and had a look at the way things had been among the kif. So all the crew did. Further things she did not want to surmise. Hilfy took Tully by the shoulders and carefully set him to the vacant side, where Khym was not, back in Chur's keeping.

There was deathly silence after that, with only the beep and flash of unliving things.

"Hilfy," Pyanfar said, and sank into her chair. "Hilfy—"— hearing those beeps and the chatter of incoming printout. "We're all tired. We're not up to this. Other ships have got other shifts, crew to spare—Geran, put a call over to Jik. Tell him fry his gods-rotted schedule; we're going offline. Hilfy: when we picked up Jik, he'd had a skirmish with the kif somewhere. He'd twisted Akkhtimakt's tail, right well. We don't know where Akkhtimakt is right now, but he wants our hides, no question of it. Sikkukkut swears it was Akkhtimakt's agents blew Kshshti docks to blazes and made a grab for you and Tully—"

"Does it matter which gods-rotted kif—"

"Shut up and listen. Sikkukkut grabbed you instead, for his own reasons. And it doesn't call for gratitude. Just common sense. Akkhtimakt's agents ran from Kshshti. They'll have gotten back to him; and that means we've got precious little time. Chances are there's one of Akkhtimakt's spotters hovering about Kshshti system. It's hard to find those kind of things til they transmit. And if that's the case he'll find out where we went the minute he skims through Kshshti system, he'll get the whole story of what happened there before he dumps speed, and gods help them if he stays to settle things with them. We don't think he will. We think he'll come for us non-stop. But we can't bet on that. We also have a report that earless stsho that just ran out of here took the Kefk route home, to spill everything *gtst* knows in the process, don't doubt it. We've got problems here, niece."

"We're within a one-jump of Maing Tol or Idunspol, for the gods' own sakes! What happened to getting Tully there? Where did that priority go?"

"With Banny Ayhar, from Kshshti. *Prosperity* couriered Tully's packet on, with a human-language translation tape, updated. If Banny didn't run into something, that packet's already at Maing Tol. Or will be." Her mind had trouble with trans-light figures, tired as she was. "We're faster than we were. And think of this—if you're so concerned for Tully's welfare. If we do take him to the mahendo'sat at Maing Tol, they'll grab him sure. Why'd you think I wouldn't give him to Jik out there? They'd lock him up and go at him til he's spilled everything. You want that for him, huh? Maybe he still knows something. Maybe I'm crazy not to get him off my hands; but I'm not doing *that* to him. It'd kill him, after this. Hear? They'd *never* let him loose."

"You were ready enough to turn him over at Kshshti!" Hilfy yelled, and over at her side there was a constant drone from the translating com-unit at Tully's side. His eyes were dark and wide.

"That was *before*," Pyanfar said, "gods rot it, *before* the thing blew up, before we—"

"—ended up in debt. Admit it. He's for sale. He's expendable if it gets us out of hock. *That's* what you're holding out for! A better gods-be deal!"

"Mind your mouth, whelp!"

"Well, isn't it the truth?"

"Gods and thunders, *no*, it's not. Not—"—since that hall, she thought. Not since she went into a kifish stronghold after him. And had a look at how it was. "Not any more, it isn't."

"So we ally with them? Risk all our lives when we're within a one-jump of mahen space?"

"We got a debt. Like you said. And it's *mahen* space. Under mahen law. Mahen politics. You want to walk into it, throw ourselves on their charity? You want to gamble everything you got on someone else's priorities?"

"I thought we were falling-down grateful to our allies here. I thought it was debt. Them to us. Now it's something else."

"Maybe if I gods-be knew what it *was*, niece, I wouldn't be going along with this. Mahendo'sat go on status. You want Jik killed, do you? Want him to go—and what happens to his Personage then, and what happens to his friends, like Goldtooth and like us? We got interests in this. And they don't call for blind trust."

"We're not a warship, aunt!"

"No," she said. Her gut hurt. Missed meal? Missed sleep? Raw fear? "We're a trading ship without a cargo, in debt up to our noses, and the *han* deputy's got enough in her files to ruin us, the stsho at Meetpoint are bound to send their own complaint back to the *han*—I don't trust that bastard Stle stles stlen further than I can see him; and we got a kif loose who's got us down as number one target in the whole gods-forsaken universe. Akkhtimakt wants to be head kif over all the kif, and if he makes it you can make your own guess what our personal chances are. So you want to know why I take alliance with the mahendo'sat?"

"You don't think they'll let us have fair chance at any human trade. They'll double-deal us, they will, all our precious allies, first chance."

"I expect they'll try. They're good at that. But right now they're all the credit we've got. You want to go to Maing Tol, try to limp the long way back to Meetpoint to bail out our cargo—*what with*, niece? Go back to Anuurn and try to argue away all the charges in the *han?* When this gets back, your father's going to have challenges; every whelp with ambitions is going to try him, Ehrran's going to make double-sure of that—and Kohan's getting old, imp. He can't take *everyone*. That's the way it is."

"So we risk *The Pride?*"

"That's the way I choose."

No one moved. Hilfy stood there trying to catch her breath. There was a persistent beep from com.

"What we do," Pyanfar said, "we take the rest we're due. We back up this lunatic mission of Jik's and we guard the deputy's blackbreeched backside. And we hope to all the gods Goldtooth's in reach. The best we can do is keep the mahendo'sat well-disposed. Sikkukkut's only normal crazy. You got out alive. What I hear about Akkhtimakt I don't half like. That kif's got a real grudge against us. Sikkukkut's only half mean—that's the truth, niece. Listen to me. You want Akkhtimakt to be the great *hakkikt*, the one that unites the worlds, the leader the kif have been waiting on since they discovered piracy? Or you want Sikkukkut, who at least has limits? Maybe we *have* got a personal stake in this kif fight, huh?"

"So we let Sikkukkut into bed?"

The coarseness set her ears back. "We don't let the bastard anywhere. Yes, we made a deal. It benefits both sides."

"I'm sorry, I'm *sorry*, I've had that bastard's hands on me, I've had drugs and shocks and every lousy trick that kif could think of—gods know what all they did to Tully: he couldn't even tell me—You want me to approve this deal?"

"No. I don't. I didn't ask." She rested her head back. "I just tried to let you know what happened. You want to ride this one out in quarters, go on. You're due the rest. I *don't* recommend you get off here at Mkks. It's going to be real hot here in a little while. Real hot, about the time the word gets to Maing Tol and to Akkt. We're talking about the mahendo'sat losing a star station, hear? Or the kif taking one. And no one's just real happy. You're not alone in troubles. Gods know what the mahendo'sat will do or how good Jik's credit still is back home. We've lost any backing we might have had from the *han*. All we've got is Jik. And Goldtooth. And if they go, we've got nothing. *Nothing.* Chances are *they'll* double-deal us just the way you say. But if they go—chances are the Personage they work for goes down; and there'll be a new Personage. New deal. New policies. I'm not sure we'd like that. I'm not sure even Ehrran would."

Hilfy's shoulders fell. She had a look of pain. The beep from com went on. It was her station. She waved a hand in defeat and went over and picked up the earplug, pushed the button. "*Pride of Chanur,*" she said to someone. "Com officer speaking."

Hilfy sat down. Back turned. Got to work.

"Tully," Pyanfar said. She held out her hand and he came over to her chair. He gave her that blue-eyed, thinking stare. But he took her hand gently as he had learned; and she curled her claws round his hand, not enough to prick his soft skin. "Go below. Go rest. It's all right. It's all right, Tully. It's just a discussion. It's just talk. Go on below and rest."

"I'm crew. Scan tech. I work."

"You're mincemeat; and you can't read our boards, let alone work our controls without a probe. You want to work? Go get some sleep. You work later. Go." She freed her hand and gave him a swat on the rump to send him off, but Tully failed to move. Khym was standing there watching all of this. It set her teeth on edge. Her husband. This male. And an adolescent with a gut-deep hurt and gods knew what notions acquired in a kifish cell. "We all go off duty and get some rest. Sleep. Food. All right?" A second swat, clawtips out. He did move, startled-like, and looked back at her in shock. "Get," she said in a no-nonsense way, ears back; and he backed up.

"Aunt," Hilfy said. Business voice, sane and sensible. "It's *Aja Jin*. Captain's compliments and he's got a problem. He says he's got to talk to you direct. He won't take no. You want to talk to him?"

"I'll take it." Anything—*anything*—to maintain Hilfy's quiet. "I can guess." She swung her chair about. "Tully; Khym; Chur; Geran; get out of here, get fed, get to bed. Now. Move it. Hilfy. You too.—One other thing, Hilfy."

"Aye?" Defensively.

"Kif says Tahar's friendly with Akkhtimakt."

"*Moon Rising?*" Hilfy's eyes widened.

"Since Gaohn. Makes sense, doesn't it? She played close with Akkukkak; after Gaohn, where else could she go? *Vigilance* is *real* interested. Thought you'd like to know."

"Gods rot. Aunt—"

"Mind that language. You're back in civilization, niece." She punched the contact in as Haral switched it, a solid stream of mahen exigency in her ear. "Gods-be, Jik—"

"—*time. You got take comp feed. What you want, wait Akkhtimakt, wait Harak kif?*"

"What you want, my crew loses it in jump?"

"Got no damn time this rest. I got same station authority my neck, got same want board ship. I got explain kif you want sleep, a?"

She raked her mane back and flicked her ears. Rings chimed, light and constant. "Then *I'll* explain to the *hakkikt*, friend. You want that?"

A moment of silence from the other end. *"I talk hakkikt. Damn."*

"Thanks."

"Before sign off, maybe get comp feed through. Deal, a?"

"No! My crew's gone the limit, understand? *No more!*"

"We got stsho run go Kefk."

"We can't do it, Jik."

"I send crew."

"Not on my deck, you don't. No way."

"You want I come over there explain? We got stationer trouble, got urgent request we clear dock, got big fear, Pyanfar. Got kif trouble. What I say to kif? Sorry, hani got take nap?"

"Explain all you like. I got fall on my face, bastard. I'm out, through; whole crew's going offshift."

"Got finish comp feed."

"Twelve hours. *Then* we do it."

"Nine."

"Eleven."

"Damn, hani, this not merchant deal. Nine. Nine all we possible got. We cover you tail that long. Listen."

"Nine," she muttered. "Nine." She punched the contact out, turned the chair and got up.

Hilfy and Chur had gone. Khym and Geran. But Tully lingered, alone against the bulkhead door frame, hands behind him.

Looking at her.

"Scared you, huh?"

"Pyanfar."

"I'm not mad at you. I give you an order, *na* Tully, you move, hear? Did I say get?"

"Pyanfar." He stood his ground. His mouth was set, his eyes showed panic. But he stood away from his wall and came as far

91

as the observer seat—came further suddenly and flung his arms about her. She hated that. But it spoke more than Tully could. She patted his head, pushed him back and looked at him.

Trust. Gods knew he had no reason.

"You're a gods-be fool, Tully."

"Hilfy say you come."

"Hilfy's another." But it touched her all the same. And what had he thought when she left him with Sikkukkut? What had he believed then—not being hani, not being kin or anything but trouble to them? "You go rest, huh? We take care of you."

"I don't go kif."

"No. You don't go to the kif. Not to anybody. We keep you with us." She thought things over and poked him with a foreclaw to get his attention. "We got a kif aboard. Hilfy tell you that?"

"Kif—on *The Pride?*"

"Prisoner. Name's Skkukuk. Know him?"

A shake of his head. "No. # # prisoner?"

"Missed some of that. Sikkukkut gave him to us. That's where we got him. You don't be afraid, huh?"

A second shake of his head. "Hilfy—Hilfy—want # say—she # kif."

"Missed that too. She's not happy. I know that. But we take care of her."

"She's good. Good."

"I know that too." She cuffed him gently on the arm. "They get some food for you?"

"Not want."

"Not want. Come on." She took Tully by the arm and led him across the bridge. Stopped and looked at Haral and Tirun, whose eyes wept dark streams from exhaustion. Her own watered. She wiped at them. "Get off duty."

"You," Haral said.

"Me," she said. "I am." She held Tully by the wrist and headed up the gentle curve to the galley. Behind them, chairs hummed and there were sounds of switches thrown.

There was activity in the galley: Geran and Khym had gone that way, and gods, she ought to have flinched at dragging Tully in there with Khym, but she was beyond it all. "Sit down," she said to Tully, and he did that, in the nearest spot, took the cup Geran put into his hands—Geran's own. He drank. "Going to have to take some food down to Hilfy," she said. "And Chur."

"I will," Geran said, and dumped more into the brewer as Haral and Tirun showed up and went over to haunt the counter and rummage the supplies.

"Here. You need it." Khym shoved a cup into Pyanfar's hands. "Sit down yourself."

"Huh." She subsided onto the bench and drank the steaming cup from both hands, set it down and wiped her mane back from her face.

Com beeped.

"Gods rot," Haral said, and took it from pocket com. "*Pride of Chanur*: you got our recording; we're on shut-down. Is this an emergency?"

"*I have a personal message from the* hakkikt. *I am waiting at your dockside.*"

"Gods and thunders," Pyanfar moaned. "Kif."

"Don't go," Khym said. "Send it away."

"You can end up regretting a thing like that." She swallowed a massive gulp of gfi. "Tell it come up. Tell Ehrran's guards let it pass. I'll deal with it below."

"Kif," Tully said softly. His alien eyes shifted this way and that in evident alarm. "Kif come—"

Pyanfar signed for quiet. Haral relayed the message.

"It's coming up," Haral said. And with a lifting of her jaw. "You know those gods-be Ehrran are going to report this business."

"I know." Pyanfar stood up. "You coming?"

"I'll come," Khym said.

"No sense all of us going. Just monitor from up here. Wouldn't want to give the impression we were worried, would we?"

"Maybe Sikkukkut's sent to get that kif back," Haral said, when they were riding the lift to lowerdeck.

93

"It would solve a problem. I'd give it with ribbons on. But I don't have any hope."

The door whisked open. They walked out.

The kif was already in the corridor, a dark shadow against the lights, arms tucked out of sight in its capacious sleeves.

So was Pyanfar's hand in her pocket, finger curled about the trigger of her pistol. Haral's too, she reckoned.

The kif bowed as they approached. She neglected the courtesy. "Well?"

Dark, thin hands came empty from the sleeves. It was a tall one, impressively tall. A silver medal glinted on its chest, multi-faceted.

"You come from the *hakkikt?*"

"Hunter Pyanfar, you will never learn to tell us one from the other."

She looked more sharply. "*Sikkukkut?*"

The *hakkikt* spread his hands, palm outward. "Messengers are not to be trusted in this, hunter Pyanfar. And doubtless they would miss nuances. There will be a computer feed; are you getting it?"

"Relayed from *Aja Jin.* Yes."

Sikkukkut lifted his head to stare down a long, soft-skinned snout. Veins stood out about it. The eyes were bright. "You have confidence in your allies."

"Let's say our interests coincide."

"You have too much *sfik* to coincide with their interests."

"Is this a deal of some kind?"

"I have offered gold."

"Doesn't interest me."

"And you a merchant."

"Not in every kind of goods."

"Your human would not speak for me. Not a word."

"Huh." She drew a deep breath, ignoring the ammonia smell.

"I didn't try too hard. But doubtless his comrades on *Ijir* talked to Akkhtimakt when he took that ship. And what would they tell? That humans are determined on trade links . . . which will destroy the Compact? Annoy the methane breathers? Distress the stsho? Do you see the forces ranged against you, *ker*

Pyanfar? Your own *han* is against you. You ally yourselves with mahendo'sat, and you know their motives."

"Tell me them."

"To diminish us. To bring in yet another species at our backs as they brought hani to shield their left hand. On Ninan Hol there are listening posts. Mahendo'sat turn their ears to space beyond Ninan Hol; they send out probes constantly hoping for some other contact they might use. They have their hands in everything. Like my old friend Keia."

"Friend, huh?"

"Our interests coincide. He wants me to defeat Akkhtimakt, disliking Akkhtimakt's immediate objectives. I want the same, of course. So should you."

"Maybe I do."

Sikkukkut's snout wrinkled and unwrinkled. "Kkkt. Let us assume we are allies. Remember this at Kefk. Should things go amiss, *come* to me."

She stared at him a long, long moment. "That what you've come to say?"

"I find you of interest."

"Gods, thanks."

More wrinkles. "You are ingenuous. You have enemies at home."

Her ears sank. "What's that got to do with here and now?"

"Much to do with the future. Will you sell me this human?"

"No."

"What will you do with him? Tell me. I confess to curiosity."

"I don't know I'll do anything. He's *crew.*"

"Hani perplex me. But you've promised, haven't you? You'll give me Kefk."

"Jik said as much. Does it take a private deal with me?"

"I offer you *pukkukkta* on all our enemies."

"Revenge I don't need."

"Do you not? Tc'a sing your name. I have heard it."

The hair stood up on her back. "Fine. I imagine they gossip a lot of things."

"*Pukkukkta.*" The dark lips drew back and exposed keen in-

95

cisors with their v-form gap; one arm flourished outward, with a flare of dark sleeve. "Hani, there will be a day you want it."

"What by the gods does that mean?"

But Sikkukkut had turned and walked away, a diminishing blot on the light. He stopped and turned half about, always graceful. "You'll have to let me out, of course. Friend."

"*Tirun.* We got a visitor leaving. Let him out."

"*Aye,*" the answer came back. Sikkukkut walked on in serene dignity and Pyanfar tautened the skin at her back to smooth the fur. Muscles resisted and turned the motion into a shiver.

"Gods," Haral muttered.

"See he gets off," Pyanfar said; and Haral strode off down the corridor in that direction, where the kif had disappeared around the corner, headed for the lock.

Her hair did not unbristle until Haral reappeared and walked back to join her.

"You record that, Tirun?" she asked of the empty air.

"*I got it,*" Khym's voice came back. "*I wasn't Mahn's back-room lawyer for nothing.*"

She drew a whole breath and spat out a laugh. It was as if some thunderstorm had blown through *The Pride*'s corridor and the sun had come out again.

But then Haral froze, looking down the corridor beyond her shoulder.

Pyanfar turned abruptly. Hilfy stood there with a pistol in hand.

"What do you think you're doing?" Pyanfar yelled.

"I heard the hatch," Hilfy said. Too quietly.

"We handled it. Get back to quarters, huh?"

"Aye," Hilfy said. The safety clicked back on. Hilfy pocketed the gun and disappeared around the corner.

"Why did I yell?" Pyanfar muttered to Haral, to no one in particular. "I didn't have to yell, gods rot it."

"She's all right," Haral said.

"Sure."

But she did not get the cold of it out of her gut until she had gotten back to the bridge and into the galley.

"What he want?" Tully asked, worried-looking, half-rising

96

from the table; but Pyanfar pushed him down again, her hand on his shoulder.

"Nothing but nuisance."

"He give money. Want me."

"He knows I wouldn't take it." She sank down onto the bench and reached for her abandoned cup. *So what* did *he want?*.

Khym took the cup before her hand got there and slid a hot one into her hand.

"Good," Khym said.

She looked up at her husband, puzzled.

"Good," Khym said again, meaning just, she thought, good job. She doubted it. But she sipped the gfi and looked up at him. She saw patience in his amber eyes. Patience he had won the hard way.

"Your cabin's taken," she said pointedly.

"Huh." He looked embarrassed at the invitation when he had realized it. Geran was there. Another male was.

Then he looked pleased in spite of himself. His ears flicked.

Gods. Tc'a. Methane-breathers. She remembered the knnn that had paced them out of Meetpoint and the hair wanted to stand up on her back again.

Something he said was important. Something was worth the trip here. Him. Would-be lord of all the kif. Visiting me.

Let us assume we are allies. Remember this at Kefk.

"Something wrong?" he asked.

Revenge on all our enemies. Hani, there will be a day you want it.

"Not yet," she said. She caught the plastic-wrapped confection Geran spun her way on the tabletop. Haral and Tirun blundered back in, hunting gfi and food. She tore the plastic and swallowed the mince in hunks, guaranteed to make for hiccups. She chased it with gfi. "Gods, tofi." The spice made her sneeze.

"Slow down, for the gods' sake."

"What, slow down? We've got eight and a half hours to sleep." She stood up and grabbed Khym's arm. "Come on, husband. Suddenly I'm in the mood."

"Gods, Py."

"Who notices? Finish the gfi. Come on."

97

Six

Eight and a half hours was not enough. The alarm went off like attack and mayhem and universal doom. Pyanfar climbed over Khym to kill it, but there was nothing for it then but to remember where she was and what there was waiting, and to pull herself and her half-conscious husband out of bed and face it.

She faced it in a plain twill pair of blue trousers, common-spacer-like, because they were headed out, and otherside of that jump was likely no time for washup or amenities. She saved her brightest silk pair for after-cleanup on the docks at Kefk.

Healthiest to think in those terms, that there *would* be the need of red silk trousers and all the finery.

But she did put on the ruby pendant earring, among the others, that winked and shone ferociously in the red-gold sweep of her tufted, many-ringed ear. It advised all who wanted to argue with a rather plainly dressed hani that she held a captaincy. On such a day she needed all the convincing it could lend.

"Feed the gods-rotted kif," she ordered Tirun when she found her on the bridge.

"Feed it *what?*" Tirun asked, and forthwith turned her stomach.

"I don't know: thaw something. Throw a steak through the door. Don't get near it. And don't carry weapons."

"Gods, it's just one kif. I can—"

"*Don't go near it. How much more trouble do we need on this ship?*"

"Aye," Tirun said, and swallowed all further argument.

They were all up, all functioning: Chur came out from Khym's former cabin to sit check-out on the bridge; Haral and Hilfy and Geran arrived from below; and Tully came up too, stiff and sore and pottering about the galley with Khym (gods!) and Hilfy, getting breakfast. On the bridge the com-flow started and *The Pride* began to drink down the information *Aja Jin* and *Vigilance* had been awake through the down-watches composing. Haral and Geran and Chur were in charge there, while Tirun went off to kif-feeding.

"We got a request," Chur reported, "from *Aja Jin*. They want conference when you can."

"Fine," Pyanfar said, martyred. "Fine. I'll get to it."

"Checks are running fine. We just take *Aja Jin*'s course the way it stands?"

"We take whatever they give us. I'm not quarreling with their comp." She leaned over Chur's seat and took a look at station output. It was mahen language again. Mkks began to have the feel of normalcy in its operations.

Any kif on Mkks who valued his life, she reckoned, was headed for Sikkukkut's ships. She thought of others of the non-involved, non-kif, wishing they could have evacuated the entire station. But that was impossible. Mahendo'sat and stsho had to stay and trust the few conventions of non-involvement and neutrality even kif observed in the Compact. Tc'a and chi were safe. Indisputably. And they protected the other, oxy-breathing residents by their own immunity and their insanity.

"What's our count?"

"Hour three minutes to undock," Haral said.

"Good gods, they're going with it, are they?"

"That mahe's a stubborn bastard."

"We on count?"

"We're catching up."

She put her own board live. Ran a survey of systems and recent com messages.

From *Aja Jin*: You got no problem, you come in on coordinate number one good. . . .

Another optimist, she thought. "Put in a call to Jik."

"Aye," Geran said. And a moment later. "He's not answering."

"*What*, not answering? We're in countdown. Remind him who's asking, huh?"

Another delay. "Captain, his first is on if you want to talk to her."

100

She punched it in. "This is Pyanfar Chanur. Have we got a problem?"

"This Soje Kesurinan. Not got problem. Fix good."

Unease ran up and down her spine. There was a *don't ask* implicit in the mahe's tone.

(So what for godsakes is *the matter?)*

"Want me to come over there?"

"No need. All fine, honored captain."

"Pride out." She punched it off. Gods, likely every kif on Mkks had access to that com transmission. She caught Haral's worried look.

"He's not there," Pyanfar said.

Haral's brow wrinkled.

"I'm betting," Pyanfar said, "he's not aboard. Geran, get me Rhif Ehrran."

"Aye." Geran made the call. "She's on, captain."

That quick. So he's not there, and Rhif's at the boards.

"Ker Rhif. Letting you know we're back online."

"We have your count. We assume it's accurate."

"It's accurate. Do we have a sequencing yet?"

"Can't this be processed at some other level, Chanur? Or is this a social call?"

"Just wondering, Ehrran." She broke the contact without the protocols. Looked at Haral.

"He's with the kif or he's loose on the docks somewhere."

"Gods-rotted lousy time to take a walk."

"I figure he knows what he's doing." She got back to the messages. A Mkks consortium lodged protests. A mahen prophet babbled something about retribution and visions. A self-claimed psychic saw humans descending on Mkks in their thousands and bringing some invention that would make antimatter obsolete—

"Good gods, Geran, you screen this stuff?"

"Sorry, captain. That's the good ones. We got crazier. Thought you'd like the local temperature, huh?"

"They're scared. Can't blame them for that." She tried not to think about it. "Where's *Vigilance's* complaint about visiting kif?"

"They never logged it with us."

101

"Huh." *That* bothered her. She bit at a snagging underclaw and watched the readout run past. Khym arrived with gfi for everyone on the bridge, regulations fractured. But it was her rule, and she broke it with a grateful sigh.

"I reckon," Geran said, "they expect us to take a lot of this data during system transit."

"They better." She sipped the gfi and looked up again as breakfast arrived, Hilfy with a tray of rolled sandwiches. "Thanks, imp."

Hilfy glanced at her in a strange, ears-back way as if the little-girl word had jarred. Perhaps it had. Pyanfar noted that as Hilfy turned away and served the rest, with Khym and Tully. Tully's moves this watch were full of winces. Besides the usual spacer's breeches he wore a white, stsho-made shirt, likely the last he had. It covered the wounds. His mane and beard were combed and neat. His eyes, always light and unnerving-quick, darted and danced in a kind of desperate counterpoint to Hilfy's quiet. He smiled. He looked happy. It had the look of desperation.

Fear of them? she wondered uncomfortably; and then caught Tully's look at Hilfy's back, that one glance in which the smile died and something else showed through until Hilfy pricked up her ears in a semblance of good humor—

—*for her*, she thought; he wore the cheerfulness for Hilfy's sake; and the inside-out of it shivered through her nerves. He moved like a woman walking round some man on the edge of his control. *Don't jostle, be pleasant, have your temper elsewhere.* Hilfy might see it or might not.

Human instinct?

Or were they tied together, one holding onto sanity because of the other—and Hilfy further gone than she suspected?

"Captain?"

Pyanfar blinked and gulped down a large part of the sandwich, turning to the board. "Thanks." Data turned up. She swallowed the other half in two bites and punched a key. The nav-system engaged and ran the data.

"Three quarters hour," Haral said.

"We aren't getting checkout from our friends out there."

"I'm—" Geran said; then: "We got a call from *Aja Jin*'s first."

"About gods-rotted time. What does she have to say?"

There was a stir at her side. Hilfy slid into her seat and started checkout. Tully edged in next to Chur.

"That's Khym's seat," Chur said sotto voce. "Take the one the other side of Tirun's."

"Captain, Jik's on his way over here. So his bridge says."

"Huh." Pyanfar's eyes went to the time ticking away in the corner of main-monitor. Small alarms went prickling up and down her spine. She sipped at the gfi. "Coming up on the half hour mark and Jik pays social calls. Are those Ehrran guards still on watch in our lock?"

"Had a call from *Vigilance* a few minutes ago," Haral said. "They say they're going to pull them out at the half hour mark. I gave them thank-you and told them we'd take care of ourselves from then on out."

"Gods-rotted pointless anyhow. Gods-rotted Ehrran priggish gods-be punctilious nonsense that keeps an Ehrran ear to Chanur business, that's what they're up to. Sealed lock and they've got to set guards in it." Pyanfar's lip twitched. A thought came through. "That blackbreeched bastard *knows* something's interesting in our downside corridor. Never mind what passes through our lock."

"You think?" That rated a turn of Haral's head.

"Khym was on guard down there when Ehrran first came aboard. That kif Skukkuk walked up to our ship and never came off; you want to bet no one on the dock saw that? And that Rhif Ehrran hasn't been sniffing round everyone she can interview on this station? If she missed any of that, she heard me ask Sikkukkut what to do with the bastard: by the gods she knows. Knows about Sikkukkut coming here to talk. And she's waiting on me to cave in and send some explanation what we're doing with the kif."

"File's got to fill whole banks by this time."

"Doesn't it? I swear I'll give that kif to her." She gulped the last of the gfi, looked around for someone free to carry it to the galley. Tully sat beside Tirun. Khym was rattling about in galley; latches snapped and thumped.

Tully turned wide eyes on her, blue and holding that perpetual hint of panic. "Trouble?" he asked Chur, with a glance her way.

"Explain it to him." Pyanfar shoved the empty cup down the security-bin. "I'm going down to talk to Jik when he comes in."

"Want company?" Haral asked.

"Sit on things here. Who's going to do that undock?"

"Central says they've got crew moving up. Mahendo'sat."

"Fine." Pyanfar headed for the door. "Fine.—Get Tully's drugs for jump. Tully, hear?"

"I got." Tully patted his pocket. "But kif—"

"Thank the gods. Brains."

"I work jump."

"You work, huh? You work it flat on your back. You go to bed, hear? And, Chur, *you're* going to quarters on this, from undock out."

"Captain—" Chur powered the chair about and opened her mouth to protest.

"You heard me. You're still not sound. Haven't got time to take care of you. Don't make me problems."

"I'm begging you this one. Captain. I'm going to be fit. It's a rough one. *I want to be there.*"

"Huh," Pyanfar said. Thought about it a moment too long and shook her head. "Gods rot it, all right, take duty."

"I," Tully said. "I work."

Another unanswerable stare, blue-eyed this time. His mouth trembled in that way he had when he had gone his limit.

She remembered then she had put a thing in her pocket, transferred from yesterday's plain trousers. She had meant to give it to him. Now it took on a superstitious feel, like saying no to Chur. She fished it out between thumb and foreclaw and took his hand and laid it there, a small gold ring meant for human-hands, not ears.

He closed his fist on the small bit of gold that had belonged to some lost friend. It meant something profound to him. "Where get?"

"Just keep it on your hand this time."

He put it on his finger. Looked up again with fever in his eyes. Then he clasped her hand with a fierceness that disarranged joints and claws; she flexed claws out in self-protection, strength opposed to strength, and he let go. "You sit this chair, huh?" *You sit here, stay steady, keep Hilfy—gods, keep her thinking. Shame her into it. Don't let her be a fool, Tully.*

"I work, captain."

"Captain. Huh." Someone had taught him that. He managed it in hani, confounding the overworked translator, which sputtered through the com at his belt. "Takes orders, does he? Huh. Tully, you watch."

She walked out.

The lift opened and let her out on the lower main. Tirun was in the corridor. She expected that.

That Tirun waited there with her back against the wall and that trouble-look on her face, she did not expect.

She slowed down, distracted from one crisis for one that confronted her, and Tirun's ears sank further, tight-folded. "Captain."

"Spill it."

"Kif won't eat the frozen stuff. He wants to talk to you personally."

She let go a long slow breath. "Wonderful. Tell him we'll have a long friendly talk at our next port of call."

"I told him you're busy."

"He said?"

"That you were a fool. Captain." Staring straight ahead, not a twitch of a tightly-folded ear. "I asked who was sitting in the washroom of someone else's ship. It said hani humor is unsubtle."

"You leave it the frozen stuff?"

"I left it. Thawed. I could puree the stuff."

"Kif's got teeth." She walked off.

"Captain. I could—bribe a docker, maybe, well, get one of those small live things—"

She looked back, at Tirun standing there with a revolted look. "Reason with it."

"I *tried*."

"Try again." She headed for the lock, jammed hands in pockets, past the butt of a gun in the righthand one. Gods. Live food. Raw was one thing. Raw and protesting was another.

She entered the short lock corridor and hooked the recessed button on the panel with a foreclaw. The inner hatch shot back unexpectedly and she glowered at the two Ehrran clanswomen on guard there, who faced her with an aborted leveling of rifles.

"Who you planning on firing on from this side? Escaping crew?"

"Captain." Politeness must have choked the Ehrran. And when Pyanfar walked through their midst and reached toward the com panel to tell Haral to open up the lock, an Ehrran arm shot into her way: "Captain, begging pardon, but it's a half hour—"

Pyanfar turned and looked, nose to nose with the Ehrran crewwoman. The ears wilted first, the arm dropped next, and the body went third, a backstep that got the Ehrran not quite out of her reach.

"Haral."

"*Aye, captain.*"

"Open us up down here."

The outer hatch shot back. Pyanfar heard it, felt the chill draft. She still glared at the Ehrran eye to eye. "You," she said to the Ehrran. "You want to walk out there into the access and see if captain Nomesteturjai's anywhere about?"

"I'm not to leave my post."

"What? Even if I cycle the airlock? You're a lunatic."

"I don't think it's a case—"

"—about the same. A lot the same."

"What, captain?"

"Arguing with me. *Get!*"

They flinched, the pair of them; they both flinched, and then it was too late. Pyanfar took the ground they gave, backed them up against the threshold of the open hatch, and it was suddenly a case of resisting a captain on her own deck or moving from their post. "*Out!*"

For a moment she thought they would actually stand fast, rifles and all; and her claws came out and her nose rumpled into a grin. But then one Ehrran's foot hit the hatch-rim and threw her off-balance. The Ehrran caught herself and backed up; the other did, and then they were both in retreat down the chill yellow accessway.

Pyanfar followed in long strides, one hand on the gun in her pocket—it was still a kifish dockside once around that bend and into the rampway. She heard the thunder of hastening feet on the plates; and when she had reached the righthand turn she saw a tall mahen figure upward bound toward the black-breeched hani, a mahe garishly dressed in red-striped green and laden with gold chains and bracelets and a monstrous large sidearm slung at his hip.

Mahen guards, far below, held the foot of the ramp. Jik strolled up the center, and the outbound hani caught-step to avoid him and passed him in great haste.

Jik stared back over his shoulder, faced forward and came on with a shrug. "What they got?" he asked with a gesture backward.

"Both ears," Pyanfar spat. She was shaking—gods, she had been in dockside brawls and barfights and a set-to with her son and never lost her head like that. The peripheries around Jik refused to come clear: hunter-vision had set in. Her ears were plastered tight against her skull and her muscles shuddered. Jik stopped—just stopped, dead still and quiet.

Pyanfar sucked air. Spat in the accessway. "You want something."

"You got time?" Judiciously and from safe distance.

A third spit. "I got time." The peripheries of her vision began to clear. She jerked a hand back toward the lock, led the way, and as they rounded the turn, she saw Tirun standing there with ears flat and a pistol in her fist.

"Haral said there was trouble," Tirun said.

"Over now. Get. Haral needs help up there. We got mahen guards outside."

"Aye." Tirun went at a run.

"Come on." Pyanfar brought Jik on through the airlock into the inner corridor, and punched the com panel. "Haral. It's all clear. Seal both hatches."

"*Aye—*"—from the bridge, without comment.

SSSShhhh-t. The door went. Sealed with an electric thunk.

She looked at Jik. Her lip still twitched. She flicked her ears with a jingling of rings. "I tell you, Jik, the *han*'s changed. It's *changed.* Hani used to go where they liked, do what they liked without some gods-rotted government note-taker stalking and lurking—"

"You think you make mistake, a?"

"I think I just made a gods-rotted big one. *Mistake!* When'd it get to be a mistake to throw two lousy insolent spies off my deck? When'd it happen, Jik?"

"Maybe—" Jik cleared his throat. "Maybe you make, Pyanfar. You bring lot strangers to Anuurn. Anuurn hani—they not got used to outside. They scare. Lot scare, Pyanfar. They got hani renegade Tahar go work for kif. You know what think? I think this Ehrran got lot suspicion Chanur got too much power—"

"Too *much?* We got debts, friend—we got debts up to our noses, my brother's not getting any younger—he'll go down one day, and gods even know if it'll be a Chanur that takes him. My nephews are all fools." It was too much to say. Far too much already. She shrugged and looked elsewhere down the corridor.

"Chanur got *space,*" Jik said. "Maybe Chanur bring back thing these world-hani not want, a?"

She slanted an ear back and looked at him then, this hunter-captain who was way, way up in mahen councils. Mahendo'sat had brought hani into space. Given them ships. Created, if hani ever admitted it, the very concept of the *han.* And Jik understood that. He understood it very well indeed. "You longtime got your hands in every nest in the Compact, mahe—" She slipped deep into the pidgin, facing wrinkle-ringed brown eyes, a sober, too-wise stare. "You *know* this Rhif Ehrran?"

She expected a shrug from Jik, denial, some glib answer. Instead: "Maybe Chanur enemy get organize, a? Maybe you watch you back, friend. I make big mistake at Kshshti, bring Ehrran in this thing. Big mistake."

"I believe you," she said. "*Now* I believe you.—What you want here, huh?"

"Want say same thing. Want make sure you not come 'cross bow with *Vigilance* at Kekt. I like you one piece, hani."

"Come here."

"A?"

She grabbed him by the arm and brought him down the corridor, around the corner and down again, where the lowerdecks washroom was. She pushed the button and the door shot back.

The kif sat on a folded several blankets on the tiles against the far wall. Its robes were tucked close about it. It had dropped its hood. Now its head came up and it rose in one muscular glide and bowed, showing empty hands, before it looked up again.

Courtesy of a killer-kind.

"Is it *ker* Pyanfar?"

"It's me. This is the captain of *Aja Jin.*"

"Sssstk." A deep nod of the head. "I am impressed. Nomesteturjai."

"Kif," Jik said.

"His name is Skkukuk. He says he's mine. A gift, from Sikkukkut."

"A.—A noikkhe?"

"Skku nik kktitik kuikkht kehtk tok nif fik pukkukk."

—*Why?* Pyanfar followed threads of it.

—*Subordinate, weapon, for pride, revenge—*

"Nfkokkth shokku hakhoth nkki to skohut."

"A," Jik said.

"Well?" said Pyanfar.

"You got kif," Jik said, and shrugged.

"I am starving," it said.

She shut the door, laid her ears back and looked at Jik. "What do I do with it, huh? Put it out the hatch?"

"They kill him sure."

"Well, gods rot it, do I run a charity for kif?"

Another shrug. "Sikkukkut give you crewman. Not number one important. Maybe fellow make mistake—"

"Maybe a crewman whose loyalty's in question? Maybe even one off that disabled ship?"

Jik's eyes flickered. "Maybe so. All same, he belong you. You got deal, a?"

"Gods rot, *you* want him?"

109

Jik rubbed at his nose. "Tell you truth. That give you *sfik* away. I friend, say no do."

"You mean status with that gods-rotted kif? Sikkukkut?"

"Best thing you kill this kif. Send same pieces to Sikkukkut."

"Huh."

"No do, a? Maybe you turn him out naked on dock."

"So they kill him."

"He same kill few, maybe."

"I've traded up and down docks from Jininsai to Meetpoint, and I've never heard the like. *You* understand it? What's Sikkukkut up to?"

"I fight kif long time. Long time, Pyanfar. Kif at Meetpoint, they quiet kif. This be border. Dis-pu-ted Zone. This space *no one* got. Where we go next, this be true kif space. You not see before. Not see before these thing. No hani see—'cept maybe Tahar. And she lot crazy."

"You've *seen* Tahar?"

"I talk with her, one time, two. She strange. Lot strange—" He touched his brow.

"She was strange before she ditched us and turned tail at Gaohn; and took kif money—"

"Hani law."

"You gods-rotted right, hani law. A lot of hani'd like to get a piece of that ship."

"Maybe do."

"Maybe do. Rhif Ehrran was already headed for Kefk when we picked her up at Kshshti. You know why?"

"Maybe you know."

"I don't. That *worries* me, Jik."

"Worry me too."

"What's an honest hani doing going Kefk way? What's an honest hani know about a kifish system?"

Jik ducked his head and rubbed his nose. "Tell you, hani, few ship I know sometime maybe got rig turn off ID squeal. Sure you not know such thing. Maybe ship also got rig make fake ID to beacon. *Vigilance* hunter-ship, a? Got lot stuff. *Lot* stuff. Also maybe know Kefk pretty good."

"*Been* there?"

"Stsho been there. Come, go. Stsho know lot stuff. Maybe sell in-for-mation."

"I'll believe that. But what's she doing there?"

"Kefk be Tahar port," Jik said. "She hunt Tahar. Also—maybe—maybe she got stsho interest. Stsho business. You think, hani: stsho don't fight. Stsho always hire guard. Who they hire?"

"Mahendo'—" The suspicion got through. She looked up into mahen brown eyes, murkier and darker than any hani's. "Good gods, they count us barbarians. They wouldn't hire hani for anything but—"

"Who else they got hire when got falling-out with mahendo'sat? Hire kif? They not fools. No, maybe all sudden they got idea hani not bad neighbor—maybe all sudden want make good friend with the *han*. Maybe one day there be hani guard at Meetpoint, not mahendo'sat. Big advantage to hani. To some hani. Lot money. Lot *stsho* money—and they plenty rich. I tell you truth, friend. I tell you truth. Ehrran want stop all hani make problem this deal. *Moon Rising*. You."

"You put us in the same—"

"*Ehrran* do."

"Gods." She flung a gesture up, put distance between herself and Jik. Stared at him.

"I tell you, you got lot enemy, hani."

She stood there a long moment. Jik made his mouth a thin, in-turned line, as if more might get out.

"What you do?" he asked finally.

"What do I do? What do I do? I ought to gods-be head out of here and leave you and Ehrran to the kif."

"You not do."

"Try me."

"No, you not do. Where go? Maing Tol? *Han* got 'nough suspicion already. Also—you not stsho. Chanur don't go hide in fight, wait for thing be better, let friend die. . . ."

"Friend!"

"I save you neck."

"For politics, for—"

"—same good reason, a?"

"Gods rot you, Jik."

"I try save you now. Want you at Kefk. *Need* you. Need you stay 'live, hani."

She looked off across the corridor. Anywhere else. Jik's voice was dim. Her ears lay flat against her skull. "So what do I do with the gods-be kif in my washroom, huh?"

"You keep. I want you keep. He yours. He got nowhere to go, a? You got plenty *sfik* he fight like devil kill you enemy."

"And if he decides I don't have?"

"You kill him quick. He offer you weapons, a?"

"Huh."

"He tell truth. Kif truth." Jik laid a careful hand on her shoulder. "You keep him lock up tight. A? Later I take. I got reason."

"I'm sure you do." Her nose wrinkled. She endured the hand, that was no small weight, and turned and stared up into his face. "So what's the game at Kefk? What's Sikkukkut want? He wanted *me*. Before you ever got into it. He got *me* to Mkks. What's he want, dragging me into this Kefk business?"

"You got damn lot *sfik*."

"You're crazy." She shook the hand off. "He's crazy."

"You got think like kif."

"I'm sure you're good at it."

"You friend."

"Friend, my—"

"Maybe kif play same game like Ehrran." He shrugged, hands in the back of his belt. "He kif. Kif mind got twists. One, he hate Akkhtimakt. Two, he want take opposite from Akkhtimakt. Three, he got no heart. Got no way understand you not all time mad like kif. You add all up, think like kif. He give you kif advisor—he number one smart: you take kif advice, he hope know what you do. You got lot *sfik* with him. Also you got tame human."

"What's *that* got to do with it?"

"Kif all time got disadvantage, try predict what outsider do. Sikkukkut *lot* curious 'bout hu-man-ity. Same way stsho not understand kif: stsho want make deal with Akkhtimakt, want make same deal with Sikkukkut, same with Ehrran hani, a? Someone eat they heart someday. Maybe Sikkukkut. Meanwhile, Sikkukkut want get me, a? Want also get human. Human be *big* problem soon. Same tc'a. Stsho—they nothing without make alliance with hani, if they not more trust mahendo'sat. Anuurn hani damn fool get involve in this politic."

"They're not the only ones."

"You *born* involve, Pyanfar. You *spacer* hani. You too smart."

"Then why am I here?"

"You got stake. We all got stake."

"Like what, like hani do all the fighting and mahendo'sat pick up all the eggs? Same as you and your partner did to me at Gaohn? Same as get me barred from Meetpoint—same as—"

"Pyanfar. We all got stake. This Mkks be half mahen station, a? I go take walk, I talk few people. Learn thing."

"Learned what?"

An expansive shrug. "Like knnn be upset. Like tc'a big disturb. Chi crazy like always. Like big rumor on methane-side got lot human come. *Lot* human. Stsho damn upset."

Mahen visionaries. Prophecies on the com. "Gods-be." It was there to have been read. She raked a hand through her mane. "Geran said."

"What say?"

"Rumor's all over Mkks. Thousands of humans coming. Where are they coming to?"

"I think maybe Tt'a'va'o."

"Good gods." *Tc'a.* Tc'a territory, right up to Meetpoint. "What fool set that up?"

"Kif know. I think they know damn sure."

"Then what are we getting into at Kefk? For godssakes, Jik—"

"Big game. Number one big game, hani."

"Game. Gods rot it, human ships have *fired* at knnn."

Jik's jaw dropped. He closed it.

"Tully told me. Now you trade me one, partner. Tell me the gods-be *truth!*"

"*What* you know 'bout knnn business?"

"Nothing else. Absolutely nothing. But a knnn ship was tracking me directly after Goldtooth gave me Tully; stayed with me when I left Meetpoint headed for Urtur. I lost it. I don't know where it went. But it was on me. It could have been at Urtur. It might even know I went to Kshshti. Hear? We did have tc'a activity there."

"Damn," Jik said. "Damn."

"Let me tell you something else. I don't trust that tc'a stationmaster at Kshshti. I don't know *what* it heard. I don't like it, hear?"

"What tc'a do?"

"Do? It was scared witless, that's what. Mention knnn near it and it went into gibbering lunacy. *Avoid*, it said. It talked about hani dying at Mkks. It talked—talked about *three* sets of kif to watch out for, one of them the kifish homeworld."

"I hear this. Not surprise. Homeworld kif wait see who win, a? They not stupid."

"No, they're not stupid, just a lunatic mahe who thinks I'm going to play tag with the knnn and politics with the gods-be kif—"

"You listen." Jik looked her in the eyes and jabbed her in the chest with a blunt-clawed finger. "I tell you truth, tell you truth, hani and mahendo'sat be longtime friend, a? Stsho friend only to *stsho*, same like kif. We got Sikkukkut, got same this fellow in the loo, a? We got lot *sfik*, this kif Sikkukkut get some from us; he go be number one kif. *Safe* kif."

"I'm not so sure he is."

"I tell you this: Sikkukkut got same interest we got. He want keep thing lot same like now. Want make quiet. Sure, he lot dangerous. But you respect him, he got *sfik*, not need kill you. This Akkhtimakt, he oppose Sikkukkut: he got kill all Sikkukkut deal with. That be long list, a? Sikkukkut enemy all be kif; but I tell you, Pyanfar—lot people be Akkhtimakt enemy who *not* be kif. Whole damn Compact. Humanity. Where he stop, huh? And we already got knnn trouble. How much trouble we need?"

"They're all crazy."

"You hani, you like too much law. Kif, they got Personage. Sen-si-ble, like mahendo'sat. Make life more simple." He touched her shoulder again. "You see why I want you 'live? You don't cross *Vigilance*, a?"

A clank sounded from outside, the noise of the line connections being withdrawn.

114

"This fancy ID system I'm not supposed to ask if you got—any chance it can fool the beacon at Kefk?"

He rubbed the bridge of his nose and gave her an anxious glance. "I not say got."

"Can you?"

"Maybe I run—little ahead main group. Maybe we get beacon. One good look all I need."

"Maybe! Kite in there alone?"

"A, got good kif friend, good friend *Vigilance* follow real close."

"Sure, sure."

"Hey, you no worry—you damn smart pilot, a?"

"Sure. No worry. No worry. *Gods rot it*, that's a binary system, Jik, and that's a kif you've got to rely on!"

"Got you come."

"Gods, what do you think I am? You're crazy, you know that? This whole thing is crazy! You're going to trip that zenith guardpost all alone out there—"

"Ana be right. You got nice eyes."

"You—"

"Hey, I got go," Jik said, holding up his hands. And with a lift of brows: "A." He reached into one of his belt-pockets and pulled out a small square packet. "Want give you this."

"What?" Her ears went down flat. "Gods-be, Jik, no more tricks! No more—"

"You take." He pulled her hand forward and slapped the packet into her palm. "Things go bad you take, run, go Meetpoint, find help."

"What *is* this thing?"

"Record. Got same microfiche. You don't worry." A blithe mahen grin. "All code."

"Jik—"

"I trust." *The Pride*'s bow rang to a second thump; the ventilation fans died and started up with a different, more rapid sound. They were on their own. "I got hurry, Pyanfar. They take ramp soon." He started away down the corridor and looked back. "You be smart, Pyanfar."

"Go on, you'll miss the ramp." She pocketed the microfiches

115

and picked up the pocket com. "Haral. Stand by to let Jik out. His people still outside?"

"Still there. I've been keeping an eye on them, captain. They're all right."

"Huh. Good." She broke the contact and walked back the other way, not without a misgiving glance at the washroom door.

More thumps from the bow. The dockers were working fast. Anxious to get them out, one guessed.

Pyanfar headed for the lift. A cold lump had settled in her stomach, indigestible.

Gods, gods, and Jik himself never told all the truth. Not ever the part that told what *he* would do.

Seven

It was chaos in the bridgeward corridor as Pyanfar headed out of the lift. Tully was there with Hilfy, doing final latch-check on doors, which meant Khym was busy somewhere and not doing that. Tirun came running to catch the lift door with a covered bowl in either hand.

"Hurry it," Pyanfar yelled as Tirun darted past.

"Aye," Tirun said.

"And don't go in with it!"

The door shut. Upship, Chur was at her cabin door, with Geran; she had a new and tightly wrapped bandage round her middle. There was a crash from lowerdecks, another seal in place. "You sure about this," Pyanfar said in passing.

"Absolutely," said Chur.

"Captain," Geran said in courtesy, and Pyanfar left them both behind, headed bridgeward in long strides.

Haral was at her post, the only one as yet, but Chur and Geran were trailing in at Pyanfar's back. The boards were lit and *The Pride*'s initial systems were all up, with ready-lights on the rest. Pyanfar threw herself into her own chair and powered it about.

"Captain." Haral acknowledged the command transfer with a dip of her many-ringed ears, never a turn of her head or a missed beat in the routine switch-flicking of power-up. Pyanfar shoved the com plug into her own left ear and leaned, fished the microfiche packet out of her pocket and shoved it in the security bin.

"That it?" Haral said.

"That's the latest bit of trouble. Gods, I'm tired of mail-carrying. Gods give that Ehrran—"

Khym showed up, from the galleyward corridor, his hands full of food-packets, his face all cheerful.

—sons, the ancient curse went. Pyanfar swallowed it and listened to the com. The voice out of central was mahendo'sat,

117

likewise the docking chief talking to them on the outside line. One could believe the universe safe and sane; and then a kif spoke up from down the row, giving them its outbound time.

Khym reached past her to clip the concentrates at her elbow. Three packets, one of water. "Thanks," Pyanfar muttered. And to Haral: "You mark what Jik's trying?"

"Uhhhn."

"*That*'s not on the plan. Something recent. Real recent. Didn't want to use that system in front of the kif, that's what, and Sikkukkut wasn't going to use his—eggs'll get pearls *Harukk*'s got that equipment too and Sikkukkut won't use it."

"That where Jik was, you think? Push-and-shove with the kif? Trying to get them to—"

"Might've been. Gods know. Gods know if Ehrran knows what he's up to."

"He's *got* to fill her in. If she comes in alone with the kif—"

Clang-thunk! The accessway was loose. *Crash!* The grapples from Mkks station retracted. They had their own grip on Mkks and they were against the docking boom: that was all that held them now.

"He didn't want to tell us," Pyanfar said. "He wasn't going to. You get that all business down there on tape?"

"Hhhuun, yes. Want it logged?"

Pyanfar gnawed her mustaches. "It's enough to give Ehrran our skins. No. But don't erase it either." She looked across the dividing console, met Haral's gold-eyed hani stare. Different than Jik's. Uncomplex in honor and greatly complex in loyalties. "Stow it in my personal file, huh? You don't need to be part of it."

Haral's ears went back. Offended. "Aye. If you want it that way."

"I do. Who heard?"

"Me."

"Huh." Pyanfar looked to the controls and brought her board up. A seat hissed under weight. She half-turned and saw Tully settle in next to Chur. "Tully."

"Captain?" Tully turned his head, not using com and the translator.

"You crew, huh?"

"I—" Tully misunderstood the question and fished up a small syringe from the chairside pocket. "I sleep at jump, wake at Kefk. I work."

It sounded chancy. Gods made humans and stsho that way, that jump made them crazy. So they ran ships in and out of jump unconscious. Lunatics. "No fear, huh?"

A primate grin, quickly compressed to a hani smile. "I scared."

"Huh. Us too."

"Hurry it up!" Haral said over shipwide com. The voice echoed through the bridge and corridors. "Tirun, move it."

"*Vigilance* lodge a protest?" Pyanfar asked, swinging round.

"Aye," Haral said, and wrinkled her nose and laid her ears back. "I'd give this voyage's profits to've been in range of one of that pair in that lock."

"Huh." *Profits.* She laughed. But humor died. "It was a stupid thing. Stupid, that's what it was. Like a gods-rotted—"

Khym was on the bridge and Pyanfar swallowed that ancient comparison down too. Called up the outbound schedule. "Log that Ehrran business. Right down to the exit from the lock."

A hesitation. A key pushed. "I already had it separated."

"I'll lay it out for the rest of us—Put Geran wise to it, huh?"

(Gods, Khym back there, coming and going in all this business between her and Haral, between mahendo'sat in the lower corridor, and not a question out of him, not a What's going on? or a Why? The world was out of shape. But she and Khym had both said a lot of things in the dark. Last watch.)

She glanced aside. Khym settled into observer one, between Hilfy's as yet vacant post and Geran's seat, flicking switches. He brought com live there, backup now to Hilfy. Geran would sit Chur's post at scan one; Tully observer two; Chur moved to second scan; and Tirun, with below-decks cargo ops and second-bridge shut down, was left observer three, when she got to it, as auxiliary switcher, comp operator, engineer, and if things went amiss, backup at armaments. When she got to it.

Pyanfar punched in lowerdeck monitoring. "Tirun. You all right down there?"

"I'm coming," said a breathless, moving source. The sound of running feet in main corridor below. Pyanfar broke the contact. Hilfy took her post. Pyanfar caught the reflection in the monitor, against the light from Khym's boards.

Back in place. Home again. A ready light came on her board from Hilfy.

A mahen voice sputtered in her ear: "Clear when ready. You got clear, *Pride of Chanur*."

Hilfy acknowledged the station communication Khym had brought through, taking over. "Thank you, Mkks." Routine and cool. *Thank you, Mkks.* Pyanfar's blood went cold.

Aft, the lift worked. That would be Tirun.

"Geran," Haral said, "put *Vigilance* on the guard-it list right along with the kif."

A moment's silence. "You serious, huh?"

"Real serious. Jik says."

"Uhhhhn." No further comment. *That* got done. Their scan operators were onto it.

"*Aja Jin* to *Pride*, you got number one depart, go, go."

Running footsteps in the topside corridor behind.

"*Gods rot,*" Haral said into the mike, "*sister, we're going, move, move, move!*"

Footsteps reached the bridge, a body dropped into a chair and Haral hit the ungrapple program.

Clank-bang. They were under power then, a little queasiness as *The Pride* came off station and gave herself that little bit of thrust that got her outbound.

Nothing showy. *The Pride* could move. It was not a fact they cared to advertise to the kif or to any other watchers at Mkks. Haral brought *The Pride* about at leisure and took her time. They might have been hauling eggshells.

"We got an update on the entry projections," Pyanfar said. "Jik's got a—"

Then: "Priority," said Hilfy, that dreadful word from a post with bad news.

It got switched. "*—same advise you,*" from Mkks central's ice-clear voice, "*we got tc'a go outbound. Navigation caution.*"

"Gods rot!" Pyanfar exclaimed.

"—Tell it power down and wait," Hilfy was saying over com. "Mkks station,—"

Com transcripting was all over second monitor, kif protests, protests from Jik and *Vigilance*. . . .

"Got a blip," said Geran. "Confirm something outbound from the methane-sector—"

"That's a kif away," Haral said, overriding. "Scan two. Comp, get that tc'a figured."

"I'm on it," Tirun said. "Stand by, Geran."

Pyanfar gnawed her mustaches and snatched helm function to her board while Haral sorted priorities. Thank gods for full crew: com was babble from three prime sources and a dozen unauthorized outputs; Geran was on station scan output and Chur tried to sort out blips exploding off Mkks station about them like seeds from a pod.

Pyanfar kicked the rotation in, for *The Pride*'s internal *G*; and rolled them up in a move that got to the pre-set course the hard way. Gods, they were on a hair-breadth schedule out to that jump-point, they had everything calculated down to the instant for that tandem jump, and the situation behind them looked like feathers in a windstorm.

"Schedule's blown to a mahen hell," Haral said. "Gods blast that split-brained fool! We got a lunatic mess back there!"

"Hilfy—" From Khym, urgently.

"Priority," Hilfy said. "Station transmission, general to all ships."

Image turned up on second monitor. Violet light: a writhing serpent-shape, gold-mottled, that dipped and wove before the lens.

Methane-sector was talking to them: methane traffic control on visual output. The yellow, sticklike form of a chi raced up and down the tc'a's uplifted back, darted about its head in frenetic attentions to its—whatever a tc'a was to a chi: master; comrade; friend or pet. The tc'a wailed, the multipart harmonics of its segmented brain and speech apparatus, multiple minds, multiple viewpoints in matrix translated at the bottom of the screen.

Tc'a	tc'a	hani	hani	mahe	kif	kif
Mkks	Kefk	Kefk	Kefk	Kefk	Kefk	Kefk
give	go	go	go	go	go	go

121

```
tell    chi     go      go      go      go      go
chi     tc'a    go      go      go      go      go
knnn    knnn    knnn    knnn    knnn    knnn    knnn
```

A cold wind went up Pyanfar's back. "Hilfy: get comp on that. Tirun, go to com one."

"Aye," Hilfy said.

Not a word of criticism. No outcry from the crew. The tc'a ship was out ahead of them, likely to foul their schedule; a tc'a official onstation was talking about knnn, and no one sane wanted *them* involved. No one could talk to knnn but tc'a; and tc'a talked like *that*, in matrices that had to be read in all directions at once. It spoke of two tc'a presences, one at Mkks, going, perhaps—(give a chi?)—to tc'a at Kefk; while knnn were involved all across everyone's motivations, and of two kinds of kif (Kefk-bound?) and two kinds of hani (gods, did it pick that schism up?) only one lot of kif was going to fight?

"*. . . abort this lunacy!*" a hani voice said, Rhif Ehrran from *Vigilance*, fairly yelling over com. "Aja Jin, *pull us back!*"

"*You want what,*" Jik's answer came back. "*Give time Kefk know we come? Sure thing they blow us to hell,* Vigilance. *You stay on course, stay on course, you hear?*"

"Khoihktkt mahe kefkefkti—"—from the kif: *The mahe's agreeing with us.*

"Aunt, comp's got nothing better. The tc'a's talking about notifying knnn and says that tc'a's going with us to Kefk. Comp's not sure about the rest, but it's got a conjecture—"

"*Vigilance* is on," Geran said, "wanting the captain direct."

"Refuse," said Haral.

"Call on three," Khym said. "It's *Harukk*. Their com wants the captain."

"Refuse: get Jik."

"Belay that," Pyanfar said, biting her mustaches and reading comp's conjectures on the tc'a, not far off her own. "Jik'll talk when he can. Give me output. Compose a message to the tc'a and tell it we go and it waits."

"Aye." From Hilfy, tautly. *No* ship talked to methane-breathers without filling out abundant official queries afterward. There were reasons. Like methane-breather logic, which could

122

take something fatally amiss. They were *different*. Very. And went berserk very easily. Tc'a were the peaceful lot.

Knnn—were something else.

"Aunt—here's the set-up; approve it before it goes."

hani	hani	mahe	kif	kif	tc'a	t'ca
ship	ship	ship	ship	ship	Mkks	ship
go	go	go	go	go	Mkks	wait
danger	danger	danger	danger	danger	danger	danger

"Makes sense to me," Pyanfar muttered as it came up on the screen. "Log and send it. Send to *Aja Jin*: quote: We're on schedule and proceeding. We've advised the tc'a of navigation hazard."

"Jik's on already," Geran said. "He's saying go with it. Still go."

"Fine." It was not the answer she had rather have had, but it was the one she expected. Go with it. Go ahead. Take the chance.

Jump with a tc'a in their midst. Tc'a navigated like snakes. They *were* snakes. Come in at Kefk blind with a tc'a liable to pop out of hyperspace any gods-rotted where off-mark and the faster hunter-ships plotting to overjump them in hyperspace. . . . It was asking for disaster. Collision.

"We'll shine bright enough for Anuurn to see, if we kink this one," Pyanfar said. "Someone want to calculate the size of the fireball?"

"Gods-rotted bright one," Haral said.

"*Vigilance* advises us," said Khym, "she's filing a—"

Hysterical laughter broke out in sneezes, short and wild. They were hair-triggered. Hani. Hell-bent on course for kifish zones.

"What's that Ehrran think she is?" Hilfy cried over it all, as if there had never been kif, never been those awful days. Hilfy: youth and outrage. "What's been going *on?*"

"Welcome back, kid," Haral said dryly, never turning around. "You want a list?"

"Chanur's got trouble," Geran said, from Hilfy's right. "Ehrran's the name of it. She's after our hide. Any way she can get it. We don't cross her bows. That's the word on it. We take this jump, we thank the gods this time we're coming in a little slower than that ship of Ehrran's. She'll be in front of us at Kefk. Don't want her on our tail, no thanks."

"Prefer the kif instead, huh?"

A small shiver in the air.

"Gods-rotted safer," Tirun said. "Temporarily."

Silence then.

"Niece," said Pyanfar. "We don't forget either."

Silence still.

"What after Kefk?" Hilfy asked then, finally, in a normal voice. "Where do we go? You got an idea—captain?" Respectfully. "Have I been left out of briefings?"

Pyanfar flexed her fingers on controls, worked her elbow in the stress-brace. Drew a whole breath. "Some. You want it in a capsule? That engine-pack back there, this fancy new rig—nothing's free, is it? We're in hock, Hilfy Chanur. Nothing money pays for. And that Ehrran business—"

Lines trued up. They were on, headed for their mark. The tc'a was out in front of them now, having gotten up to its speed: no more turns now, even for it. Nothing but a knnn played games with physics.

"Gods-rotted tc'a's going to be in front all the way," Pyanfar said. "Gods only know where it'll be after jump. I can tell you this. Jik's got an idea he's going to fake an ID signal at Kefk—break through there a shade ahead of the rest and get that scan for us before it shuts down."

"Gods," Tirun said. "How much ahead?"

"He didn't say. No schema. Nothing. I tell you this, if he doesn't make it, we got trouble. Real trouble. We got a nest of kif for one thing. We got some other things too. What are we getting on com? We got some quiet out there?"

"Nothing worth listening to," Haral said. "Lot of kif stuff."

"*Vigilance* has stopped transmitting," Geran said.

"So's *Aja Jin*," Hilfy said.

"All right. Geran, I want you com backup right now; take number one scan after jump."

"Got it."

"Hilfy."

"Aunt?"

"You asked about Ehrran. I'll tell you what I've guessed so far in this business. Our troubles aren't just bad luck. They've been coordinated."

"*Ehrran?*"

"Oh, higher than that, imp. We settled that dustup at Gaohn, we busted our hani enemies out of Kohan's way, drove Tahar clan into near collapse, pushed *Moon Rising* into exile—We brought mahendo'sat to the homeworld, we brought humans and we brought knnn, which sets off the isolationists back home right proper, doesn't it? Naur. *Her* bunch. Llun clan got chewed up helping us at Gaohn; so'd others of our friends. Tahar, enemy that they were—we broke them and broke their power over their allies; and that left vacuum, and *that* let some other clans move up in the *han.*"

"Naur and Jimun and Schunan," Haral muttered. "Ehrran's precious patrons."

"That's precisely the shape of it. We were better off with Tahar for enemies. They were bastards, but they were spacing bastards. What we got left is the worldbound old eggsuckers like Naur; and those fat old women'd just as soon see us all back in kilts and *sofhyn.*"

"It's me," Khym said.

"Swallow it, Khym."

"Look, if I'd stayed downworld—"

"If not that, some other thing. We brought outworlders into Anuurn system—"

"—and got a male offworld."

"So we got every bigot in the *han* stirred up. The spacing clans got chewed up bad at Gaohn; among the Immunes, our Llun friends lost too gods-rotted many good women; and Ehrran's been itching after a piece of their rumps for years. Sure, Ehrran'll kiss-foot for the Naur; they got themselves that shiny ship, got themselves big ears and notebooks, and the stsho—those fluttering bastards have got their fingers in the stew. The mahendo'sat leaned on the stsho to get our papers reinstated because Goldtooth suddenly wanted our help—wanted *spacing* hani on his side. So the stsho bent, they always will—but straightway they ran and got Ehrran's ear and sucked that fool

125

right in. Ehrran was out at Meetpoint hunting down Tahar and doing any other bit of business the *han* wanted with the stsho—like secret negotiations, maybe, for a whole lot of things—and then the stsho up and offered them our hides for a bonus."

"Stle stles stlen," said Hilfy.

"Stsho got humanity coming in at their backs. They waffled on Goldtooth at Meetpoint. Gods know what they spilled to Ehrran; and I think if Stle stles stlen were less corrupt and less scared of Goldtooth the old bastard would have sold Tully to the kif right off. But *we* were there, and Ehrran *didn't* bribe them, iron-spined fool that she is. Rotted stsho xenophobes are climbing all over each other, thinking about humans coming in at their backs and straight up against stsho territory. But Ehrran played politics and got outbid—I'm guessing. Stle stles stlen lost his nerve about doublecrossing Goldtooth when we turned up with a virtual blank check and high-level mahen authorizations. But I wouldn't be surprised if old Stle stles stlen worries a lot nowadays about the mahen guards at his door at night. And I've got to tell you something else. Something you'd better hear. Haral—you got that tape from down in the corridor?"

"Aye."

"Run it. That and the one with Sikkukkut.—We've been getting a lot of offers, cousins. On all sides."

It was a long, long silence on the bridge, except for that thread of sound. Operations interrupted it. Pyanfar listened with one ear and winced now and again, kept *The Pride* running, tried not to think what Hilfy was going to say. Or what the translator was doing with it in Tully's ear.

Tc'a. Tc'a. Methane-breathers were upset, Jik had said.

Jik had been out in the station at large. In secret. Conniving with gods knew what agencies; and tc'a were high on the list of possibilities.

Right along with Sikkukkut.

The tape finished. There was silence after, too.

"I've got us into a mess," Pyanfar said. "One gods-be mess. I thought you'd like to know just what kind."

"Sounds like—" Tirun said, "sounds like Jik's right. We were

126

born involved. Being Chanur. When we get home—I'm betting we won't find the *han* what we left."

"I'm betting we won't," Pyanfar said. "But what is, nowadays?"

Another long silence.

"Well, *I'm* with you," Tirun said.

"Same," Chur said; and: "Same," her sister said.

"Aunt, I—"

"Maybe you want to think about it, niece."

The beep and tick of instruments went on. Tc'a matrix came up as comp sorted it, but it was all the same.

"Tully," Pyanfar said, "you understand even half of it?"

"I hear some."

Pyanfar could not see his face, saw only a shadowy reflection in a monitor, one un-hani silhouette.

"I hani," he said. "I *hani.*"

She blinked, thinking *that* through. But it made a warm spot all the same. "Khym," she said.

"My opinion?" he said. A great sigh gusted into com, a low rumbling. "Pity Ehrran's Immune."

"But they are," Hilfy said. "They'll go at father. They'll go for him at home. We may not *have* Chanur any more."

"I figure," said Pyanfar, "I figure Kohan Chanur's still no easy mark, niece. My brother and your father's no fool. Neither's any of our sisters, to let the bastards maneuver them out of the house. They'll be holding on. Long as we're in space, long as there's Chanur ships loose to worry about—Naur and her pets'll use some caution about dirty tricks. Kohan can still take anything that I know about, if the fight's fair."

And she thought of Khym when she said it, and felt an old pang of guilt: *If I'd been home when Kara challenged him, if I'd been there to prevent hangers-on from interfering—*

Khym might still be lord in Mahn if she had been home—if she had come blasting in for him the way Chanur clan had rallied for Kohan Chanur against her son Kara Mahn. Khym might not be in exile now if she had been there—even alone. Even when the rest of his wives and sisters and daughters deserted him. *She* might have stood by him against their son and

127

their blackguard daughter. Chanur might then have had its best ally intact, in Khym lord Mahn. And the likes of Ehrran would not have risen and the world would not have changed.

"Nav fix positive," said Haral.

"Wonder if that tc'a up there understands the flight plan," Tirun said.

"We'll find out, I guess," said Geran. "Want to lay bets against, *na* Khym?"

"She's cheating again," Tirun said. "She always collects."

"We got formation behind us," Haral said. "The kif are making mark. Looks like we're really going."

"Looks like," Pyanfar said. Her nerves tingled. Her forearm shed fur on the panel-edge. Sheer terror. Doubtless the rest of them were flutter-nerved as well.

"I'm with you," Hilfy said hoarsely.

"Thanks, niece.—Stand by, everybody. We're coming up on jump. Tully. You better use the drugs. Help him, Chur. Make sure he's out."

"Aye," Chur said.

She punched in all-ship. "Kif—Skkukuk. Get ready: we're going for jump."

"I offer you your enemies."

"Fine, that's real fine, kif." She broke the contact quickly. A vague guilt still gnawed at her. For a kif.

As well talk to the walls. It talked good hani; they talked good hani back to it; and nothing intelligible got said to either mind.

I offer you your enemies.

There was stress in its voice. Maybe it was scared, alone on a hani ship. Maybe it was trying to bargain.

Maybe it *would* starve, helpless and unattended in that washroom. Or break its bones in maneuver.

It was, gods knew, as trapped in its fortunes as they were— their good luck talisman; or their personal jinx.

"Jump plus ninety," Haral said. "Fixed on Kefk."

"Get it in your heads," Pyanfar said, because the other side of jump, things fuzzed and habits took over. "Jik might not make it. If he doesn't, we've got to move fast: get position first. Locate *Harukk* next. Remember that, hear? We're going in with *G.*

We'll make it that easy on ourselves. If it goes real sour we've got a few options. The second we come out, we lock reference on Tt'av'a'o; we run for Meetpoint if we have to. That's not Jik's plan; it's *mine*. We've got those three guardstations to keep track of at Kefk. We've got heavy debris in that system, it's a close binary stirring that stuff up, and kif made our map. Even if Jik gets us one. Remember that. Remember it, all the time."

"We got those numbers," Tirun said, "I got 'em up. Gods send Jik's anywhere along his entry line and we'll track him."

"Nasty place," Chur said. "Real nasty."

"Set systems," Haral said in calm, cold tones, and switch-flicking went on apace, systems-check, line-up. Pyanfar coordinated with her, shed the anxieties and called up the computer prompt program, comparing plan against tc'a-problems and Jik's intentions. Shifted a priority in the prompts. Re-ran it. Fed it in with the press of a key. Other stations were doing similar things. Haral was running master-check, making sure all jobs were sequenced.

There was most need of locating themselves on the passive-scan; getting absolute position to start with.

Then find Jik, find *Harukk* and *Vigilance* and ride down their trail to Kefk's heart.

"Sure one lunatic way to run a starsystem," Tirun said.

"We can try telling them that."

The numbers ticked away.

"There goes the tc'a," Geran said.

"Gods help us," Haral said.

"Tully?" Pyanfar asked.

"He's under," Chur said.

"Minus five," Haral said.

Gods, a tc'a loose in their pattern.

And Jik had been out of pocket before undock. Talking about methane-breathers and visiting spies—

Could Jik bribe a tc'a? Was that what he had been up to, in his furtive sortie onto Mkks station docks just before they left?

Navigation help? Precision?

Was that what Jik had been after—a way to cut it fine enough to keep *Harukk* on his tail—using tc'a computers and tc'a charts to get one critical spacetime calculation—

—on a kifish system?—against *Harukk*'s wishes and beyond what *Harukk* wanted to provide them?

My gods—

"Minus one."

They were gone.

—*there* again.

   —falling—

      —material and solid. Lights were blinking, the dopplered instruments gathering input and reading it—

"Kefk," Haral said. "Spectrum-match."

"Mark, where's our mark?"

"Searching," Geran said. "It's—*gods rot*—That's—in tolerance."

"Unnnh." The mind wanted to wander off at tangents and seek its former nowhere. The lights danced, hypnotic, led the eye in patterns: there was the sunlight on the hills—

—home.

"Aunt Pyanfar," the little girl cried, running breakneck down the hill, ears laid back and small limbs pumping with all their might, "aunt Pyanfar! you're home!"

Wide eyes and all ears, was Hilfy Chanur, her father's darling daughter, her aunt's surrogate for her own faithless Tahy—

—in Chanur's yard at night: "Aunt Pyanfar, name me that star—"

"—That's Kjohi; it's a white, much, much too far and too hot anyway. We don't go there.—See that little one below? That's a yellow. That's Tt'a'va'o."

"Have you been there?"

"No hani has, yet. That's a tc'a star. Tc'a have a whole hand of brains; they sing when they talk; they have seven voices all at once. I knew one once. Its name was So'o'ai'na'a'o."

Hilfy laughed. "Say that again—"

—"*Where's that gods-be tc'a? Geran! Chur! where's our own schema, we got any position on anybody?*"

130

"Negative, negative, I got the other map integrated almost—got it, got it, got it—It's coming through. . . ."

The image turned up on Pyanfar's board. Kefk-system schematic, adjusted to their entry-point. Sikkukkut's best current map—at least of things like major rocks that could be long-term mapped and tracked in their chaotic orbits through Kefk system.

A huge starstation—gods, she knew it must be be big. The kif's only legitimate outlet to Compact trade, after all. Fifty ships in port and miner-craft scattered like red stars among the yellow ones of asteroids; and no one of those ships where a ship was indicated. It was only a for-instance of a map. *Beware, hani: ships might exist. And they do.*

It showed kif and tc'a and chi in port. Likely. Again a for-instance. Gods knew what else.

"Stand by dump. Haral, double-check me."

"Aye."

—Use the wits, remember, wake up. *Aja Jin* out front by now—gods, *where? Harukk* and half the kif and *Vigilance,* with more kif due in at any instant.

—Down again.

—"Aunt Pyanfar—teach me the stars—"

Her own daughter, Tahy Mahn: "You're never here. You always come back too late. It's all over now. Kara's gone. *I* sent him to Hermitage—"

Son and daughter gone. Each in different ways—

"So. I've got things to do, Tahy. I'm sorry."

"You'll *always* have them. You don't *live* in this world. It's that ship! It's that ship! I don't know you, I never will—"

—And up.

Back to realspace. Pyanfar's eyes rolled and centered on the lights, her fingers scantly aware of the controls; her elbow ached.

"Third dump. Come on, line us up, look alive back there—"

"Got it—*we got Jik, he's out there!*"

—"Pyanfar," Kohan said, his broad face, his golden eyes gone all gentle, unlike the scowl he wore for show. "Sister—for the gods' own sake—be careful this time."

—She was selfish. He was not. He omitted to mention the real reason for his worry. Khym. Her private madness. His own public embarrassment. They had talked about it once.

—"They'll go for you," Kohan said. "All our enemies. They'll be trying."

—"Law out there's different, brother of mine. Safer. Folk accept what's strange."

—"I hope so," Kohan said. "I do hope so."

—And he walked away.

—*"We're on, we're all right. Got signal, got signal—He's got us a beacon-image, he got it!"*

"Star-fix, get that star-fix, Haral."

"Affirmative. Tt'a'va'o. We've acquired."

"Uhhhnnn." She felt the drain of strength, the wobble in her hand. They were inertial. *G* pushed her decidedly down, not back. The arm ached in the brace. She freed it and pulled loose one of the concentrate packets from its clip, bit a hole in it and drank. The stuff hit bottom in her stomach and lay there like lead.

Gods, gods—Figures ripped past like lunacy. And coincided.

"We're on," Haral said. "By the gods, we did it twice, and blind; and Jik and all of 'em—"

"I'll believe it when we find that tc'a," Geran said. "Where *is* that lunatic? *GOOD GODS!*"

Scan broke up. Lights went red. The siren howled. *"Haaaa!"* from Khym; and for a moment there was a nausea like dump-down; but not—

"*V* check," Pyanfar yelled into the mike. "Gods blast—"

—*dump*, this time, with a sluggish awful nausea.

The tc'a had come in close. Ripped past and dumped speed with two rapid flares of its field. And it was *there*, a large lump on scan matched with them in *V*.

"We just found the tc'a," Tirun said.

"Gods and thunders," said Pyanfar. Her blood ran hot and cold, her joints went weak; the concentrate fought to come up again. Someone *was* throwing up. On scan there were sane blips again, but one was far too close.

Human babble. Tully had come to.

"*V* plus point zero eight," Haral said. "That bastard gave us *V!*"

"Let it ride; we burn it off later." Pyanfar swallowed hard and blinked her eyes and tried not to listen to the retching off over at com. "We got—while yet before Jik's AOS on Kefk—gods-rotted tc'a: it saying anything?"

Someone over at com managed to get transmission to her screen.

tc'a	chi	hani	kif	kif	kif	kif
Mkks	Mkks	Mkks	Mkks	Mkks	Mkks	Kefk
Kefk	Kefk	Kefk	Kefk	Kefk	Kefk	Kefk

"It's saying, I think—" Hilfy said hoarsely, "it's come from Mkks to Kefk with a hani and lots of kif. Hello."

"They won't shoot," Pyanfar said, as the thought got through. *Jik. That earless bastard, Jik's called in another debt and snagged us a tc'a. It knows our flight plan. It must.* "Gods, that son's riding us close out there—they won't shoot. Kefk wouldn't dare." She leaned back, turned her head. "Chur. You all right?"

"Fine." The voice sounded weak. "I'm on-duty."

"Khym?"

He was the sick one. She had thought so. No answer but a moan.

"We're nominal on equipment," Tirun said.

"We still got the kif back there," Geran said. "Got another ship just blipped in behind us. *Ikkiktk...* I think ... right on mark, five minutes Light."

Everywhere about them the tick and blip of instruments went on, *The Pride*'s ordinary functions, unflappable mechanical processes.

"Tully?" Chur said. "Tully, you all right?"

"What that?" A slurred, faint voice on com. "What?"

"Tc'a got friendly. Gods-rotted closest we ever came to collision. Closest I ever want to hear about."

"That's blip two: second kif in."

"We just got a message from the lead kif back there," Hilfy said. "It's confirming it's behind us, that's all."

"Acknowledge," Pyanfar said. Their realscan showed their own little packet of space; their passive-signal pickup, half a roundtrip quicker than bounce-signal scan, showed them the stars and the things that reflected light, and the lead ships' recent emission-trails. A lot of them.

"We've got time-calc on that image," Tirun said. "Jik's doing fine. Jik, Ehrran, Sikkukkut and a flock of the *hakkikt*'s best. *Haaa*—we got *Harukk* scan now—Clear, clear, clear!"

"Good luck to 'em," Haral muttered. "Even the gods-be kif."

"Hope those earless bastards at Kefk haven't moved any rocks," Geran said.

"We're running into old chatter," Hilfy said. "Kefk isn't aware yet of anything, on this timeline. Geran, I'm going to feed you sequencing on this stuff. See if you can do a locator on it, get an update on these positions."

"Lot of scatter," Geran said. "Chur, take scan one."

Down the time line again, racing their own incoming wave-front to Kefk station. Waiting for the message to come back. But this time they had shed a lot of speed. Kif talked behind them and in another time-reference, station-kif talked, and that clicking chatter occupied com.

More kif dropped in behind them.

And the tc'a glided along beside.

"We're getting reaction now," Hilfy said. "That's a guard-station talking, I think. They're challenging. That's minus twelve Light."

Two guardstations, one at Kefk 1 nadir, to stop escapees; one at Kefk 1 zenith, not so far away. The third off in Kefk 2's ecliptic. And Kefk station itself was armed, by Sikkukkut's admission, which violated more Compact laws.

"*Harukk* just answered," Hilfy said. "*Harukk* ordered Kefk system to surrender. Challenge goes on. . . . I can't make out if they've launched anything. Translator, Khym; help; gods-be—"

"Is that it?"

"—Back it up. Geran."

"Sorry," Khym said. "I'm sorry—"

"I got it," Geran said. "That's affirmative on launch. Two interceptors away from Kefk 1 on Jik's contact-moment."

"Intercept vector for Jik," Hilfy said.

"Kif behind us report—" Khym said, "they just heard that defense-engage."

Pyanfar bit her mustaches, watched the steady rotation of images Haral shunted past her screens.

"Unchanged," Hilfy said.

"Tc'a's unchanged," Chur said. "Still by us."

"Let's hope it stays put," Haral said.

"Unchanged," Hilfy droned on. Then: "Wait, we're beginning to get some comment out of station now. They're real disturbed and they're speaking pidgin as well as main-kifish. We won't get the guardstation transmission to station or to Jik's bunch at their angle."

"What's it doing?" Khym's first out-of-line question, in a careful, quiet voice. "What the godssakes is it up to?"

"Easy." Haral's voice. "We're not skinned yet."

"Kif," Tully said sharply.

"Tully's right," Chur said from scan. "Another one of our party just came in."

"Huh," Geran said, "By the gods all and sundry, we may just make it."

"That's a *hakkikt*, five kif hunter ships, *Aja Jin* and a *han* deputy telling them there's a tc'a inbound at their tail," Tirun muttered. "And they don't know what more or how many. You think that won't shake them up? If I was kif with my nose to station or a desk-sitter in central I'd be real upset just now. They'll fold. Sikkukkut's not half crazy."

"Huh," Pyanfar muttered. Crew talked themselves to confidence. Her stomach fought her again and she fought it back. Comp asked a question, offered choices. She kept her eyes focussed, read comp's suggestion, scanned two other monitors and punched confirm.

Another desperate swallow. Her hand shook, terror catching up to her in a chill when the moment was long past. The tc'a *could* have hit them. Gods. How much closer? How much closer before they got pulled apart? Or before they made one ball of fire, hani, tc'a and kif together?

"They friend?" Tully asked and no one had time.

"Tc'a insystem are upset," Hilfy said. "We're starting to get chatter out of our own tc'a. It identifies itself and us. They're sixteen minutes down the timeline."

Camera image came up on the screens: Haral had gotten them image . . . at this range, a bright orange sun washing out the stars. There was a red dwarf companion, Kefk 2, invisible or inconspicuous. Everything else was still too far. Heavy debris orbited Kefk, by Sikkukkut's outdated charts.

And four stations all told, with a lot of disturbed kif.

"Transmission," Hilfy said. "It's them!"—forgetting protocols. "It's Jik!"

"—*Hold course*," the message reached Pyanfar via Haral's switching. "*You hold course. We go ahead in. Got no trouble yet—*"

"They know the guard ships are on their track?" Khym wondered.

"Can't tell," Haral said. "They ought to. That's—ten minutes Light. We're still getting output . . . just chatter. Jik's bunch isn't upset, and they're further into the timeline than we are."

"Looking good," Geran said.

Pyanfar let out a breath. A chill went up her back. To cut it that fine, to *do* it, by the gods, to come in blind like that and pick up signal on the mark, with all the kif behind them.

Navigation like that was a hunter-ship trick. Not for honest merchant-folk. But they did it.

They had done it.

They were alive so far.

"Haral," Hilfy exclaimed, "we just got beacon!"

Image flashed up on monitor. Full current system composite: it showed Sikkukkut's cluster of ships inbound for the main station; showed a skein of ships inbound where they themselves ought to be . . . the kif, the tc'a, *The Pride.* And the interceptors.

Three guardstations; a belt full of miners; an outbound ship; a schema of the main station that showed forty six ships in dock, origin indeterminate. Same as Jik's initial snatch of image before beacon shut down.

Give or take their own presence. And the interceptors.

"We believe that thing?" Tirun asked.

"Kefk's talking," Hilfy said. "It's a guardstation, I think. It's—welcoming us in."

"Gods," Haral said. "Now it's really working I don't like it."

Pyanfar gnawed her mustaches. "I don't either. Message. Relay Jik what it sent and put our wrap around it."

"Aye."

"Kif are talking," Khym said. Haral switched it. "Behind us."

"—*kkthos fikkthi kthtokkuri ktokkt* Harukkur *shokkuin.*"

"They're querying *Harukk,*" Pyanfar translated. "Sounds like they're confused as we are."

"*That's* good news," Haral muttered.

"Our tc'a's transmitting too," said Hilfy. "Same stuff as before. 'I'm coming in with hani and kif'."

"That's the reason for our welcome," Geran said. "That lunatic tc'a. They *can't* shoot."

"Yet," said Pyanfar, and chewed her mustache-ends. She reached for another packet and drank it in one forced series of gulps. Put her head back and contemplated the situation while *The Pride* hurtled at *C*-residual *V* toward a kifish stronghold that wanted to let them in. Past a doubtless armed guard-station.

Get them onto the docks, she could imagine the counsels in that chunk of fragile metal up ahead. *We outnumber them. Lure them out of their ships if possible. Send poison through their ventilation tubes if not. Let the tc'a dock peacefully in the methane-sector and then destroy the intruders on the oxy side.*

"We brought our own private kif along, didn't we?" Pyanfar said. "Tirun. Khym. We've got a little time inertial. I want you two to go down, get some flex, and bring our guest in the washroom up here. His name's Skkukuk. Be polite. Tell him I sent for him."

"Aye," Tirun said.

A moment later. "Aye," said Khym.

Kif on *The Pride*'s bridge. The other side of Mkks, she would have sooner died.

Eight

The lift worked, down-bound, two hani kif-hunting in the lowerdeck; and soon enough, one kif coming up topside, near sensitive controls. Unease crawled up and down Pyanfar's spine. She flicked switches at her board, taking some of *The Pride*'s automatic reflexes under her own hand while Tirun and Khym, where that lift let out, entered corridors that could become a four story plunge straight down if *The Pride*'s thrust cut in for some unexpected reason—like an avoid-alert.

They were perhaps cavalier about such scramblings-about while *The Pride* was inbound at some commercial port, with safe lanes and the prospect of a long, sedate voyage under inertia.

Kefk lacked all such guarantees.

"You stay course." Jik's voice sputtered into the complug in Pyanfar's left ear: Haral had relayed it, on slight delay. Pyanfar flicked her ears back, looked at the time-differential of several situations ticking away on the upper margin of the number four monitor. Not enough time for her query to have gotten Jik's direct response: half that. He had anticipated the question, she reckoned, when he himself had acquired beacon image from some source, maybe one from Kefk station itself.

"Sikkukkut's transmitting," Hilfy said. "Same sort of thing."

If anything short-flashed between *Harukk* and *Aja Jin* or *Vigilance*, close as they were riding within their own little band of kif, Jik gave no clue to this. *"We got system scan now, got Kefk output, they not want trouble, a? Nice friendly port."*

Gods. "We stay it," Pyanfar said to the crew about her. She twitched in misery; fatigue settled like a hot iron between her shoulderblades and into that shoulder and elbow locked into the brace above the control board. She sweated and stank and shed hair; crew were no better. The hunter-ships would likely have had a shift to backup crew now and again, all crew seated in a touchy situation like this, but taking the shunt to give main-crew a chance to stretch and eat and take the kinks out of their backs. The hunter-ships would have that luxury; so would the kif incoming at their backs and up ahead; and gods only knew if the multibrained tc'a even *needed* relief. She left shed fur on what she touched. And the aches—*gods.*

"Jik says they've asked for a ship list over and over again. No response from station."

"*That*'s not good," Haral said.

"Not at all friendly of them," Chur said.

"Hope that tc'a stays real close," said Pyanfar.

"The tc'a's still transmitting," Hilfy said. "Same stuff."

"How are you doing, Chur?" Pyanfar asked.

"Uhhhn. Lost a bit of weight. Gods-be concentrates . . . we got to get a hot-box on the bridge if we keep this up. Nice warm food."

"Food?" Tully asked.

"He has a hard time biting through the packets," Geran said. "Here . . . now. You got to have the teeth for it, friend . . . He's catching on with the equipment. Knows what he's looking at, just fine."

"Math," Tully said.

"Help if he could read," Pyanfar said.

"Sure might."

No knowing whether human instrumentation was anything like their own. And his blunt-nailed hands had no hope of hani recessed buttons. Thank the gods. There was nothing he could push.

But a kif's retractable claws were quite another matter.

She should, she thought, have gone down to the lower deck herself and left the ship in Haral's capable hands. Not called a kif to the bridge.

It was too late to do otherwise. She saw the flash from the optional-telltale that was presently linked to lift operation and withdrew her arm from the brace. "Haral. You've got it."

"Aye."

"We got a kif coming up. All of you—" Pyanfar rotated her chair crew-ward. "All of you keep your minds on your work, huh? Is this going to be a problem for anyone?"

Silence.

"Even if it gets interesting."

"Aye." From multiple throats.

Tully turned a bewildered look her way. Hilfy never budged.

"Geran, take over com for now. Hilfy wants a relief."

"Aye, captain."

Hilfy swung her chair half about. Her ears were back. "I didn't say—"

"I know you didn't. I want you on guard. Something wrong with that?"

"No, aunt," Hilfy said, a quiet voice. She spun back to the board and looked up as Geran released restraints and prepared to shift.

Pyanfar spun her chair the other way and undid her own restraints.

"Is this a test?" Hilfy asked.

"No," Pyanfar said. "It isn't. It's the real thing. I figure you know the kif well enough. Don't you? Maybe your considered opinion's worth something."

Hilfy's ears slanted back. Her adolescent mustaches drew down in a look of distress. "Putting it on me, are you?"

"Yes."

"Don't by-the-gods patronize me."

"Don't by-the-gods foul up."

Hilfy's mouth opened; she shut it definitively. The ears struggled erect. There was a nick in one. A gold ring swung from the sweep of the other.

"All right?"

Ears twitched. "All right." Hilfy's voice shed its edge. The eyes stayed black.

Down the corridor the lift-door had opened. "We've got company."

Silence then. Pyanfar stood up, facing that oncoming set, in the center of which was a tall, robed darkness that set her teeth on edge.

So a kif arrived on the bridge, in the doorway, Tirun and Khym on either side. Hilfy stood up and Geran switched seats.

"Tirun. Take scan one."

Tirun took the indicated post without question. Khym stayed

141

still at Skkukuk's side, tall as the kif, twice its size in other ways. Tirun could have cracked its bones barehanded. Khym could take it apart. Its hands were bound before it: kif limbs did not flex back conveniently.

"Captain," Skkukuk said.

Tully had turned in his seat, just once and briefly. Something had touched his face—wariness, surely. Maybe something else. But he was eyes-to-the-scope again, his back turned to the kif. Pyanfar noted it, and her estimation of the human went up another notch with that.

"You all right, Skkukuk?" Politely posed.

Skkukuk lifted his bound hands and let them fall. His dark, red-rimmed eyes wept tears of eyestrain in the light. "This is stupidity," Skkukuk said. "Behind the neck, hani, is far more effective. We can bite through wire."

"Thanks. We'll remember that next time. Do you know where we are?"

"Kefk, I suppose."

"Why do you suppose that?"

Yet another shrug. "It was the *hakkikt*'s intent."

"Sikkukkut's."

"That *hakkikt*. Yes."

"He took you into confidence, did he?"

"It was well known among his ships."

"Were you—among his ships?"

Skkukuk ducked his head.

"You were Akkhtimakt's, huh?"

"I am yours now." The dark head lifted, the jaws worked. "I lend you my *sfik*. I am formidable, even now."

"You lend me confidence. Tell me, Skkukuk. Do you know Kefk?"

"Yes. Thoroughly."

"Why do you suppose Kefk hasn't launched a defense?"

"You want my assistance."

"I'm asking you, kif."

Skkukuk gave a kifish shrug and lifted his hands toward the scan posts, miming request. "Show me the situation."

"Haral, put the scan image up on main."

It arrived. The kif's face lifted to the overhead, where the big screen was.

"What we've got here," Pyanfar said, "is *Vigilance* and *Aja Jin* and *Harukk* out in front, headed into Kefk with several other ships. Kefk guard ship've gone inertial now. No great hurry on them. Beyond that interval, ourselves. A tc'a beside us. The rest of the kif with a ship named *Ikkiktk* in charge of the rest."

"A tc'a."

"That ship's named *So'oa'ai.*"

Another small gesture of joined hands. "This is ominous."

"Why?"

Skkukuk's eyes went to her and Hilfy. The stink of unwashed hani and human was already on the bridge. Now there was a strong ammonia scent. "The methane folk are unpredictable."

"Have you got reason to say that? They've *been* stirred up. Haven't they?"

"Yes." The ammonia reek was very strong. Kif sweat. "I advise caution. Don't offend this thing. Don't speak to it. Let it dock."

"That's what the station seems to be doing."

"That's the wisest thing."

"We conduct our little disagreement in a crowded house, is that it?"

"Kkkt. That's adequate. Yes. We do. There are always the methane folk."

"What were you—before you offended Sikkukkut?"

"*Skku* to him. Subordinate."

Her ears went back. She pricked them up again. "Friend of Akkhtimakt's, huh?"

"*Skku* to him also."

"You have one chance, kif, to tell all the truth in terms I understand. You play games with me and I'll serve you back to Sikkukkut for dinner. After I give you to the human and my niece for their amusement. Hear?"

The kif's head drew subtly lower between his shoulders. The hands lifted and fell. "I hear, hani."

"*Then tell the gods-be truth!*"

"I've offered you my weapons. I will give you your enemies.

143

Name them to me. Or let me hunt them out. I will lend you *sfik*. Hani can be fools."

"So can kif, *friend*. What about that invitation from Kefk? Those ahead of us are going in. Sikkukkut says come in. Is it a trap, kif?"

"Of course it's a trap!"

"Whose?"

"Sikkukkut's. And theirs. No one is to be trusted. Keep your speed, blast all and run." Thin hands spread as best they could. "Perhaps the station and its defenses would take out the rest. But strike *Aja Jin* and cripple him; Nomesteturjai would pursue you to the death. *Harukk* would be the lesser danger in those circumstances. Kif would desert the *hakkikt* in such an attack. But strike him if you have time, the same with *Vigilance*. Still—" The hands fell, the shoulders hunched. "Your ship lacks weapons; and hani would not respect your *sfik*. Do these things and go to the *hakkikt* Akkhtimakt. Bring him your weapons and he will welcome you."

"Gods be," Pyanfar said. Her fur bristled down her back. Her ears had lain down. She got them up again. By the kif's shoulder, Khym stood with ears still flat. And Hilfy—

"He would," Hilfy said. "Our kifish ally would do that. What's he waiting for?"

"Shall I answer this person?"

"Answer her," Pyanfar said, "and respect my crew, rot your guts. You belong to all of us."

Again a hunch of the shoulders, a sinking of the hooded head. "I answer. Sikkukkut thinks he has *sfik* enough to lure Akkhtimakt to a place of his choosing. He thinks he has *sfik* enough that Kefk will offer him its weapons—"

"—meaning what?"

"—that. They will be part of his *sfik*. He will hold Kefk temporarily, beyond doubt. Possibly he will take it completely."

"Make sense," said Khym.

"It's truth." Skkukuk turned that way and theirs again, opening his narrow hands before him. "Am I to blame that Sikkukkut is a fool? And you lend him *sfik*. I nourish hope this is a strategem."

"You hate Sikkukkut, huh?"

"I would spit him from my mouth."

Her stomach turned. "How are we doing, Haral?"

"Steady on. Transmission from our lead still says come ahead. Other situations unchanged."

Maybe there was time to put this atrocity safely back in its confinement. Maybe not. "Get him to a seat," Pyanfar said to Khym and Hilfy: "Move. We don't know what we're into. Belt it in real tight."

"There is no need. I tell you I could free myself."

"See he doesn't."

"Don't be a fool," Skkukuk said, straightening as Khym took him by one arm and Hilfy moved to take the other.

"One moment," Pyanfar said.

Motion stopped.

"Question," Pyanfar said. "Is there a hani ship named *Moon Rising* with Akkhtimakt?"

"I've met them. Several times. Kif know this ship. They are— kthok kakatk kthi nankkhi sfikun—of diminishing *sfik*. They brought some of the *sfik* of Akkukkak to Akkhtimakt, but it wasn't much by then. They've been of use. Ktoht-sfik. A good knife has that. But without ornateness. One values it. One can take another."

Gods, the logic. "Go sit down. *Trust* me, kif."

"The captain jokes. Further, I am hungry. I protest this treatment."

Pyanfar hissed and sank into her chair.

"I wish to tell the captain—"

"Sit it down. And hurry it up." Her back was still bristled; she looked back again, to see Hilfy and Khym drop the kif into observer four and jerk the restraints tight over his arms.

Tully looked her way. There was stark fear in his eyes. Observer four was a non-working post one seat removed from him—much too close, by Tully's evident reckoning.

"I don't blame you," Pyanfar muttered. "Me too—" And louder: "You've got a job, Tully. Do it, huh? *Work*."

"Aye," Tully said, and swung about and glued himself to the

scope. Chur muttered something to him. He muttered something back.

Pyanfar spun her chair about.

"Kif says it's a trap," Haral said.

"Figured that," Pyanfar said. "From the start, didn't we?"

"Sounded like good kifish advice."

"I'm sure it is."

A moment's silence. "Wonder what Jik's got in mind," Haral said. And after a moment more: "Captain—That business about *Vigilance* I've got no trouble believing. I know Jik's saved our necks before."

"But?"

"But coming in here like this—Captain, you ever remotely wonder if Jik's been working the dark spots—a bit too long?"

"It occurs to me." Pyanfar drew a deep, deep breath. "Occurs to me real strong lately. It's going to be a lot stronger feeling on that dock."

There was quiet on the bridge, except for the occasional beep from a system needing the crew's attention. "Revert to posts?" Tirun queried.

"When you're covered," Haral said.

Seats whispered and hummed, Hilfy and Khym settling in. Ready-lights came live in the sorting-out of crew.

"Kkkk-kkt." From the kif.

"Shut it *down*." (Tirun's voice.)

"Jik's response," Hilfy said. "He says to our query, just stay it. *Vigilance* says, quote: Follow orders."

"No reply," Pyanfar said.

So what's Vigilance *up to, huh?* Ehrran was still going along with it—at this range.

And Jik with that ship at his side—

Strike first, the kif advised, knowing his own kind. Kif would.

A dire, ugly thought offered itself in the wake of that musing: that all chaos might break out just about the time those ships came in; among all those kif, with projectiles loosed, *accidents* might happen, ships losing track of where fire had been laid down—

146

—if things went wrong, if they were betrayed and shooting started—

A very easy accident. Like one hani ship running into the other's fire.

—blast *Vigilance*'s vanes and leave them for the kif. Take out the witnesses and all those records—

It was not Chanur's style. It was, gods help them, Sikkukkut's own simple way.

—*want make sure you not come 'cross bow with* Vigilance *at Kefk*—

Take out the witnesses.

With *The Pride* lost—there were piles of evidence and charges in *Vigilance*'s databanks. And *Vigilance* could go back to the *han* and offer it all uncontested, how Chanur betrayed hani and the *han*. Take *The Pride* out and accuse Chanur, and let Kohan Chanur fall; then the carrion-lovers moved in and homeworld took the course Ehrran and her ilk longed for.

But accidents could go either direction—if the shooting started.

A gods-cursed kif put such thoughts into her head. *Vigilance* had no kif to advise them: could an Anuurn hani ever think of such a vile thing unhelped?

—Out in the dark spots too long, Haral said of Jik.

Maybe, she thought, it described an aging hani captain all too well.

"We're getting dock assignment," Haral said at last, as if they were approaching any port in all the Compact. "Number 12. That's Jik beyond Ehrran, *Harukk* way down the row."

"Methane-side's transmitting," Tirun said, "docking for the tc'a."

"Looks like a Compact standard setup," Haral said while Pyanfar kept her attention on business. "Give or take the guns and the guardstations. No ship-names, rot their eyes. But we got a knnn in there, along with six tc'a."

"I don't like that," Pyanfar said. "Gods, I don't like that."

A handful of tc'a in port and two more insystem, busy, doubtless, with tc'a/chi affairs, which was mostly mining and some cultivation, in their side of the station, of the cultures which methane-breathers relished, part furniture, part food. No threat there.

But anomalous behavior around a knnn—drew attention. Undoubtedly they had its notice. It was sitting still. Minding its own business. Watching, maybe, the curious madness of oxy-breathers.

"Acknowledge the instruction," Pyanfar said.

"Kkkkt." From the kif.

They were far past the mark when they should have started realspace braking in any friendly system. Lagtime between themselves and Jik stayed constant. Between them and station collectively it had decreased.

Suddenly Jik's number started ticking down.

"Jik's group is braking," Chur said in the same moment.

"We get a confirm on com," Tirun said.

"Looks like here we go."

"Transmission from *Harukk*," Tirun said. "They want—get that!—Orders to the kif to brake."

"Priority: *Aja Jin*: Quote: *Stay with the tc'a.*"

"'Stay with the tc'a,'" Haral muttered, switch-flicking. "Match moves with a polybrained gods-be snake—Good gods. What's he think we *are*?"

"A prime target," Pyanfar said. "That's what. He's next to Sikkukkut. He wants us in the old snake's shadow, right up to station. Like we were real cozy. I'm willing if it is." She reached and snapped the restraints in place, chest-belt and arm-brace. "Snug in. Gods, Chur—you fit for this? Straight answer."

"I'm fit. Soon be in this chair as walking that corridor back to quarters, I'll tell you."

"You play hero I'll send you for a walk." The tc'a-blip stayed steady on, ghosting along inertial as if it knew it served as shield. She reached for another concentrates packet, solids, this time. It tasted horrid. Her stomach rebelled and she shuddered. Beside her, Haral took the same opportunity, trying to keep reactions quick and brain functioning. By this time the hunters-ships were surely on their second shift of well-rested crews.

"The tc'a's being real reasonable so far," Haral said.

"Does it understand?" Khym asked from com. "Are those things ever friendly?"

"Those things do what they want and gods forbid it zigs or zags. It *will* when it gets to approach *V*."

"Knnn, now," Haral said, "have fewer rules."

Vid came up on last-monitor, a collection of spheres and drive-pack with five vanes irregularly spaced about it.

"That tc'a?" Tully asked.

"Closest you'll ever want to see one in motion," Haral said. "Yes, it's tc'a."

"*Kkkt.*" From Skkukuk. "Kkkkt. Kkkkt," a soft droning, talking to himself.

Gods-rotted kif. Skkukuk's advice was what *Skkukuk* would do. If he had the guts. The *sfik*. The self-assurance. Shoot anything that moved.

Loyalty was measured on that status-scale. *Skku*, the kifish word was . . . which meant vassal.

What's Skkukuk *mean, then? Faithful servant?*

Slave?

"Skkukuk. Were you born with that name?"

A silence. "Kkkkt. No." From across the bridge, out of its furthrest corner. "I've had it seven years."

"How old are you?"

"Thirty six. Captain, I am in discomfort."

Mysteries and mysteries.

Doubtless hani puzzled Skkukuk too.

"Kkkkt," it said. "Kkkkt."

"Kif, *shut up.*"

There was silence then.

"Tc'a," Khym said in distress. "Hilfy, tc'a—"

Communications matrix came up on-screen. "Priority. It's going to—"

The Pride yawed, and power slammed in. "*Gods and thunders!*" Pyanfar swore.

"—maneuver," Hilfy said.

Stable again. *Gods-be earless gods-be lunatic*—A stream of profanity, holding the concentrates that wanted to crawl back up her throat.

Pyanfar shook. Steadied her arm. Heard Khym's deep gasp. *The Pride* kept up the braking thrust.

Clang!

"Rock," Haral said.

"No alarms," Tirun said.

Two more rang off the hull. *Ping. Boom.*

"Daughter of a—!" Pyanfar kicked in the braking full.

"We're sound," Tirun said.

"Kif back there aren't happy," Geran said.

"Neither am I," Pyanfar muttered. "Gods *rot*—"

The tc'a left them, rolled and slewed off in an approach maneuver that made sense to a multibrained snake.

She held course. "No following that. We're on our own."

"The tc'a's transmitting," Hilfy said. "We're getting *Aja Jin*—"

Scan image crossed to main monitor. The lead ships were moving in on docking approach.

"Guard ship's braking," Haral said.

"Message from *Harukk*: Sikkukkut's compliments and he invites our docking. Says Kefk has surrendered."

"Tc'a—" said Khym.

"I've got it—" Hilfy's voice, weak and strained. "That's station, docking instructions for the tc'a."

"Kkkkt."

"Skkukuk." Pyanfar shifted her eyes to look up at a reflection of the bridge. "What's your opinion, huh?"

"The station has surrendered."

"Where's the trap now?"

"Kkkt. They will let you dock. Beware Sikkukkut. Beware your allies. Return my weapons, hani. Arm me with the best you have. I will be an advantage."

"To which side?"

"Kkkt. To the side of advantage. Sikkukkut has none for me. Kkkotok kto ufikki Sikkukkutik nifikekk nok Akkhtimaktok kektkhikt nok nokktokme—kkkt."

Something about Akkhtimakt and meals and unique objects.

Her screen lit with a transcription, mute, from Hilfy's post: Sikkukkut having derived service from me would find it a twice unique treasure to feast on me in the face of Akkhtimakt.

"Sounds like he's got a problem," Haral muttered, "if one could believe the son. Which I don't, not half."

"That's confirmed from Jik," Hilfy said. "Jik's committing himself to dock. *Harukk*'s transmitting."

"Gods rot it." Pyanfar flexed her hand in the brace and laid her ears back. The pulse kept on hammering in her ears. "We're fools. Gods-be kif station, gods-be lunatic mahe—" *Where's our shiplist, Jik?*

"What's he up to?" Haral asked. So Haral had thought much the same, in the secrecy of her old and wily heart, that at the last moment Jik might pull something.

"I don't know. Hilfy; feed the schema down to Skkukuk's screen."

"Aye."

"Does that look normal, kif?"

"The traffic is heavy here, but it often is. They give you no ship names."

"No."

"That is alarming."

"*Vigilance* going in," Khym said.

"That's the one," Haral said, "I wonder about."

"Sure thought that son would bolt," Tirun said.

"Skkukuk. What will they do?"

"They will surrender. Slowly. Testing *sfik* against *sfik*. Withholding the shiplist may be the station's test of the *hakkikt*."

"Or Sikkukkut's order?"

"He has no motive to withhold it. The ships about us obey him. No, it's a test of him. It will be an expensive test if they are not careful. Kukottki-skki pukkuk. Sikkukkut may interest himself to find the one who withstood him. Do you wish to gain *sfik* at Sikkukkut's expense? Discover this fool on the station and kill him before Sikkukkut does. Captain, I tell you, it is a waste—"

"*Priority!*" Chur yelled, simultaneously with Tully. "System entry, ecliptic 23-45, *V* z-70-aught factor 9—"

Pyanfar's heart stopped. A lurking ship was on a nine-*G* startup and headed in; a kifish beacon carried its image to them, and relayed as it came—"*Relay on!*" she ordered, and Hilfy already had the system set: the message went, calmly: "This is *The Pride*. We've got an incoming, *Aja Jin*. Take—"

And over-riding her own message: "Priority," Hilfy said. "Aunt, it's *Mahijiru!* That's Goldtooth coming in! The kif—*Harukk*'s sending. Don't fire, he's telling his ships, don't fire, it's allied."

Keep your speed, blast all and run, the kif advised. *No one is to be trusted.*

They were hani. Not kif. "Send," Pyanfar said past the nausea in her throat. "*Pride* to *Mahijiru*. Gods fry you, Goldtooth, it's about time you showed up!"

Nine

Harukk went into dock; *Aja Jin*; *Vigilance* and the advance kif guard followed in final approach: *"The* hakkikt *take dock now,"* word came from *Aja Jin* then; and shortly after that docking a voice from Kefk central: *"Oxy-side traffic control will shut down briefly,"* first in main-kifish and then in hani. "Pride of Chanur, *this is Kefk central: oxy-side traffic control will shut down trans-mission briefly and resume with* Harukk *personnel, compliments of the* hakkikt *Sikkukkut an'nikktukktin; methane-side operations will continue. Please stand by."*

"Skkukuk?" Pyanfar asked.

"The *hakkikt* Sikkukkut has secured the dock around his ship," the kif said from his seat across the bridge. "His force is on its way to take station central; central indicates no resistence. Hani, I am suffering. Kkkt. I am—"

"So are all of us. Shut up."

"Beware traps. Beware—Sikkukkut knows them. Beware hidden resistance. There will be—Kkkt. Hidden resistance."

"Where?"

"Hidden. Hidden."

"Lot of help, kif."

"Kkkt. Ktkot kifik kifai. . . ."

"Well, we're *not* kif. Thank gods."

"Fool. Kkkt. Fool."

"Shut him up!" (From Hilfy, harsh and desperate.)

"Quiet. Kif, shut it down."

"Kkkkt." (Subdued.) "Kkk—kt."

"Shut it down." (Tirun.) "Or I'll break your gods-be arm."

Quiet then, excepting a few clicks. Profound silence, around Hilfy's station. *You lost it, kid, everyone knows it, the kif knows it. Pick it up again, huh, niece? Let's pick it up, mind on business, you're doing all right, kid.*

And a little later: "Aunt," Hilfy said; and from com: "*—This is Kefk traffic control, compliments of the* hakkikt *resuming trans-*

mission. Ikkiktk, continue as instructed.—Pride of Chanur, *compliments of the* hakkikt, *continue as instructed. This is Tikkukka, skku to Sikkukkut an'nikktukktin* akki-hakkikt pakkuk Kefktoki. *Compliments of the* hakkikt *your docking will be berth 12 as assigned.*—Ikkiktk, *honor to the* hakkikt, *you will occupy berth 14;* Makkurik, *honor to the* hakkikt, *you will occupy berth 25*—"

"Politeness," Chur muttered. "*Politeness.* Listen to 'em."

"Skkukuk?" Pyanfar asked. "You hear that?"

"It seems straightforward," Skkukuk said from his post at the rear of the bridge. "The *hakkikt* has secured station central control. Hani, I am weary of this chair; the wire cuts my wrists. I need food—Kkkt. Kkkt. I warn you my services will be wasted—"

"Just shut up about it, kif. Answer me straight. What's likely up there?"

"What will the mahendo'sat do? Kkkt. Kkkt. What does your incoming ally intend? Kkkt. If the mahendo'sat try treachery against the *hakkikt* we will not be wise to dock."

Goldtooth's *Mahijiru* was still coming, inertial now. Not hurrying as much as he might. But decidedly on his way.

"Aunt," Hilfy said, "*Aja Jin* advises we dock and take no connections but shielded line and personnel access."

"Affirm and acknowledge."

"Kkkt. Most of all beware your allies. Beware—"

"Shut it down, kif."

"Fools, I have been given to fools."

They kept coming. Ahead of them their lone tc'a escort underwent its lunatic evolutions on its way to docking on Kefk's methane side. Kefk's methane-side control sent out data matrices in tc'a communication. And camera image came up now on monitor 4, Haral's sending. Kefk station shone in its own floods like a baleful star, lit in orange and red.

"Gods-be mahen hell," Chur said.

"Kif have a hell?" Tirun wondered. "How about it, Skkukuk?"

No answer.

"They don't swear, either," Hilfy said. "Kif don't swear, do they, kif?"

"Mind on your business," Pyanfar said shortly.

"Kefk," Haral said, and switched a call through—likeliest from Khym's board. Kefk stats started up, and Tirun sorted them on comp, searching for anomalies and trouble. "All clear, all clear," Tirun said, "we got a normal approach at this V, all standard for Kefk's size."

More numbers started rolling in. "Auto this?" Haral wondered. "Affirm," Pyanfar said. There was no reason not to. *The Pride* took the numbers in as Haral punched into the auto-approach: tired, gods, they were all tired. A red light blinked urgently, comp's advisement that armament was live and it was being asked to violate the law. Pyanfar overrode with a triple key-punch and logged that decision with another press of a key.

"Approach under hostile conditions," she muttered into the recorder. "Armaments will stay live until dock." The vid screen caught her eye. There was a tone-difference in the slowly rotating station, a few ships not taking the floods in the same way as others docked at Kefk, three, not two bright spots in Kefk's as-yet indistinguishable row of oxy-breather ships, beside the methane-sector rim. She keyed in a tighter shot. Tighter still.

"I'm not picking up any heat," Haral said, "except on the ships I think are ours."

Meaning no hostile ship's engines were hot and no one unanticipated was lately come or about to bolt dock. Yet.

"We got more than kif at this station," Pyanfar said. "Haral, have a look at vid one. We've got more bright spots on that rim than we ought to have."

"I see it. Maybe the spare's our fugitive stsho. Maybe it docked here. Maybe it had to."

"Might be."

"Or more of Jik's gods-be conniving?"

"Or Goldtooth's."

The Pride trimmed up and lines trued on: Kefk station kept talking, realtime now for all practical consideration. The system schematic indicated a scatter of miner craft, all insystem and hardly more maneuverable than the asteroids themselves. There were the guardships, which had shed their *V* and began a sedate return to their base. And *Mahijiru* advancing with the only speed in the system besides their own that still warranted a flashing red line on the course-plot.

"*Aja Jin* says they've got the dock secure," Hilfy said. "*Mahijiru*'s requesting docking instructions."

"Huh," Haral said, and: "thank the gods," from Geran.

Not going to attack then. Once the braking started in earnest—Goldtooth meant to come in.

Why? for the gods' sakes, when he was safe and secret out where he was?

Why leave cover, Goldtooth? What are you up to—friend of mine? Another doublecross?

Or did Jik always know you were here?

"Captain," Haral said, and gave her station-image. "Vid one. That anomaly looks mahen-type."

Pyanfar looked. The brightness among the dull grim shapes of kifish vessels resolved itself. It was indeed another ship of mahendo'sat design.

That meant an unanticipated mahen ship at Kefk dock—or a hani.

Closer and closer. Pyanfar wiped her eyes. *Fool, stay awake, stay alert, or you won't have to worry.* Kif-taint had permeated the bridge. Her nose twitched in the promise of a sneeze. She restrained it, and it crept up again and erupted. She wiped her nose. Another revolution.

Aja Jin and *Vigilance* and one bright-shining ship too many. "That's about berth 18 or 20," Haral said. "I'd sure like to know what it is."

"So would I," said Pyanfar. *Ask Jik,* Haral meant. But Jik was not saying anything about the discrepancy. No one was talking. Neither Jik nor *Vigilance*. "Put in a call to *Vigilance*. Ask them to confirm status dockside."

"Aye," Hilfy said, and it went. Pyanfar bit at a hangnail and watched Kefk station in its slow turning at the highest magnification *The Pride* could use. Definitely mahen-type craft. Definitely. Not their stsho. That stsho had to have gotten through unscathed: it would take phenomenal luck for even hair-triggered kif guardstations to stop a through-bound starship that meant to jump out again without pausing. There was small chance a sedentary force could fire anything that could intercept a high-V transit—unless they were virtually in its path. That was the nature of stations. That was their vulnerability. And the vulnerability of ships that shed V and went to dock.

"Message from *Vigilance*," Hilfy said. "They confirm. Central's secured. They indicate we're to come ahead with caution."

"Thank them," Pyanfar muttered absently. *They haven't noticed? Ehrran came into a kif station denied a shiplist and never tried the vid? Jik didn't? In a mahen hell. Jik knows there's a ship here that doesn't belong. And Rhif Ehrran can't be that much of a fool. What are they together on? Do they know that ship?*

She fired retros. Hard.

"Huhhh!" Haral said. Hearts must have leapt all across the bridge.

"We're off-pattern," Tirun said calmly then; and Hilfy: "Message from Kefk, from our escort, they query—"

"We just missed a rock," Pyanfar said. "Tell them sweep their lousy lanes, huh?"

"We going to take a look at that ship?" Haral asked, having figured it out for herself.

"Gods-be right we are." She had just thrown *The Pride* off the auto-approach timing with the station's revolutions. Now they had to revise their figures and fuss about with revised lane-assignment and approach. A few judicious pulses might put them closer to station on a timing that would swing that surplus ship under the camera's scrutiny.

"Gods," Haral said, "priority, priority—we show that knnn's engines live on the rim."

"Gods be." Pyanfar scanned a ripple of new information across her screens, heard Khym talking urgently on one channel while Hilfy queried the other—"We've got that information," Khym said. "—*Py*, Jik says—"

—a new image came up. Scan.

"—it's moving out from dock, gods, gods, *look* at that thing travel."

"Get it, get it—Chur, help, I've fouled it!"
"Kkkt. Kkkkt."
—"Priority, priority—it's transmitting—Tc'a's answering."
Knnn-song wailed over com. Tc'a-matrix flashed up, totally numerical.
"What's that?" From Khym.
"I've got translator on it," Hilfy said. "Our tc'a escort's talking to the knnn."
"Kefk transmission," Tirun said. "Methane-side's talking on several wavelengths."
"Keep going," Pyanfar said and gnawed her mustaches. "We keep on approach until they try to stop us."
"—Priority: Translation: *query, query, query,* from the knnn. Tc'a response: indeterminate. Translator can't get it. Shall we query?"
"Negative, negative on the query. Steady as we go."
More matrix came up.

Tc'a	knnn	kif	kif	hani	mahe	mahe
Mkks	Kefk	Mkks	Kefk	Mkks	Kefk	Mkks
Kefk	go	Kefk	Kefk	Kefk	Kefk	Kefk

"Sounds like it's just talking to the knnn," Haral muttered.
"Tc'a's holding course, on the average. Gods—knnn's shifting to match—o good *gods*—"
"—Priority," Hilfy said. "Kefk's giving us a new lane assignment. They're scheduling us on in."
"Knnn?" Tully asked. "What do, what do?"
"Hush," said Chur. "Quiet. It's not . . . not . . . doing anything, it's just out there."
"We're just going on in, Tully. Quiet."
"Kkkkt. Kkkkkt. Kkkkkt."
"Shut *up.*" From Tirun. "Or we give you to it."
"Easy, easy," Pyanfar muttered. "Chur—you all right?"
"Priority—Jik's advising us come on."
"Knnn's close—close to our line; intercept with the tc'a, looks like—"
"There—it's not on our numbers—" Geran said.
"That's match with the—Tc'a's moving. There's the knnn—"
"Track it. Get vid."
"Trying," Haral said. "Gods-be—"

158

Image came up, magnified in a series of jolts, the tc'a's jumbled planes in its running lights and floods: the flare of fire where the knnn was—no running lights, no numbers, no names: the knnn took no care in navigation at all and obeyed no lanes. It was out there, that was all—it showed on scan. Fire showed. Braking.

"That's intercept with the tc'a," Geran reported. "Minus 23, 22, 21—"

Goldtooth was back there—minutes outside the timeline and taking cues from what old information got to him. He might have spotted the knnn by now. Might be doing anything. Or he might be waiting on cues from them. Slowing down—continuing at *V—anything* was potential provocation with a knnn. Pyanfar gnawed her mustaches and spat them out again, her heart pounding against her ribs.

". . . . 3, 2—Priority."

Scan image came up. The knnn was moving into pattern with the tc'a. Was matching *V* with it—that quickly, that easily. Dead stop to course-reverse: metal could never stand it. Bodies would flatten.

Tully muttered to himself. It sounded like oaths, a steady drone of them. The tc'a and knnn began to accelerate together, the joint blip moving faster and faster away from the station vicinity.

"Gods," Geran muttered, "they're going, they're going. Plus 10, 25—*Look* at that!"

The other way. The knnn was heading outsystem, nadir with the tc'a either grappled or close in pattern. Colors shifted on the scope, incredible acceleration.

"Ah!" Tully said.

"It's jumped!"

"Kkkt. Kkkkt."

"Minds on business!" Pyanfar snapped. Nothing had stopped, least of all *The Pride* hurtling inbound to station and the chrono flicking numbers down. It was over. The tc'a was gone. Lost. And Nav-comp was flashing red lines on second monitor. "Off the mark, off the mark, gods rot it, Haral—I want that flyby. Get that equipment up, get it, hear?"

159

"Aye, aye, up and coming."

"We are observed," Skkukuk said faintly. "Kkkkt. The methane folk, I warned you. Pull us out of here. Kkkt. Fools."

"Shut up," Tirun said.

"There is no profit to this!"

"Skkukuk," Pyanfar snarled, "*shut it up.*"

Silence then. The beep and click from instruments went on. Kif ships talked to each other. "—*honor to the* hakkikt," the station took up the refrain again, "*there is no damage. We are secure. Continue in pattern. Please acknowledge.*"

And from *Mahijiru,* incoming, silence, while the knnn business unfolded on Goldtooth's timeline.

"Stand by," Pyanfar said, "Tirun, I want that approach calc. Take stats and set me up again."

"Got it, got it, I'm working."

And a little later, when station handed revised schedules down the line: "Bastards! I just had that!"

"They're not going to bump us down-schedule," Haral said. "They're going to revise the whole list of ships behind us. They want us in before the kif just real bad, don't they?"

No one answered.

"Run that schedule," Pyanfar said. "Can we do it? Are they going to route us blind to that ship again?"

"We got it, we got it," Tirun said after a moment, and a course plot came up.

Closer then and closer. Vid clarified. One full revolution of Kefk station. Two.

"Come on, Haral, I want that ship," Pyanfar muttered. "Digital-record. If we miss it on sight we'll try that."

The station revolved slowly past *The Pride*'s dome cameras. No need of amplification. The serial numbers showed plain on the next station revolution, on a bright vane column.

Hani ship. 686 YAAV.

"*Moon Rising,*" Haral muttered. "That's *Moon Rising.* Tahar!" Oaths went through com all over the bridge.

Pyanfar sat silent. Not surprised, no. It fit. It fit very well. *So how large does this party get? How did Goldtooth know to meet us here? Gods, what have I got us into?*

It was the red trousers, a dash of perfume enough to mask the sweating she was likely to do in hours ahead—Pyanfar took time for that, with *The Pride* only tentatively in dock. Shielded com line and personnel accessway connections were still all that any of their ships took from station, and station dockers made weak protest about safety and undue strain on the grapples, but they swallowed it. Sikkukkut's ships stayed ready to move; and so did they.

It was not vanity, this scrub-down: *one* of them ought to look and smell presentable to kifish hosts, and she made feverish haste about it. Three of them were off-shift at the moment. She had gotten Chur to rest, over protests she should go on sitting duty while her captain took showers; *"Up,"* Pyanfar had said, and Chur disengaged herself and headed down the corridor from the bridge to Khym's cabin, wobbling as she walked. The wrapped bandage about Chur's side had gone looser, her draw-stringed trousers tending perilously low on the hips. "Get her bedded down and fed," Pyanfar ordered Geran, laying a hand on Geran's chair-back. "See she's all right, huh?—Khym—" She paused for more assignments, reviewing what useable crew she had: the personnel-combination worked out wrong, but she took what there was. "Khym, you get the galley up, Tully, you help him, hear?"

And: "Aye," Tully said with never a flinching on his part and only an unreadable look from Khym as he got out of his chair and headed galleyward.

Pyanfar came pattering out of her quarters still damp, still putting on her bracelets as she headed down the main corridor bridgeward. Tully was coming out of Chur's cabin, having brought food in, she supposed. "She all right?" Pyanfar asked.

Tully laid a hand on his side. "Hurt," he said in hani, and by his look had more to say he did not trust the translator for. He blocked her path. Gestured at the door. "See. Go see, captain."

"Huh." She lowered her ears. Tully tended to anxieties: deaf to most that went on, he got the wrong of most crises. There was no time at present for them or him. But the worry was quiet

this time, anguished; and Chur—"Get," she said. "Go bathe."
He was the worst of them save the kif. "I'll see about Chur.
Go."

"Chur—" He refused to be moved. "Bad hurt."

"Get!" She waved a half-hearted blow to be rid of him, turned
and punched the door control.

Geran turned from Chur's bedside as the door hissed back,
quick and quick about getting her ears up and her face com-
posed. Chur lay there with one arm on the covers. Indeed things
were not right—not right, Chur's listlessness. Not right, the tray
sitting on the table, untouched by a spacer just out of jump.

"How's she doing?" Pyanfar asked and let the door shut.

"She's pretty tired," Geran said.

"Fine," Chur said.

"Sure. Sure, you are. You're not working next jump." Pyanfar
caught Geran's eyes with a glance. *I'll talk to you later.* And to
herself: *Gods, gods, gods.*. "You get food down her. Huh? I don't
care if she doesn't want it."

"Right," Chur said, and stirred in bed. She propped herself up
on her arms. "My side's doing a lot better. I'm a lot better,
swear I am."

Pyanfar walked up to her bedside and swiped a hand across
Chur's shoulder. Dead fur came away. Too much of it.

"I'll see to her," Geran said. "Captain, she's all right. She's
doing all right. Just a little drained."

Pyanfar laid her ears back and wiped the hand on her
trousers. "Take care of her," she said. "Chur, you stay put, hear
me?"

"I'll be fine, captain."

Pyanfar stood there a moment. It was a conspiracy of silence.
Chur and Geran—Chur always the busier one of the sisters, the
cheerfulest, quickest wit.

—the ancient hall in the house of Chanur, in the days of *na*
Dothon Chanur. The day the cousins had come down from their
mountain home to apply to Chanur for domicile—

—Chur answering always, laughing, dissembling a rage at fate
and the fall of Anify to its new lord. Geran dour and grim; and
letting Chur do the talking, letting Chur make light of the awful

decision to desert their own new lord to his folly. "Lord Chanur, that man's a fool," Chur had said. "And worse, he's boring." While Geran sat silent as a grave-wraith and tongue-tied in her wrath.

—Geran looking to Chur when Pyanfar spoke to her now; brief answer and a reflexive glance Chur's way—*Cover for me, sister, talk for me, deal with them—*

Geran had come out of her reticence once she took to space and freedom: she had found her own competence, learned to laugh, learned to deal with strangers, swaggered with rings in her ear and a spacer's easy grace.

But suddenly it was Chanur's hall again. Two sisters arrived homeless and self-exiled from the far hills; Chur doing the thinking and Geran with the knife. Conspiracy. And it was clear again who in that pair ran it all.

"Huh," Pyanfar said. "Huh." Chur beckoned for the tray on the table. Her ears were up. Geran moved the tray to Chur's lap.

"She's all right," Geran said.

Pyanfar walked out and closed the door. She punched the pocket com. "Hilfy—are we still all right up there?"

"We're all right," Hilfy's voice came back from the bridge, even while Pyanfar walked. *"We got a call from Jik, just told us take it easy, he's handling what needs be; Goldtooth's on a leisurely approach and he's in no great hurry to make dock as long as things are the least bit unsettled. No one's doing much right now, they've got a little set-to in the methane side—got a couple of tc'a/chi locals in some kind of upset and the chi are running wild over there. The kif aren't talking about it. At least there aren't any more knnn in port, and things are getting calmed down over there on methane-side, it sounds as if. Gods hope."*

Pyanfar overtook the voice, walking onto the bridge, and wrinkled up her nose with the pungent aroma of the kif. Skkukuk lay listless and neglected in his chair, still secured, a mere heap of black, while Hilfy and Tirun fended calls and Haral ran ops. At least his chatter had stopped.

The kif was one more problem on her mind. One more neglected and suffering piece of protoplasm. She paused by the

163

kif, her hand on the chairback. Skkukuk turned his long-jawed head and gazed at her with red-rimmed eyes. "Kkkkt. Captain. I protest this treatment."

"Fine, fine." The ammonia reek was overwhelming. She felt pity and loathing at once. And a desire to sneeze. "Hilfy, Tirun, go offshift—get this kif down below, get him fed, let him wash up." She let go the buckle of Skkukuk's restraints herself and hauled on the kif's bound arm. "Up."

Skkukuk cooperated, as far as the edge of the seat. "Captain," he said.

And plummeted through her hands. Pyanfar recoiled as Skkukuk hit her legs and folded the rest of the way down onto his face in a black-robed, ammonia-smelling heap. Hilfy and Tirun rose from their chairs and Haral looked and quickly swung back to business.

"Gods," Pyanfar muttered, between dismay and disgust, and squatted down as the kif began to stir and Tirun moved to help.

—Chur. Chur lying abed, the hair peeling from her skin, Chur, of the red-gold coat, the shining mane that got second looks from every man she met—fading out. Wasting under their eyes—

She grasped the kif's thin, robed shoulder and remembered jaws that could bite wire in two. It was a shoulder hard as stone. "Watch it," she said as Tirun tried to pull him over by the hip, but Skkukuk levered himself up on one elbow and his bound hands. His hood had fallen back. He lifted his bare head in a dazed way, blinking and looking from her to Tirun. "Get him water," Pyanfar said. Hilfy stood there. It was Tirun who got up and went. "Get your hands back from it, aunt," Hilfy said.

It was, reckoning those jaws, only sensible advice. "Help me," Pyanfar said, got a grip on the shoulders of Skkukuk's robe and hauled the kif upright. "Get his feet."

Hilfy grimaced and gathered the knees up; the two of them heaved the kif into the chair he had fallen from.

Tirun came back across the bridge in haste, bringing a cup of water. Pyanfar took it and held it under Skkukuk's mouth. His tongue darted and the water level dropped to a last soft gurgle as the cup emptied. Then he leaned his head back against the headrest and blinked listlessly.

"So he warned us," Pyanfar muttered. "Get to galley—get something thawed." Tirun left again in haste; and she put an unwilling hand up Skkukuk's sleeve and felt the abnormal chill of his arm. "He's gone into shock, that's what. Gods rot, I don't want to lose him."

Hilfy looked at her in a guarded, hostile way.

"You want him?" Hilfy asked coldly.

"I by the gods don't want him dying like this. Come out of it, niece. Is that my teaching—or something you learned in other company?"

Hilfy's ears went back. Nostrils flared and pinched. And Hilfy turned and walked away to the corridor with businesslike dispatch.

"Where do you think you're going?"

"*To fix your gods-be kif,*" Hilfy snapped. "Captain. By your leave, *ker* Pyanfar."

"Niece—" Pyanfar muttered.

But what she had was Hilfy's back as Hilfy headed away down main corridor; and an all-but-limp kif in her custody. "Gods. Gods *be.*" She unwound the flex which had bitten into the kif's wrists. His hands were cold and limp, and he regarded her hazily, unresponsive to a fight among hani that might have greatly amused him on a better day. "Kkkkt. Kkkkt," was all the sound he made in his misery.

Shut up, they had told him when he had begun to make that noise.

Khym came in from the galley and stood there with his ears back. Tully came in after him, and stood observing the situation with one of those inscrutable expressions that evidenced something going on in his blond-maned head. Perhaps, like Hilfy, he wanted the kif's death. Perhaps he was afraid, or wanted to warn them of the danger in this creature, and lacked words to do it. "Get cleaned up," Pyanfar snapped at them both. "You think we got time to stare? Gods-be kif's wilted on us, that's all. Move it. The rest of us want their break. Go. Get to it. The rest of us are waiting on you."

165

"Food—" Tully said lamely, and pointed back at the galley.

"Come on," Khym said, and caught him by the arm and took him on through the bridge to the corridor. Tully went, with a backward look from the bulkhead doorway.

"Get!" Pyanfar said.

"Captain," Haral said from her post. "*Harukk* calling. The *hakkikt* advises us the guardstations have officially surrendered."

"Thank the gods for that. Acknowledge."

"Aye."

Tirun came back from the galley, carrying a cup of chopped raw meat that reeked of thawing and chill even at arm's length. "Kkkkt," Skkukuk moaned, and averted his face when Tirun offered it.

Pyanfar scowled. "Shut up and eat it, hear me, kif? I haven't got time for your stupid preferences."

"Kkkkt. Kkkkt. Kkkkt."

"Gods fry you."—She took the cup from Tirun's hand and held it under Skkukuk's mouth. "*Eat* it. I don't care what you don't like. I haven't got time for this."

"Kkkkt." And the jaws clamped together with a swelling of muscle down their long length. The nostrils drew inward. Skkukuk gave a long shiver, and kept his face averted, his eyes shut, his throat spasming.

Pyanfar took the cup back. "He eat anything we gave him before jump?"

"I'm not sure," Tirun said. "A lot of it had dried up."

"Captain," Haral said, "We got a definitive whereabouts on that stsho that went out from Mkks: kited through here this morning and never stopped for hellos."

"Gods rot. Naturally it did. What's happened to Tahar? Any word on *Moon Rising?*"

"Make inquiry?" Haral said.

"Has anyone else?"

"Negative."

"Gods. Now you'd expect that question out of *Vigilance*, wouldn't you? No. Don't ask. Just go on listening."

"Maybe we ought to ask the *hakkikt* advice in kif-feeding,"

Tirun muttered at her side. "Captain—maybe if we ask the kif to get something—"

Pyanfar turned a flat-eared look on her and Tirun tucked the stinking cup back into her hands and covered it and shut up.

And Hilfy came back from down the hall. With another cup in hand. "He eat anything?"

"No."

Hilfy offered hers. It smelled of blood. It was. Pyanfar drew in her nostrils as Hilfy extended it past her face.

"Where in the gods' good sense did you get this?"

"Med stores," Hilfy said, ears back, jaw set.

There was already a twitch of kifish nostrils. The head turned, the eyes opened and a desperate tongue investigated the air. Skkukuk lifted his own hands to cup Hilfy's holding the vessel; and the darkish red contents disappeared in an energetic palpitation of the kif's long jaw-muscles.

"Good gods," Tirun said.

"Just selective," Hilfy said. "A real delicate appetite. Freezer-stuff's just too far gone for him."

"Get him cleaned up," Pyanfar said. "Feed him again if you have to. But don't by the gods get generous. We *need* those supplies. And you—"

Reprimand died in her mouth and left a bad taste after. Hilfy was on the edge. She saw it in the look in Hilfy's eyes, the set of her jaw. "Get some rest," she said to Hilfy; and that brought Hilfy's ears down as quickly as a blow to the face would have.

"I'm fit."

"Are you?"

Hilfy said nothing. The ears stayed down. The eyes stayed dark.

Get him off this ship, off my deck, send him back to Sikkukkut.

Gods, gods, gods, the med supplies. How often do we have to bleed to feed this thing?

"Kkk-t," Skkukuk breathed. Pyanfar looked at the kif, and saw already a focus to the eyes as Tirun made shift to move him out of the chair. "Kkkkt," he said softly, "kkkt—"—trying to get his booted feet under him. His head came up and the reddened eyes looked at Pyanfar. He knew what he had drunk. *After the rest of it, are you, kif?*

Tirun got him on his feet. Hilfy took an arm and they led him away, slowly, holding onto him and holding him up at the same time. *Ought to bind those jaws when we handle him.* There was a patch on her left arm where the fur grew wrong: plastic surgery, once and long ago, in her wilder youth. *Wonder if he'd smother—the nostrils run close to the surface.*

Gods, get him off my ship, that's all!

And get Hilfy away from him.

"Going to give that bastard to Jik," Pyanfar muttered, settling into her own seat up by Haral's side. And before Haral could venture comment into a family situation: "Go on. Get yourself cleaned up. I can handle things solo a while. We've got enough gods-be problems. I don't know how long we're going to be in this port. Not long, I'll guess. Hours, maybe. Maybe a day or so. With luck."

"Aye," Haral said, no demur, no comment, and no delay in shunting things to her board and bailing out of her seat. "Anything you need below?"

"Negative. Just hurry at it. Send Hilfy and Tirun to the same when you see them."

"Aye." Haral headed off at all deliberate speed. Throw water and soap on herself, pull on fresh trousers, stagger back to the galley if there was time and get food in her belly.

None of them carried any spare fat nowadays. A gaunt and haunted look hung about all the crew, standing watch and watch without meals or sleep except in snatches, while jump after jump burned them up from inside. There was a physiological penalty for every jump. The kif paid it. They did. She found herself eating from knowledge that she had to, not because food appealed to her, when she should have been ravenous. Only the wobbles signaled need for food: no appetite. *Another jump—gods, another jump and we'll begin to feel it for sure. No one can stand this schedule.*

Chur—can't. I was a fool to listen to her at Kshshti. She's in serious trouble, thinner and thinner. Bone and hair goes next. Bowel function. Kidneys. Heart. It's not only kifish fire that can

168

kill us. We can't run now. If anything goes wrong here we can't pull out. Chur needs those hours. Needs days here.

Get a med? Whose?

No. No. Chur's on the mend. The side's healed. The jump took a lot of minerals out of her system. Healing leached everything. Feed her vitamins. Lots of red meat. She'll make it now. She's past the crisis and she's still got reserves.

But I shed a lot. The kif collapsed. Pyanfar tongued a sore spot in her mouth, a tooth that promised soreness after brushing. *So we've been running hard. Gods-be kif wilted after one jump. We've been—gods, how many jumps on short rations and short sleep?— and we're still holding on.*

We need a hani med, gods rot it. Not mahendo'sat, someone who knows *what the margin is. And hani medical personnel are scarce out here. If I ask* Vigilance—

In a mahen hell.

But her hand punched through to ship-to-ship while her mind was still arguing the matter. *"Vigilance.* This is *The Pride of Chanur,* Pyanfar Chanur speaking. Put me through to your med staff."

(*Gods, Chur's going to chew sticks if we call over a* Vigilance *med. But by the gods, let her. I don't like this. I don't like that look in her.*)

"Pride of Chanur, *this is* Vigilance *watch. Captain, we have operations in progress. Our boards are busy. I'll put your request through and call you back."*

She read between the lines, a big lazy ship with personnel to spare, crew on rest, backup crew on duty, Rhif Ehrran was off-shift along with her high officers to shower and sleep and eat at leisure. And not wanting advertisement of their status.

Telling their ships' internal schedules and habits to the kif none of them any good.

"All right, *Vigilance."* She shifted to Jik's channel. *"Aja Jin,* this is *The Pride."*

"Aja Jin here, got all personnel busy. This emergency?"

It's Pyanfar Chanur, rot your hide, get me Jik! But that was panic. Jik was in communication with *Mahijiru,* likely, *Aja Jin's* crew up to its noses in running codes and communications with

169

Goldtooth as he continued on approach. *Aja Jin* was trying to keep track of that situation and take the whole operations load off *Vigilance* because they had no trust for that ship, and off *The Pride* because *The Pride* had no crew available to carry it.

"No," Pyanfar told *Aja Jin*'s com officer. "Put it through when things settle down."

There was a delicate question—how to get in touch with Jik and get Jik to twist Ehrran's ear for that medic without being too evident about it. They had made light of the stack of charges Ehrran accumulated. But they needed no more of them. Nothing to complete the pattern and damn them with the *han*.

Follow channels. Do it the safe way. Keep to protocols.

There had to be time. Even if that stsho had run for Meetpoint and babbled all *gtst* knew; even if knnn were stirring about. Goldtooth and Jik acted as if there were time. They laid plans. Goldtooth was still coming in to dock, which meant he expected at least a number of hours before trouble hit, at least personal business here to make the trip worthwhile.

But Chur—

Geran's covering for her, that's what. And Geran's scared. So am I. Gods rot it, I never should have let her come past Kshshti.

But we needed her. We still need her.

Gods, she's not getting better. She's worse.

Com chatter kept up, Kefk adjusting to the reality of its occupation. Methane-sector was settling down at last—only a small portion of Kefk's territory, but a precinct with which kif did not trifle and out of which little coherent information came: the chaos at least seemed less. And there were no more knnn involved.

Geran came back to the bridge. Came and leaned on Pyanfar's chair, and Pyanfar turned it about to face her. "She all right?" Pyanfar asked Geran.

No. Not all right, Pyanfar thought with a sudden chill. Geran's mouth was clamped tight, jaw clenched.

Tongue-tied again. Like in the hall. Like things that touched on resisting Chur. She watched Geran's mouth twist, the strain of her throat, just to get words out. "She couldn't keep it down, captain."

"Listen, cousin, I've already got a call in for a med."

"Aye," Geran said, and to her surprise made no argument. Then with a look more naked and more wretched: "I really think you'd better. Captain, she choked pretty bad trying to eat. She's that weak. She couldn't get her breath."

No words for a moment or so. Mortal equations. Points of no return. Healing in jump cost and cost. And if the wound drew too profoundly on Chur's resources and the jump-stretch went on—

There was another jump beyond this; it might come in a day—or hours; and if things went really wrong here, there might be jump and jump and jump with kif on their track and somewhere, somewhen down that course—having to send *The Pride* into jump knowing of a certainty Chur would die in it. That was what they faced.

"All right," Pyanfar said quietly. "All right, we do it. We get that med in here right now. A hani med. *Vigilance* has got staff. I'll get one. I don't care what it takes."

Another convulsive effort to speak. "Let me. Captain, let me." And quietly, the dam broke: "Begging your pardon—but maybe I can talk to staff, go the quiet route, huh? Kin-right."

Without the arrogance of captains involved, Geran meant.

"Do it," Pyanfar said without rancor. "They've got a com-hold on. You'll have to get past it."

"Aye." Geran took com one post, sat down and went on the com, quietly, urgently.

It was not a thing Pyanfar cared to listen to—Geran pleading Chur's case with an Ehrran crewwoman who wanted to argue channels in the matter of a Chanur life.

I should have done it before now. Begged them. Gods, I don't care, we've got to get a hurry-up on this. But it was more likely Geran could win it. Doubtless it would come to captains and her having to plead with Ehrran personally before all was done; but something still had to be sacred among hani—like kin-right and the bond between sisters. A ship incoming with family crisis on Anuurn outranked all other traffic. A woman homebound in

171

such events could board any plane, commandeer any conveyance without stopping for formalities like fares till later. Kin-right could unsnarl red tape, overcome barriers, silence opposition and objections. There was law higher than *han* law. There had always been. *Vigilance* had to respect that.

"Captain. They want your request on file."

Pyanfar turned the chair and met an anguished stare with a quiet one before she took the call. "This is Pyanfar Chanur," she said to com.

"Chanur." It was Rhif Ehrran in person. *"You want your crewwoman transferred to our facilities?"*

"Treated here, if you can do it." Gods, to put Chur in Ehrran hands. "I've got a next-of-kin request, *ker* Rhif." Humbly. Quietly. With as much of Chanur dignity as she could save. "Geran Anify *par* Pyruun: she's got the right to go with her sister if she has to be taken off." *You'll have an able Chanur loose on your ship if you take them, you eggsucking Ehrran bastard, no luck getting your hands on one of us helpless and undefended—and we'll be two crewwomen down, blast your eyes, and you'll have two hostages and you know it.* "I'd take it kindly, captain, if you could get a little speed on this. She's pretty sick."

A long delay. *"Dispatch the case records. Such as you have. My medical staff doesn't work on suppositions."*

"You know I haven't got a medical staff, Ehrran."

"You expect me to take on the liability without adequate records. I'll want a release from Geran Anify as next of kin and from you as clan senior here before my staff touches her."

"You'll get it." *Cover your backside, you gods-be parasite. Protect yourself. You give me the chance and it won't be a lawsuit when I go for you.* "With respect, can we get this underway? We don't know how long we've got in this port."

"It's waiting on that release, Chanur. Or if you'd rather have the mahendo'sat or the kif see to your problem—"

"We'll get your release. Thank you, *ker* Rhif. I owe you one."

The contact went discourteously dead.

"Gods fry her," Geran muttered.

"By the gods," Pyanfar said, turning and matching Geran's

look with one of her own, "we owe her one, *Chanur* owes her one for this."

"Aye," Geran rasped. The breath came from the depths of her gut, as if it strangled on its way. "Hearth and blood, captain. When we get a chance."

"When." Pyanfar flicked her ears. Rings chimed, reminder of voyages and experience. They dealt with an Immune. Unchallengeable, by every principle of civilized law. But Chanur was older than any Immune clan. Older than Ehrran in all senses. "Get that release. Get Khym in here. And get the automed and relay Chur's vital signs over to *Vigilance*; let's give the meds all the help we can and save the Ehrran for our own time, not Chur's."

Khym came onto the bridge and got to legal files; Tully strayed through the door: "Here," Pyanfar said, called Tully over and leaned aside in her chair to fish a size three probe out of the under-console toolkit. She extended one claw in demonstration, punched a harmless button with the probe while Tully watched, and turned and slapped the probe into his palm. His blue eyes lighted with sudden understanding and he clenched his hand on the tool.

"We get Chur help," she said. "Meanwhile we need crewman, huh? Understand? Buttons. Controls. Gods, you can't read. Use your imagination. Go to Khym, tell him you do what he says, can you?"

"I understand," he said. "I do. I work, I help."

"Good for you." She patted an available leg and sent him off, the halt to help the inexperienced, and both to do what they could. Gods, gods. She dropped her head against her hands and wiped her mane back. She was shaking with fatigue. She heard someone else come onto the bridge. Geran had come back with stats from the little medical equipment they had, and she flung herself into Haral's vacant seat to put the data through to *Vigilance*, no motion wasted.

Gods know how long we'll be here. Geran guesses the risk we're at—if we have to run for it on the sudden. Chur—gods know if

173

she's thinking straight at all now. Or thinks she's dying anyway and won't burden us with helping her. Gods-be stubborn hillwomen. We go to space. We never get home out of the blood. Gods, gods—There had been a look on Geran's face for a moment in the dealings with *Vigilance,* a look such as she had seen on Hilfy's with the kif, and neither expression looked much toward personal survival. Her own heart beat hard when she thought on Ehrran, when she reflected on herself, on a fool who had gotten a little ship and a merchant crew involved in the affairs of Personages and *hakkiktun* and gods forbid, the knnn.

There was nowhere left to run but home, nothing but charges and challenge there, and no way with a sick woman aboard to do that running without killing her. They could get back to Mkks from here. Or reach Tt'a'va'o, in space no hani had ever visited and where no hani was welcome; or run for Meetpoint— where *The Pride* had no welcome either and no few agencies wanted their hides. Chur might not live to get to any of those places and *The Pride* itself might not last much longer than their arrival.

She gave her mane a second wipe, flicked the rings on her ears into order and listened to Geran getting the data through and insisting on an acknowledgement from the Ehrran medical staff.

Haral came back onto the bridge, still wet from her bath, as Khym got up from his board and quietly handed Geran the legal release for fax-transmission to *Vigilance.*

"What's underway?" Haral asked.

"Getting a *Vigilance* med over here," Pyanfar said quietly; and Haral's damp ears went back in quiet acknowledgement. Haral knew who; why; was relieved, and avowed she had not been worried it would get done, all in that one twitch. It comforted her, such friendly familiarity, close as her own mind. There had been times in their youth when she and Haral had come to blows. Never on *The Pride's* deck. Never since they took to sitting side by side at *The Pride's* controls. "Chur's not so good, huh?" Haral asked.

"Not critical," Pyanfar said, "but none too good. It's not *now* that worries me."

Haral added up other unspoken things right too, with a scowl for their luck and Chur's and for allies they had to rely on.

"Goldtooth's on—"—*insertion approach* Pyanfar started to say, and com started flashing an attention-light. She reached and leaned over the mike. *"Pride of Chanur.* You've reached the captain."

It was neither Ehrran nor Jik. It was the tinny sputter of the shielded dockside line. *"—kokkitta ktogotki, Chanur-hakto. Kgoto naktki tkki skthokkikt."*

"Gods rot it, I'm not opening that hatch."

"—kohogot kakkti hakkiktu."

"Not even for him."

"—Khotakku. Sphitktit ikkti ktoghogot."

"Speak pidgin!"

"—Gift. From the hakkikt."

Pyanfar drew in a long breath and looked up at Haral. Haral's ears were back. Don't ask me, that look meant. You know what choice we've got.

"I'm coming," Pyanfar said into the com. "Kgakki tkki, skku-hakkiktu." Politeness grated. And when the contact was broken: "Gods, what else did we need? Khym. Tully. Haral and I are headed for the lock. Get on the com and tell Tirun and Hilfy meet us down in lowerdecks—armed, and hurry it. Geran: get that camera on." She flung herself to her feet as Haral headed for the weapons-locker. "And, Khym, when you've done that get on shortrange and advise Jik we've got kif arriving with presents at our lock. *Don't use the station lines! Hear?"*

"Aye," Khym said, and shifted himself into Hilfy's vacant place, already throwing com switches. No argument. Gods, the menfolk had settled in and become useful—somewhere *something* had happened, and the uphill weight she had been shoving against since Anuurn port began to move on its own impulse. She took the light pistol Haral handed her, checked the safety in haste and headed out of the bridge a step in front of Haral.

"Gifts," Pyanfar muttered as Haral overtook her in the main corridor. "Gifts! That's how we got into this gods-forsaken mess in the first place. Knnn. Chur sick. *Vigilance* playing games. And a gods-be kif wants to give us presents."

175

With Goldtooth in the last stages of his docking approach, they were losing their free-space shield; and from here on, it was stand prepped for a hasty undock and a mad scramble for defense at any moment.

They had caught station with its defenses low. It was an easy trick to take a starstation out—a few C-charged rocks carried through jump and let fly—if an attacker had no scruples.

And, she kept recalling, Akkhtimakt's reputation included none, even among kif.

Ten

Tirun and Hilfy met them in front of the lift lowerdecks, armed with pistols from the downside locker, ears laid back and both of them wetter than Haral had been. "What have we got?" Tirun asked as they headed down the corridor to the lock.

"We got a present coming from Sikkukkut," Pyanfar muttered, and gave a look Hilfy's direction; Hilfy showed nothing now but a clear-eyed attention to business. "That's what they say out there, at least; I didn't like the last present much; and b'gods, if Sikkukkut gives me another earless hanger-on I'll feed it to Skkukuk and solve two problems."

"I don't like this," Haral said. "I don't like it at all. Captain, let Tirun and me sort this out in the lock. We might get more kif than we bargained for and they could sabotage that hatch—"

"Airlock gives them advantage of position," Pyanfar said. "*Geran*, you got image on them?"

"*No, captain—one's in sight at the bend; there's more, but they're staying back and that accessway light's lousy.*"

"Gods-be mess," Pyanfar muttered. "Stand by, Geran."

A single shot from their airlock toward the accessway might blow them to hard vacuum, even with light pistols; and Kefk was rife with potential suicides willing to bet their lives hani would hesitate one necessary instant to take the opposition with them.

"We could take it from lowerdeck ops," Haral said.

"*Sfik*," Pyanfar said, and took her gun from her pocket and threw the safety off. "Besides, sabotage at that hatch we don't need. Airlock it is. You and I go in, cousin. Hilfy and Tirun hold the rear and keep your hand on that close-switch. And, Geran, you look sharp up there."

"*I'm on it,*" Geran said.

Tirun's ears were back. Tirun had the clear ruthless sense to throw the emergency seal, backup to Geran; Hilfy was there because Hilfy happened to be belowdecks, and sending her topside would say something Pyanfar had no wish to say.

"Huh," Tirun said, commentary on it all.

They rounded the corner toward the lock. "Geran. Inner hatch only, Geran."

Sssssnnk. The big inner hatch went back on the instant, and the lock glared white with lights. Tirun took up position where the hatch rim gave some cover from fire and a split-second longer survival in an explosive decompression, her left hand set on the emergency switch. Hilfy stood armed on the opposite side of the hatchway.

"Easy," Pyanfar said; and walked into the airlock with Haral behind her. "Geran, open her up."

The outer hatch whisked back. A single kif who stood there a distance down the orange-lighted access, its hands in plain sight. It looked not at all startled at the pair of guns it faced; and it wisely refrained from all sudden movement.

Sikkukkut himself? Pyanfar wondered. But it was not so tall as Sikkukkut. It smelled different. She caught the different smell of Kefk station, musty and ammoniac, that came wafting in with it, fit to raise the hairs on a hani's back. Her nose twitched. *Gods, I'm* allergic *to the bastards—*

"The *hakkikt* sends," it said. "Will you accept the gift?"

"*What* gift?"

The kif made a slow turn. "—Kktanankki!" he called out. *Bring it*—a word that implied other things beyond *bring*, like a present that was able to walk under its own power.

A faint sound came from further down, around the corner of the accessway. More kif arrived, a massed drift of shadow with the red-gold of a hani in their midst, a hani in torn blue silk breeches.

Pyanfar's heart lurched, first in startlement and then in recognition of that face, the tangled mane with the bronze tone of Anuurn's southlands; left ear ripped, a black scar that raked mouth and chin.

"Dur Tahar." Pyanfar said.

The captain of *Moon Rising* raised her eyes as the kif brought her to the threshold of the lock. She blinked and the ears came

178

up and flattened as the first kif and two more took her inside, under the white light. Her eyes were the same bronze as her mane, wild and hard and crazed-looking. "Pyanfar Chanur," Tahar said, in a distant, hoarse voice.

"The *hakkikt* gives you your enemy," the foremost kif said. "His compliments, Chanur."

"Mine to him," Pyanfar muttered.

"Kkt," the kif said, and turned with a sweep of its robes and left, taking its dark companions with it, in kifish economy of courtesy.

"My crew," Dur Tahar said. Her voice struggled for composure and failed. "For the gods' own sake, Chanur—go after them! *Ask* for them; get them out of there!"

Pyanfar expelled one breath, sucked in a new one and strode out into the accessway in pursuit of the departing kif. "Captain!" Haral called after her; but Pyanfar went only as far as the bend, where she had view of the down-bound knot of kif on the ramp. "*Skku-hakkiktu!*" she yelled after the collective shadow. "I want the rest of the hani! Hear?"

The kif came to a leisurely halt, and gazed up at her as his band halted around him.

"Tell the *hakkikt*," Pyanfar called down the icy chute of the ramp, "I appreciate his gift. Tell the *hakkikt* I want the rest of the hani. I set importance on that. *Tell* him so!"

"Kkt. Chanur-hakto. Akktut okkukkun nakth hakti-hakkikta."

Something about passing the message on. Modes eluded her, the subtleties of when or how fast, woven into the words kif used with each other like fine-edged knives.

"*See to it!*" she yelled back.

The kif bowed like a slide of oil, turned and walked on down the ramp with his companions around him. Pyanfar scowled, snicked the safety onto the pistol, then turned and hastened back into the airlock.

"Shut it, Geran!" Pyanfar yelled up at com. "And lock her up good!"

The door hissed behind her, and the electronic seals clashed and thumped.

"Where *are* your crew?" Pyanfar asked Tahar.

179

"Station Central. Last I knew." Tahar staggered as Haral took her by one bound arm and pulled her through into the warm corridor outside. As she passed Tahar looked from Hilfy at her left to Tirun at her right; and with Hilfy whose mother was Faha-clan there was a feud as grievous as Chanur's own. But Dur Tahar showed not a spark of defiance, only weary acquiescence as Pyanfar pushed her over to stand against the corridor wall.

"Get them out!" Tahar said hoarsely. "Chanur, anything you want, just get them out. Fast."

"Tirun, you got a knife?"

"I got it." Tirun drew her folding-knife from her pocket, turned Tahar's face to the wall and sawed through the binding cords that held her hands, turned her about again and cut the one that circled her throat—stuffed the cut cord into her pocket, spacer's neatness, while Dur Tahar leaned against the wall, rubbing the blood back into her hands, her eyes glassy with shock.

"I sure didn't fancy to meet you under these circumstances," Pyanfar said.

"We were off our ship when you came in. They held us in the offices—Gods, I don't care what you do to me, *just get them away from the kif.*"

"I'm going to try. I sent Sikkukkut a message out there in the accessway. I'm not sure I've got enough credit the *hakkikt's* going to listen, but I think I've got enough it'll get to him."

Dur Tahar pushed away from the wall. "You can do better than that, Chanur!"

"Listen, you make me trouble, Tahar, you'll die earless. Hear me?"

"I hear. Just get on it. *Talk* to them. You know what they'll do—"

"I know. But that message has to get there before I can do anything. You should know that well as any. I'm going to call *Harukk* on com. Suppose you tell me what you're doing in port; where Akkhtimakt is. Maybe you can give me some coin to bargain with, huh?"

Tahar's mouth tightened. She gestured vaguely outward, elsewhere, anywhere, with a lifting of her eyes. "There. Out there.

Kshshti, likeliest." It was the ghost of a voice. "You want our word, you have it from me. Anything. Just for the gods' sakes don't let them die like that."

Pyanfar stood staring at her. Old-fashioned words meant something on Anuurn; like *our word*, like *clan* and *law* and other things alien to the far dark place they had gotten to, in the modern age of *Vigilance* and stsho connivance. "It's a long way from home. A long way, Tahar."

Dur Tahar leaned her head back against the wall and shut her eyes. "They'll turn on you. Mahendo'sat same as kif. They will. Take my example—get out of here. Shed all of them and run, Chanur."

"You know a place to run to?"

Dur Tahar opened her eyes and looked at her, such a look as ached with exhaustion and terror and months and years of running. "No. Not ultimately. Not if you're like me. And you're getting there real fast, aren't you, Chanur?"

It was not a sight any of them would ever have looked for— *Moon Rising*'s captain sitting at *The Pride*'s galley table up by the bridge, taking a cup of gfi Geran pressed on her. Dur Tahar drank, and Pyanfar sat across the table with a cup in her own hands and more of the crew lounging against the cabinets with whatever bits of food Tully had scrounged: two males in the galley—so beaten Dur Tahar was that she hardly spared more than a misgiving glance at Tully and less than that at Khym.

She knew Tully was with us, Pyanfar noted. *Or at least knew he might be. So the rumor's got to Akkhtimakt.* Tirun was back on duty, trying to query *Vigilance* on the medical assistance and get Jik's attention to the Tahar matter—("Let me take this round," Tirun had offered, while Geran was back seeing to Chur. "Do it," Pyanfar said. And between the two of them: "Put the fire under *Vigilance*, huh? Discreetly. Gods rot them. Get some hurry out of them.")

Khym and Haral and Hilfy and Tully—they lounged about the walls, guns on hips, all of them armed but Tully; and Tahar drank her gfi in silence, eyes at infinity. "I want it straight," Pyanfar said to her. "I want the whole story, *ker* Dur. And fast. Tell it to me."

Focus came back. "My crew—"

"*Mahijiru*'s in dock; Goldtooth's hooking up the com lines right now. We'll begin to get some movement out of the kif soon now. Ships are on short crew, same as us. Even the kif. Your cousins'll be safe enough for the time being—the kif'll hold off till they've got some direct order from Sikkukkut, or until Sikkukkut's free to see to them; and Sikkukkut's real occupied just now. Depend on it. Drink that down. My watch officer's sending to *Aja Jin*. We're doing more than it looks like we are. But you play me for a fool, Dur, and I'll—"

"No." Tahar took a swallow. The cup trembled in her hands. "You run in rough company. This *hakkikt* of yours—"

"Not mine."

"—he's winning, do you understand that? The kif think Akkhtimakt's already lost. The word's spreading—How well do you know the kif?"

"About as well as serves, and better than I want to."

"*I* know them, gods, believe me that I do. *Sfik*. Gods-forsaken kif change sides quick as stsho in a situation like this, two kif at the top of the heap and both of them near-matched: Sikkukkut and Akkhtimakt—they both served Akkukkak in different capacities till he went, and now the two of them have all kif space in chaos. Every wind, every whisper that comes along, ordinary kif sniff it and change their politics. And all of a sudden Akkhtimakt's small stuff. His move against Kita was a big threat; gods, he's from Akkht, he's big stuff there—got powerful *skkukun* hunting down all his rivals on homeworld, while Sikkukkut's just a jumped-up provincial boss from Mirkti, for the gods' sake. *But the mahendo'sat know him.* Sikkukkut's a longtime neighbor of theirs, someone they're used to dealing with; and they're *dealing* with him. Do you see? All of a sudden Akkhtimakt looks like a kif a long way from his power base and losing it. Sikkukkut's operating in his own home territory, using old connections, and Sikkukkut's cut Akkhtimakt bad—thanks to you and the mahendo'sat. Real bad."

Pyanfar leaned her elbows on the table. "Where's *humanity* fit into this, huh?"

The whites showed around Tahar's eyes, a slight tic in Tully's direction, but Tahar did not turn her head, not even when Geran drifted quietly into the room and stood there with arms folded and her face like boding storm. "Humans," Tahar said, "are coming in. They're moving slowly—but your ally ought to be able to tell you that."

"Sikkukkut, you mean?"

"This human. *Or* the mahendo'sat. Akkhtimakt's program was to stop the human ships; keep them out of Compact space. Or prey on them one by one on the fringes. Humans are mahen allies, the way the kif read it. But Sikkukkut's got the mahendo'sat working with *him*. He's got you, got himself the Eyes of the *han*, for the gods' sweet sake. Got a pet human of his own. How do you fight a combination like that? Kefk took one look at that situation and all of Akkhtimakt's partisans here started looking at their neighbors and refiguring every tie they had—I've been through it before. A kif looks at a situation, adds up his own *sfik* and whether he's got any advantage to the other side, and if he doesn't, he'll know his neighbors are adding it up too, and one of them may try to get more *sfik* by killing him. If he kills his attacker he's got more *sfik* for the moment, but if he suddenly gets *too* much, he may look like a threat and lose all the benefit of it. It's a bloody game, Chanur. I've played it for two years."

"Looks like you missed a step, doesn't it?"

"Oh, I tried. Kif don't understand hani, that's all; they don't know how our minds work, not in crises—but they do know we're different and the way we choose sides isn't predictable or sensible by their lights. So that's what happened to us. We didn't get a chance to switch sides. We were in an office—the staff just turned without warning and killed one kif who was too high up—too much *sfik* to trust; and they rounded up others to hand over to Sikkukkut for—o gods." Tahar shuddered and set the cup down with both hands. "My *crew*, Chanur, my crew—Sikkukkut handed me on for a gift. *I've* got *sfik* enough. The situation has. But my cousins—if you don't get them out of there—Chanur, I've seen what happens when a kif wants to throw a celebration. I've seen it."

"I'm working on it. My word on it, Tahar. Gods know I'd cheerfully break your neck if things were different. But not here and not now and not that way. I'm applying every leverage I've got. Want a warm-up on that?"

"No."

"Take it anyway. You can use it." She retrieved Dur Tahar's cup, held it for Tirun to fill and set it back in front of Tahar's hands. "You get news from home?"

Tahar raised her eyes with apprehension.

"Short and straight," Pyanfar said. Gods, it had a bad taste in her mouth when delivering the news once would have been revenge in itself. "Tahar's in deep trouble—but you'd figure that. I don't know how bad or how much internally, or what's going on at Anuurn at the moment, but you could figure it. Tahar was having trouble getting cargoes last year. *Victory, Sunfire* and *Golden Ring* are all working over farside, last that I know about it, as far from kif as they can get. If they haul their own cargo, someone raises a question whether it might be pirated goods being dumped; if they haul someone else's they have to post a bond of guarantee in the case they should decide to pirate it themselves."

"Cut it, Chanur!"

"I'm telling you the truth. What do you *expect* you've done for Tahar's reputation? Gods rot it, you knew it when you bolted with the rest of the kif at Gaohn! You might as well listen to it."

Tahar's ears were back, she set the cup down hard and looked as if she were coming over the tabletop in the next breath; but then the wind went out of her in a long shuddering sigh, and she bowed her head and flexed her claws out, points on the hard table surface. "You gave me gods-be little choice. Do what? Come home and face my brother? Go on running Tahar cargoes after what the kif did to hani at Gaohn?"

"You knew they were kif when you bedded down with them."

"So do you know it." Tahar's head came up, red-bronze eyes dark-centered and burning. "Remember that. *Remember* that,

184

Pyanfar Chanur. You can't shed your clan. You never can. What you do comes back on your kin at home. And kif are kif and hani are hani, and one can't trust the other in the end. Get us out of here. Get my crew out and let's go *home*, Chanur, for the gods' sake, I'm begging you, let's both of us go home!"

"*Captain.*" Tirun's voice came over the com on the wall. "*Vigilance is sending: Quote: 'You've boarded Tahar personnel.' I'm reading it exact, captain. 'We require you stand by to transfer this person to Immune custody.'*"

"Gods rot them," Pyanfar muttered, and slid out of the bench.

"Ehrran," Dur Tahar murmured darkly, and started to her feet in a move that brought Chanur out of their leisured poses all about the galley. Tahar's ears went flat in alarm and she subsided back into the seat.

"The law," Pyanfar said. "They're here, Tahar. *Han* law. They've been hunting you for two years."

"Chanur—take my parole!"

Take custody, Tahar meant; clan to clan. Take her back to Anuurn justice in Chanur custody. It might even one-up Chanur enemies; and humiliate Rhif Ehrran. That was what Tahar offered, knowing what she offered.

It also might backfire.

Pyanfar stared at Dur Tahar eye to eye within the half-ring of Chanur crew and the hair bristled down her back. *Gods, that I have to be afraid. That one hani has to look at another like this, and worry about the* han.

She brushed past and headed for the bridge.

"*Chanur!*"

Pyanfar looked back, at Tahar with Haral's hand clamped in a firm grip on her arm. Pyanfar jerked her chin up in a gesture that freed the Tahar captain, turned and walked the narrow, curve-floored corridor to the bridge.

"They still on?" she asked Tirun, at com one, as she settled into her own chair.

"Your two," Tirun said, and Pyanfar spun her chair about, and punched that channel in on speaker, along with the recorder.

"Pyanfar Chanur speaking."

185

"Rhif Ehrran," the answer came back, delivered over speaker from the board, as others gathered on the bridge to hear it. *"We understand the kif have turned one of the Tahar over to you."*

"That's correct, *ker* Rhif. Dur Tahar. She's advised us that her kin are still in the custody of the *hakkikt's* forces, and that they're in imminent danger. We made immediate application through all channels for their release. We're holding her pending a quieter situation on the docks—"

"You undertook this without notifying us."

"The notification to the *hakkikt* was a matter of emergency. Hani lives are in danger. Regarding the general situation, Tahar showed up at my lock in kif custody without advance warning. And let me remind the deputy this is not a secure communication."

"You're obstructing a han *order, Chanur."*

"As a matter of record, Tahar has appealed to us to take her parole."

Dead silence on the other end for a moment. Then: *"Cooperation, Chanur. You don't take that parole. Hear me? Hear me? You want ours, we get yours. You'll turn her over."*

Pyanfar's pulse skipped. She flicked a glance at the recorder light's green glow. It was being logged on *Vigilance* and assuredly she wanted it on *The Pride's* tapes. "You're implying, are you, that our request for medical assistance to injured personnel hinges on our rejecting Tahar's appeal?"

More silence. The trap was too obvious. Rhif Ehrran was too wary to confirm that with any chance of it being logged verbatim. *"Nothing of the kind, Chanur. But I don't send my crew into a situation I don't trust. And pending resolution of this matter, I'm putting that request on hold."*

"Gods rot you, you're talking about a critically ill woman and a gods-be short schedule! You're—"

Click.

"Gods blast you!"

Tirun's voice quietly: "Log it?"

"Log it. Log that cut-off, to the minute." Pyanfar cut the recorder off. She was shaking when she spun the chair about, and her heart hurt her when she looked at the faces about her;

Geran's face; and Tahar's. "Geran," Pyanfar said quietly, to the killing-rage she saw in Geran's eyes. And with profoundest shame: "Tahar. I'm still trying."

"What are they doing?" Tahar asked in a hollow voice. "Chanur, what's going on?"

"The *law*. The law that wants you is telling me they'll by the gods let Chur Anify die if we don't hand you over on the spot. That's what's happened on Anuurn since Gaohn. That's what the *han*'s come to nowadays, spies and note-takers out to prove their case at any cost. Law by innuendo, by threat, by payoff and profit and political gain. That's what we've got. Deals with the stsho. Buy-outs and sell-outs. Hani so gods-be anxious to get the advantage of their rivals they don't see anything else—like you and me, Tahar. Like both us gods-be fools. I watched you and you watched me and we fought each other, and our menfolk did, and all the while the old women in Naur and Schunan licked their whiskers and planned how to skin us both. They sent Ehrran out. The stsho found a chink and they're using it— stsho money; and hani gods-be stupidity. Incarnate in Ehrran. By the gods, Tahar, I'll help your crew, I swear to you. But they're demanding I turn you and them over to Ehrran. And I don't see a way out of it. I've got a sick woman aboard with another jump to go, gods know when. They've got the medic that can help her; and they're going to play dirty."

"My sister," Geran said quietly. Her voice achieved a pitch of deep hoarseness it had never reached. And stopped though it was clear Geran had more to say than that. Shame, shame to have a transaction like that to Chanur's account and Anify's, and there was nothing else to do.

"Chanur," Tahar said, hands clenched on the co-pilot's cushion till the claws gouged. "Chanur, I'm a gift. A *kifish* gift, hear? You want the *hakkikt* to think Chanur can't hold what they give you?"

"Gods, you argue like a kif."

"You're dealing with kif, Chanur. You're in their station. This is their game. Not the *han*'s. Not yours. You give me to the *han* you lose *sfik*. And you can lose your life for it. You can lose all you've got."

"Shut it down, Tahar!"

"Don't send me yet! Gods, Chanur, if you're going to throw it all away, at least get my crew out first, while you still have the *sfik* to bargain with!"

"I've got a woman sick, I've got gods-be little time to bargain in."

"They'll kill you. The kif will kill you if you slip. You hear me? Where's Chur Anify or any of you then, huh? You think Tahar's the only lives at stake at this gods-forsaken station?"

More silence, profound and dreadful. The crew listened; Tully's face was set and pale, for what small amount he followed.

"Maybe—" Geran's voice came softly, hoarse and hollow. "Maybe a mahen doctor—Captain, maybe Chur'd be better off with someone not Rhif Ehrran's pick in the first place. I trust her that little. And I know how Chur feels about it."

What for godssakes has gotten into us? A darkness closed about Pyanfar's vision, a narrowing tunnel in which one course leapt out with white-edged clarity. *"By the gods,* no! We're not taking this from that blackbreeched foot-licker. Tirun! Get me Jik." Pyanfar spun her chair about to the board and hit the recorder and the com. "Priority—" The com came live. *"The Pride of Chanur* to *Aja Jin,* priority, priority; this is Pyanfar Chanur. Get the captain on—" And as a mahen voice droned back: *"Move it, crewman——*Tirun, gods rot it, give me those med stats." She punched buttons, hunting in two banks. "Where in a mahen hell'd you put that gods-be file?"

"Four, captain, it's your comp four, I'm getting it—"

"Stand by comp transmission, *Aja Jin,* priority—*Where's Jik, gods blast your eyes!"*

"I got," a deeper voice came back.

"Jik, get our comp-send and get a med over here, priority, priority one! Mahen, hani, I don't care what, just hurry, code one, hear? *Hurry* it, Jik!"

"You got. Ready you send."

She sent, two keystrokes.

"Got. We go, go."

"Go!" She broke the contact and spun the chair about. "Tirun. Log a medical emergency. Log the call." She leaned back in the cushions and stared at her crew and at Tahar, darkly smug. "There's more than one way to get something done around here. *Now* let Ehrran play politics with an emergency call."

It was not safe. Sudden moves in a stationful of nervous kif might open something else up.

No move at all was unthinkable. She looked at Geran, whose ears were canted back, whose eyes were white-edged about the amber and black.

"So we get Jik in on it," Pyanfar said. "And by the gods if he can get Blackbreeches to Kefk he can gods-be sure get that hani medic over here whether Rhif Ehrran likes it or not, and by the gods she'll do her job."

Geran gave a smile far from pleasant, prim pursing of her mouth. No smile at all from the rest of the crew; a wary look from Khym; a warier one yet from Tahar; and from Tully a lost and worried stare. He laid a hand on Haral's arm, questioned her with a look.

"We get help for Chur," Pyanfar said in simplicity, for him, and got up from her chair. "Tahar, your crew gets my help nonconditional. I'm not Rhif Ehrran. If you doublecross me or get in my way I'll just break your neck right off and send the remains to the kif. And let me make one thing more clear: my crew's not in any state to be patient with your mouth. We're short on sleep and gods-be mad, and I don't know if I'd save you if you cross one of us again. *Hear it?*"

Tahar's ears went back, a visible flinching. It was the truth, at least the first part. And maybe the second. And Tahar gave no sign of doubting it.

"Better be ready on that access," Pyanfar said, and turned a look toward Haral. "Tirun, stay your post. You know who you've talked to. Hilfy, Khym, put Tahar in Tully's room a while." It was one of the few places on the ship relatively damage-proof, and it at least had a bed. "Move it. Geran—see to Chur, that's all."

Crew scattered, except Tully. He still had that lost look—anxious, frightened. *Chur.* That was all he could likely make out. Next to Hilfy, the closest friend he had. Pyanfar walked over to him and set a hand on his arm. Claws half out. He had that dis-

189

connected look of hysteria, and she gripped his arm to wake him up. "Hey," Pyanfar said. "It's all right, huh?"

"Tahar," he said. "Kif. Kefk. What do, Pyanfar? What do, what do?"

What are you up to? What kind of game are you playing? I trusted you. What's going on, Pyanfar?

"Captain," Tirun said, "Jik's lot're headed up the dock. Estimate three minutes. *Mahijiru* queries: assistance wanted?"

"Affirmative." She left Tully, walked over to Tirun's side and leaned there.

"Kif query," Tirun said. "It's *Harukk*."

Then the minuses of the trick came home to nest. "Respond: medical emergency. Injured crew."

Tirun relayed it. "We have a call already in—" Tirun added, reminder to the kif on the other end. And: "We understand that. Will you go on trying?" Another incoming-light lit. Haral snatched the call. . . ." Right. We got you. We'll open for you. Captain, it's the meds."

"Tell Hilfy intercept them as they come in. Tully—go help Geran. Go to Chur. Take Geran's orders."

Tully went without question. It was off the bridge, it kept him from underfoot and he could fetch and carry if someone could get it through to him what was wanted. *Loyal,* she thought; he was that. *Friend.*

And alien and dangerous as the mahendo'sat when matters got beneath his skin.

There was a coming and going belowdecks, grim mahen personnel bristling with weapons taking up station in the accessway, along the lowerdeck main corridor and at the lift.

And on the upperdeck main, where a frowning Ehrran medic worked with a tall black Ksota mahendo'sat, and Chanur's off-duty and motley assortment standing grim and glowering round the walls of Chur's sickroom—two males, either one of whom might have raised the Ehrran's hackles for completely different reasons; Geran Anify and Hilfy Chanur, Hilfy standing there with her hand consciously or unconsciously on the butt of a pistol. They went armed, with the airlock standing open under mahen guard; and it was not only the kif that concerned them.

Pyanfar hovered by the door, with a complug in one ear, listening to operations as Tirun sorted them past.

The medics exchanged surly technicalities. "No gods-rotted good," the hani said; and Geran moved closer, hands in her belt and a frown clenching her jaw. "What isn't good?"

"Captain," the medic protested, not for the first time. "I'd like this room cleared."

"That's all right," Pyanfar said from the doorway. "We're all friends. I'm sure Chur doesn't mind."

"Get *them* out of here—" With a look at *The Pride*'s two menfolk.

"Why?" Pyanfar said. "You going to object to your professional colleague too?"—who was male, and mahendo'sat.

The hani medic gave a bleak hard stare and turned and laid out supplies. Plainly she did object to males in medicine, whatever the species, and swallowed it.

"Better be good," Geran said.

The medic hesitated with a bottle in her hand.

"Mistake might damage your career real bad," Hilfy said, hand still on the gunbutt.

"I didn't come here to take abuse and threats from junior crew."

"Better be right," Chur said for herself, rousing herself to tilt her head back on the pillow and look at the drip stand the medic-assistants were setting up by her side. "Mahe, haosti." *Check it, will you?*

"Shishti," the mahe agreed.

The hani medic glared, and handed the bottles and the bags over to the mahe one by one. "Seals," the hani said, pointing out the tops. "This woman never should have left Kshshti. By the gods she never should have sat a post—"

"You going to quote us another regulation?" Khym asked in his deep rumble. "I'll quote you laws. Like criminal negligence, malpractice, and kin-right."

"Get him out of here."

"Huh," Pyanfar said, and leaned on the doorframe and turned with it at her back until she was in the hall.

"*Captain,*" the voice came from com. "*Medic down with Skku-kuk says he's fit enough. Says we got a diet problem with him, they want to send some stuff over.*"

"Live?"

"*They say—well, the things are real dumb and they breed fast.*"

Pyanfar grimaced. The skin between her shoulders drew tight. "Vermin, huh? What's *it* eat?"

A moment of silence. "*I'll ask.*"

She rolled back around the corner and looked into the room. Looked askance again when the lift door opened down the corridor and let in another band of mahendo'sat. For one moment the grim look of them sent Pyanfar's hand instinctively to the gunbutt.

Then recognition took over, and she flung herself from the doorframe and strode down the dead middle of the corridor.

"Goldtooth!" she spat.

"Ha, *Pyanfar*—" He was a black mahendo'sat, and he came in the somber black of his companions, not a flash of gold except when he smiled wide and glittery. He towered there in that dark company on whom the only metal was the black sheen of AP guns and belts and buckles. And the grin died a fast death. "Say Chur she all right, huh?"

"No thanks to you, you rag-eared bastard!" She jerked the com-plug from her ear and looked up at his black, worried face. "I got my tail wrecked at Urtur, got my crew shot up at Kshshti—"

"Message go."

"Yes, rot you, your gods-be message went. Banny Ayhar and *Prosperity* took it on, if she got through alive." She recalled the open door and the Ehrran medic, snagged Goldtooth by a lanky, powerful arm and dragged him toward her own cabin. "Stay out!" she snapped at his gun-bearing escort as she opened the door and pulled Goldtooth inside.

She closed it in the faces of his guards and turned and glared at him in the privacy and soundproofing of her own quarters. "So no more merchant. No more play-acting. This is your real face, huh, *hunter-captain?* Leave us a message at Urtur—head us at Jik and never tell us. You play games, you earless bastard, and we do the bleeding, all over Kshshti docks. You good-humor me right now and I'll break your gods-be neck. *Where have you been?"*

Goldtooth's small ears were back. He had a different look than he was wont, no humor at all. "You want list?" His voice was hoarse and quiet, unlike himself. "Jik number one fool, Pyanfar, he fool listen to this kif."

A cold feeling settled into her, worse than before. "He's your *friend*, gods rot it! You sent him after me at Kshshti. Didn't you?"

"I send. He friend. He same time number one fool. Maybe work, this thing. Maybe I fool, same." Goldtooth sought a place to sit down and sank down on her rumpled bed, leaning back on one arm to look at her. "We got trouble, Pyanfar. Fool Jik talk tc'a. Knnn take tc'a. We got lot human ship, come Tt'a'va'o 'bout now. We got human come in, got knnn disturb, got stsho disturb, got kif make fight—Jik *know* this Sikkukkut. He say—got beat Akkhtimakt. Sikkukkut do. Jik say this kif he be poor pro-vin-cial, going make big lousy mess deal with homeworld, lot longtime trouble. I think Jik wrong. I think he big wrong. This kif not small problem. Got number one *hakkikt* want be real friendly with mahendo'sat, with you—You watch, you watch, Pyanfar. Sikkukkut be no dumb kif."

"I don't think he is."

"Fool. Big fool, Jik."

"So what are *you* doing here?"

Goldtooth's ears went up and back again. "Maybe try make kif lot busy. I come, go, hit here, there. I close kif route to Meetpoint. They lot upset." A flash of gilded teeth. "Keep Akkhtimakt lot busy, a? That kif want my heart number one urgent, three time try."

"What's *Sikkukkut* going to do now you're here? Answer me that, huh?"

"He got no grudge on me. I bring him lot *sfik*. Same you, hani. Same Jik. Same *Vigilance*. We give that kif so damn much *sfik* he eat whole Compact."

It made sense. It made an uncomfortable lot of sense.

"So why did you come in?"

The ears flicked. Dark mahen eyes half-lidded. "Maybe I got no more choice. Maybe Jik got whole thing."

A fist closed about her heart. "You're lying to me, Goldtooth. I've had enough of it."

Long silence. "Maybe good thing one smart mahe come stand real close this kif, huh?"

"You're planning to *kill* him?"

"A. You maybe got idea, hani."

"You think other kif haven't tried?"

"Kif no do. Kif no try. They kif, they want *live*, Pyanfar. We mahendo'sat, we little crazy, a? I tell you truth, Pyanfar. You talk that kif I die real slow. You know same, a?"

"Gods, I don't want to hear this! Don't make me your co-conspirator!"

"Old friend."

"Friend!" She strode over to her dressing table, unlatched the drawer and searched inside it for a small presentation box. Goldtooth had sat up straight; she tossed it and he caught it.

"What this?"

"Expensive present. From Stle stles stlen, your precious friend at Meetpoint. The stsho you told me to trust. A note. Go on. Read it. It's short."

He opened the lid, unfolded the paper and his ears tightened against his skull. "Bastard!"

"*Gtst* nearly Phased on me. Maybe he had a bad attack of treachery. *Don't trust Goldtooth.* That piece of advice cost your government plenty. And that stsho bastard's been dealing with Rhif Ehrran and the kif and the tc'a, I don't doubt. *And* you. *And* me. And every landless daughter in the Compact's been sniffing round for advantage. That son was real help, oh, yes! So was your stationmaster at Kshshti. Same gods-rotted kind of help as Stle stles stlen. Gods fry you, you sent me across the Compact like a gods-be lightning rod for every piece of double-dealing for forty lightyears round!"

Goldtooth got to his feet. Tossed the case back. Pyanfar caught it, threw it in the drawer, slammed and latched it.

"You got lot reason be upset, Pyanfar. But you got lot smart. You never 'preciate same. You best damn captain Anuurn got. I got lot confidence you. You almost same good like me. Maybe better pilot, a?"

"Oh, no. No you don't. No more favors. Gods rot it, I got no more crew, I got a gods-be zoo! I got a human scan tech, a kif who neglected to present his papers, and they want to feed him little live vermin—"

"You want mahe? Lend you number one fine fellow. Two, three guard."

On my ship? Fine fellow to report every move I make? "No thanks. I got enough on file with *Vigilance*. Taking on mahen crew would about do it, friend."

"You take. You got need. They take you order. Swear. I give you five."

"No. No way! I can handle it."

"We got lot trouble come. Akkhtimakt—he go Meetpoint."

"Oh, good gods—" It was credible. It was all too credible. The matter spread itself out like a piece of whole cloth. "He's going to sell himself to Stle stles stlen."

"You right."

"Hani are allied with the other side!"

"'Cept you; 'cept maybe Tahar. Friend."

Oaths failed her. She stood there staring up at Goldtooth; breath hung in her throat and the dark was all about them both. She coughed her throat clear and a shiver gathered in her gut and ran outward. "You," she said finally, "you—"

"You no fool, Pyanfar. You got brain. You, me, Jik—not matter *look* right; matter what we *do*. Akkhtimakt got hani, got stsho ally, he make them fool. Where hani guns, a? Two, three ship. Stsho got none. Got proverb, hani—you go bed with some people half hour you got hundred year kid, and he got kids and they got in-laws. Same make deal with kif when you got no gun."

She stood there silent, staring up at this mahe, this somber self Goldtooth never showed on docksides. *I kill this kif,* he had said. Deal and double-deal. He could do it. Strike at Sikkukkut

195

after the whole fragile structure was built and it would all tumble into chaos again.

More lives and ships. More years of hazard. And knnn with their black legs into it, weaving gods-knew-what about the fringes of the Compact, with humans trying to come and go.

Mahendo'sat. He's fighting for mahen survival. His *whole species is in danger.*

And where's hani survival?

Not, for sure, with Akkhtimakt.

She drew a deep breath and folded her arms. "So. So you got me listening, mahe. But you'd better know this: that tc'a the knnn snatched wasn't the only thing we lost out of here. A stsho craft bolted Mkks, and it came this way, full sail for Meetpoint."

"Ah, no. Not Meetpoint. Go out Tt'av'a'o vector." A small flash of gilt teeth. "Try maybe take short cut, a? to Llyene?"

"Into the human ships?"

"Xenophobe stsho got big surprise, a?"

"The gods-rotted stsho are cozy with the tc'a, friend."

"Maybe we fix."

"O gods, gods, human lunacy's *catching*—you're playing tag with the *knnn,* you rag-eared bastard!"

"That do be problem, true."

She stared into his dark eyes and had another cold moment of doubt. "More secrets? Where are the humans going, friend? Where next? Here? *Meetpoint?*"

Goldtooth's humor had fallen away like a shed cloak. He gazed at her long and thoughtfully. "Maybe we make deal with knnn. Maybe *e-qui-librium.* Tape you got, tape I give you at Meetpoint, you say Banny Ayhar take on—one thing in this tape be knnn record; hani, we got hope this thing get to Maing Tol. You courier *knnn* message."

"Good gods."

"Tully—he be cover for message. He know. And I know you take good care this human. He got paper say he crew of *The Pride.* You fight save him if you not fight for me."

"You bastard. You son of a—"

"You listen." He held up a hand and with the other reached into his belt-pouch.

"What's *that?*"

"From Jik. You got fine new comp unit downstair, a? You feed this. Got code sort. You process our private message real good, you get talk to us. *Ehrran* not got."

"Best present I've had in a while." She took it and tucked the envelope into her pocket.

"Also," Goldtooth said, "my medic get look stats on Chur Anify; we got piece equipment we bring aboard. Number one fine she go through jump. Same like be in hospital, give her all she need."

"Gods rot it, why didn't Jik give us that at Mkks?"

"He not got. This from *Mahijiru.* We big ship—got zonal command post. Big hospital. *Aja Jin,* he maybe more fast, *Mahijiru* got more crew—got need have this thing. Save few lives. Now you got need, a?" He set his hands on her shoulders, hard and heavy. "We settle detail later. I got go, not like be longtime off my ship. Damn lousy place, Kefk. But one thing more I give—" He reached into his belt pouch and took some other small thing from it, took her hand and hooked over her finger an earring, with one great perfect pearl.

"Best I find. I owe you long time for welders, a? Come from Llyene oceans, number one most beau-ti-ful."

"Goldtooth—Ismehanan-min—" But for the second time words failed her, and Goldtooth laid his hand on the door switch. "You fine woman," he said. "Beau-ti-ful thing belong you."

"Where are they going? Gods rot it, what's their route?"

"Always want talk business," he sighed, and opened the door and walked out into the corridor.

"Goldtooth, gods rot you—"

She pursued to the doorway, stopped abruptly as a pair of mahendo'sat came dollying a large polystyrene crate past the door. Goldtooth pressed himself against the wall on the other side of the corridor til it passed, waved his hand cheerfully toward the crate that headed for Chur's room. "There, see, we move quick. I promise. It be done." He gave an engaging grin. "You trust. You *trust,* Pyanfar."

"Ismehanan-min—"

"Chur do fine now," Goldtooth said definitely, and walked off toward the lift, with a nod of his head gathering up his dark-clad crew that hulked along on all sides of him, formidable and irresistible.

She stood alone in the doorway with the pearl clenched in her hand. And felt entirely numb.

Eleven

"She's not to get out of that bed," the hani medic said. The Ehrran's ears were back, her nose drawn taut about the nostrils as she stood in the corridor prepared to leave. She looked up at Pyanfar the half-hand of difference in their height. "Whatever you imply about my ethics, captain, I did the best for her I could do, and the mahendo'sat have moved in a gods-rotted expensive piece of equipment she'll stay hooked up to during jump. It'll take the load off her heart and kidneys and prevent any more deterioration. With luck—" Geran had showed up in the corridor and stood there with a face like thunder. "With luck she even may build back a little on the trip. Depends on a lot of things. You're lucky this far. So is she. We don't have that kind of resources. We can't buy it." There was bitterness in the woman, a tight-jawed hani anger at outsider wealth, and the laws and agreements between mahendo'sat and stsho that forever shut hani out. And that was an old story Pyanfar well understood.

"I appreciate your professional effort," Pyanfar said quietly. And could not forbear adding: "And I do understand you, Ehrran."

"Thanks," Geran said for her part. The word all but strangled on its way out.

The hani medic nodded curtly and hitched the strap of her carry-sack higher on her shoulder as the mahen medic came out of the room. "She explain?" the mahe asked. "I hook up machine, she stay connect. No take off. You get list procedure. I leave supply in cabinet."

"She explained it. Yes. Thank you. Mashini-to, a?"

"A." The mahe grinned and bowed and swung off down main corridor with the hani slogging along beside, an unlikely pair headed for the lift. Mahen guards peeled themselves out of the corridor in their wake and followed, Goldtooth's remaining intrusion withdrawing itself.

Geran looked drawn and shaken. Silent even yet. Pyanfar put her hand on Geran's shoulder. "Hey, she's going to be all right. Best new-fangled stuff Iji's come out with. Good as hospital. And more good news. I don't think we're pulling out of here real soon, not like we were afraid we might. Day or so, maybe. Maybe more. We know where Akkhtimakt is; I just got word from Goldtooth, and it looks like we're going to have a little chance to breathe. There's more to it than that, but for Chur's sake it's the best news we could come up with on short notice."

Geran said nothing. But her face went defenseless and ordinary as if she had come back to them finally. Pyanfar pressed with her hand and Geran drew a deep breath. "What did Goldtooth have to say?"

"A lot of stuff that takes explaining." Pyanfar looked in on Chur, leaned there in the doorway of a room which had a great lot of machinery sitting over against the wall; and a crowd of visitors: Hilfy and Tully and Khym still lingered. "Hey, you," Pyanfar said, "out of there and let Chur rest, will you?" And as the file passed her in the doorway: "Chur. Cousin, you hear me?"

"Uh?" Chur lifted her head from the pillow.

"We just got a present, a little while to rest. We got a message where Akkhtimakt is and we've got time for a litle R and R. You don't be getting out of that bed or you walk back to Kshshti."

"Gods-be needles," Chur said. "I hate needles."

"Got more news for you. You get more of them on the way. Get some sleep, huh?"

"Trying," Chur said, and shifted in the bed and settled as flat as the tubes and one arm strapped outward let her.

Pyanfar shut the door and looked at the somber gathering in the hall.

"So what is it, captain?" Geran asked.

"Not something I much want to dump on you right now," Pyanfar said. "But I'd better."

"Chur—"

"Not about her. Us. Bridge. Everyone."

The four of them followed her. Tirun and Haral turned their

chairs about as they walked in. Pyanfar went to her own seat near Haral and leaned on the back of it while the rest of the crew settled on chair-arms and against cabinets. "Haral, Tirun, you catch that business in the corridor?"

"Aye," Haral said. "Both of us. Good news on Chur. Thank the gods."

"Thank the gods and friends where we have 'em. Such as they are. We got anything essential running now?"

"No."

"All right." She took Goldtooth's code-strip packet from her pocket and put that down on the counter by her seat, powered her chair about to face the crew and sat down.

"Humans are moving out from Tt'a'va'o. I don't know what route they took; maybe you do, Tully, but the choices from there are real limited. I've *talked* to Goldtooth. I know a lot of things." She watched Tully's face, saw anxiety—the least little flicker of his strange eyes. "Humans on the move. And that's not the worst of it. Goldtooth's been lurking about Kefk regions keeping the Meetpoint route closed and creating a real difficulty for Akkhtimakt—Jik said sometime back that Goldtooth might be up to something hereabouts. But it turns out they don't check things out with each other real well. It seems Jik took off on his own and made the deal with Sikkukkut. Unauthorized, as it were. Or at least without consulting. Forced Goldtooth's hand. Tully, I'll try to use small words. Goldtooth had come in from deep space—at least from outside the Compact—with Tully aboard, off *Ijir*. He left *Ijir* to go its way—but he had a duplicate of the message packet *Ijir* carried. He had Tully. And he had gotten something else—some kind of message from the knnn. *From* the knnn, gods help us. At least that's what Goldtooth hints. Meanwhile Akkhtimakt aimed to take Kita Point, while his agents were busy eliminating all opposition on the kifish homeworld—setting himself up as *hakkikt* of all the kif, that's what he was after. And back at that stage, a few months ago, Sikkukkut was no more than a provincial boss from Mirkti—with ambitions. Sikkukkut courted his old mahen connections at Meetpoint, approached Goldtooth trying to outflank Akkhtimakt, probing for every weakness he could get—

Meetpoint's always a good place for intrigues. A real good place
to pick up rumors. And right around that time rumors were
running heavy—like hani deals with the stsho; mahen deals—
everybody who was high up enough to get advance warnings was
trying to get the best advantage against this new kifish *hakkikt.*
Against Akkhtimakt.

"But Sikkukkut had a spy with Akkhtimakt, gods know how
or where. Undoubtedly he had some stsho on the take at Meetpoint. He *knew* about the courier-ship falling into Akkhtimakt's
hands. He knew—I suspect from his spy with Akkhtimakt, the
same way he probably got the ring—that Goldtooth had Tully
aboard. And it wasn't too hard to figure Goldtooth had handed
Tully to us at Meetpoint, when we showed up with our papers
cleared with a gods-awful monstrous bribe from the mahendo'sat.
Which we didn't know about. But Sikkukkut may have.

"Sikkukkut set us up, deliberately put us in a bind at Meetpoint. He snagged us into his reach, he snagged Ehrran, and
Ayhar; and he steered us out of Akkhtimakt's trap at Kita.
Steered us right for his own front yard, step by step. *And*
snagged Jik by having us in his net, while he was at it. By that
business at Kshshti he gathered himself enough *sfik* to take
Mkks on his own; and now he's got Kefk. So all of a sudden
momentum's on his side and deserting Akkhtimakt.
Akkhtimakt's supporters are beginning to desert him. Fast. Kifish logic: shoot your former allies in the back and run for the
winning side. Akkhtimakt's got to be worried.

"Part two: Jik. *Jik's* got this idea mahendo'sat are a lot better
off with their old familiar neighbor from Mirkti as *hakkikt* over
all the kif. And Jik got Ehrran in on it; and he got us. Never
mind Mkks' safety. That wasn't all he was after in those negotiations at Mkks. And Ehrran's on a lot more than Tahar's track
now if she's got half sense—she's up at the top of this little information pyramid. She's got access to highlevel strategy—and if
she's not a total fool, and if she knows anything about this, it's a
lot more than Tahar got her to come to Kefk. Treaty law, yes.
Jik's got credentials clear from the top, I'm sure he has. And
what he specifically said to her that got her out of Mkks and
headed this way—gods know. I have an idea the whole urgency

behind Ehrran's search for Tahar has a whole lot to do with the *han*'s negotiations with the stsho and the fear of the kif getting a leader. *I* think they wanted Tahar dead. Wanted to eliminate any possibility of her advising and helping a *hakkikt* predict what hani would do. Xenophobia again. But in this case, xenophobia with a real good reason. I'm guessing Ehrran's real and immediate motive in going along with this lunatic expedition is because she knew she hadn't a spit in a hurricane of getting back to Meetpoint and hani lanes in one piece if she didn't tag close by Jik—and learn what he was up to. Meanwhile Akkhtimakt supposedly held Kita, remember."

"Supposedly?" Haral said.

"I think Jik gods-be *knew* where Goldtooth went when he left Meetpoint: straight for deep stsho-tc'a space; right for a rendezvous with *someone* who was going to guide the humans in. And then he was supposed to go—probably from Tt'a'va'o (the tc'a connection again!) to Kefk—harassing Akkhtimakt, making him divide his efforts between holding Kita and trying to keep the Kefk lane open, while Goldtooth set himself to keep it shut. So Meetpoint's had a two-way stranglehold on it, trade cut off by the kif at Kita; and by Goldtooth at Kefk. Goldtooth's plan was to bring Akkhtimakt down by weakening him—lessening his credibility—all the while playing another game designed to soften up this whole gods-be zone from Kefk to Meetpoint because he *knew* humans were going to come through in this vicinity. If he could link up a mahen-human traderoute right past kifish borders, he'd ruin Akkhtimakt's credibility once and for all. Devastate him.

"Meanwhile the kifish homeworld is in complete chaos with hunter-squads and assassinations, trying to handle Goldtooth and hunt humans and balance its attentions between two rival *hakkiktun*. And the *kif* get information what's going on at Kefk; and some of that information goes to Mkks . . . to kif, but not to mahen authorities—unless the tc'a talked, and they may not have, to unauthorized mahendo'sat. No, Sikkukkut knew exactly where Goldtooth was all the time. But I'm not sure Jik did, when he accepted Sikkukkut's deal to move on Kefk. I don't think Jik even knew for sure whether Goldtooth was alive. So when he was offered a deal that might provide a *hakkikt* that mahendo'sat could deal with—he took it. It'd take him to Kefk. It would let him link up with Goldtooth, if Goldtooth was still alive. I think mahen information broke down at that one really critical point; and now *Goldtooth's* in danger—because I think Sikkukkut sees a lot more of Goldtooth's thinking than Goldtooth thinks he sees—a lot more even than Jik may be aware of. Sikkukkut's drawn Goldtooth into the open now. Sikkukkut's got him accessible; and Goldtooth's come in, on his own, real close to Sikkukkut. Not playing coy at all. You see?"

"We got trouble," Haral said. "Gods, we got trouble."

"Oh, it gets worse, cousin. Jik used some kind of credit at Mkks to get that tc'a to go with us. The knnn are definitely into it. They've already sent one message to Maing Tol—that packet that we sent on with Banny Ayhar, if you can believe Goldtooth that far. I don't know what else Jik did at Mkks, but I'm betting he gave the tc'a stationmaster our navigation data and got a tc'a to run cover for us and make sure Kefk fell without a shot. The knnn may consent to it. Or the knnn may have taken exception to it. Gods-rotted sure they took the tc'a. We don't know *how* they think. Or what they want. But humanity, remember, is cutting real close to the knnn's territory in getting here, if they haven't cut right through it: gods know where the knnn think their zones extend—if they even understand borders. And Tully says humans have fired at knnn ships."

Eyes dilated all round the bridge. Ears flattened.

"So here we are," Pyanfar said. "We moved into Kefk and caught Kefk by surprise and a high dice roll, and Kefk did the kifish thing and bellied down to the deck fast as they could spit. Sikkukkut takes everything on the table.

"Except for one thing. Akkhtimakt's got one recourse. The stsho hire mahen guards for top security, right? The stsho don't trust hani for anything but the lowest level guard jobs, and they trust kif for bully-jobs. But. *But.* Mahendo'sat are trying to get the humans into the Compact, same way they bullied the stsho into admitting hani once upon a time. Now *we* have a common border with mahendo'sat that kept us satisfied with trade in that direction for a long time; and we've got a natural barrier on the stsho side, with a gulf our ships can't jump. Hani haven't been bad neighbors for the stsho. It's a lot different with humanity. Humanity wants *through* stsho space. Wants through tc'a and knnn space. Through kif space, if it can't get the other routes. That's got the stsho worried. Real worried. And meanwhile, on Anuurn, we've got a division: we've got hani who took to space and we've got hani who're gods-be near as xenophobic as the stsho. Old-fashioned hani who don't know the stsho. They aren't capable of knowing the stsho—gods, they aren't capable of *imagining* the stsho. But stsho money gets to them and buys votes in the *han*. Sets up new hani authorities of a mindset the stsho approve. That takes care of one border problem. Hire hani guards, then. Displace the mahendo'sat from every security post they hold on stsho property. Get them out. That takes care of the in-office stuff and gets rid of the mahen stranglehold; and gets mahen fingers out of stsho lines of communication. But there's one more thing the stsho need to stop the humans, something the nonspacing faction of the *han* can't provide them and no stsho can possibly handle *gtst*self. Armed ships. In numbers."

"O my gods," Tirun said.

"You've got it, cousin. The humans are headed either for Meetpoint or for Kefk. Goldtooth planned it that way. Put pressure on the stsho to get closer to the mahendo'sat. *Make* 'em deal with humanity. Bring Akkhtimakt down hard when he can't stop the human advance right under kifish noses. But the plan's backfired, partially thanks to Jik and thanks to us. By taking Kefk Sikkukkut just piled a pressure on Akkhtimakt that's forcing Akkhtimakt to do something he'd never ordinarily do—he *can't* handle Sikkukkut and the mahendo'sat and the humans without more help than he's got. So Akkhtimakt's headed to Meetpoint to deal with the stsho. Same as the *han* is. The *han*'s just ended up on Akkhtimakt's side."

There was profound silence. Sound whispered from a loose complug; the ducts hissed.

"Well, we got a real problem, don't we?" Haral said.

"Well, it's the *han!*" Geran said. "It's the likes of Ehrran, it's the likes of Naur and all of them back home, the gods-be fools!"

"We end up," Pyanfar said, "alone on this side with the

mahendo'sat. And the kif. We're headed for Meetpoint. *That*'s where the *hakkikt* will take this party for sure. *If* he's sure humanity's going there and not coming here to take Kefk. That's the one thing he's got to be scared of—the one thing that could sink him, destroy everything he's built—and Goldtooth might do it to him. He wants to know that. He desperately wants to know that, and Goldtooth isn't talking. If you want other possible motives for Goldtooth coming tamely in to dock—try the possibility that he's got help coming. A lot of it. That has to worry Sikkukkut. He daren't move til he has some way to cover himself and he daren't stay here and lose his momentum with his own followers. Goldtooth's got him worried bad, and Goldtooth wants to keep it it that way.

"One other thing you can figure: Ehrran. Ehrran'll turn on us the moment we hit Meetpoint space. At the least, she'll run for home—straight for the *han* to try to get a policy decision. And she'll take them everything in those records. Everything. Our troubles may come to a head at home before we can possibly get there; *if* we can get there at all. And there's no way we can get word to the House and Kohan what's coming. No way we can warn them—unless we break and run for home ourselves. I'm not about to tell Chur what's up: she can't stand this right now. But the rest of you had better know. You'd better think about it real hard. We can tear out of here at first excuse and go home. We can lay course straight from Meetpoint, run for all we're worth the second we hit that system, while everyone else is busy. And we can face whatever we have to back at Anuurn. We can't outrun *Vigilance*. But we might get there in time to meet charges. Tie it up in the *han*. Organize a fight—when, gods help us—it may have already been lost out here.

"Or we can stay and fight with the mahendo'sat, when it comes, against Akkhtimakt and whatever force the *han* may have set to assist the stsho at Meetpoint. You can guess what captains they might have talked into it. And where that ends then, I don't know. But I do know this beyond a doubt: if Akkhtimakt should win—he'll own Meetpoint, he'll move in on the stsho with no one to stop him, once he's past their security systems; and gods know what the knnn and the humans and the *han* will do in their separate craziness. But I don't decide this one. On this one you tell me."

"What do you think we ought to do?" Haral asked.

"I've told you."

"Tell us plain."

"Aye," Tirun muttered. "You've seen through this much of it—how much else do you see?"

Pyanfar drew a deep breath, pressed her hands against her eyes. Time went in loops. Anuurn sunset. The old vine on the estate wall. Hilfy playing in the dirt.

A ship at Meetpoint, dying because it happened to be hani, and in the wrong place—

Tully, crouching naked on her deck, writing numbers in his own blood—

Chur, handing them a white plastic packet, as she lay bleeding on a Kshshti dock—A kifish den. Jik's ridiculous smoke—playing *sfik*-games with the kif.

"I'd go with the mahendo'sat. Maybe I'm a fool. Maybe it's the worst kind of a fool—but being a fool hasn't stopped Ehrran from dealing left and right, has it? We can't do worse. We can't do worse than the *han*'s done. Maybe that's a fool's arrogance too. Maybe, maybe, and maybe. Maybe it's Anuurn's last chance. Last chance for hani to do anything independent in the universe—sounds funny, too gods-rotted high for us; but that's the plain truth. I'm not sure where we'll end up, or what we'll do to Chanur back at home, or how they'll survive this. Or what we'll be even if we win—on Sikkukkut's side. But I don't want to see what happens when Akkhtimakt laps up the stsho like an appetizer. That's what I think. If you think the same, we get our minds on short-term business and we ride the waves the best we can. If it's go home, you tell me and we go that way long and hard as we can, while we can."

"I'm on your side," Haral muttered. "The stsho go down—we haven't seen trouble yet."

"Same," Tirun said; and: "Same," said Geran. "No question."

"Same with me," said Hilfy quietly. "No choice, is there?"

Pyanfar found her claws clenched on the upholstery and carefully drew them in. "I owe you an apology for this," she said.

Understatement. But her voice threatened not to work. She bestirred herself to the side and picked up the code-packet from the counter and handed it to Haral. "Mahen codes. We just got made official. As of now, we're guilty of everything in *Vigilance*'s files. I just don't want to spook *Vigilance* out of our company too fast. So we go on doing what we've been doing and we don't give any hints, if by some wild chance Ehrran hasn't guessed what Goldtooth's up to, and what Jik's done. Gods help us, if we were really lucky, Ehrran would catch some common sense and side with us, and drag the *han* over to our side, out of the mess it's in. But that's about the last hope I entertain."

"She's snake enough to twist two ways at once," Tirun said.

"Inside out if I had my choice," Geran said.

"Meanwhile," Pyanfar said, "while we've got some time, we don't have much, and work goes on. Hilfy, Tully, Khym, they're sending over some stuff for the kif. I'd like to get rid of him, but I don't see a way to do it without creating a problem with Sikkukkut, and we don't need that. On the other hand, whatever he is, he's stood about what he can. I want him transferred to a regular cabin, I want the room safed, understand. We're going to have some sort of live stuff to take care of. Skkukuk can do his own vermin-herding. I want it decontaminated. Never mind the docking-check on this watch, except the filters, the ops and the lifesupport; we'll catch the little things next. Someone looks in on Chur now and again in Geran's off-watch; you arrange that, Geran. Don't wear yourself out. Tirun, call down to Tahar and tell her we're still working on the problem. She's probably chewing sticks down there. I haven't got time to talk to her. Tirun and Geran, Hilfy and Haral when you've got time, I want this code-strip fed in and checked against the translator. And when you get all that done, I want a regular dinner set up, none of those gods-be sandwiches."

There was dismay in tired faces until the matter of the dinner. "We'll go off-shift," Pyanfar said, "at need. When there's a lull, sleep. Feel free to trade off jobs and watches—I don't care who does it, just so it gets done before watch-end, and it gets done with due precautions: no one visits Skkukuk or Tahar alone. Sorry about the schedule. Goldtooth offered a full crew but I turned him down. Trust is fine; but I'm not handing over *The Pride*'s codes to anybody. Not these days."

"Gods-rotted right," Haral said, and, "Aye," from the rest, with a flick of ears and a tautness of jaws.

"So get it done, huh?" She nodded a dismissal. Hilfy got up and walked out with Geran, down the corridor. Tirun turned back to com and Haral turned to the main board and systems-checks again. The menfolk were last on their way out, separately. And—"Khym," Pyanfar said before he could go: "You all right in this? Tully?"

Khym stopped and stuck his hands in his belt, glanced at the deck with a deference natural in Chanur matters. "You pick the fight, I'll settle the bastards, wasn't it something like that we promised each other fifty years ago?" It was their marriage vow, less elegantly phrased. But then he looked up, and a curious quirk came and went she had not seen in years. "But I think you'll have to help, though, wife."

She laughed despite it all and he grinned as if pleased to have pleased her. She watched the straightening of his shoulders as he walked off the bridge. Somewhere he had got a swagger in his step.

The ache in her own bones felt less, for that.

"Py-anfar?"

"Tully." She rose from her chair. Walked over near him as he stood there with confusion on his face. "Tully. Did you follow what I was saying to the crew? You understood?"

He nodded his head energetically—*yes*, that peculiar gesture meant. "I work," he said. "I work." And he turned his shoulder to her, there by the scan panel, his hands busy with some printout which he could no more read than he could breathe vacuum.

Avoidance.

"Tully," she said. "Tully."

"I work," he said.

"Put those ridiculous papers down." She snatched them from his hand and flung them onto the counter. He backed up, hit the chair and caught himself with an arm against the seat-back, eyes wide and flickering. He smelled of human sweat and Anuurn flowers. And sudden terror. Tirun half-turned her chair, and kept staring in distress. Tully stayed frozen, stsho-pale. Fear. Indeed, fear. It set her heart to pounding and touched off her aggressive reflexes; but *child* she made herself think, dismissing hunter-mind; and *alien* and *friend* and *hair-triggered male.*

It was not her move that had frightened him. He was beyond that. He knew she would never lay hands on him; she knew that he knew. It was a deeper thing.

"You worried about something, Tully?"

"Not understand lot you say—" He waved a vague gesture at the room. At the scan panel. "I work. I don't need any understand."

"Tully, old friend." Pyanfar laid a hand on his shoulder and felt the slight shift of muscles as if he had rather not have it resting there; she smelled his sweat despite that their air was cool for a human. "Listen—I know you doublecrossed me." The translator sputtered through the com Tully wore at his belt. She wore no earplug: she needed none at this range. "You and Goldtooth worked together. He told me. Gods rot you, Tully, you did set me up—"

The translator rendered something in its flat, Tully-voiced way, and he sank down on the chair arm to evade her hand, out of room to retreat.

"You tell me the truth, huh, Tully. What's got the wind up your back? Something I said?"

"Not understand."

"Sure. Let's talk about things. Like things maybe I might like to know—What's the humans' course?"

"Ta-va—"

"Tt'a'va'o. You heard that from me just now. Maybe you know more than that. Maybe you know what Goldtooth's not saying. *Truth, Tully, gods blast you!*"

He flinched violently. "Truth," he said. The translator gave him a woman's voice in the return, but the pitch was not far from his own. "I don't lie, I don't lie."

"Where before that?"

"Not sure. Ta-vik. Think Tavik."

"Tvk. At least one kifish port. Tvk. I'll guess they didn't stop to say hello. Skimmed it and out. And then to Chchchcho, not Akkti, not likely. Chchchcho. The chi homeworld. That's a real fine route, Tully. Real great. Who planned it?"

"I come—*Ijir*."

"You mean you don't know."

"Not know."

"Tully. That packet. Packet. Understand? What did it say?"

"Make offer trade."

"To whom? Who to, Tully?"

A desperate wave of the hand. "All. All Compact."

"Kif too, huh?"

"Mahe. Hani."

"Tully, what else was in there? A knnn message, for instance. Knnn. You know that?"

A shake of the head. That was no. The eyes were wide and blue and anxious. "Not. Not know knnn thing. Py-anfar—I tell you, I tell you all thing. # # I don't lie to you."

"Funny thing how that translator always spits on sentences I'd really like not to doubt."

"I'm friend, I'm your friend, Py-anfar!"

"Yeah. I know."

"You think I lie."

"Didn't say you lied. Just wish you'd tell the truth *before* things get hot, huh? I just don't like the feeling there's something still rattling round back of those pretty blue eyes of yours. Something's been there since a long while back." She raked his mane back from his face with a judicious claw—let the hand rest on his shoulder again, gently. "Look, Tully—you're not scared of me, are you?"

"No."

"Then why don't you tell me the truth? Why'd you keep things from me when we started this voyage?"

"I tell."

"About the ships, yes. You did try. Why not the rest of it?"

"I try—try tell—You all time # busy not #—"

"Knnn's a word would get my attention real fast, Tully. You ever talk about the knnn with Goldtooth, huh? You tell him about firing on the knnn?"

211

A blink, a shake of the head, a shift of the eyes. Evasion.

"Well, you've been real helpful to a lot of people, haven't you? You tell me the truth about him taking you off that courier ship?"

"Truth."

"He personally?"

"Goldtooth."

"Ever hear anything about another ship? Another hunter-ship out there—someone with the rest of the humans?"

"No."

"You mean these human ships are just careening about Compact space on their own. No charts, no guide? No one watching them? Come on, Tully. How many?"

"I don't know."

"Two. Ten?"

"Not know. Ten. Maybe ten. Maybe more."

"More."

"I don't know!"

"Where'd these ships come from, Tully? Who's bringing them? Who told them to? You know about that?"

"Not know."

"Goldtooth knew. *Truth*, Tully. What do you know about these other humans?"

A darting of the eyes aside, elsewhere, back, away again.

"Huh?" she asked. "What do you know, Tully?"

"Come fight kif. They come fight kif."

"Uhhnnn." She caught his stare and held it. His eyes darted and jerked and stayed centered, dilated wide in the bright light of the bridge. "How do they sort out which kif, huh, Tully? Who tells them?"

"Kif is kif."

"Think so? What kind of plan is that? Take on the whole by the gods kif *species?* You're crazy, Tully. No. The mahendo'sat don't deal with crazy people. And you're dealing with the mahendo'sat, aren't you?"

"I ask go to bring you, bring you, Pyanfar, I don't # the mahendo'sat."

"Say again."

"Mahendo'sat don't speak all truth. I'm scared. I don't know what they do. I think maybe they want help us but I—*I!*" He laid a hand on his chest and said it in hani, sending the translator into sputters. "I Tully—I scare, Py-anfar."

"Of what? What scares you?"

"I think the mahendo'sat more want help self. Maybe hani have want help self. I don't know. I don't understand too much. The translator makes wrong words. I scare—I don't know—"

"You're talking real clear now, Tully. You understand me. And I don't want any more evasions. You don't tell me you don't understand, hear? You know what kind of mess we're in."

"I don't understand."

"Oh, yes, you do. *Who's with the ships*, Tully? What's the arrangement they made? Where are they going next?"

"I don't understand."

"I told you I don't want to hear that. I want to know what you know. Tell me this, Tully—what questions did Sikkukkut ask you? What did he ask you, all alone?"

"Not—not—" His eyes widened. He twisted suddenly and looked behind him. Pyanfar glanced beyond, where Hilfy stood. Reflection and movement in the dead monitor screen. That had caught Tully's eye; and he seized on the chance.

"Hilfy," Tully said, pleaded. "*Hilfy—*"

"Something wrong?" Hilfy asked.

"We're just talking," Pyanfar said. *Gods rot the timing.* "Go see how Chur's doing, huh?"

"Geran's with her. Was just there." Blind to hints. Or ignoring them.

"Fine. Go see about the filters. You want to walk through, walk."

Hilfy's ears went down. She stood there.

"I go help," Tully offered, making to get up.

"You stay put." She shoved him back down on the chair arm. "I'm not through with you. Hilfy. Get."

"What's the matter? What's going on?"

Fear. Human sweat. It was distinct and general in the air. The quiet on the bridge despite two stations working, the look on Tully's face—

213

"We're discussing routes," Pyanfar said evenly, quietly, and laid a quiet hand on Tully's shoulder. He flinched from under it and glanced round in panic. "Discussing what things he may still know. What he might have told without realizing it, to the mahendo'sat. To the kif in particular."

"I don't talk, Hilfy, I don't."

"Didn't say you were a liar, Tully. I asked you what Sikkuk-kut asked you. I want to know what Sikkukkut wanted to know."

"For godssakes, aunt—"

There was sweat on Tully's face. His skin had gone white. He looked up at her.

"Let him alone, gods rot it, aunt, he's had enough."

"I know he's had enough. I know what he went through—"

"You *don't* know! Keep your hands off him!"

Panic. Killing rage. *O gods. Gods, Hilfy.* Whoever wore that look was not a child, had never been a child. "Tully. All right. Get." She gave him a shove to move him. "Go on, I'll talk to you later."

"We send out ships," Tully said, suddenly, perversely clinging to his place. He poured the words out, clutched her wrist when she made a gesture of dismissal, and he looked from Hilfy to her, to Tirun and Haral and back, his alien eyes flickering and distracted. "It long time—long time—I try—They leave the Earth, understand. They make # self a #—" And when she shifted in the pain of his grip, he held the harder. "You listen, *listen*, Pyanfar, I tell you—"

"Make sense, gods rot it, the translator's frying half you say."

"We send ships—" He let go her bruised wrist to make a vague and desperate gesture of displacement, of going away. "Ships go from Earth, from homeworld, they make #self # law, make #self # Compact. They don't like Earth. We fight # long with these human. Now we get no trade # be # to Earth. There be *two* human Compacts. They # want #. Want Earth. We want be free. We want make our # law. We want go—out in space—not the same direction like before. We find new direction, new trade. We find your Compact, find you. We want trade. This is the truth. If we get trade we make three

214

Compact. Earth # be the third. Earth # be the # friend to hani, to mahendo'sat."

"*Two* human compacts." Pyanfar blinked and wiped her mane back with a sore hand and looked at Hilfy, who looked confused.

"Three," Tully said. "Also Earth. My homeworld. We got trouble # two humanities. We want trade. We the home of humanity we need this #. We want make way into Compact space, come and go # # #."

"You know about this?" Pyanfar asked Hilfy.

"No," Hilfy said. "No, I don't know what he's talking about."

"# #. Human be three kind." Tully held up as many digits. "#. #. Earth. I be Earth-man."

"Politics," Pyanfar muttered. "We got gods-be human politics, that's what. Well, who's telling the human ships where to go?"

"Earth. Earth tell."

"And what are you, Tully?"

"I spacer."

"You're so gods-be quick with that."

"Aunt."

"You want to ask him?"

"Gods blast it, take it easy on him!"

Pyanfar drew a deep breath. "Look, maybe he never talked to the kif. I'll take that on his say-so. Maybe he never spoke a word. But he doesn't lie real good. He never did."

"Not to us."

"He speaks the language, niece. Watch the eyes when you ask him questions, never mind the ears, watch the eyes. He's a lousy liar. He was alone with Sikkukkut. With drugs. With questions. All right, you know what and I don't. Even if he didn't talk—he may have spilled something *he* doesn't know he spilled. You think of that?"

"You ever ask me what *I* gave them?"

Pyanfar blinked in shock. Shook her head at the thought.

"A cracked skull and nothing else," Hilfy said. "I didn't give them anything. And they tried, aunt, that precious kifish friend of yours did try. You take my word, take his. I know he didn't."

215

"They had him quite a few hours to themselves, Hilfy. With all the pieces to this fractured mess starting to fit in Sikkukkut's brain, with us in port and leaving Sikkukkut a last few precious hours to try for what he could get out of Tully—*along with* what he learned from other kif living at Mkks. So you want to be some help here and let Tully for godssakes answer for himself?"

"He's told you. No! He didn't talk! I *know* him."

"*Sure* you do," Pyanfar drawled, and the inside of Hilfy's ears went suddenly deep rose; and they folded. Eyes reacted. Everything shouted reaction and shame. It was not what she had meant. Pyanfar felt her own ears go hot; the flinch was unavoidable, the instantaneous glance aside from the matter they had skirted round and skirted round. She covered it with a cough and a wave of her hand. "Look, niece—"

"I know him real well," Hilfy said with cold deliberation. "Maybe you take my word for something, huh, aunt? Maybe you trust *I* got out of there with my wits about me, huh? And I'm telling you how he was, and how he handled himself, and I'm telling you, he's not a boy and he's not the fool you take him for. Don't talk to him like that."

Pyanfar looked at her. Saw no child, no petulance. "I never said he was a fool. I'm saying you and he may be a little out of your territory—and smart, niece, smart is *knowing* when you are. If you're not as clever as your enemy, you by the gods hope he's over-confident: you sure as rain falls don't need to make a mistake in that department. That kif's not a dockfront tough; that kif's smart enough to put the *han*'s tail in a vise; and con Jik; and outwit Akkhtimakt down the line; and by all the gods near take over the Compact. You want to tell me he couldn't just ask you questions and watch your reactions? You don't want to remember that time. Fine. You don't want to think. All right. But that cripples you. And if you're number two in wit, you don't need another handicap. We're in it up to our noses. Remember what I said a while ago—what the stakes are right now? We've got a problem, Hilfy Chanur. I need a straight answer out of our friend here. I need to know what that gods-be kif's onto and what he's not; and I need to know whether hu-

216

mans are going to be here or Meetpoint, which is what Sikkuk-kut would give a whole lot to learn right now. You think the Compact's a tangled mess of ambitions? I'm betting what drives humanity is the same thing—politics we don't understand. Three Compacts, good gods! I'll tell you something else. It's a good bet Tully *doesn't* know the answers I'd really want. You think they'd let him know everything and send him off with the mahendo'sat? No. *That* kind of thing gets known by long-toothed old women in high councils. Politics is politics, at least in the oxy-breathing kinds *we* can talk to. I don't take anything for granted. I think any thought that needs thinking. Like what deals Goldtooth's made. Or Jik. Or—" She looked at Tully. "—what Sikkukkut and you could have talked about in those few hours when he knew by the gods for certain you speak hani. What about it, Tully? What'd he ask? What'd he say?"

Tully's pupils dilated and contracted and dilated again. He tried to speak and his voice failed him. "He say—say he know my friends die, he tell me—tell me # # # they #. Say I talk to him, what be human deal with mahendo'sat. What deal with you. Lot time ask. He want know route. Same you. He know human come. Not know where. # # #."

"Lost that."

Tully's lips trembled. "Lot time. Lot time. Hurt me. # #. You make deal # this kif?"

"I'm not his friend, Tully."

"I *know* this kif."

"Know him." Pyanfar looked from him to a sudden shift of Hilfy's stance.

"Sikkukkut said—" Hilfy's voice was quiet, subdued. "Said he knew Tully from before."

"On Akkukkak's ship."

Tully nodded. Emphatic. His eyes focussed elsewhere, on something ugly. Came back to them. "He be Akkukkak # # #. Long time he ask me, my friend question."

"Gods. Akkukkak's interrogator. Is that what? Is that where you know him from?"

"He kill my friend," Tully said. "He kill my friend, Py-anfar. With his hands."

217

"O good gods." She sat down against the counter edge, hands on knees. "Tully—"

"Tully asked me when we got back," Hilfy said, "just how close you're friends with Sikkukkut. Now I know why."

"Gods," Pyanfar said. "I'm *not*, Tully. I'm trying to save our lives, you understand me? Did you tell him anything, did you give him anything?"

Tully shook his head. It was not the naive look, not the clear blue stare he generally had. It was a different Tully. Tully-inside, calm and cold and thinking. She knew it when she saw it, long as it had been. "I say nothing, don't look at him. I go far away. I wait. I not be. You say you come to get me. So I wait for you."

Pyanfar let go a long, long breath. The silence stayed there a moment. "Politics," she said. "All politics. You understand politics, Tully? Kif aren't anyone's friends. Not mine. Not anyone's. But there's kif and there's worse kif. You know why I'm dealing with him? You understand? *Can* you understand?"

"Politics," Tully said. Not naive, no. "I know you come take me from kif. That be *your* politics."

"I'm not any friend of Sikkukkut's. Believe that."

"Bad thing happen. I don't understand. You lot scare. Where we go? What we fight? We got enemy be friend, hani and sts-sts—"

"Stsho."

"—be enemy. You don't trust Goldtooth, don't trust Jik. Don't trust hani. Don't trust kif."

"Goldtooth and Jik are friends. We just can't trust them much. Not where it crosses mahendo'sat interests."

"Where be hani?"

Pyanfar glanced Hilfy's way, felt Tirun's stare at her side. She slouched against the console. "Good question."

"What I do?" Tully asked. "What I do, Py-anfar?"

"What *did* you do? What are you *going* to do? I wish I had an answer for either one. *Friend*, Tully. That's all I can tell you. Same's Goldtooth's my friend; and yours. Gods know what it counts for. Wish I had an answer for you. Wish you had one for me."

"I fight," he said. "I crewman on *The Pride*. You want fight #, hani, kif, I don't # to die with #."

"Gods rot that translator. Do you understand me at all? Have we got it fouled up again?"

"You be my friend. You. Hilfy. All. I die with you."

"Gods, thanks," Pyanfar murmured bedazedly. A superstitious chill went down her spine. "Translator again. I hope." Hilfy's ears had flagged. "I sure hope you come up with a better idea."

Perhaps he did not take the humor. His face stayed void of it. Of everything but anxiety.

"Friend," he said.

"You've got duties. Get. Hilfy. Get."

"Aye," Hilfy said. And touched the seat-back. "Tully."

He rose from the chair arm. At the other side Tirun had just turned attention to something from the com-plug in her ear and turned half about again with a flick of the ears and a tilt of the head. Some new difficulty. An incoming call. Pyanfar gave Tully room to get up, laid a hand on his back as he passed, a slight pat of consolation. "Friend. Go help Hilfy, huh? She wanted you for something.—Uhhhnnn. Tully."

He looked back at her, all unprepared and trying to collect it again.

"*Is* there anything you know that we don't?"

Flicker.

"Uhhhn," she said again, eyes half-lidded.

"Py-anfar—"

"You think of something, huh, you come to me. You come and tell me. All right?"

The kif had used shocks with him and got nothing. The mahendo'sat used wit; and achieved something. She stared him in the eyes without any mercy at all. And tried for a piece of him.

"Don't trust," he said suddenly, miserably. "Don't trust humanity, Py-anfar." And he fled out the door—walked out, but it was flight, all the same. Hilfy delayed at his back with one anguished look toward her. And turned and went after him.

Pyanfar was unamazed, except by Tully's unequivocal thoroughness. It was doublecross. Goldtooth's. Jik's. Hers.

219

Humanity's. Everyone's but Tully's—who, along with Chanur, had just betrayed his own kind. Gods knew his reasons.

What drove him?

Anything hani-like? Where was family, clan, House? What was he?

He.

Male. Houseless. Sisterless. Wifeless. Renegade. *Nau hauruun.*

But not hani. There was no analogy in Tully to that kind of destructive orphan, who killed and stalked at random. *Nau hauruun.*

Not Tully their friend. Tully no-name. Tully from distant Earth, of the ships and the strangers.

"Captain," Tirun said quietly. "Captain—Ehrran's on. 'Fraid they've been on hold a while. They're getting pretty hot."

"Good," Pyanfar said flatly; and went and flung herself into her well-worn chair and powered it about to the boards. *Mind on business, Pyanfar Chanur. Wake up. Smell the wind and watch the branches overhead.* "I'll take it.—You got any movement out of *Harukk* on the Tahar business?"

"Not a thing," Tirun said. "I keep calling; keep getting the same answer. Sikkukkut's still not available. Business, they say."

"Gods-be *sfik* games. I begin to get the feel of it. And I don't like what's going on. Put that call through again as soon as I finish with Ehrran. Have them tell Sikkukkut I'm *personally* interested in the Tahar crew. Tell him we've got *sfik* involved here."

That got a look from Haral, beside her. "Captain. Begging your pardon—"

Haral left it unfinished. It was hani lives at stake, feud with Tahar or no feud. A miscalculation with the kif might touch something off and get the Tahar crew killed outright. Jik might even be working near to success on the matter. All these things she thought of, and thought of again under that worried glance from Haral, and a like one from Tirun past Haral's back. A twitch of many-ringed ears. A deep frown.

"Send it," Pyanfar said. "Be tactful, that's all."

"Tactful," Tirun muttered, and turned to execute the first order.

Pyanfar turned her chair again and touched the button to bring the long-waiting call through from Rhif Ehrran; listened to Tirun address the *Vigilance* com officer.

More games of politics and captainly protocols. The com officer insisted on getting response from *The Pride*'s captain before putting her own on.

"I'll take it," Pyanfar said—curiously, pride with Ehrran had just diminished in importance. She failed even to feel a twinge of temper with the Ehrran officer who tried to provoke her and put it on record. "This is Pyanfar Chanur."

Keep Ehrran quiet. Get the essentials done. Tahar was the emergency. Chur was safe. Tully assured her nothing critical had spilled into kif hands. There were things Sikkukkut still needed. And that meant at once a safer and a less predictible kif.

"*Vigilance. Com officer speaking. One more moment, captain. I'm afraid the captain's gone off line a moment.*" Cold and calculatedly insolent. Games of provocation.

Three human compacts? Fights between them?

One human Compact, Earth, the human homeworld, trying to counter two rival human powers with new trading routes? Or *was* it trade they were interested in?

That was a *big* section of space, if it had room for three starfaring economies . . . correction: *two*. And one that just *wanted* to be bigger.

Did Goldtooth know the situation inside human space? Mahendo'sat with their scientists and their mad delving into oddities—always poking and prodding at things, hoping—hoping what? For new species? New alliances?

New situations they could use to deal with their old neighbors the kif?

Beware of Goldtooth. Thus the stsho, who had double-dealing down to an art.

"*Ker Pyanfar, this is Rhif Ehrran. I trust whatever emergency kept you wasn't serious.*"

"No. It's all handled. No further problem. Unless you have one."

"*No. I'm going to relieve you of one. I'm sending a detail over to pick up Tahar.*"

221

"Afraid not. I've accepted her appeal for parole. Sorry, Ehrran. She's under a Chanur roof, so to speak. And I'm head of
house—out here."

"*This isn't Anuurn and we're not in the age of* sofhyn *and
spears, you hear me,* Chanur?"

"No. We play with bigger toys nowadays, don't we? You're
fond of quoting the law. Me, I like the old laws right fine: like
kinright. The kind of law you can't quote by the book, Ehrran."

"*Put Tahar on.*"

"Maybe you ought to concentrate on her crew. *They*'ve got a
real problem. They might appreciate your intervention. But Dur
Tahar's comfortable enough where she is. Is that all you want?"

Click.

"Log that," Pyanfar said. "Put the other call through."

"Aye," Tirun said.

"Good shot," Haral said with a dip of her ears. Meaning Rhif
Ehrran and a genteel stroll to the brink.

"Huh," Pyanfar said. "Why couldn't the kif grab *her*, huh? Do
us a favor."

"Make a trade?" Haral suggested brightly.

"Gods, that's a—"

"Captain." Tirun lifted a hand, signaling quiet. "*Harukk*'s
going through real procedures this time—I think they're going to
try to put the call through. Maybe—*Yes.* The captain's waiting,
Harukk com, if you can do that. Yes. . . . Right. Captain,
Harukk com's compliments, and they'll try to reach the *hakkikt*
if you'll put the request yourself."

Protocols. *Sfik* games again. Pyanfar flicked her ears and made
an affirmative handsign. Immediately the ready light came on
and Pyanfar keyed it. Her claws flexed. She drew in a deep
breath and killed all the anxieties, banished them to a cold, far
place without a future.

"*Harukk*," she said calmly, "this is Pyanfar Chanur. I have an
urgent message for the *hakkikt*, praise to him."

"*Honor to the* hakkikt, *he may give you his attention, hunter.*"

—*So we come up from our obscure beginnings, do we, kif? Provincial boss and chief torturer—to prince? And we by the gods set
you there.*

She waited. Coldly, calmly. Long. Eventually:

"*This is Sikkukkut,* ker *Pyanfar. What is this urgency?*"

"*Hakkikt.* I appreciate the courtesy. And the gift you sent me. I'd like to talk with you further. I understand you have *Moon Rising*'s crew in your custody. . . .''

"*Hunter Pyanfar, your forwardness would daunt a chi. Is my gift too scant for your appreciation?*"

"*Hakkikt,* I see a way to use it to your benefit and mine. There's some urgency in it. If you'll send a courier I can be more specific."

Pause. "*Hunter Pyanfar, you interest me. But I see no reason why one of my skkukun should come from my ship to yours and back again, when your own look to be in good health. And I have nothing to say to your crew. I made you a proposition at Meetpoint, you may recall, which you declined. I make it again—a rare offer. Come to* my *deck this time. If this offer has the merit you say. I trust it does. I'll expect you—within the hour.*"

Click.

She leaned back in the chair.

"Captain," Haral said, beside her, "good gods—"

She turned a look in Haral's direction. "That didn't go right."

"Now what? We call Jik?"

"Call Jik to mop up?—We just got a challenge, cousin. *I* got it. *Sfik.* The bet just got taken and doubled."

"They want to get their hands on you, good gods, they can't get Goldtooth in reach—they want *you!* You just heard Tully say what that son *is* and you said yourself what Sikkukkut wants most—Goldtooth was just here, talking to you. The kif have to know that. They *know* he could have passed us what they want to know—"

"They'll kill the prisoners. They'll kill them sure now if I fail that appointment, and they'll let us know about it. If that weren't enough, our credit with the kif hits bottom. Hard."

"You can't do it!"

"I can't duck it either. No. Sure that earless bastard is going to try us. One way or the other. And I think I'm starting to *think* in kifish; I think I read him. I'm perfectly safe to walk in

223

there—if I can keep him wondering. I'm going to need company out there. Want to take a walk?"

"Oh, sure," Haral said with a despairing shrug. "Gods, why not?"

Twelve

The air of Kefk hit like an ammonia-tainted wall. Haral coughed even on the ramp; Pyanfar sneezed and felt the sting of her eyes in spite of the antiallergents. Haral had put on her portside finery, dark spacer blue with a collection of gold earrings, a set of bracelets, an anklet with a bangle, a belt with silver and gold chains that rattled right along with a monstrous black AP gun and a belt-knife. Pyanfar wore the red silk trousers, gold bracelets and belt and gold-earrings aplenty; a knife and a pocket-gun besides the AP slung low on her hip.

"We look a right set of pirates," Haral had said before the lock sealed them out. "It's the pirates outside worry me," Tirun had retorted to them both, there in the lock.

And Khym had said other things, while Geran and Hilfy fretted and gnawed their mustaches sparse—"Huh," Geran had said, with exhaustion and worry in her eyes. "I'll go with you—"

Haral: "My job."

And Tully, later: "Where she go—*where go, Py-anfar?*"

She avoided answers with Tully. "Out," she had told him in that unwanted encounter in the downside corridor. "I got business, Tully. I'm in a hurry."

"Careful," he had said, anxious-looking. Frightened, doubtless from the time he heard that inner lock open, preparing to expose *The Pride* to the kifish docks. She reckoned the crew would tell him where they had gone after she was well on her way. Or better yet, when she and Haral got back.

When.

They walked the dockside, she and Haral, in a sodium-light hell of clinging smokes and ammonia-reek and a moist chill like a swamp at sundown. Kif moved, black wisps in the dimmer shadow along the far wall of this section of warehouses and factory fronts. There was no color anywhere about Kefk docks but the sickly sodium-glow, no brightness but the stark white of some argon spotlight on a round steel doorway.

225

"Kkkkt. Kkkkt," the sound came to them, as they walked past kifish ships. Kif, doubtless some of their erstwhile companions— had seen them walk outside and gathered in clusters to whisper—and perhaps, Pyanfar thought, to wonder whether the two hani walking down the docks of Kefk had lost their collective minds.

("Look at you," Khym had cried in dismay while she dressed for this foray. *Wear that into a den of thieves? Py, for gods-sakes!"*)

Crazy to wear that much gold into a kifish den if one had not the *sfik* to hold onto it. "So we look like trouble," Pyanfar had said to Haral when they laid their plan. "A lot of trouble, by kifish lights. That's the idea."

Advertise their presence and hold it under kifish noses till they smelled it and looked at the gold and the weapons and remembered that *The Pride*'s crew had no general reputation for being fools.

Therefore they must be the other kind. Dangerous.

They were also the *hakkikt*'s invited guests. At least on the way *to* the meeting.

"Marvelous thing about kif," Pyanfar muttered in a moment when she and Haral were well out of earshot of kif, between one gloomy ship-berth and another. "It occurs to me that these types out here on the dock aren't any more secure than we are. We're high on the wave and so are they and kif sail a rotted choppy sea. Always wondering when the wind's going to shift."

"They're different, that's a fact," Haral muttered in her turn. "No lasting grudges—and, gods be feathered, *nothing* they won't trade. Flighty folk. I don't think hani ever have got the right of them. Maybe we should have brought our friend Skkukuk on this trip, huh?"

"I did think about it. But I've got an uneasy feeling that one's a little crazy even for a kif. I don't want him near guns and knives."

"Huh. Me either, now I think on it."

A waft of something reached them down the dock. Blood. Even through the ammonia. Pyanfar hissed and cleared her throat. "Good gods," Haral swore in disgust. "That's enough to kill your appetite."

"We're nearly—"—*there*, Pyanfar started to say and suddenly lost the thread of her thought as she caught sight of the kifish numerals for 28: *Harukk*'s berth. Kif traffic was thick hereabouts and the blood-smell grew stronger.

It worsened rapidly, the closer they walked. The steel rampway rail had a series of metal poles chained to its stanchions, and a dark object sat atop each.

"Gods and thunders," Pyanfar muttered, "Haral, don't flinch."

The heads were kif. Kif came and went on that number 28 ramp, past the awful watchers; she and Haral headed that way among the rest, waiting for challenge from some guard or other.

None came. They passed the first stanchion up and Pyanfar gave the gory object atop it a cold and curious glance.

"So much for the opposition," Haral said.

"Sure ought to keep the new converts in line," Pyanfar muttered. Every kif that came into *Harukk* had to see it, victory for some, grim warning for the others.

At least, she thought in profoundest relief, none of the heads was hani.

Kif turned and stared at them as they passed, upward bound like all the rest who had business aboard *Harukk*. A knot of kif who stood at the accessway clicked and hissed as they passed but made no offer to delay them.

There were, finally, guards inside the large airlock.

"Hakktan," one said in kifish. *Captain?*

"Ukt," Haral answered with a nod at Pyanfar. *Yes.* Pyanfar stood by with her arms folded, arrogant to the slant of her ears, and let Haral do the talking. Two of the three kif kept their hands tucked within their sleeves, doubtless concealing weapons besides the guns they wore openly. They stood blocking other traffic into the lock from either direction, while the third reported their presence to the monitor above.

The answer came, orders for their admittance. The guard at the inner hatch stepped aside; and the third guard bowed with that hands-empty gesture: "Inside," that one said.

"Huh," said Pyanfar; bowed and slanted her ears back when

she did it. Haral stayed close as they passed the hatch to *Harukk*'s ammonia-smelling interior.

More kif waited in the inside corridor—one who turned out to be merely delayed traffic, who stalked on; and four tall kif rattling with weapons.

"Follow," one said, and stalked off in the lead without looking back. Three walked behind, while two stayed. And not a word of objection about the array of weapons their visitors brought aboard. Not a word of any kind. They passed kif in these dim corridors that stank of ammonia and machinery and blood and other, unidentifiable things, and no one gave them a second glance.

Kifish manners, Pyanfar thought. Don't notice the *hakkikt*'s odd guests, don't stare, don't give offense. The aura of fear and fierceness throughout the place was infectious. It bristled the back, set the pulse beating faster, sent fight-flight impulses coursing the nerves.

Hilfy knows this place, Pyanfar thought at sight after sight, with an involuntary tightening of her gut. *Hilfy was in this awful place.*

Hilfy had stood silent by Khym's side when she had broke the news to them where she and Haral proposed to go. Khym had had his opinion of it all. Like Geran. But Hilfy's ears just went flat and her nostrils drew taut; and: "Huh," Hilfy had said. "Why?" With a darkness of memory in her eyes; and an estimation, and nothing else readable. "You know it's a trap."

"I know," Pyanfar had said. "At this point there isn't a better choice."

Hilfy knew the ways of kif better than any. And gave her no argument. No offer to come either. The situation wanted cold steadiness and as little as possible chance of provoking the kif. And that put the job, by seniority and by disposition, on Haral Araun.

Haral walked along beside her now as warily easy as on a trek down one of the Compact's rougher docksides—kept her ears up and her face serene during the ride pent in a lift with the pair of kifish guards.

The lift stopped; one guard exited and the rest hung back as they had done below. And it was one more long walk down the dimly lit corridor aft from the lift; then an open doorway, and a dim chamber where a handful of kif waited attendance on one seated on an insect-legged chair, a kif who wore a silver medallion, whose black robe and hood were edged in silver that shone dimly in sodium-light.

"*Hakkikt*," Pyanfar said, approaching this grim magnificence. And bowed with a carefully rationed measure of respect and self-importance.

"Kkkt." Sikkukkut flourished his thin, dark-gray hand. "Ksithikki." Kif scurried to the corners of the room and carried back two chairs and a low table, all at a virtual run.

"Ksithti."

Pyanfar nodded and sat down in one, feet tucked. Haral took the other. More orders from Sikkukkut, and a wave of his hand in a silver-bordered sleeve. Kif scurried after pitcher and cups with as great haste; and hurried to put a cup into Sikkukkut's outstretched hand before it had had time to tire of waiting. A cup went to Pyanfar; a third to Haral. A kif had poured for Sikkukkut; and came quickly to pour for them from the same pitcher.

It was, thank the gods, parini. Liquor. Strong and straight and likely to go straight to the head; but it was nothing objectionable. Pyanfar sipped gingerly and tried not to think of obvious things like whether the off-taste was the ammonia in her nostrils or something in the drink.

But they were sitting in Sikkukkut's hall, on Sikkukkut's deck; in his starstation; in kif space; and drugged drinks here seemed as superfluous as removing their weapons, which no one had offered yet to do. Haral followed her lead and drank: Haral, whose stomach was redoubtable in station bars from Anuurn to Meetpoint and who always made her duty schedules without a hangover. For the second time she was glad it was Haral by her and not Khym.

"You turned down this invitation once at Meetpoint," Sikkukkut said.

"I remember." A sneeze threatened her dignity. And their lives. She fought it back with an effort that made her eyes water.

229

It was psychological, this aversion to kif. She had taken the pills. And gods, those pills made a hazardous combination with the liquor, dried her mouth, dulled her perceptions. And her nose still prickled.

"I told you then I looked for a change of mind someday." Sikkukkut dipped his nose into the ornate cup and drank. "And here it is. Kkkt. After an emergency on your ship. What sort of emergency, do you mind?"

Wits, get your mind working, Pyanfar Chanur. "There *was* a medical difficulty; but the emergency call to the mahendo'sat was a matter of convenience." She looked straight at the *hakkikt* and prayed the gods greater and lesser for no sudden sneezes. Attack the matter straight on. Rob the bastard of all his carefully laid traps and surprises. "Actually it was an excuse for consultation with two of my allies—without the nuisance of a third, speaking plainly. On several matters. Your gift, *hakkikt*— gives me options to deal with that nuisance. That's why I came. It may rid you of one too—since I think my annoyance and yours has one source."

"Kkkkt." Another sip, and a shadowed glance within the shadowing, silver-edged hood, black eyes reflecting the glare of sodium-light. "I take it then you don't intend to kill this Tahar hani."

"No. I don't."

"So you have asked for the crew as well as the captain. This would be a rather large gift on my part. They are unusual—kkt. Ikkthokktin. A mild rarity. Amusing. I don't say I'm personally interested, but certain of my *skkukun* would be pleased to have one or another of them. Is it perhaps a certain—ethical reluctance—on your part? Should your desires mass more than others of my captains?"

Think. "I have reasons more than amusement." *Kifish logic. Pukkukkta. Let him lead himself astray. When outclassed in wit, create plausible complications and let the enemy think himself to death.* "You have to understand, *hakkikt*, I'm sure you do—that Rhif Ehrran is no particular friend of mine. I don't doubt you've heard from her, wanting them released to her."

"And from Keia and even from Ismehanan-min. These Tahar

hani seem be a matter of some excitement in your faction. A *sfik*-item, you say. But why should I give the whole prize to you?"

"Tahar interests quite a few people, particularly hani. They're a big family, they've got wide holdings in the same continent as Chanur, as well as being spacer-hani, which also makes them valuable in some quarters. No. I'm going to ask an even larger favor of you, *hakkikt*—trusting *Moon Rising* got through the station takeover undamaged. I want that crew handed over to me—and I want their ship."

"Kkkt. Pyanfar Chanur, your audacity grows larger by the hour. First Tahar, then the crew, now the ship. Next will you ask me for Kefk? Akkht, perhaps?"

There was a hush in the room. Not a kif stirred. "You have Kefk." Pyanfar assumed her most charming smile. "Myself, *hakkikt*, my ambitions are different. I want this one small ship. And its crew. For my own reasons."

"Where are the mahendo'sat? Where is Keia? He could surely make hani reasonable to me. Kkkt. I make no assumptions when dealing with such a suicidal species. And—kkt—the emergency call and the consultation. Kkkt. Kkkt. *Who* is injured?"

"One of my crew. A minor business. It gave me the chance to talk with Goldtooth. Ismehanan-min. It has to do with the ship." (*Back to the trail*, hakkikt!) "Goldtooth delivered me some information that makes me surer than ever where my interests lie. Rhif Ehrran and I are about to come to severe difference; it's possible she'll attack us directly, but I doubt it—she wants to survive. She has the means to create difficulties for me on Anuurn. When we get to Meetpoint we'll have her to reckon with."

"To Meetpoint."

Pyanfar blinked. "Meetpoint. Definitely Meetpoint."

"You assume this."

"Where Akkhtimakt is headed. Where a certain treaty with the stsho could bring the *han* and all their ships in on Akkhtimakt's side. You don't act surprised, *hakkikt*. I didn't think you'd be."

"Only in your forthrightness. I know about the stsho treaty."

"Then explain a kif motive for me. Why haven't you taken Ehrran out, since her liability is about to outweigh her use?"

"Kkkt. She is attached to Kefk at the moment. Inconvenient and dangerous. Let's wait til she goes outbound. Explain in return: why did Keia acquire this double-edged person in the first place?"

"To keep her from going anywhere else. And for the same reason you've used her: the *sfik* of the *han*. Roughly speaking. *Hakkikt*, honor to you, I don't know how often you've monitored our communications, but Ehrran has quite a collection of reports she trusts will damage Chanur's *sfik* on Anuurn—I'm translating this as best I can—so thoroughly that the pro-stsho party can destroy us. I don't intend to let that happen. Now is my motive clear?"

"Labyrinthine as I expected. Kkkt. Once away from dock I can solve everyone's difficulty at a stroke."

"Ah, but that's another favor I ask you: leave the Ehrran ship to me. Destroying it outright might be a present convenience to me, but a difficulty in the long run, when the tale got around, and it *would* get around. Among this many ships, even among your own, some would talk, to damage me and advance themselves, I have no doubt. If that rumor got out, those records of Ehrran's wouldn't even need to get to Anuurn. The pro-stsho party would have all the ammunition it needs to do me harm. Martyr. You know that concept?"

"I haven't heard that word, no."

"It's a kind of *sfik* you get by dying in a way that makes a point, *hakkikt*. Double *sfik* because you're dead and you can't be discredited. People will die following you forever. And that makes more martyrs. Destroy Ehrran and she'll cause us twice the trouble."

"Kkkkkt. Kkkkkkt. Kkkkt." Sikkukkut's snout drew down as if something offended his nostrils. He sipped at his cup and the tongue lapped delicately around his lips. "What a concept. Kkkkkt. I think, hunter Pyanfar, the straightest course is simply to blow up the Ehrran ship in the next action, when matters are suitably confused."

"Ah, but then I'm still left with Tahar for company, which would ruin my *sfik*—unless I can first discredit Ehrran. And you can't discredit a dead hero. Bad taste. Martyrdom. No, I can put this simple hani concept in kifish without any difficulty at all: *pukkukkta*. Revenge. I have to deal with Ehrran in a hani way, in a way that shows other hani what we both know she is—an utter fool. And to do that, I need Tahar."

"Why should I risk my ships for the sake of your *puk-kukkta?*"

"*Sfik.* I'm your ally. I can put a stop to a problem. Balance, *hakkikt*. Equilibrium in the Compact. It's one thing to climb a mountain, it's quite another thing to build a house there."

Kif stirred about the room. Sikkukkut was frozen still with the cup in his hand. *Too far, gods, one step too far with him.*

But: "For a hani, you have a fine grasp of politics," Sikkukkut said, and sipped at his parini, a delicate lapping of a long, black tongue.

"*Hakkikt*, hani may be new in space, but politics is the air we breathe."

Sikkukkut's snout wrinkled. "So you want the small matter of seven more hani and a well-armed ship, the behavior of which in our midst you guarantee. And you want the Ehrran ship to deal with too. Kkkt, hani, you amuse me. You may have the Tahar crew and *Moon Rising*. Kgotok skkukun nankkafkt nok takkif hani skkukunikkt ukku kakt tokt kiffik sikku nokkuunu kok-kakkt taktakti, kkkt?"

Something about turning over a thousand kif as well. There was the sniffle of kifish laughter about the room. "So," said Sik-kukkut. "What else did Ismehanan-min have to say when he met with you?"

Gods. To the flank and in. "Beyond the warning about affairs at home, the business about Akkhtimakt moving on Meetpoint. That, mostly. And warned me about the stsho treaty with the *han*. Which I'd suspected." Turning over that much truth made a knot of foreboding in her gut, but some coin had to go on the table, and it was the thing most likely Sikkukkut already knew—with former partisans of Akkhtimakt in his hands.

"Kkkt. Yes. And the humans are coming in. Did he say that?"

"He said they were headed this way."

Another lapping at the cup. A flicker of dark eyes. "Be more specific."

"He wasn't specific."

"Tt'a'va'o," Sikkukkut said. "Go on."

Pyanfar blinked again. Surprise took no acting. Dissembling outright fright did. The little she had drunk reacted with the medicines and hummed in her blood. "Tt'a'va'o," she said. "I know the stsho are panicking. The mahendo'sat can't restrain them. This alliance with Akkhtimakt is the worst thing they could do for themselves, but it's the stsho's only hope of getting armed ships, which the *han* can't provide in numbers. The kif are a known quantity. The stsho are most afraid of what they least understand. And they think—mistakenly, I think—that they know how to cheat a kif, playing one against the other."

There was a whisper, a stirring of robes.

"Kkkkt. This place is a mine of information. All sorts of things pour into my ears. Where will the humans come next?"

"The stsho think Meetpoint. They would. I don't know." She took the slightest of sips. And took a risk that chilled the blood. "The tc'a may have some part in that decision."

Sikkukkut's snout moved. *Score one. Fear.* "Your estimation? Or the mahendo'sat's?"

"I got the impression that's the case. I don't like it, *hakkikt.*"

"You say you don't know the human's course. Kkkt. You do have one resource."

"My human crewman? *Hakkikt,* the mahendo'sat might know. Tully doesn't. I get the impression the human ships are improvising their course—going where they *can* go. And Tully left humanity—months back. He hasn't got any more idea than I do where the humans are going—less, in fact. *I*'ve talked to Goldtooth."

"Kkkt." Sikkukkut gazed at her long and thoughtfully. "Interesting. Interesting, this human. *Friend* of yours. Friend of mine. I would not take a gift amiss—since you expect my generosity."

"I'm still hani, *hakkikt.* We have our differences. I can't give up a crewman. But *pukkukkta*'s a fit gift to give a *hakkikt,* isn't it? *Pukkukkta*'s something we have in common. And if I win— Chanur's going to do some re-arranging back home. *Pukkukkta* for certain. You want no more hani-stsho treaties, *hakkikt,* I'll

give you that with my compliments. Common motives. Wasn't
that the way you described a good alliance?"

"You have aspirations on Anuurn."

"Oh, yes. On Anuurn and in space."

Another long silence. A dry sniffing. "The prisoners are inconsequence." Sikkukkut waved his left hand and set the cup
aside into a hand that appeared to take it on the instant. "Go. I
have taken time enough with this."

Pyanfar stood up, bowed; Haral did the same. "And the ship,"
Pyanfar said.

"Details." Sikkukkut waved his hand again. "See to them.
Skktotik."

Kif arrived at the lock. With deliveries.

"They can by the gods wait," Tirun said; and Hilfy turned and
looked at her, her heart pounding. Tirun was senior; Tirun
called the decisions now on *The Pride* and sat in Haral's chair.
And Hilfy only looked at her, having known Tirun Araun long
enough to know with Tirun there was impulse and there was
what Tirun had the sense to do in spite of impulse. *Don't back
up, don't show fear—*

"Gods be," Tirun muttered with fury in her eyes. "Hilfy—
they're pushing, these kif are: I don't like their timing; but it's a
real soft push right now. We got to take that delivery."

"Sure as rain falls we can't back up from them," Hilfy said.
"*I'll* go down there."

"Take Khym with you."

"Rather have Geran."

"I want a second pair of eyes up here at the boards. Take
Khym."

"Right." Hilfy punched the all-ship, on low volume. "Geran.
Tully. You're needed on the bridge. *Na* Khym, go to lower
main."

And she felt a quiver in her stomach as she got up from the
board. Raw terror. Pyanfar was out with Haral and the kif
wanted in at the lock with an innocuous delivery of a cage full
of stinking vermin and a mini-can of grain.

235

Compliments of the hakkikt.

From Sikkukkut, who had kept Pyanfar and Haral aboard a worrisome long time.

Geran reached the bridge before she had gotten across the deck to the weapons locker. "Kif below," Tirun said at her back, talking to Geran. "We got visitors."

A chair sighed with Geran's weight as Hilfy heaved the weight of an AP about her hips and gathered up a light pistol for herself and one for Khym. Her hands were shaking. She looked up as Tully arrived on the bridge. "Sit scan," Hilfy said as he looked her way. "Help Geran."

"Py-anfar got trouble?" Tully asked. There was panic in his eyes. Raw nightmare. "What do?"

"*Sit down!* Don't ask me questions!" She had not meant to snarl. Instinct delivered it; terror; vexation. Men. It was not a man's kind of fight—yet. And all she had for help down there in lowerdeck was a man not hers. Pyanfar could handle Khym. *Pyanfar* could knock reason into his thick skull, and Pyanfar was off with the kif in gods knew what trouble—

—and *na* Khym knew that.

Gods, gods. She snapped the locker shut as across the bridge Tully slipped into the chair by Geran's side, an extra pair of eyes and hands in crisis—that, at least. Skilled and illiterate. And mortally scared.

"Stay put!" Geran was saying to someone on com; and Hilfy guessed who. Chur had surely heard that bridge-call.

Hilfy hit the topside-main at a run, the heavy gun knocking at her leg, the light pistols in either hand as she headed for the lift downside.

"This way," their guide said, deep in the gut of the kifish ship, down reeking halls, down sodium-lighted corridors and through one and the other ominously sealable door.

On the far side of this last doorway were cross-barred cells.

"Wait outside, captain?" Haral said.

"Aye," Pyanfar said, and Haral stepped to the side by the outside of that door and set her hand on her gun—fast; and firm;

and she blessed her first officer's good sense as Haral got away with it.

But the kif performed a like maneuver: one of their dark guides went in and beckoned her on; while the others lingered to take up guard with Haral outside.

Move and countermove.

A species old in assassinations and treachery; and the hani species recent from the age of walled estates and bright banners and yes, by the gods, treachery of its own, House and House, with never poison in the cup but connivance and betrayal and duel aplenty. Pyanfar drew a deep breath of the tainted air as she walked in, searching it for information; and saw a touch of color in this black and gray hell, behind crossed bars. Huddled in a corner, the merest glimmer of rust-brown, a lump of hani bodies rested together in their misery.

—Hilfy—

In this place. Here. No sane hani ever built a place like this, this cage for thinking creatures, this place of horrors and torment.

She was supposed to be daunted by this place. *Sikkukkut* arranged it. No word of explanation—just guides who came to take them down to see what happened to hani here.

"—orders of the *hakkikt*," the guides had said in the corridor outside the *hakkikt*'s hall, and showed them into a lift and down and further astern in *Harukk*'s huge ring. To recover the prisoners, they promised. And the message was clear: *dare my hospitality to the depth, hani; or tell me you're afraid. Tell me that in front of my captains and my sycophants, and we'll know where hani fit in our ranks and in our future plans. We'll know how we have to deal with you—how much you can take and how much you can hold onto. Are you like Ehrran, hunter Pyanfar? Where is your flinching-point?*

Useful to know that—when we meet in space, when your nerve and mine guide ships and time their reflexes—

Where are your reactions, hunter Pyanfar—so that I can predict them?

She walked halfway to the bars and stood there. There was a small movement from the knot of hani in the corner of their cell. A tension and then a furtive fix of slitted eyes: if they had been resting at all, the opening of the outer door had gotten their attention. And now her presence did.

Chanur, their enemy, resplendent with silk and gold and weapons, standing beside their kifish guard in the heart of this prison.

"Stand behind me," Hilfy said when she and Khym got to the lock—she turned and looked up at him, great towering hulk that he was. "Cover me. Don't shoot toward the access; you can blow us all to vacuum. *You hearing me,* na *Khym?*"

"Yes," he said, and the ears flicked, so she knew he heard. But the eyes were dark. And that was trouble. So was his silence on the way down the corridor.

"You make a mistake you can kill her—*hear?* This is probably a little thing, the stuff we were supposed to get for that gods-be kif—"

"I'm not crazy," Khym said, and bristled about the shoulders. "But they're from Sikkukkut. He's trying something."

He *was* thinking. "I'm sure of it," Hilfy said, and hit the com button by the lock. "Open her up, Geran."

"*I'm on monitor,*" Tirun's voice came back. "*Careful, cousin. And don't take any stuff either.*"

The Tahar gathered themselves up. Blood had caked on their fur, in their manes. The senior—Gilan, her name was—had taken a kifish bite on the left shoulder and the awful wound glistened under plasm that had kept her from bleeding to death. It was not the only such wound. Canfy Maurn had a hand wrapped up in a rag and by the blood on it, it was a bad one.

"Get them out," Pyanfar said to the kif, with no doubt the kif was going to do that, and fast. "You've got your orders."

"Kkkt." The kif lifted his long-jawed face, contemplating mayhem. "I take no orders from you, hani."

"*Captain,* you earless bastard, and I'm sure the *hakkikt* won't miss you much."

"Ssss. My orders are only the *hakkikt*'s. Don't push, *hani*."

The airlock opened. A group of kif stood there, black knot against the orange-lit accessway, the foremost two holding a large metal cage in which dark things darted and squealed. Hilfy sucked a deep breath of the cold air that wafted in. It tasted of something obnoxious, beyond the expected ammonia-taint.

"You can set it down right there," Hilfy said, with the pistol in her fist aimed at the kif in general. "We'll take it aboard."

"But we are ordered to observe courtesy," said the leftmost kif, stepping over the threshold with his end of the cage.

"*Hold it!*" Hilfy brought the gun to both hands and remembered the danger of firing. Angle them against the wall. Make the shots true. Panic wobbled her hands.

A living red-brown wall shifted into Hilfy's way, brushing the gun aside. "She said stop," Khym rumbled, and faster than seemed likely made a grab for the kif.

"Look out!" Hilfy cried. The cage went flying up into Khym's way, clanged and hit the floor in a multiple squealing as Khym smashed it underfoot. Khym swung a fistful of robes and a live kif into the airlock wall as the rest surged forward. "Khym, get *out of the way!*"

Khym just lifted another kif onehanded and threw him at the corner, and grabbed a third. Hilfy uptilted the pistol and used the butt on a kifish snout. Escaping vermin squealed and screamed underfoot. She trod on something tough that threw her off-balance as the kif grappled for her gun. Suddenly her attacker vanished backward as Khym got it by the scruff and flung it for the hatch—not a true throw. The kif hit the wall and sprawled out, fell on a second cage on the accessway floor and drew squeals and panic from the contents as it collapsed.

A kif down the accessway leveled a gun.

"*Khym*" Hilfy howled. "*Gun!*"

He froze in the lock dead center.

And the hatch shut as fire hit it from both sides.

Hilfy wilted against the inner wall, and Khym still stood there.

"You all right?" Tirun asked them over com. *"Hilfy, Khym, you all right?"*

"Good gods," Hilfy breathed. Tirun had heard—the veteran spacer had hit the hatch control from the main board. Khym still stood there with his ears flat. He turned with an appalled look on his face.

"It's a trap," Hilfy said hoarsely to Khym and Tirun both. "They meant to take the ship. The captain and Haral are over there in *Harukk* and they're trying to take *The Pride*."

The kif glared and moved to the barred door, reaching inside its black robes to find a small key-tab. "You," it said to the Tahar crew, "file out. You go into this hani's custody. If there should be difficulty—I will shoot one of you. I'll choose at random." It inserted the key. The door went back.

"Chanur's taking you out," Pyanfar said.

"Captain's here," Gilan said hoarsely, the other side of the open door.

"She's on my ship. Come *on,* Tahar."

Gilan Tahar blinked dully, laid one hand on the doorframe and walked out, the wounded arm dangling, her step unsteady. Her crewmates followed: Naun and Vihan Tahar; Nif Angfylas; Canfy Maurn and Tav and Haury Savuun; Haury looking as if she were doing well to walk at all, holding her ribs and limping on a bloodstained leg. Ears were torn; skin had been gashed. Haury wobbled against the bars and Tav steadied her, keeping her own body between her sister and the kif.

"Come on," Pyanfar said, low and harsh—*Fast, move it—don't hold us up and don't try anything fancy, Gilan Tahar.* She gestured toward the door that led out; and a sense of overwhelming oppression closed about her. Haral was out of sight, beyond the door. The metal bars, the cruelty of the place afflicted her to the soul, infectious and bewildering. *Kill* occurred to her and *hunt,* and her claws flexed out on reflex. It was the fear-smell, everywhere about the ship, endemic among the kif.

The guide-guard turned and walked to the door, silently directing her, out of this place with the prize she had gained. A handful of hani lives. A promise—a *kifish* promise.

"The *hakkikt* will get my report," she said, not to let the chance pass. "He'll ask, kif." She walked out, relieved to find Haral still there, hand on gunbutt, at a standoff with the kifish guards. "Come on. We're leaving."

Hilfy came panting onto the bridge and leaned on Tirun's chair back as Khym arrived, as Geran and Tully turned at their places. "We lose any of that accessway?" she asked Tirun.

"It's still sound," Tirun said. "Pressure checks up. We're in contact with Jik and Goldtooth on open channels—captain'd skin us if we used that code—"

"What do they say?"

"They're not happy. Jik says he's getting some people out onto that dock—"

"Gods rot it, Tirun, Pyanfar's with the kif—we've got to get in there—"

"Hilfy—" Tirun turned around, flat-eared and dark-eyed. "For godssake you're talking about the gods-be *hakkikt!* What do you want, raid *Harukk?* They've pushed, we got 'em. What more do you want us to do? Go in shooting and get 'em both killed?"

Hilfy let her breath flow out, leaning there on Tirun's seat back and being the fool and knowing it. Her joints were loose, either the run topside or outright panic. "Get Tahar up here. It's her crew the captain's risking her hide for—and Tahar knows those kif out there."

Tirun's ears lifted and flicked back and forth in indecision. "Well, we can use the extra hands up here. *Do it,* Geran." Another wide flick of the ears, a rumpling of her broad nose and lift of her lip. "And it occurs to me we've got one other mind on this ship knows those kif."

"Skkukuk," Hilfy said. A falling feeling hit her gut. She knew her own unreason on the matter; and it was Tirun's command. Tirun's say. Not hers to argue in any case.

"If we need him," Tirun added, with another twitch of the ring-laden ears—veteran of a hundred crises, Tirun Araun, cagy and hard to take. And all the while her sister Haral was out there in trouble with Pyanfar—one forgot that the two of them had that desperately close personal bond. Tirun *made* one forget—doing what wanted doing with no hesitation, no self-interest between her and the ship. Hilfy looked at the old spacer and at Geran Anify, whose efficiency covered com and scan, trading functions back and forth with Tirun like a smoothly functioning machine while the world came apart about them; and for the first time in her adolescent life she truly knew the measure of her seniors, and knew what she had yet to reach—It hit like a blow to the gut, what she was, what they were; and she was not likely to live long enough to get there. But even that thought was a selfishness Tirun would never take the time for in a crisis. She saw it all in a flash like a shellburst, a moment of panic; and then she found the wobble in her knees had gone away and she discovered some scrap of something Tirun-like in a place she had never known she had it stored, down where she kept her temper.

To a mahen hell with yourself, Hilfy Chanur, and your fears and your precious wants—The ship's got a problem.

"—Tahar's on her way topside," Geran said; another light flared on the com panel, another call; Hilfy itched to reach out and intercept it, taking her station back, but Geran had it, Geran occupied her seat, Tully positioned next to her where Geran could assist him, with his eyes firmly on the scan, watching for any move out of Kefk: even something as small as a construction pusher could take them out, if it went crashing into their vanes; or if some saboteur EVA'd out through a service access and limpeted some explosive to *The Pride*'s big vane panels, or to the yoke. It would cripple them at the least. Make any jump out of Kefk uncertain, enough to kill them if they tried it. Enough—

—o gods, to force them to negotiate—

"Tirun," Hilfy said, leaning on Tirun's chairback. "If they damage us—they've got Pyanfar and Haral in reach. That may be what they're trying. Take us if they can; cripple us if they can't—Nothing personal on the kif's side: if you get a chance to put an uppity ally down and subordinate 'em, you do it."

Tirun's ears moved. She heard. Hilfy flung herself the few paces across the deck to take the seat next to Tully, to take over scan function with eyes that could read and hands that could use the buttons.

And:

"—They were about eight kif," Geran was saying to someone on the com. "No. No. No, captain. Let me ask my—Let me— *Let me ask our duty officer, captain.*.—Tirun, it's *Vigilance.* Ehrran's sending crew out there to secure the docks."

"Gods rot it—*Give me that.*"

"She's just broken contact."

243

Thirteen

They rode the lift in *Harukk*, nine hani and two armed kif, and the door let them out onto the access level of the ship, into the dim light and colder air of that final passageway that was open to the docks.

We're going to make it, Pyanfar thought, which she had doubted down below, in the prison-hold. She had doubted everything until the kif got them to the lift and two got inside the lift car with them, outnumbered at least at that range and within that car; and she believed it almost entirely when she saw that door open and let them out onto the right level of the ship, in a corridor with no ambushes and no waiting contingent of kifish guards—just a way out. She glanced once at Haral in the course of a look over her shoulder at the kif and the Tahar crew, and caught a flicker of Haral's ears and eyes that worked like telepathy: same thought: *We're near, captain, maybe we got a chance of getting away with this after all.*

Pyanfar turned and kept walking at the pace their guide set. This time there were stares from passers-by, curiosity at last—recalculation what kind of game was being played here, she reckoned.

What kind and by whom.

"That damn fool," Jik said over com. *"She no do, she no do—"*

And broke contact abruptly. That was Jik's comment on Rhif Ehrran's decision to go out on Kefk docks. Hilfy heard it along with the rest, and looked to her right as captain Dur Tahar arrived on the bridge at a fast pace.

"What's this about my crew?" Tahar said forthwith, out of breath.

"We're working on it," Hilfy said, and got out of her seat, scan set to alarm. Dur Tahar on *The Pride*'s bridge deserved at

245

least one crew member on her feet to fend her off Tirun's neck, and Khym had just risen to appoint himself—*not* the best situation.

"So what's going on?" Tahar asked, casting a look toward command, where Tirun, in urgent communication with Gold-tooth, had no time for talking. "What's the trouble?"

"—Well, what do they say?" the gist of that conversation ran from Tirun's side. "The *hakkikt* got any good reason why we just got our airlock shot up? Why we got gods-be vermin running loose all over our lowerdeck? Where's our captain, huh? They know?"

What *Mahijiru* command had to say to that was inaudible.

"Captain's out trying to get your crew released," Hilfy said to Tahar. "Meanwhile we just got shot at. You want to take a crew post, captain? We're up to our noses in problems. Scan would be real helpful just now. Tully doesn't read real good."

She expected objection of rank. Tahar lowered her ears and started for the indicated post with never an objection. But Tirun swung her chair about before Tahar could get to it. "Belay that. Goldtooth says he can't reach Sikkukkut. Kif are being obstinate. They're stalling. It wasn't any accident." Tirun got out of Haral's chair and with a wave at Dur Tahar, hurled herself into Pyanfar's instead. "*Sit*," she said, hitting the seat's turn-control. "Take number two, Tahar. I'll fill you in. Hilfy—Khym. Get that by the gods kif up here. I want to talk to him right now."

Hilfy caught Khym by the arm and moved.

No one sat in Pyanfar's place. But it was being done. No foreign clan sat in *The Pride*'s seats. But they did that too—they did *anything* that gave them a better chance.

They pelted down the main corridor; and of a sudden there was the electric thump of the generators coming up, a vibration all down *The Pride*'s steel spine. Khym skidded on one foot and stopped, turning back before Hilfy grabbed him by the arm.

"That's power-up!" Khym cried.

"That's precaution," Hilfy said, and hauled him about again into a run for the lift. "We're not pulling out. Tirun wouldn't do that. For godssakes follow orders."

So our systems are all the way hot. So the kif know we can move. Or shoot. They can take us out. We can take Kefk out with us, if it comes to that. That's what Tirun's letting them know.

"Kkkt," the kif said, on guard at *Harukk*'s lock—"kkkkt:" when it saw what it faced, softly and with an edge a hani could read. Pyanfar kept her hand near her gun and flattened her ears as it looked like challenge.

Then the guard waved them on with the dark flourish of a sleeve. Pyanfar strode out into the chill of the access and turned abruptly, with a scowl for the kif and a concern that *all* their party made it out clear.

The Tahar crewwomen walked as best they could, Gilan on her own, Naun and Vihan doing the best they could to support Haury between them. Nif and Canfy with Tav. Haral came last, dour and grim—*no bending, no show of weakness.* Sikkukkut had not forgotten them; Sikkukkut would be curious what they would do, would be suspicious of connivance—

—would cut their throats at the first hint things were not as represented to him; or at the first suspicion hani motives had confounded him.

Come on, keep it moving—Pyanfar put impatience into a scowl at Gilan Tahar and spun on her heel the instant Haral cleared the lock, outbound and downbound for the docks.

"Kkkkt," the kif Skkukuk said, lifting his hooded head from his nesting-spot on a clean bed in a clean cabin. "Kkkt. Young Chanur—"

"Up," Hilfy said. She kept her gun in holster and made no move to threaten. Khym was behind her, and that was more than sufficient.

"I am weak with hunger. Hani, it is a waste—"

"Get up, kif. Move. We've had a little problem with your dinner. It's all over the ship. Our hatch has a nice new burn-scar on it. That's what we want to ask you about."

"Treachery," Skkukuk said. He stirred himself and came off the bed, using a hand to catch his balance. "Kkkt. Treachery."

247

"You understand it real well," Hilfy said. "Come on. Let's go topside and discuss it with the crew."

"Not my doing," Skkukuk said, "hani, it was not my—"

"*Out!*" she said.

Skkukuk came out toward them. Khym grabbed himself a handful of kifish robe at Skkukuk's nape, and Skkukuk twisted and rolled his eyes in alarm. The jaws clicked alarmingly. "I offer no resistence, I want to go to your bridge, there is no need—"

"I'll bet you do," Hilfy muttered, and grabbed his arm while Khym took the other side, hauling the kif along clicking and protesting. Something black and small fled down the hall and scuttled around the corner into a lesser-used corridor.

"I have given you my weapons," Skkukuk hissed, struggling to free his arms. "Let me go! Let me go, hani fools! I am yours, I am loyal to the captain—"

"In a mahen hell," Hilfy muttered.

They reached the bottom of the ramp, down by the gory row of heads, and Pyanfar looked back yet again with her hand laid on the AP gun she wore. The Tahar crewwomen did the best they could, keeping Haury Savuun on her feet and keeping moving; and Haral brought up the rear—clear enough that Haral would gladly have gone faster on this stretch, but there was a limit what the Tahar kin could do; and there were several watching clutches of kif, down by the dockside and up above them on the ramp. "Kkkkt," the sound came to them from above and below. "Kkkkt."

Well, look at those fools, Pyanfar translated it to herself, and her hair bristled. She glanced a second time at the Tahar, at *Moon Rising*'s first officer in particular, the moment that they passed out of earshot from either end of the ramp. "*Ker* Dur's safe," she said quickly. "That's the truth. And I got your ship back. You're free. How are you doing?"

Gilan's eyes seemed to pass in and out of focus, a widening and narrowing of the dark-in-amber as what she had said got through. "Captain's with you—And *Moon Rising*?"

"Both in my keeping. You're safe. We're getting you back into safe territory fast as we can, going to turn you loose—*Don't you wilt on me, gods rot you, look alive!*—We've got a long way to walk, Gilan Tahar. No transport on this dock *I* want to use."

"Aye, captain." Gilan's voice was hoarse and earnest. "We're with you."

Kif were to either side of them. Kif clicked and muttered, in mirth at the sight they saw—

Sfik, Pyanfar thought with a sinking heart. This ragged crew of hani demonstrated—gods help them all—hani vulnerability. *Not enemies, the kif don't see Tahar as enemies to us. We're treating them wrong. It's a trap, by the gods, Sikkukkut's own sense of humor, not to send them with a kifish escort. To make us take them ourselves. Hoping one of them will faint on the way and make a scene.*

"Captain—" Haral said from a few paces behind.

Kif were taking up a stance along the dockside ahead, across their path. It was walk through or detour round.

"We don't bluff," Pyanfar said, and put an exaggerated swagger in her step, her hand on the gunbutt. On a second thought she took the AP from the holster and flicked the safety off, carrying it barrel-down and swinging as she walked. "*Out!*" she yelled down the way, and gestured at the kif with a wave of the gunbarrel. "Praise to the *hakkikt*, you scum, we're on his business with these prisoners and you'll keep your noses out of it!"

There was slow movement, timed, she reckoned, just to brush against them in retreat—pushing it. But they were going to move. She kept the gun free and her finger on the trigger, reckoning Haral behind her was taking a similar attitude and backing her up.

"*Hani!*"

A kifish shout behind them. She stopped at once and braced wide-legged with the gun aimed two-handed at the crowd in front; and knowing Haral was turning similarly braced toward trouble behind them.

"Three of 'em," Haral's voice reached her backturned ears; back brushing against her back. "Migods—! A kif's been hit! Someone shot a—"

249

Pyanfar let off a warning shot over the first kif's heads as she spun to Haral's side and saw one kif on the dockside deck and a second and a third in the act of falling. *Sniper-fire.* Her other foot hit the deck and she shouldered Gilan Tahar in a move toward the tangle of gantries and lines along the ship-berths. "Cover," she yelled. "Rot it, out of the open, *move* it!"

The Tahar crew ran. She stopped and spun again to see Haral covering their retreat, with fire coming from somewhere, with kif falling and kif firing back and a chittering of kifish voices in tumult.

"Get cover!" Pyanfar yelled at Haral, and Haral fell back in haste. Fire popped across the deck and exploded off something behind them with a deafening shock and a sting of particles.

"Go!" Pyanfar yelled, turning and waving the Tahar vehemently to move—to gain what ground they could; and: "Move!" Gilan Tahar echoed the order, and lent her good arm to drag at Canfy Maurn. "Come on! Let's get out of here!"

Kif firing at kif.

Akkhtimakt's partisans, rising against Sikkukkut.

"We got a revolution on our hands," Haral gasped, coming up beside her with her arm about Haury Savuun and Tav and Naun panting up behind. "Captain—we got—"

A shot exploded near, and Haral flung up her gunhand to shield her eyes, staggering. Pyanfar spun about and pasted a shot in the general direction of fire.

"By the gods, they fire this way, they get it—"

—A volley came back, a clanging thunder, an impact that flung her backward and cracked her head against the deck. She rolled and scrambled for cover, blind.

"*Captain!*" Haral cried.

"Hold it, hold it," Geran said as chaos erupted out of *The Pride*'s com, "I got it—Tirun, I got Jik on one and a kif on two—"

"Give me the kif," Tirun said; and listened while Hilfy and Khym held their own kif immobilized and furious between them.

"Shut *up!*" Hilfy said to Skkukuk; and maybe it was that or maybe it was the news pouring out over the console speaker that hushed him.

"—*Honor to the* hakkikt *Sikkukkut an'nikktukktin,*" the voice said. "*A suicide attack by rash elements has endangered your captain and her subordinate. We are presently moving in reprisal. We advise all ships in this command to exercise extreme watchfulness for external attack during this crisis.* Pride of Chanur, *refrain from rash action. The* hakkikt *will deal harshly with these adventurers.*"

"Watch him," Hilfy muttered, and dived for com. "Tully, shift down. Take number one scan—Tahar captain's got monitor up there—"

Tully bailed out. She hit the seat and snatched up a complug, coming into the tail of Geran's few seconds delayed retransmission of the kifish message down the mahendo'sat link. "Jik's got that," Geran muttered, as the kif finished and *Aja Jin* acknowledged on that channel.

"This is *The Pride of Chanur,*" Hilfy sent back on the kifish link, unauthorized and in haste. "*Harukk* com—where's our personnel? What location?"

"*I will ask authorization for that information, Chanur com.*"

"They fear," Skkukuk hissed at her back. "The *hakkikt* Sikkukkut is in distress—He does not have them prisoner. . . ."

Hilfy twisted round in her chair and stared full into the kif's red-rimmed eyes. "Why?"

"Because, young Chanur, he says they are in danger. He admits a weakness. He promises retaliation. This is not control of the situation. It is not his doing. He would not claim weakness even in subterfuge."

And on the Jik-channel, suddenly over general speaker: "*We got personnel out on dock, we got* Mahijiru *move—Where be Pyanfar,* Pride of Chanur? *You got contact?*"

"Against *what?*" Hilfy asked Skkukuk. "What's going on out there?"

"They will be Akkhtimakt's partisans, young fool. They hope for a coup. There is likely fighting even within *Harukk.* The *hakkikt* will be dealing with that personally. He will be occupied."

"Likely truth," Dur Tahar said, swinging her chair around from monitor.

Hilfy rose to her feet with her pocket pistol in hand and aimed at Tahar. "That's your recent side, Tahar, isn't it—Akkhtimakt's?"

Tahar laid her ears back. Her eyes showed white and she froze in the chair. "Shoot or listen to me, Hilfy Chanur. The kif's telling the truth. But it's local stuff—*nothing*'s coming in coordinated with this. Nothing I know about, leastwise. And I might have. No. It's a local thing. We got my crew and your captain out there on the docks. The kif's guessing but he's guessing straight—they're not where the *hakkikt* can lay hands on them right now or he would have. No, this goes right along with that assault on the lock down there. Kefk station is counterattacking—Akkhtimakt's partisans are making their move and your captain and my crew is caught in the middle, for godssakes—*listen to me and put that gods-be gun down*—"

Tirun spun her chair about, still listening to something, the complug pressed hard in one ear. Her eyes flicked. "Ehrran's just engaged the kif—Gods *rot* it, they're shooting up the docks out there—"

"I'm going out there," Khym said flatly.

"You go with the rest of us," Tirun said, and hurled herself to her feet. "Gods be, the captain's going to skin us, but when we get 'em back she can skin me first. We seal *The Pride* up tight and we get ourselves out there. *Move* it! Geran—shut her down. Put the lock on autoseal." Tirun crossed the deck at speed and opened up the weapons locker, handed a pistol toward Dur Tahar.

"I," Tully said, on his feet, holding out his hand. "*I*."

Tirun slapped her pocket gun into his hand. "Use it."

"Come on," Hilfy said to Skkukuk, and grabbed him ungently by the arm, claws out. "We put you back below."

"Leave him one of two on this ship?" Tirun said. "No thanks. This son goes. First. First out. You lead the way, kif."

Skkukuk's wiry body straightened. His head lifted to his full, gangling height. "Give me my gun back, hani."

"Suppose you *take* one," Tirun said, nose rumpling. "From the *other* side."

"Captain—" Haral leaned over her in the shelter they had reached along a towering gantry, in the red tracery of fire that speared the smoke and popped off the wall and the gantry-structure. Haral had a piece of cloth from somewhere and was daubing away at her face with a rough earnestness while her ears rang and the fire went back and forth. It was all far away; and then it came clear, Haral's anguished face and the pain in the back of her head. "Gods be," Pyanfar muttered, struck the ministering hand away and tried to move. Her skin hurt. She put a hand to her middle and wiped away a dew of blood.

Metal fragments. Splinters. She was peppered with them. She felt their prickling. Felt the slickness on her fur. She blinked at the Tahar crew's frightened faces—saw Haral looking white around the nose, and panic in Haral Araun was so out of character it shook the world.

A second shaking: this time an AP blast against the station wall over their heads, and another spatter of particles. A five-hundred-weight of severed hose plummeted to the deck close enough to kick up the wind. "Gods!" Pyanfar cried, and got over onto her knees, searching after her gun in an empty holster.

"Here." Gilan Tahar slapped the heavy butt into her hand, and she looked from the Tahar first officer to her own, saw Haral take a careful look out from their cover, and turn a dour face back toward her.

"Pretty thick out there," Haral said.

"A weather report, for godssakes—we got any cover further on?"

"We got ourselves pretty well set here—"

BANG! Another thunderclap, another shower of metal from overhead.

"They're hitting the gods-be wall!" Pyanfar yelled. "The gods-be fools are going to take this whole gods-be dock for a spacewalk—"

"That's volatiles down the dock," Haral yelled back over the

253

sudden thunder of fire, pointing at the cans down the way, cans with the deadly yellow combustibles sticker. "If we run that way we can draw fire on that and get fried real good, captain!"

"We sit here we got our choices too! How long's that sister of yours going to wait, huh?"

"I'm expecting Jik," Haral yelled.

"Well, he's *late!* And we got a fool lot of crew's going to be out here on this dock after us if they don't get assurance out of Sikkukkut, and I don't think he's in any position to give them any! We got to *move*, cousin, cans or no cans." She turned a look on Gilan Tahar, on a woman undone with bloodloss. Gilan had gotten a bandage tied on the wound in her shoulder, but it was soaked. Haury Savuun was still conscious, by what force of will the gods only knew. "Gilan—we got a long sprint ahead. We don't want to do any shooting—don't want to attract any attention near those cans." She fished in her pocket and drew out the light pistol, handed it to Gilan. "In case. But you by the gods stay with us."

"We're with you," Gilan said, and the overhead erupted and another length of hose and a length of pipe hit the deck and bounced erratically the other way—as easily into the midst of them.

"Come on!" Pyanfar yelled, and headed for the next berth in a roiling of laser-riddled smoke so thick it obscured the next support girders. She sprinted for the cans with the yellow circles, remembering then that kif were at least partially color-blind.

Vermin scampered pell-mell as they charged up to the airlock, as the hatches shot open, inner and outer, as Tirun turned to hit the lock-close in the dim orange passage. Hilfy ran, skipped aside from the collapsed cage and the can—

Explosives—Hilfy surmised in horror, explosives, if the kif were willing to decompress the dock. "Go!" she yelled, bristled all over, and Skkukuk darted past with kifish speed, Khym and Geran gaining. Tirun banged into the collapsed cage and cursed; and Hilfy clutched her gun and pelted after Khym around the bend of the passage with Tully and Dur Tahar hard after her.

"Tirun!" she yelled, half-turning there; but: "Go!" Tirun yelled back, running hard enough at the outset of their course—Tirun would do the best she could, lame in any run, and bring up their rear and cover their backs even if she commanded. "Get down there, get clear!"

Hilfy ran, passing Tully and Tahar, coming up behind Khym as they reached the pressure gates at the bottom of the ramp. There was a gentle, distant popping of fire.

A shot went off the inner wall. Skkukuk skipped and dodged, and dived for cover. "You get, get!" a mahe cried, rising from concealment near their ramp, waving a frantic arm. There were mahendo'sat holding positions over near the cargo-console, Jik's people or Goldtooth's. Hilfy sought cover immediately behind the gantry control console and the sheltering metalwork of the gantry itself, leaned there with her heart pounding in terror and glanced back to see Tirun and Tahar and Tully pelting off the hazard of that ramp. *O gods, gods, get us through this—I can't, I can't*—She flung a look the other way, thinking Khym had gone to cover in a stack of cargo-cannisters ahead.

He had not. "*Na* Khym!" she yelled in dismay, huddled in the solidity of her shelter, for Skkukuk dashed on, and Khym followed. "Gods be! Khym! Uncle! *Stop!* Wait!"

Then it all seemed clear, the direction of the kifish enemy and the direction of the fire where Pyanfar and Haral had gone, and she shook fear away to some far cold place and gave up on either survival or mortality.

Go on, *Hilfy Chanur, go on, is a man crazy who knows he's overdue to die or a kif on his way to switch sides again—Go, fool, Haral's out there, and Pyanfar—Run til the shots come your way and then you cover and shoot til they stop. It's all real simple, kid.*

Haral's voice, instruction-giving again.

And Pyanfar's: *Gods-be fool.*

Fire hit, tracing smoke puffs on the deck where Khym ran.

Pyanfar darted behind the cans of volatiles and kept running, feeling the ache in bones and head with every jolt of her feet on

255

the deckplates. The air was too thin and burned the lungs, the ammonia-smell cut with acrid smoke and laced with ozone. She sobbed another breath in a glance back and stopped to wave Gilan and Naur on with a pass of her hand, covering them without firing—wanting no notice they could avoid, but keeping her finger hard on the trigger. Vihan had Canfy by the arm, guiding her; Nif and Tav sprinted after, and hindmost, Haral with Haury flung over her shoulder, jogging along at what pace she could make, Haury no small woman and Haral not smallish either. "Go," Pyanfar yelled at Gilan's back, and ran back to intercept Haral as Haral struggled away from the explosive cans, grabbed Haury as Haral ducked out from under her body—no word of debate from Haral. Haral ran; and Pyanfar shouldered Haury to a carry and jogged on, all but blind for want of air. Fire suddenly burst on the far side of the cans—evidently kif saw the hazard marker—not hitting them. They kept going, reached a tentative shelter behind a cargo-loader. But next was an open space, and a run to scant shelter by the stress-supports. After that, another run, and another and another.

And if Jik had not reached them by now, there was something impassable in the way.

"*Na* Khym!" Hilfy cried, beckoning her uncle to safety, and he *heard*, by the gods he heard, and spun about and came sliding in by the gantry-side beside her all reeking of sweat while Geran slid in beside.

"Gods," Geran said, pointing ahead, and there was Skkukuk still going, face on with a kif who stood frozen in his path as if it were trying to analyze the matter; then it fired, twice, zig and zag, where Skkukuk *had* been, but not where he was, which was coming down right onto the kif and taking it in a rolling tangle of black robes.

"Uhhn," Khym said.

The uppermost kif's head was bearing down and down at its enemy—gods knew *what* it was at. Hilfy shuddered and looked back as Tully came sliding in, and Tahar and Tirun with him,

256

Tully desperately out of breath and white and gasping in the ki-fish air. "Where's Skkukuk?" Tirun asked. "Gone over?"

"Gods know which one's alive over there," Hilfy said. "I don't and I don't care." She lifted the gun then, not clear she was going to shoot, but not clear she was not going to either.

Tirun's hand shot out and grabbed her wrist. "What are you into? What are you into, Hilfy Chanur?"

The fury on Tirun's face bewildered her; and came home slowly. Hani. Home. And civilized behavior.

"It's a gods-be *kif!*"

"Who's in command out here?"

She let go the tension in her arm and lowered her ears in silent deference. Tirun let go her hand, ears flat.

"Py-anfar," Tully said, and took her by the shoulder, hard. "Hilfy, Py-anfar—"

She threw off his hand.

"Can we for godssakes move it?" Dur Tahar asked.

"Move," Tirun said, and led this time, until others of them outstripped her, Hilfy among the first. Like a shadow in the tail of her eye she saw the kif leap up and run into the shadows on the far dockside, saw him weave out again and into cover, and afterward, vanish.

Pyanfar stumbled, hit the deck on her knees and threw herself to save Haury's skull—but Haral and Tav were quick enough—both of them to save Haury, and Haral to grab Pyanfar by the belt and haul her into shelter of a metal console.

"O gods," Pyanfar moaned, and made shift to get her torn knees under her. Her chest and gut ached, her loins were water, the knees long gone. She leaned on Haral's arm and on Haral for a moment. "I'm too old for this—o gods—"

"Aye," Haral panted, the two of them braced against each other, holding to each other.

And the world went to fire and sound.

"Good gods!" Geran cried; and Hilfy: "Something's blown up! My gods—"

Smoke came rolling down the dock like a black wall, obscuring knots of miniaturized kif, throwing laser-fire into visibility before it swallowed everything. And there ahead was a cluster of red-brown amid all the black and gray, figures huddled together on dockside.

"Look!" Khym yelled, and headed that way, strung out as they were; and Hilfy grabbed Tully and ran. Sirens blew, decompression alert, the triple-interrupt pattern screaming alarms transspecies and translogic—the docks had gone unstable. An outer wall was in jeopardy. And gunfire never stopped. AP bursts peppered the inner walls and kif barred their way, backs turned toward their advance, kif pinning down that group of hani ahead.

Geran opened up and Hilfy did—braced for aim, then moved, for Khym risked their line of fire—rushed ahead firing as he went, and no matter his wretched marksmanship, there was no need to pick targets. The kif beseigers scattered, and Hilfy stumbled a step as a splinter hit her calf—recovered herself and kept going, in and out among the girders and cables. Shots still came and she fired back at opportunity, rounded the last corner of their cover and dashed across the open dock and in among the hani at Geran's heels.

And stopped cold.

They were Ehrran crew, blackbreeches, who stood up to face them with guns and rifles leveled.

It was the second impact for a battered skull, and Pyanfar lay there retching after breath tinged with sweat and smoke and volatiles. Sound when it returned was a chilling siren above the thump of fire. She felt something stir against her, got her eyes focussed against a tendency to cross and stared over into Haral's dazed face beside her.

"I think they got those cans," Haral commented from the horizontal. "O gods, my head." And started moving, swearing in soft incoherency. Pyanfar rolled on an elbow and sat up. "Gilan—"

The Tahar were all moving—sluggish, but moving. Haury proved life by turning on her side and trying to get up on her own; and Pyanfar swung round and looked where the sudden wild fix of Haury's eyes went. Reflex pulled the trigger of a gun she had forgotten she was holding. The shell burst on a kif in mid-leap; and the remains thudded off their sheltering can-stack onto the deck hardly a bodylength distant, while three more kif scrambled for other cover.

She sat there and shook like a beardless youngster; and got her breath and shoved her heels and one hand under her. "Keep going," she said in a voice that failed of steadiness, and looked up at the blank, unfriendly pressure-gates of a sealed ship-berth. An empty berth. Or a ship that had gone on protective internal seal. Those gates in that case could open and pour out hostile kif into their refuge at any moment. "We've got to keep going—"

"Haury," Tav objected, wobbling to her knees. "Haury—"

It was so. Haury Savuun had to be carried. None of them had the wind for it. Pyanfar sank down where she was, on her heels, and Haral rested again, holding her hands locked behind a skull that was doubtless doing what hers was, a steady throbbing to the siren that told them the dock might blow to vacuum at any moment.

"They've stopped shooting," Nif Angfylas said, her torn ears lifting despite her exhaustion. "Maybe—"

A shot hit the wall and they ducked and covered.

"Gods-be!" It was a new angle of fire, one forty five degrees oblique to their escape route, and high. "They got us pinned!"

Another shot exploded and Pyanfar tucked her head into her arms, lifted it with a sinking feeling—the *opposite* quarter, that time. "They got us *crossed*," she yelled at Haral. "Get that gods-be sniper ahead highline, and watch your head! I think he's on the second level walkway!"

She scrambled for the firepoint at the other corner of their shelter, and felt a presence close behind—Vihan Tahar, looting the dead kif's body for weapons and cartridges. Vihan ducked in close at her shoulder while Haral took the other side of the console that offered their tiny triangle of shelter from incoming fire. Smoke roiled up and drifted in blinding clouds. Whatever had gone up had gone in a hurry—it smelled like fuel; but a lake of it still burned on the dock, sending a hellish glare up to the smoke-palled overhead. No fans working up there. The air ducts had gone sealed, not to encourage the fire.

It did not encourage breathing either. Her nose ran. She wiped her eyes with a gritty hand and checked the AP's cartridges. Down to six. No reloads. "We don't waste any fire," she said to Vihan, at her back. "Anything compatible on that kif?"

"Got two rounds," Vihan said, pressing them into her hand. "His gun's in pieces."

"Get over there and see if Haral needs them worse; I got—"

Fire came back; Pyanfar took a chance shot the moment she saw the brighter flare of a rifle aimed their way, and dived aside, shouldering Vihan to the ground.

Thunder broke and particles showered. Pyanfar bobbed up again and restrained herself from spending another round. "May have got the son—I can't tell—"

Kif moved, a number of black distant figures cavorting in rolling smoke, about a lake of golden fire. *Sikkukkut's? Akkhtimakt's?*

BOOM! from the other side. She spun about and plastered herself flat against the console with Vihan and Naur crouching tightly by her; and rolled a glance at Haral, who had pressed herself mirror-image to the far corner of the console. "Get him?"

"Dunno," Haral said, and wiped watering eyes with a bloody fist. "Gods-be smoke—"

Pyanfar looked up, where the smoke got lower and lower, obscuring most of the gantry now, lowering a black, asphyxiating ceiling over their heads. "They by the gods got to get those fans going soon." A cough threatened. Her own eyes were pouring water and her throat was raw.

"We got four berths to go to next dock," Haral said.

"We got a gods-be blockade up there," Gilan said. "We got kif between us and any way out of here. Snipers got your own people pinned for sure. Sikkukkut's *losing* this one—"

"Console—" Pyanfar said suddenly; and twisted onto her knee, found the storage panel at her back with the kifish lettering that said EMERGENCY.

She ripped it open and hauled out the first aid kit. Plasm foam. A few plastic bandages. She shoved the contents in Gilan Tahar's direction. No injectables. No class two supplies. No oxygen.

A second glance up. There was a console call-post up over their heads, if anyone wanted to stand tall enough to try for it. And tell the kif in central their precise position when it got to that. But the sirens warned of more imminent disasters. The smoke worsened.

She thrust herself onto her knees and risked her head standing up, a quick snatch at the mike and jab at the recessed channel buttons. The connection failed. "Captain," Haral cried in anguish as she tried the input again.

"Gods-be short gods-be cord—*Pride,* hello, *Pride,* do you receive?"

"Try *Mahijiru!*" Haral shouted from a crouch a little below her shoulder. "And get your head down!"

"*Captain,*" a hani voice came back, hoarse and weak and static-riddled. "*What's going on?*"

"Chur? *Chur?* Where's Tirun? We need help—"

Something whistled past her head and blew at her back; and something seized her about the legs and got her down, hard, Haral wrapped about her as a second burst blew the corner off the control console and roiled up a stinging smoke. Somewhere in the murk overhead, bending metal shrieked and groaned in protest, something huge giving way—

"Gantry's going!" Nif Angfylas cried. "Migods, the gantry's going down—"

Pyanfar rolled, as the metal-sound rose to a shrill grinding. She was not the only one to grab for Haury; Tav Savuun had her sister's other arm—there was general collision of well-meaning help; and in the smoke above, the gantry's dissolution progressed one shrieking degree at a time, impelled by inexorable station-spin and its own steel mass. Cables dropped down and writhed like snakes.

261

"Run!" Pyanfar yelled, struggling to stand and pull Haury with her. Her knees wobbled as she drove against the weight. *"Run!"*

"Where's my aunt?" Hilfy Chanur yelled at the Ehrran over the noise of fire, of a horrendous crash from somewhere down docks. "What's their position? Have you seen them?"

"Out there!" the seniormost Ehrran crewwoman yelled back with a wave at the stinging smoke. "How should I know?" The Ehrran's mouth fell open as Tully came panting up with Tirun. "My gods—you fools!"

Hilfy shot out an arm: Tully evaded the Ehrran's grasp with a suck of gut and a spin onto the off foot—and Hilfy flung herself with a hard body-check into the path of the Ehrran officer.

"You bastard whelp—" The Ehrran raked a left hand full of claws into her shoulder, and out of nowhere a heavy blow shot past Hilfy's shoulder and the Ehrran rocked back with a curse.

Tirun's arm. Tirun, ears flat and with an AP gun in the other fist.

"Go!" Pyanfar yelled, seeing the gantry hit and bounce and thunder like a perversely living thing, now toward the kifish positions and now toward their own, broken and in several places achieving independent motion. Smoke skirled and billowed in the shock.

And for a precious moment there lingered that random violence on the docks as great as the kif and bouncing the kif's way.

"Go!" Pyanfar yelled. Tahar crew grabbed Haury by one arm and the other, and they limped along. Pyanfar spent one precious shot toward the far side of the dock to keep kifish heads down: Haral fired another of their diminishing few rounds and Gilan Tahar let off a third as they ran and lurched their way behind the cover the careening wreckage gave them.

"Come on!" Tirun shouted at the Ehrran officer. "Save it for later, Ehrran—we got troubles down there! You want to talk about it later, fine. Let's get the rest of us off that dock down there!"

"That's Tahar!" The Ehrran pointed at Dur Tahar. "By the gods, Chanur—"

"Save it," Tirun yelled. "Settle it later, hear? You're talking to a ship's chief officer, woman, and we got hani lives at stake!"

"I don't regard any Chanur patents. You got a man out here carrying arms, you got a non-citizen alien and a known fugitive with weapons—" The Ehrran raised her gun. "You're under arrest, you, all of you!"

"You gods-be lunatic," Khym roared, and waded forward. A shot went off and he spun half-about—

—"Gods!" Hilfy cried. Muscles jumped and she launched herself at the same time as Geran and Tirun and Tully.

But Khym had never stopped; he made his spin full about, landed a sweeping blow and the Ehrran went flying across the dock. Hilfy's own particular target had her mouth still open when Hilfy hit her and sent her knee up into an unprepared gut—straightened the Ehrran up with a gunbarrel under the chin and shoved her back. "AP," Hilfy snarled, in case the Ehrran crewwoman had any doubts what was at her jaw. "Drop yours— *drop it!*"

The woman rolled her eyes and a gun thudded to the deck. Hilfy shoved her loose. Ehrran were scattering, in full flight, two delaying to pick up their senior, unconscious on the deck. Tully was picking himself up off the deck, bleeding at the nose and wobbling, but he still had his gun in hand, and the last Ehrran lit out running. Hilfy sucked wind and aimed the AP into the running midst of them—

Her finger froze. Her hand shook. None of them fired. None of them did. The blackbreeches crossed the open area, plunging through a group of oncoming mahendo'sat who had appeared out of cover.

"Mahend' nai casheni-te!" Tirun yelled at them. "Hai na Jik!"

"Pau nai!" the shout came back, with waving of arms. *Wait!*

"Blast you, *help!*"

Fire spattered the dock. The mahendo'sat dived back pellmell.

"Gods-be!" Tirun yelled, not her voice but a hoarse, cracking sound; and they dived for cover on their side.

"You all right, Khym, you all right?" Geran asked.

"Uhhhnn," he muttered, hand on his upper arm. Blood leaked through. His eyes were dark and dreadful to see. "Let's move."

"Come on," Tirun said; and leapt up. Down-docks. Into the fighting. The only way any of them chose to go.

"*Where's Tahar?*" Hilfy yelled, suddenly missing the captain as they started to run. "Tirun—Tahar—"

"Go," Tully yelled, waving his arm to indicate direction, gasping for breath as he tried to keep pace. "Tahar go!"

Ahead of them.

Pyanfar stopped and turned and sent another shot toward the inner wall of the docks, covering the three carrying Haury Savuun, putting herself and another of their last rounds from the AP gun between Haury's all-too-exposed person and the chance of another shot.

A shot came back low and exploded off the downed gantry in a hail of fragments. A second shot went past her: hit the back wall. She staggered and flung herself to the minimal cover they had, wiping a haze from her eyes.

"We got to keep going," she said, shoving Nif aside to drag at Haury's limp arm one-handed. "We got no more choice, we're out of cover—"

"Where's Jik?" Haral gasped, as they kept moving, as a shot whumped off the far wall and something blew up behind. "Gods rot that earless son, where *is* he?"

Where's Tirun? Pyanfar translated that. Haral did not ask that, neither of them wondered *that* aloud.

And from overhead, everywhere, thundering through the public address:

". . . Ktogot ktoti nakekkekt makthaikki. . . . kothoggi go-thikkt nakst . . . sotkot naikkta . . . hakkikktu . . . skthsikki . . . nak sogkt makgotk Kefku. . . ."

264

"Sikkukkut's—claiming—victory," Naun Tahar gasped, laboring along with Canfy Maurn against her.

"Good luck to him," Pyanfar gasped, and grabbed Canfy from the other side as Canfy stumbled.

And stopped, blinking tears in the smoke. A lone figure sprinted toward them, hani and armed.

Fourteen

"Gods," Pyanfar cried, "that's Dur! *Tahar!—where's the rest?*"

Dur Tahar yelled something back, and came sprinting through the fire-zone into Gilan Tahar's path—cousin and cousin in the stinging smoke, Gilan and Vihan, the distant kin, in hasty embrace—A glance round as Pyanfar struggled up with Canfy in tow and Haral came running, glancing at every third stride to the darkened farside where sniping went on unabated.

"Where?" Pyanfar yelled at Dur Tahar. "Gods rot it, *where's my crew?*"

"Ehrran—" Tahar gasped, and whirled and caught her by both arms, "they tangled with Ehrran—Pyanfar—" Tahar gasped a second mouthful of air. "Come *on—*"

Pyanfar scanned her up and down in hopes of AP rounds; there was nothing, nothing but the smallish gun in Tahar's grip against her arm. Her heart sank. "Tahar, where's Jik? You seen Jik or Ismehanan-min?"

"Gods-be mahendo'sat're off across the docks holding their own positions—I don't know."

"Captain!" Haral sang out, and Pyanfar looked beyond Tahar's shoulder to more oncoming figures, red-brown hides and one white shirt that shone through the smoke like a natural target.

"Gods rot it!" Pyanfar screamed at the lot of them, "we got snipers! *Run!*"

Her heart was up in her throat as her own crew came charging up through the smoke. Tirun, Geran, Hilfy, Khym and Tully, all of them armed; Khym bleeding down his arm, Hilfy from the calf, Tirun limping along hindmost and grimacing in pain.

"What kept you?" Haral yelled at her sister.

"Hey," said Tirun, panting to a halt in front of Haral, swinging a gesture back at the smoke-hazed dockside. "What'd you want? Next time you arrange a party, Hal, for godsakes give us the address!"

"Let's get out of here!" Pyanfar yelled, and waved an arm. "Get the injured on their feet, let's get out of here!"

Khym gathered Haury Savuun up in his arms, leaking blood on both of them, and Tirun and Geran flung an arm each around Canfy Maurn as they gathered breath and wits and headed through the smoke and the din of sirens—the deep bass sirens of dock-emergency alternate with loudspeakers that clicked and hissed and thundered with kifish threats and instructions.

A sudden glare of sodium-light broke through the smoke-haze at the left, close, a light alive with shadows as robed figures came pouring out of a ship-access.

A hundred kif, a whole ship's crew headed out toward them at some summons; or having finally made its collective mind up which side to join. New sirens wailed, high-pitched. Fire hailed about them from the flank as other kif aimed at the sudden breakout.

"*Run!*" Pyanfar yelled, and veered off across the dock, limping. She turned and let off her last shot where it counted, into the heaviest firepoint that was putting shots past their ears; and turned again and ran, breathless and all but blind toward a set of girders near the main freight-chute, where a conveyor went up into the station's upper levels.

And stopped cold as she rounded the corner and saw the band of kif in front of her, APs leveled dead at her and her empty gun.

Gods-be, she had time to think, in profound self-disgust.

An AP shell landed in the full middle of the kif. Her forearm flew up on instinct to save her eyes, her legs flung her sideways and sprawling to confuse hostile aim; and she rolled to her knees staring up at a single standing kif who held his AP gun widely to the side, non-combatant beside a smoking heap that had been five of his fellows.

"Captain," Skkukuk said as cheerfully as she had ever heard a kif speak, about the time her crew poured about her and made a defensive wall.

She struggled for her feet, almost sprawled again, but Tully, closest to her, caught her arm and saved her balance.

"I feared treachery," said Skkukuk with a wave of his hand at the rest of the crew. "And so I followed you my own way, captain, to be of service."

"Gods save us," Tirun muttered.

"I would advise," Skkukuk said, "going back to the ship. The *hakkikt* Sikkukkut will reward you for that prudence."

"You're a gods-be agent of his!" Pyanfar cried.

A flourish of dark sleeves and weapon-hand toward the smoking pile of kifish corpses. "Did I not offer you my weapons? I am *skku* to Chanur, no other, and I have given you your enemies." Skkukuk turned and pointed down the docks toward their own berth. "The mahendo'sat have secured the docks a little further on. Come and I will show you a safe route."

"Then move," Pyanfar said numbly. "Get!"

"Keep this one from my back!" Skkukuk pointed a claw in Hilfy's direction. "This one—"

"You gods-be filth!" Hilfy cried, and headed for him, but Pyanfar caught her arm. "*Move* it!" Pyanfar yelled at the kif.

The kif turned and started off in a dash for other cover. "Go," Pyanfar said, still holding Hilfy's arm, and hurled her into free, passing her in the tracks of the kif who sped as a darting wisp of black in the smoke.

Whump! Overhead, power went up full: lights glared; the distant burr of fans reasserted itself. Kefk station was trying to live. The loudspeaker blared, inaudible in the other din.

There was a sudden fading-out of fire; as if entropy had set in—decreasing organization and increasing desire on the part of kif still involved to exit the affair with whatever gains they had: alive. Defense only, at this point.

Follow the kif. Trust the kif who had saved her skin. They were within com range of *The Pride*. Pyanfar reached for the pocket com in her limping jog, coughing as she went, blinking smoke-stung tears and hoping to the gods all the rest were still behind her as she tracked the light-footed kif from cover to cover. "Chur," she gasped into the com. "Chur, it's Pyanfar—do you hear me?"

No answer.

A dozen strides more. "*Chur!*"

269

Silence from the com. It could have gotten broken in a fall. It could have.

Skkukuk came to a sudden halt in the shelter of a set of girders just ahead, and plastered himself against it. Strobe-light flashes lit the smoke ahead, a ceiling-towering series of upward cycling lights that sent ice to a spacer's heart.

Of a sudden the whole station shuddered. Pyanfar flailed wildly for balance and found it next Skkukuk in a thunder of rollers and hydraulics and an airshock that made the ears ache.

"O gods," she said, braced against the column and staring into that roiling cloud as the rest of the company reached them. The great doors of the section seal had shut. *The Pride*'s dock, *Mahijiru*'s, *Vigilance*—*Aja Jin*—They were cut off.

"What—" Khym's voice came in gasps, subdued and frightened. He leaned there gasping, his back to the girder cross-brace, Haury limp in his arms. "What happened?"

"I don't know," Pyanfar said. The whole station seemed suddenly quiet. The sirens were silenced. "Could've been holed—" *The Pride.* O gods. "We're cut off." She tried the pocket com again. "Chur. Chur, you receiving?"

She expected no answer. She got none. She flicked it to standby again and met Geran's eyes by accident. "Probably can't get through," Pyanfar said on a gasp. "Range is marginal through that seal."

"*Ktiot ktkifik!*" the PA thundered—*EMERGENCY.* And went on and on—Skkukuk lifted his dark, long face the better to hear, but the kifish words garbled in the echoes.

Another burst of loudspeaker sound, from another direction, likewise kifish, groundlevel.

"Captain!" Haral caught her arm and pointed, where four brightly-garbed mahendo'sat had broken from cover and begun to run their way, close at hand.

Desperately.

"Gods be," Pyanfar said, "*Jik*—Jik, you gods-be earless— *What's going on over there?*"

Jik came panting up and caught her arms, at the end of his breath. "You come—got go—other way. Got no go ship, no go ship—"

"*What happened over there?*"

"Got trouble. Got *Vigilance*—I think she blow dock. I think she go—go Meetpoint."

"Where's *Mahijiru*? What's *Aja Jin* doing, for godssakes? You got contact? Clip a vane off her! Stop her!"

Jik blinked and gasped. "I lose contact *Aja Jin*—*Mahijiru* power up. *Mahijiru*—*Vigilance*—go."

"He's after her."

"He no shoot, no shoot. Pyanfar, I not know what he do—*Get off dock, we got get off dock! My partner—he—he not shoot!*"

"You mean he's going *with* her? He's going out with *Vigilance?*"

"A," Jik gasped, shaking at her. "We got—problem—"

"Kkkt," said Skkukuk. "Understatement. The *hakkikt* will not be pleased with mahendo'sat or hani today."

"Shut *up!*" Pyanfar snarled; and Skkukuk lowered his head between his shoulders.

"Look about you," said Skkukuk.

"Uuhhhnn," Haral said; and Pyanfar looked.

Shadows appeared throughout the smoke-haze, robed shadows converging on them from all sides, with caution and deliberation. And leveled rifles.

"These will be the *hakkikt*'s," Skkukuk said. "Since they aren't shooting. They will get us back to your ships. Or not, at the *hakkikt*'s pleasure. Kkkt. I trust you did not offend him in your interview."

"Beware of Goldtooth," Pyanfar muttered distractedly. "Beware of Ismehanan-min."

"What say?" asked Jik. "What talk, Pyanfar?"

"Not me. Stle stles stlen. The stsho warned me at Meetpoint. From the start. I paid a lot for that advice. A whole lot." She shoved her empty gun into its holster and stared bleakly at the narrowing circle of kif. "Everyone stand easy. Let's just hang onto the guns if we can."

"Kkkkt. Parini, *ker* Pyanfar?"

"Appreciated, *hakkikt*." Pyanfar reached out a sooty, blood-

271

caked hand as an attendant brought a cup to her side, there in *Harukk*'s dim hall.

Back to starting-point. The blood and stink of the docks still clung about them. They bled from wounds. The *hakkikt* elected to have his nose offended; or delighted in the sweat and discomfort of the opposition.

All of them were there—Hilfy, Tully—seated at Sikkukkut's low table, on insect-legged chairs: Haral; Dur Tahar; Jik; the others of all three crews, hani and mahendo'sat alike, were back in the shadows along the wall, among armed kif—except Haury Savuun. The kif had taken her over objections as violent as they dared make. To no avail. It was surely mockery that set Hilfy and Tully as guests at Sikkukkut's table; with Dur Tahar: and unsubtle mockery that set Skkukuk to crouch on the floor near the *hakkikt*'s chair, robed knees up near hooded head, arms tucked out of sight, a very, very quiet Skkukuk, as small as he could make himself.

Sikkukkut sipped his own cup. It was not parini. Dark eyes glittered. "Should I wish a dockside destroyed in future," Sikkukkut said, "I will only invite my friend Pyanfar. First the stsho, then the mahendo'sat, and now the kif. You are an expensive guest."

"I'd like to contact my ship."

"Of course you would. Kkkt. Chur Anify has stayed aboard. Wounded, you say. But perhaps still capable at controls. Who knows? While, Keia, the complement you left on *Aja Jin* is— virtually complete. Except yourself and the four with you. You and Ismehanan-min withdrew your crews from the docks simultaneously with those of *Vigilance*. To put it directly—*why?*"

"A. Because—" Jik fished in his pouch for something and came up with a smoke and a light. He carried the stick to his lips and lit the lighter.

"*No,*" said Sikkukkut definitively, and Jik paused and looked his way, fire burning and smokestick unlit. "No," Sikkukkut said again.

Jik froze a moment as if undecided, then deftly snapped out the lighter, palmed the smokestick and returned both to the pouch.

"Well?" said Sikkukkut.

"Number one sure thing *Vigilance* got make trouble." Jik hooked a thumb toward the company over by the wall, and gestured loosely toward Tahar immediately at his right. "Ehrran go out, they think maybe they get hands on Tahar. Want bad. No good try. *Pride* don't let. Things go bad quick, shooting start, those hani they get recall order. *Pride* crew, they try find captain, a? Try cross dock—they same time save Ehrran hides all by accident. They run like hell, board ship. When I see *Vigilance* crew go off dock, I get quick nervous."

"You knew what she would do." Sikkukkut sipped at his cup, flicked his tongue delicately about his lips. "Well, as we sit here at our ease, *Vigilance* is still outbound—on Meetpoint vector, without a doubt. Your colleague and partner Ismehanan-min is running hard behind her, not a shot fired on either side. Does that surprise you, Keia?"

"Damn sure surprise," Jik said darkly.

"And yourself, *ker* Pyanfar?"

Pyanfar lowered her ears. "*Hakkikt*, I told you what Ehrran would do the minute she got the chance. No, I'm not at all surprised."

That did not well please the *hakkikt*. She saw the tension in the hand that held the cup, the relief of tendons and veins under the dark gray skin. But the snout gracefully lifted from the cup again. The dark eyes blinked ingenuously. "What would you do, *skth skku?*"

Vassal of mine. Pyanfar flattened her ears further. "What's necessary to do. The *hakkikt* has no need of my advice, but our motives still coincide. *Pukkukkta.* Ehrran plainly aims to kill us, and I don't intend to let her have a sitting target. By your leave, *hakkikt.* What I said before the fighting started is still the truth."

"Sktothk nef mahe fikt." Safety snicked off a gun close at hand. A guard held a pistol close to Jik's head and Jik never flinched, but picked up his wine and took a measured sip.

"Do you trust our friend Keia?" Sikkukkut asked.

"*He's* still here. He was doublecrossed in this, same as us."

"Was he, truly? Second question. Is he *my* friend?"

"Like always," Jik said with a tilt of his imperiled head, and the cheerfulness faded to a frown. "*Hakkikt*, long time I work with Ana Ismehanan-min. He sometime crazy. I think maybe he got idea, maybe go this place—"

"*Humans*." Sikkukkut leaned forward, set down the cup on the low table and rested his hands on both his knees, long jaw outthrust. "Ismehanan-min knows precisely what he is working for. *Mahen* interests—which have perhaps very little to do with mine.—Or even yours, *ker* Pyanfar. I wonder what those two discussed with each other before Ismehanan-min left dock. I wonder what agreements exist. Would *you* know these things?"

"I've never found Goldtooth forthcoming on his plans." Exhaustion threatened her with shivers; or it was the cold; or a sick dread of the narrow path they walked, and where it might turn next. The gun stayed at Jik's head; and there was ice in her stomach and her nose ran. "He left Jik here. So he didn't tell Jik anything. Same as me. Didn't trust me with what he was up to."

"But he trusted—I do dislike that concept—*trusted* this Rhif Ehrran."

"That isn't necessarily so, *hakkikt*. I don't think he *trusts* anyone."

"But Ehrran has a ship on her tail and at last report, she isn't firing. Is this characteristic of Ehrran?"

"It is if she's got a hunter-ship on her back. She's only brave on docksides. I haven't seen her style in space. But I know she's no match for Goldtooth in a fight. *Couldn't* be, if he's got position on her. Fancy ship, fancy computers, lot of programmed stuff. Programs for everything. But I wouldn't bet *Vigilance*'s arms systems against *Mahijiru* and I sure wouldn't bet her crew. Evidently she thinks the same."

"There's another possibility. Ismehanan-min boarded *Vigilance* during his time in port."

Her ears pricked up. It took no acting. "After or before he came to me, *hakkikt?*"

"After. Does it suggest something to you?"

"It might still have been on our business." The sweat stung in her wounds. Across the chamber, against the wall, Canfy Tahar

274

slowly slumped to the deck, not fainting, but at her limit. Tav knelt by her; and kifish guns angled toward them. They still had their own weapons: kifish etiquette. But theirs were not out of holsters; and the kif's were.

And the gun never left Jik's temple. He sipped carefully at his drink and ignored it. But that was calculated and dangerous too.

"I doubt it was," Sikkukkut said. "If they are not acquaintances, who sleep in one bed, they will be by morning. Is that not a hani proverb?"

She blinked. "A hundred year child. That's a mahen proverb. Longtime trouble from a single act. Goldtooth's either making a serious mistake, *hakkikt*, or he's still acting in your interest. He'll be at Meetpoint. Where he's useful. And it's not his style to consult with his partners."

"What of that, Keia?"

"I *like* that smoke now, *hakkikt*."

"Answer."

Jik's eyes came slowly to Sikkukkut's. "She right. I think maybe Ana got idea put self where make lot trouble."

Sikkukkut's long nose drew down somewhat. It was not a pleasant expression. He folded his long fingers beneath his outthrust jaw. "Kkkkt. Shall I observe, Keia, that your position is uncomfortable? That I presently have ships proceeding toward jump, to warn my enemies. That this whole diversion on the docks—*diversion*, Keia!—was perhaps created to give those two ships time to get away."

"They be kif who fight, *hakkikt*."

"They are worms who lacked initiative until someone moved! Don't tell *me* kifish motives! Don't play the innocent with me, mahe, or you will find me other than civil!"

Pyanfar flexed claws and tried to think past the pounding of her heart. Hunter-vision tried to take over. She forced the black edges back. "She was in port with him."

"Him," Sikkukkut said sharply. The kif turned his attention in her direction, went off one hunter-fix and onto her. "Who?"

"Goldtooth was at Meetpoint at the same time as Rhif Ehrran; same time as you, *hakkikt*. I'm wondering who was talking to whom back then. You talked to Goldtooth. He intimated that

275

much. But who met with the stsho? And who met with whom in stsho offices?"

"No," Sikkukkut said, as if he had turned a thing over in his mouth and decided to eject it, delicately, his eyes burning and full of estimations. "No. I don't credit the stsho with that much nerve."

"Then," said Pyanfar, "the stsho at least thought they were on the inside of this business. They *thought* they were ahead of the hunt. Or leading the hunters where they liked."

"Suppositions are a shaky bridge, *ker* Pyanfar. Particularly when the waters are deep. You wish to distract me. You see—I know *friendship*. I put it with *martyrdom*—in the category of terms useful to know. Friendship—is also subject to rearrangement of loyalties. At the most disadvantageous moments. Believe me that I understand the exigencies of allegiance-trading and advantage. Let's operate within them. Shall we? Let's consider what prompted this attempt on my life . . . since that's surely what it was. Let's consider how it incidentally created the timing for escape—*Vigilance* uses its guns as it parts our company and breaches an entire dock to hard vacuum, a dock conveniently free of mahen or hani casualties. Not of kif. But remarkably your crew and the crews of *Mahijiru*, *Aja Jin*—Keia; and of course *Vigilance*—were not on that dock when it decompressed."

"We weren't in a favorable situation ourselves, *hakkikt!*"

"Be still, *ker* Pyanfar, and let my old friend Keia do this explaining. Let him tell me how *Aja Jin* was so fortunate in its timing. Do you want your smoke, Keia?—*Take* it. Perhaps it will facilitate your thinking."

"A." Jik reached again into the pouch, kept his movements measured: I am not in a hurry, they said. You do not force me.

And that sudden patience on Sikkukkut's part raised the hair on Pyanfar's nape. Stalk and circle. *Take* it. Have what you want at my hand. When I choose. If I choose. Your addiction is your vulnerability and I control it, I demonstrate it to these others and you must bear with that.

And soon with other things.

See, hunter Pyanfar, how easy and how perilous the fall from my favor.

276

Friendship and kinship is your addiction. I can twist that knife too.

Godssakes—as Hilfy let go a long, careful breath—*sit still, niece.*

The smoke rose, gray wisp against the orange sodium-glow; and swirled above Jik's head, taken by the ventilation. "I tell you," Jik said easily, and gods, there was only the faintest fear-smell: he was that steady. The strong smoke subdued other olfactory cues, deliberate strategem, perhaps. "I tell you, I not happy. Ana be old friend. But politic make different. We be mahendo'sat, *hakkikt.* I know what he do. He hedge bet." He made a gesture with the smokestick and put the lighter away. "He call me fool. Maybe I be. We not trust Ehrran either one. I know damn sure when Ehrran crew make fast withdraw from dock we got trouble. *Mahijiru* already got close up tight hatch. I send all crew aboard, tell get hell off dock, try get damn fool hani—" He gestured Pyanfar's direction, and over his shoulder at the others. "They going find captain. Damn sure *I* got no way stop. Damn good idea anyhow. Pyanfar be val-u-able ally. Maybe do favor to *hakkikt,* a? Rescue Pyanfar." Another large drag at the smoke. It leaked slowly from his nostrils. "I *not* like whole ship company go out from *The Pride*—but they go quick get off dock. This number one good idea. I don't trust Ehrran. I run like hell, try catch these hani. No good. We get pin down. *We* got no *hakkikt* permission be on dock, a? Every damn fool out there want shoot us. *Hani* go through. We stuck. So got one job then—hold way open for hani, back to ship. We do. We hope Ana take care Ehrran. I think he do. He *follow* her. I still got hope he got good idea. Maybe help. He not like tell what he do. This maybe make friend lot nervous. Make me damn nervous now, a? I be like you, *hakkikt.* I always like know what my friend do."

"Your *friend* has left you in a precarious position. Or you've elected to stay and lie to me."

"A. No lie. Got know truth to make lie. I not know. He not talk to me."

"Meaning nothing can extract this truth from you."

"Not got. What want? I say give you Kefk. I give."

"Kefk is in ruins, Keia. It seems a dubious gift."

"You got lot *sfik*. You step on Kefk, go 'way, take lot more prize, a? Akkhtimakt no got. You be rich, you fix, easy."

"Ah. But you still suppose Ismehanan-min is going to support us at Meetpoint."

"He no like Akkhtimakt."

"I take that for granted. You yourself serve your Personage and not me. As he does. Doesn't this mean some agreement of action?"

Jik drew another large breath of smoke and sought a place for the ash afterward. There was none. He tapped it and let it fall to the floor. "I serve Personage. I tell you plain I got reason want see you be *hakkikt*. I think this be good for all. So I serve Personage. Serve you. Balance, *hakkikt*. You be Personage we recog-nize. You got lot *sfik* with mahendo'sat. These be crazy times. Better kif got good smart Personage, a?"

"Flattery, base flattery, Keia. Diversion again. I tell you I am not persuaded it was kif who began that fight on the docks. And this—"

—in a blink Sikkukkut's arm shot out, and guards pounced on Skkukuk, hauling him upright.

"Kkkt!" Skkukuk's protest was throat-deep and anguished.

"He's *mine*," Pyanfar said tautly. *Never back up, never back down, never let a kif get away with any property.* "A present from you, *hakkikt*."

Dangerous. O gods, dangerous. So was flinching when that long-jawed face turned her way.

"It remains yours," Sikkukkut said.

"It gained a little *sfik*," said Pyanfar. "In our service out there. I'd like to keep it."

"Kothogot ktktak tkto fik nak fakakkt?"

The question went to Skkukuk; and Skkukuk drew his head back as if he wanted to be far from Sikkukkut's sight.

"Nak gothtak hani, hakkikta."

"Nakt soghot puk mahendo'satkun?"

"Hukkta. Hukktaki soghotk. Hani gothok nak uman Taharkta makkt oktktaikki, hakkikta."

—No. Desperately. *I saw no collusion. The hani argued over possession of the human and Tahar and left, hakkikt.*

A wave of Sikkukkut's hand. The guards let Skkukuk go and he collapsed back into a head-down chittering heap beside the table.

"So he attests your behavior," Sikkukkut said. "Your *sfik* still powerfully attracts his service. I wonder is it hope of you or dread of me so impels him."

"He's useful."

"And as we speak, *Vigilance* and Ismehanan-min hasten to betray us at Meetpoint. What attraction can they find there, I wonder, that impels Ismehanan-min to abandon Keia here to my pleasure—Do I not correctly recall a mahen proverb, Keia my friend, that green leaves fall in storms and the strongest friendships in politics?"

"Long time friend, Ana Ismehanan-min."

"But he would let you die."

"Like you say, politic. Also—" Jik pinched out the smoke and dropped the butt into his pouch. "Also Ana lot mad with me." Jik's eyes came up, liquid and vulnerable and without the least doubt. "He know I work with tc'a. Fool, he say; Jik, you be damn fool involve methane-folk. Ana, I say, I not much worry, I long time talk tc'a. Got lot tc'a know me, long time. I want tc'a come here to Kefk—fine. Dangerous, maybe. I think now maybe knnn got interest. Maybe good, maybe bad—"

O, deft, Jik. The methane-breather connection. That's one thing Sikkukkut has to be afraid of. For godsakes don't overdo it.

Jik shrugged. "So, Ana be lot upset. Lot knnn interest this human thing. *Lot* interest."

Profound silence. Pyanfar found herself holding her breath and daring not get rid of it. She kept the ears still; and even that betrayed the tension every posture in the room already betrayed, kif and hani alike. Tully's eyes darted to Jik, to her, to the kif, the solitary, sapphire-glittering motion in a gray and black world.

"Yes," Sikkukkut said. "There would be interest on their part. And it has also occurred to me that we have a source of information here among us. At this table. Tully—you do understand me, Tully."

O gods—She saw Hilfy's minute flinching; the tension of muscles in her, in Tully, in Haral—*Look this way, Tully*—

"I understand," Tully said at his clearest, looking straight at Sikkukkut with never a look or a pause for advice. "I not know, *hakkikt*. I not know route. I not know time. I know humans come quick."

A long moment Sikkukkut gazed at him as she glanced between them. A visible shiver began in Tully's arms, his hands upon his knees. "You and I have met before on this matter," Sikkukkut said. "But how fluent you've become."

"I be crewman, *hakkikt*, on *The Pride*. I belong captain Pyanfar. She say talk, I talk."

Gods help us, be careful, *Tully.*

"Where will they likely come?"

Now Tully looked her way, one calmly desperate look.

"Do you know?" Pyanfar asked, pretense, not-pretense. He continually baffled her. "Tully, gods rot it, *talk*."

He looked back toward Sikkukkut. "I not know. I think humanity come Meetpoint. I think Goldtooth know."

"Kkkkt. Yes. I think so too. So does Akkhtimakt, who stripped that knowledge from your shipmates. Who has what that courier carried, information that—doubtless—has sped to points in mahen space. Truth, finally, arrives from the least likely source. You amuse me—Tully. You endlessly amuse me. What shall I do with Keia?"

"Friend," Tully said quietly, evenly. His best word. Almost his first word. His fall-back word when he was lost.

"But whose?"

There was silence. Long silence.

"I think that Keia will be my guest a while. Go back to your ships. I shall release your crew, Keia—in time. I wouldn't impair your ship's operation. And I'm sure your first officer is quite competent."

Jik reached for another smokestick. No one interfered. He slid a look Pyanfar's way. *Go.*

"Right," Pyanfar said in a low voice. "I take it we're dismissed, *hakkikt?*"

"Take all I have given you. You'll board by lighter. The dock access is not useable."

"Understood." She rose from the insect-chair, in the murk and the orange glare; and signed to her crew and to Tahar. Jik sat there lighting his second smoke and looking as if that were the most ordinary of companies to be left in.

O gods, Jik. What else can I do?

"The *hakkikt* promised *all*," Pyanfar said to the guard, her ears flattened and her nose rumpled. "I want the wounded hani. Savuun. Haury Savuun. You'll know where she is. You'll bring her."

It pushed—about as far as they could push. "Yes," the kif in charge said, stiff—all over stiff. The hostility was palpable. Not hate. There was no *hate* in question. It was assessment—what the foreigners' credit was with the *hakkikt*. When to kill. When to advance and when retreat in the *hakkikt's* name. A kif did not make two mistakes.

Yes. It turned and gave orders to that effect.

It was a silent trip after that—down through *Harukk's* gut to the hangar-bay; and no relief at all until they had gotten down near the large boarding-room, and Haury arrived on the other lift—dazed, wobbling on her feet as they brought her out, but limping along with kifish help. From Haury a lift of the head, a momentary prick of the ears and widening of hazed eyes that betrayed confusion, then a taciturn expression, a wandering sweep of the eye that took in friends and guards and the boarding-lock. Gods knew what she had expected being brought down the lift. But only the tautness about her jaw still betrayed emotion—a hani long-accustomed to kif, grim and quiet. Eternally playing the game that kept a kif alive.

"We're getting out of here," Dur Tahar said when Haury and her guards came up close. "You all right?"

"Fine," Haury said in a hoarse whisper of a voice. That was all. She gave Pyanfar one long uncommunicative look; and took her sister Tav's help in place of the kif's. There were bandages about her ribs. Plasm on her wounds. The kif had done something for her at the least . . . with what courtesy was another question.

"Go," said the kif on the docks, with the wave of a dark hand toward the waiting lighter-access. "Compliments of the *hakkikt*."

Praise to him stuck in the throat. Pyanfar favored the kif with a stare and stood there with hands in her belt, near her empty weapons, while both crews boarded. Haral stood with her. They went aboard together, down the short, dark tube past the hatch.

No suits necessary in the lighter, thank the gods: nothing kifish would have fit. Pyanfar walked the center aisle into the dim, utilitarian rear of the cargo lighter, where Chanur and Tahar sat side by side on the deep benches. Up front, the kifish pilot gave confirmation to the launch crew in hisses and clicks and gutturals. Pyanfar sat down, belted in as the lighter whined in final launch-prep, sealing its hatch to the ship. The lighting, such as it was, limned the pilot and co-pilot up front in lurid orange, making shadows as they moved. The cold air stank of ammonia and machinery.

No one spoke. They swayed and braced as the lighter moved out of the bay on the launch boom—smooth, not a shudder in the arm. Well-maintained, was *Harukk*. Pyanfar noted such details, recalling the balky loader *The Pride* had tolerated for years. No glitches in this sleek killer-ship. No little flaws even in things that had tolerance. One knew something about a captain from such detail as this, and Pyanfar stored the information away among the other things she knew of Sikkukkut an'nikktukktin, inquisitor for Akkukkak, conniver from Mirkti, prince and lord over ruined Kefk.

The boom grapple thunked and let them free in their armored little shell as the shadow-pilot reached out a thin arm and put in a gentle thrust aft. Beyond their shadow and the glare, the massive side of a neighboring kifish ship hove up in the double viewport and spun off as the lighter accelerated and maneuvered at once, leaving the rotational plane and letting station spin bring *The Pride* to its approach-point.

Arrogant, Pyanfar thought, irritated with the cavalier exit maneuver. *There's a flaw for you.*

Grandstanding for the passengers. Sikkukkut would have this pilot's hide for that. Then, remembering the access ramp to *Harukk* and its awful ornaments. *Literally. O gods, gods, Jik—*

Kif talked to kif as the viewplate dimmed to dark. They went inertial now, freefall. From here on out the tricky business was up to the onboard computers and Kefk's guidance—nastiest of all maneuvers, getting up to the emergency access of a ship at dock, on computerized intercept among the vanes and projections of ships locked to a rotating body. They did not propose to use the cable-grapple and winch in, but to engage *The Pride*'s own docking boom and come in on *The Pride*'s power. That took one access code to activate the hatch and boom—one precious key into *The Pride*'s computers, handed to the kif. That code had to be changed immediately when they got aboard. *Damage my ship, hotshot, and I'll have your ears.*

Easier to worry about a botched dock or a code switch than worry about other things. Like no contact with *The Pride*. "Your ship does not respond," the kifish officer had said when she had asked the docking request transmitted. And that meant Chur was not answering. Chur *could* not answer. Geran knew it and sat back there with the rest, silent and uncommunicative and with no expression at all when Pyanfar chanced to look her way.

Chanur estate. The courtyard gate where Geran and Chur walked in one day, young and catching eyes wherever they went with their delicate Anify beauty—Chur all pleasantness and Geran sullen-silent even while Chur was asking favors of the Chanur lord and a place in Chanur's household. "Watch them both," the old lord had said, *na* Dothon, her father. "Watch them both." Chur of the ready smile and Geran of the ready knife.

It was the knife in Geran's mind now. Bloodfeud. Pyanfar knew. She gnawed her mustaches with dread of what might already exist on *The Pride*, and fretted at the delay of using the lighter; and loathed the procedures and the kif with their dark hand into *The Pride*'s codes, their presence at her vulnerable downside access. Allies. Allies—while they did gods-knew-what to Jik.

Traitor, was a word she thought, among other words for Ana Ismehanan-min. *Vigilance* had to be going for jump by now and *Mahijiru* sped after—Goldtooth knowing, by the gods, *knowing* he was leaving Jik in a desperate bind—But *not* knowing he had left Jik a prisoner. She refused to believe Goldtooth had known his gods-be fool of a partner would have *not* gone immediately back aboard *Aja Jin* with his crew, that the loyal fool would have headed down that dockside personally, hunting a hani friend, trying to get them clear of that threatened dock and clear of kifish retaliation.

And gotten himself caught by the kif. Alone.

Soje Kesurinan commanded *Aja Jin* now—an able woman: all Jik's people were first-rate, and his second in command was no fool. Would not become one, she hoped. Gods, she hoped.

Treachery on all sides. Only the kif had betrayed no one. Only the kif had stood by their word. Like Skkukuk, back there, a forgettable lump of shadow at the lighter's extreme rear. Skkukuk, who had never yet played them false.

Loyalty?

Your sfik still attracts his service, Sikkukkut had said of Skkukuk.

And wondered in the next breath whether it was the alternative which compelled Skkukuk's devotion to his new captain.

Chur. Jik. The cold of the air penetrated Pyanfar's skin and she sat numb while the *G* force of rollover hit and a vast white mass hove up in the viewport. Braking started in earnest as white and black alternated—as station rotation carried a kifish ship past their bow. Slower and slower. Lower and lower toward the place *The Pride* would occupy as the rotation carried it round. Doing it on the first pass, thank the gods. No waiting round. The access code would have gone out. *The Pride* would have her docking boom extended, waiting for them to make contact, continually tracking them, aligning the cone precisely with their approach.

The rim of the cone came up, gargantuan on their relative scales. The co-pilot reached and hydraulics whined, extending the lighter's own docking-stops, a ring of partials about the bow to prevent the cone swallowing them entire. They shoved forward into the green-lit interior.

Contact and gentle hydraulic rebound as the lighter's ring absorbed the shock and locked hard. Not a grind or grate. Perfect dock.

Arrogant and good, Pyanfar acknowledged. *But if he isn't, a kif's not a* Harukk *pilot, is he?* A dozen worries gnawed at her, tumbling in suddenly as she ran out of concerns to distract her. Another whine from the lighter's systems, a shuddering as *The Pride*'s years-unused boom dragged them down against the hullport, lock beeping at lock until the boom knew how much extension to leave on it.

They had stable *G* now, linked via *The Pride*'s boom to station's rotation. She unbuckled and felt her way over Khym's knee and Haral's til both of them unbuckled and made room for her next Dur Tahar. "Dur," she said, "you're welcome aboard. Want to tell you that again. We've still got a little time here, I hope to the gods."

"You've got your own troubles."

"We got medical equipment. *Moon Rising*—"

"We're pretty well set up to handle it. Got some nice stuff. Piracy—pays, Pyanfar. We'll see to Haury. And the rest of us."

She nodded, started to get up and make her way back forward as the deck rocked to final contact. The accessway whined, starting into place overhead.

Dur Tahar caught her arm. "What you did—going after my crew; staying *with* them—they told me how you and Haral carried Haury down that dock—"

"Yeah, well—"

"Hey." The hand bit hard. "Chanur. You want my word? You want anything we have? You've got it."

"You follow my lead in this?"

"Hearth and blood, Chanur."

She nodded slowly. There were things not to say aboard, where every word they whispered might be monitored up front; or outright recorded. Even dialect was unsafe: there might be kif translators. And there was a plenitude of things not to hint at—

285

like plans for Meetpoint; and what they were going to do if they found hani lined up on the other side.

Like what *Moon Rising* might do to her credit with the *hakkikt* if it ran.

"I vouched for you," Pyanfar said, "way out on the cliff's edge."

"We're with you, I said."

She looked long into Tahar's shadowy face, as the final contact boomed home, as the hatch opened and her crew unbuckled. She calculated again that they might be recorded: she gestured with her eyes toward the overhead, saw the little lowering of Dur Tahar's lids that acknowledged she was also thinking of it. "There's one ship in particular I want," Pyanfar said.

"Meaning *Vigilance*," said Tahar.

"Meaning *Vigilance*."

"No argument from me."

"Huh." An orange glare flooded in from overhead as the lighter hatch whined open. She turned and reached for the ladder without a courtesy to the kifish crew, as Haral scrambled up it ahead of her, where the pale circle of *The Pride*'s hatch was mated up to the dark access-clamps. Haral whipped a wad of kifish cloth from her pocket, grasped the space-cold lever and yanked. The hatch retracted in a puff of unmatched airpressure, a breath of clean cold wind. Haral looked down from the top of the ladder, in a bath of white light; Pyanfar waved her on, protocols be hanged; and Haral clambered up and through.

Pyanfar scrambled after, feeling the ladder shake as someone else hit it in haste. She came up in the brilliant white light of *The Pride*'s emergency airlock, turned round with Haral to pull Tirun through, and Geran next, and Tully, and Hilfy, and Khym with his arm bleeding again after the quick plasm-spray the kif had given it. She forgot, she outright forgot and had straightened to see to Khym when she heard something else hit the ladder and saw a shadow scramble up to them.

She bent and offered her hand: Haral was not about to. Skkukuk's dark, bony fingers hooked to hers and he sprang up into the hatch with kifish agility, head up and wide-eyed.

So the captain helped him with her own hand. Skkukuk's eyes

glittered and his nostrils flared in excitement, and she felt a frustrated disgust. The hatch whined down and thumped into seal under Haral's pushbutton command. The inner hatch shot open on the E-corridor. "Geran," Pyanfar said on the instant, turning. "Get!"

"Aye!"

And the smallish woman headed out of the lock at a dead run ahead of them. "Seal us!" Pyanfar yelled at the crew in general, leaving security to them, and lit out on Geran's heels, headed for topside, for—gods help them, whatever there was to find up there on the bridge.

She heard the hatch seal. Lights came on in the corridor ahead as the monitor picked up the sound of Geran's running footsteps and stayed on to the sound of hers.

The E-lift was in place, automatically downsided by the hatch-open command. The lift door opened instantly to Geran's push of the call button, and Pyanfar skidded in after and emergencied the door shut as Geran punched the code to send them on their way, up and then sideways as the car shot down the inner tracks for the main lift shaft.

Geran was panting. Her ears were laid flat, her eyes showing white at the corners. She was close to panic and she would not look Pyanfar's direction, staring only at the sequencing marker-lights as the lift ran its course up, up-ship and up again to the main lift-shaft and the corridor to the bridge.

There was no time for comfort now. And no use in it.

They hit the main-corridor running—a small, dark thing squealed and eeled away down a side passage, and another scuttled ahead of them in panic—*gods, what* is *it?*—Pyanfar let it go, her mind on one thing and only that; and one quick glance into the open door as they passed Chur's borrowed room—showed where Chur was not. The bed was empty, sheets flung back, tubes left hanging, the lifesupport machinery flashing with malfunction lights. Pyanfar spun on one foot and ran all-out after Geran, on and pellmell onto the bridge, where a thin, red-brown figure lay slumped in Hilfy's chair, head-down on the counter. A pistol lay by Chur's shoulder. Her arm hung limp over the chair arm.

Geran brought up, hand against the chair, and lifted Chur's head—used both hands to prop her back against the seat. Chur's jaw hung slack. Pyanfar reached to offer what she could of help, her own hands shaking.

Chur's ears twitched, the jaw shut, the eyes opened half, and she made a wild lunge for the counter and the gun.

Pyanfar caught her. "'S all right, it's all right," Pyanfar said, bracing her up and putting her face where the wild fix of Chur's eyes could register who it was. "It's us."

"Gods," Geran said, and sank down to her knees on the spot, against the chair. Her ears were back. She was shaking visibly as she clung to the chair arm. "Gods rot it, Chur—*What*'re you doing here?"

Chur's ears twitched and slanted her sister's way as she turned her head. "Everybody get out?" she asked, the faintest ghost of a voice.

The lift was cycling. "They're on their way up," Pyanfar said. "Even got Skkukuk back, worse luck."

"He with you?" Chur asked thickly. "Gods, I thought he was loose on the ship. Been seeing things—little black things— Couldn't find anybody aboard—Gods." Chur lay back against the seat-back and blinked, licked her mouth. "*Vigilance*—went, captain. I tried to get the guns to bear, tried to stop 'er. Missed my fix. Armament's still live—" She made a loose gesture toward Haral's seat. "Got back here—I don't remember— Gods-be little black things in the corridors—"

Pyanfar got up and walked over to her own post. The armament ready-light was flashing red on the boards. She shut it down and capped it and looked up as the lift door opened down the hall and their ill-assorted crew came running, kif and all. "She's all right!" she yelled out to them from the bridge, violating her own cardinal rule; and went back to Chur, only then realizing Chur had not a stitch on. "Migods," she muttered, with not a blanket to be had and two men—no, three—arriving on the bridge; and then decided no one cared. They were all crew. Even the kif Skkukuk, brought along willy-nilly. Tully

288

came rushing over among the rest, and Chur grinned and reached up and patted his anxious face right in front of Khym and everyone.

"Let's get you back to bed," Pyanfar said. "Gods-be med-machine's blowing its fuses in there."

"Uhhnn." Chur put a hand on the chair arm to lever herself up, and fell back. "Goldtooth," she said suddenly, hazily. "Goldtooth."

"What about Goldtooth?"

"Took out after Ehrran—blasted out this message—"

"*You get it?*"

Chur waved her hand at the com board. "In there somewhere. In the decoding—function—"

Pyanfar started to bring it through on the spot; and stopped with her hand on the board, remembering Skkukuk standing there. She turned and waved a hand at the crew. "Tirun, take station. I want a systems checkout. Fast. Geran, Hilfy, get Chur to bed. Haral, Khym, Tully, take Skkukuk to his room, then go wash up, patch up, and get back here double-quick. We got ops to run."

Haral's ears slanted. "You're worse hurt than I am."

The metal particles stung at every move; most of her exposed fur was matted with blood from pinprick punctures. Her battered skull throbbed with so many impacts she had gotten used to the pain. It was likely true she was the worse case. But: "Get," she said, because there was that message from Goldtooth in the decoder; and Haral read her by that silent way they had of thinking down the same line. Protest filed, Haral turned and made to gather up Skkukuk as she went.

"I am a valued ally," Skkukuk said, drawing himself up in offense. "Captain, I am not to have my door locked, I am not—"

"Shut up," Hilfy said, facing him by Chur's side. "Move it."

"This one means harm," Skkukuk said. "Kkkt. Kkkt. Captain—" He dodged as Khym reached for his arm. "They have taken my weapons! I warn you their intentions—"

"*Get!*" Pyanfar said. Skkukuk flinched and ducked his head, and Haral motioned to him again. *Shouldn't have yelled,* Pyanfar thought. *I shouldn't have yelled; the son did save my life, fair and plain.*

But he's kif.

They led him out and down the corridor, Haral and Tully and Khym together. And Hilfy and Geran turned Chur's chair about and with tenderest care bent down and lifted Chur out of it. "I can walk," Chur said. "I c'n walk, I just got tired—" But they swept her off her feet between them and carried her anyway, off the bridge and down the corridor, Chur mumbling protests all the way, only then and loudly realizing she had forgotten her breeches.

Pyanfar sank into the vacated chair and punched the recycle on the com-system. Nothing came up. Frustration welled up, changes in the systems, every time they looked, some new gew-gaw in the works. "Gods-be, what's access on the decoder?"

"That's CVA12," Tirun said from Haral's post. "To your one, I got it, I'm getting it."

It ran.

"Gods rot, it's in mahensi!" She cycled it again and sent it through the translator.

"Situation deteriorating," came the translator's droning voice. "Advise you human destination Meetpoint. Same mine. I got talk to one Stle stles stlen. Make maybe deal. Ehrran go; I go, same. Keep company. You clear dock number one fast, both. Got little fracas start."

"Gods blast him!"

"—Best chance I can give."

"Blast him to his own hell!—You know what you did, you smug bastard, you know where you left your partner?"

The message ended. Pyanfar cut it off with a shaking hand. Sat there with both fists clenched, until the black edges cleared from her vision. Then she carefully punched in another call. *"Aja Jin,* this is Pyanfar Chanur, come in."

Not on coder program. The kif down the row, the kif in station command—were undoubtedly monitoring even the so-called shielded-line. Everything. It was not politic to be too closely associated with *Aja Jin* just now. Or to talk in secret.

290

"Captain, this Soje Kesurinan, Aja Jin. *You back? You got news?"*

"Bad news, Kesurinan. Your captain's been detained. Him. Those with him. In the *hakkikt*'s custody. I think your personnel are going to be released. No word like that on your captain. The *hakkikt*—" Keep it neutral, keep it ambiguous, tip Kesurinan off to the situation as much as she could read between the lines. "— the *hakkikt* sort of wants to assure *Aja Jin*'s good behavior. After *Mahijiru* lit out. And to discuss the matter. You got any news on that?"

"They jump," Kesurinan said after a moment. *"Confirm. You got word captain's status?"*

"Just that the *hakkikt*, honor to him, wanted to talk to him. Alone. I left him in good health."

Honor to him.—*We're being spied on, Kesurinan, remember that; we're in real trouble. Don't press me with questions.*

A long pause on the other side. *"You got suggestion, captain?"*

"I suggest if you've got a good explanation what *Mahijiru*'s up to with Ehrran, it sure might help."

"I get," Kesurinan said. The strain came through the accent and the com-garble. *"I do number one quick."*

"If you learn anything let us know double-quick. I think your captain's situation is extremely delicate. I don't think he knows what the *hakkikt*, praise to him, wants from him. If you can come up with that it might help. Understood? We'll use what good influence we have."

A second long pause. *"Yes, understand. Thank you, Chanur captain. Thank you call us."*

"I'm sorry," she said, heartfelt, and broke the transmission. Propped her throbbing head on her hands and winced helplessly at touching one of several lumps on her skull. It bled. She felt the dampness and looked at the stain on the fur between her pads. She began to shiver. "I'm going to wash up," she told Tirun. "Can you carry on a while?"

"Aye," Tirun said without turning around. On the boards rapid checks were going, searches after surreptitious exterior damage which, if not the kif, Ehrran might have done to them.

291

Or *Mahijiru.* She could not believe in *Mahijiru*'s desertion. Could not believe Goldtooth had turned on them.

But it was politics. Like *han* politics, like the scramble for power that put herself and Ehrran at odds. In this case it was two partners who violently disagreed on how to deal with the kif—Jik who wanted compromise, and Goldtooth who played some other game, involving knnn; a game in which the stakes were perhaps too high, too unthinkably high, to put friendship anywhere in the equation.

The affairs of rulers, of Personages. Hani had never tolerated any divine right but the right of clans to decide their own affairs; or the rights of groups of clans to hold a territory: and hani never by the gods bent the knee to anyone but kin and house lord.

Honor to him. Honor to a prince of pirates who tortured her friends and laughed inside when a hani had to mouth politeness to him.

I'd pay him any pretty speech he likes for Jik's life; and I'll pay him something by the gods else, the first chance I get.

Likely he knows it too.

He wanted me before he wanted the mahendo'sat. Offered me alliance back at Meetpoint. He couldn't trust the mahendo'sat. He knew that. He knew how a hani could be snared: he appreciates what Chanur could be and do—the way the han *appreciates it, oh, yes, the* han *wants our hides on the wall. The* han *saw it before the kif did . . . what we were capable of after we took out Akkukkak, after we contacted humans. They saw it coming . . . if we were ambitious. And they thought we were. And they pushed us to it.*

She walked off the bridge, paused for a moment at the door of Chur's room, where Hilfy and Geran had settled Chur in again.

"Gods-cursed needles," Chur said to her.

"Sure. You tear loose of that again I'll have a word with you."

"Goldtooth's message."

"Ambiguous as ever." She saw the glance Hilfy and Haral gave her. "I don't know what he's up to." They would not have told Chur about Jik and his companions, not spilled any more bad news on her than they could avoid. "Stay put, huh?"

"Where's he going?"

"He thinks he's going to Meetpoint. So's everyone else we know. Big party going to happen."

"We?"

"Oh, yes. You can lay bets on that, cousin. We'll be there."

Chur blinked, turned her head to the side, where Geran was taping tubes at her elbow. "Captain's not telling all of it, is she?"

Geran pursed her mouth. Said nothing.

"Conspiracy," Chur muttered. And shut her eyes, exhausted.

"She did a good job," Pyanfar said, reckoning Chur could hear that.

"Yes," Geran said.

Pyanfar lingered there a moment, studied the three of them. Chur; Geran; Hilfy. None of them the same as they had been, excepting Chur, excepting maybe Chur. Geran's movements were quiet, economical, delicate; her manner was wry cheerfulness, and it was a mask. Chur sensed it, surely, knew the killing rage buried under it, Geran of the knife, Geran the silent one. Geran who smiled with the mouth nowadays and not with the eyes. And Hilfy. Hilfy had gone to whipcord and hairtriggered temper. No more young Hilfy; no more young at all. Hilfy had gone fine-honed and when she was quiet there was always a shadow-play behind the eyes, where things moved Hilfy Chanur did not talk about. There was sodium-fire and dark; and no bath took away the ammonia-stink and the blood.

But Hilfy had sat there in that hall listening to her tread the narrow line with this kif, the same as Geran had sat there consumed with worry about her sister and never betrayed it; and Tirun had done her job down to the line same as Haral, where they were needed.

And sitting there side by side in that dark council hall—Tully, answering the kif calmly; and Khym, whose self-control had never broken, two males who had held their anger quiet inside and waited for orders from their captain. Crew. Same as the rest of them. The best. *The Pride.* Something the kif would never own.

C. J. Cherryh

"Huh," Pyanfar said, summation, and walked away down the corridor.

Continued in
CHANUR'S HOMECOMING